"Circle up folks," David said, motioning to the rug which now lay spread upon the deck. His father, he noted, sat as far as civility allowed from the Faeries. Once they'd all arranged themselves, Nuada reached into the neck of his tunic and drew out a gold disc on a fine gold chain. A deft motion of his silver hand freed the disc; a tweak of those metal fingers set it spinning. A *word*, and it was glowing. Another woke images there.

Something was wrong, David realized instantly. For while he'd rarely seen one of those devices in action, he could tell by the creases that barred Nuada's brow that all was not well. Images did form—but they never clarified. It was like TV with interference. Once, David was certain, he caught a glimpse of Lugh's face: tense, wild-eyed, and contorted with pain. Once, too, he glimpsed the body of a naked man, with chains running off into some obscure distance, but it dispersed as he watched, as though fire had burned it away. Indeed, fire was the most pervasive image, and eventually there was nothing *but* fire: a sphere of the stuff, like a small sun, with a sense of something bubbling and seething nearby.

Nuada inhaled sharply, muttered yet another *word*, and the red glare vanished. The disc clinked to the deck, its glass totally dark.

Nuada's face was as grim as David had ever seen it.

Warstalker's Track

TOM DEITZ

AVON · EOS

AVON BOOKS, INC.
1350 Avenue of the Americas
New York, New York 10019

Copyright © 1999 by Thomas F. Deitz
Library of Congress Catalog Card Number: 98-93289
ISBN: 0-380-78650-8
www.avonbooks.com/eos

First Avon Eos Printing: April 1999

AVON EOS TRADEMARK REG. U.S. PAT. OFF. AND IN OTHER COUNTRIES, MARCA REGISTRADA, HECHO EN U.S.A.

Printed in the U.S.A.

WCD   10 9 8 7 6 5 4 3 2 1

This one is for Deena
and
in memory of Monnie and George

ACKNOWLEDGMENTS

Jennifer Brehl
Diana Gill
Amy Goldschlager
Brenda Hull
Linda Jean Jeffery
Tom Jeffery
Deena McKinney
Howard Morhaim

And, once again,
a special bow of appreciation to
Buck Marchinton
for general expertise on guns, warfare, and critters
and for lending me John Devlin

Scott Gresham's Journal

(Sunday, June 22)

Testing . . . testing . . . one . . . two . . . three. Oops! Wrong medium . . .

Hmmm: What do I say? I've finally got around to puzzling out this fancy laptop the Mystic Mountain folks gave me last week, so I guess I ought to put something official in it, like a journal, which is what I've called this. Only something tells me the stuff I *really* ought to include isn't the boring day-to-day log of me trying to put one over on my employers about this staff-geologist-thing they've hired me to do and which I've suddenly found out I ought *not* to do, and to lay out all this magic stuff instead: this stuff that's had me freaked-to-avoidance since that business at Scarboro Faire a couple of years ago, when I first found out there was such a thing as Faerie.

Thing is, I wasn't the first. Myra's brother's friend David Sullivan was first. He accidentally got the Second Sight back when he was in high school and found out the *Sidhe*, who are basically the Irish Faeries, lived in an invisible world that overlapped his corner of north Georgia but which only he could see. Short form (long form later), he knew they were there, they knew he knew, and some of 'em liked it and some of 'em didn't—which didn't stop him and his buds bouncing back and forth between here and there off and on for the next umpteen years. Up until now, I guess.

(God, I'm rambling! Maybe I'll just think of this as an outline and fill in the details some other time—not that I'm likely to keep this, anyway.)

Anyway . . . David's crowd and my old Athens crowd

eventually got together and started holding these yearly pic-
nics near a Straight Track (which is a kind of road between
the Worlds), down in Athens, on one of the days the Faeries
are supposed to ride in procession. Nothing's ever happened,
but then this year something *did* happen. I was supposed to
be with 'em, only I'd just that day been offered this job with
Mystic Mountain Properties as staff geologist and had to
come up here to Enotah County, thinking I had this neat new
job I needed really badly, doing surveying for a resort a
bunch of money men from Atlanta wanted to build near some
of David's old turf. But anyway, *this* year a kid from Faerie,
whose name I don't remember, came riding up and told 'em
that they were summoned to an audience with Lugh, who's
High King in Tir-Nan-Og, which is the local Faerie realm.
Short form (again): Lugh's apparently in a bad political situation because iron from our World's been burning through
over there a lot, and this resort I'm working on is kind of
like the last straw, so he summoned every human who knew
anything about the existence of his folks to a big council to
pick their brains, except he also gave them an ultimatum:
stop the resort or he'd flood Sullivan Cove, which is where
the resort's going to be. Somewhere in there, too, there was
an attack on the mortal-types, and David's crowd had to retreat back here—right on top of my campsite, actually—so
they figured they'd see what they could do. Bottom line was
that a bunch of 'em decided to seek aid from some really
powerful dudes who live over near (I believe) Wales, and
have gone there. The rest of us are supposed to try to slow
things down here, which I'm doing by dragging my heels
and trying a bit of very clandestine industrial espionage, like
sugar in gas tanks and stuff like that. And some more folks
are going to see what they can do to mess up things via the
Net, while my old friend LaWanda and David's friend Calvin
(who's a for-real Cherokee) are supposed to be trying to
delay things here by making it rain, only I'll believe that
when I see it. Shoot, I wouldn't believe it at all if I hadn't
seen some other things to kind of make me believe. So here
I sit, in this nice paid-for motel room in Enotah County,
wondering what I'm gonna do, because I thought I was look-

ing out for myself, only I've wound up being on the side of the bad guys. And . . .

Shit. I don't feel like playing the self-analysis thing right now. It'd just make me more depressed. Sun's out, so maybe I better go up to Sullivan Cove and pretend to look for a sapphire mine somebody told me was around there.

Gotta figure out how to hide this file, too. Shit. I hate computers.

Prelude:
The Prisoner

(a dubious place—high summer)

It was the first time in the uncounted ages since his birth, unreckonably far away in time *and* space, that Lugh Samildinach had ever been unconscious.

Against his will, anyway, for even the Sidhe must sleep; their bodies were not so unlike those of mortal kind to preclude *that* necessity—besides which, without sleep there could be no dreaming, which was in itself an art to one as skilled in the shaping of Power as he. And of course there had been revels uncounted: drunkenness, drugs of every kind, besottedness on sensuality that might as well have been unconsciousness. But never had he passed from full awareness to the realm inside his skull abruptly, without consent.

He had even been dead. Immortal he was, and yet could die; for what was death to one of his kind save the severing of the bond 'twixt soul and flesh? Indeed, he had died so many times—all before his last rebirth, in Ethlinn's Tower—that he was expert at it. It was amazing what meat, bone, and blood could withstand. Swords had pierced him, poison ravaged him, starvation—once, on a dare—reduced him to a shriveled shell. But he was strong—the strongest of his kind in this fourth of Faerie—and Power, which was to spirit as energy was to matter, was his in profligate amounts to command. As long as he—himself: his soul—had Power . . . well, the body that housed it was of no real consequence. Time would (as mortals said) heal all wounds. And time he had aplenty.

He did not think much of it, this unconsciousness. It was

4

darkness without dreams, dull heavy pain with only the ghostly hope of relief. But it was *not* forever.

He blinked—and saw naught save the same colorless geometries that spun behind closed lids in the darkest caves of his realm. Blinked again, and saw neither more nor less. But he noticed three things at once.

The most imminent were the bonds that held him spread-eagled and naked in midair: shackled at wrist, neck, and ankles. *Iron* it was that gripped him: iron, which none in Faerie could work, for the fires that had wakened in that metal at the Worlds' first making never cooled. Iron that contained his limbs but did not touch them, shielded by the thinnest sheets of impervious wyvern skin, so that he felt the pain of proximity where those fetters clasped his flesh but did not—quite—consume it.

Iron was the second thing he noted as well; for not only did it restrain him but chains of it stretched away into unguessable dark, to bind his bonds to a greater mass of that metal that entombed him like the shell of an egg in which he was embryo. Or the core of a ball of flame: a sun, perhaps—irony there, for mortal men had styled him Sun God and given him a feast-day to prove it: Lughnasadh, celebrated in that World and Faerie alike.

But the iron sun had him now, and not one of the Powers at his command could win through that fierce ferrous fire and escape. Not even thought.

The third thing he noticed was how very badly he missed the Land. He had *lost* the Land, though his rational aspect, that every second fought past panic and pain to greater ascendancy, knew that as long as he lived and Tir-Nan-Og endured that bond could not be severed.

Which set him to thinking more alertly, as impressions gave way to knowledge and supposition bowed to the force of fact.

Fact. He had not become thus of his own free will. He had drunk wine—poisoned, probably—and dozed in his bath, not yet dreaming—and awareness had simply vanished into darkness, like a candle blown out. And before he could rally his Power and recover, there simply was no air. *Too quickly.* His substance had needed that support before spirit could muster itself to flee, and so he had *thought* one urgent plea for help, and one command—and passed out.

Fact. Whatever had occurred had required intervention by another conscious will. Which could not have been accidental. Which in turn awoke that word he had long, in his most secret parts, dreaded.

Rebellion.

Someone—*many* someones, likely, else his guard were more lax than he had cause to assume—had won through a palace crammed with defenses mundane and arcane and stolen a reigning sovereign from the heart of his own realm. He had to admire their bravery—their audacity, anyway—and already had an idea what group had worked his downfall.

The Sons of Ailill.

But why was he a prisoner?

One reply alone made sense: the same reason there had been talk of rebellion before and increased disaffection among the smaller Fay as recently as yesterday.

The mortal situation.

He should have listened, he supposed, to the tidings Nuada brought him, he who was closest observer of what chanced in the Lands of Men. But also to what everyone of late had seemed to whisper: that the Lands of Men were grown too close, that Holes were burning through the World Walls everywhere, and ever nearer to the heart of Tir-Nan-Og. That by ones and twos, in families and clans, the folk of his realm were fleeing, claiming shelter with Rhiannon of Ys, or Arawn of Annwyn, or Finvarra of Erenn—or simply seeking some new World upon the Tracks.

Lugh wasn't certain he blamed them. But he strongly disapproved of how they had chosen to resolve the situation, when he had just set the final stone in his own plan to counter the increasing encroachment of the Lands of Men.

Which brought him to the boy.

The *mortal* boy. David Sullivan—who, though not by design, had already brought him too much pain.

And then whatever—wherever—it was that held him shifted, as the weight of bodies came upon it. For the briefest instant, fresh air flowed in, and Lugh thought he might be on the verge of release. He inhaled—

—and breathed agony beyond belief, while more pain spread like flowing lava across his body. It was dust: some fine powder riding in with that air to settle upon his sweat-soaked skin and form a thin film there.

No ordinary dust, however—

They had coated him with powdered iron!

Perhaps, he reflected, as his dark prison echoed with the grinding of immortal teeth, unconsciousness was no bad thing after all.

Prologue:
Holed Up

(near Tir-Nan-Og—high summer)

Firelight woke dancers of black and red upon the cave's rough granite walls. Dancers already posed there, however, their shapes crude yet graceful, their forms human, yet not quite so, the paint with which they were limned clear though dulled with years uncounted. Blood bound that pigment (not all of it based on hemoglobin), and the fat of beasts as well, whose genes sometimes showed a fifth and sixth amino acid. Handprints showed there, too, outlined in ocher blown through bone: five-fingered hands, but with some of the digits oddly attenuated or smaller than those of the smallest child.

And the beasts—most had four legs, but many also sported wings, and some showed equal parts bird and fish, or mammal and reptile, and (not all that rarely) aspects of all four. There was writing, too, perhaps, though neither of the men watching that firelight dance among those painted revelers could have read that curling script. It had been there when the older man's folk had entered that land. The younger's kin had dwelt in caves then, and wrought art of their own: painted horses, fat women of clay, and scrimshaw work on ivory and horn.

The fire burned in a cavern a hundred yards from the fractured cliff face that masked its mouth. The floor was sand washed in by centuries. The air was chill because the rocks were, but the fire warmed it, and gave light and security. Fish baked in clay shells beneath the coals, but no smoke

8

fouled the air, for Power whisked it away before it could torment either set of lungs.

Both men were magicians, after the notions of their kind. One was mortal, one was not.

The immortal—taller, fair-haired, and with the smooth, unlined face of a twenty-year-old and the eyes of the eons-aged—leaned back against the pillow he had contrived from what remained of a fine white velvet cloak, laced fingers cased in leather and silver metal across the flat plane of his chest, and regarded the other with the wry, wary stare of the warrior he was.

"You were wise not to sleep in the palace," that one observed, careful to avoid names here where names had Power and those who presently commanded Power were even now reshaping the order of the World nearest without.

The other—the mortal; once also a warrior, now called *poet*—looked rougher. He wore new jeans, a black T-shirt, and a jacket of faded denim. And a leather glove on his left hand. His hair was short, auburn-brown—and unkempt. He looked older than the other, with experience if not actual wear, but was tenscore centuries younger. His teeth caught the light when he grinned, and the warrior recalled that they were both, by some obscure linkage, born as tearers of meat.

"I was . . . warned," the poet confided. "I'd prefer you didn't ask how, and surely you already know why."

The warrior smiled in turn. "The keeping of secrets is an art well practiced among the Sidhe—in exchange, I fear, for crafting such as this, though something about the proportions of these hands we see around us makes me wonder."

"I wonder that you never found it," the poet snorted, reaching out to prod the coals with a stick of wood already vitreous with petrification.

"I never looked," the warrior admitted. "One must hold some mysteries in reserve when one is immortal."

"Good thing for both of us," the poet acknowledged. "The food was good, though—in the palace, I mean."

"No better than those fish I smell cooking there."

"Found 'em in a pool further back. Blind. Caught 'em one-handed, but kinda hated to."

The warrior raised his leather-gloved hand and studied it

absently, flexing the fingers, noting how they still stung from his night's work with sword and Power. He could have healed himself, of course, but this was not—quite— Tir-Nan-Og, for all that, as best he could tell, this little bolt-hole had once been part of that Land until it had broken away. Or been eaten off by the taint of iron in the Lands of Men and drifted here along a Track, changing as it went, acquiring its own existential conventions.

"I am also glad I found *you* . . . Poet," the warrior said at last, with a knowing twinkle in his eye.

"I was wonderin' about that . . . Warrior," the poet replied. "Figured it was rude to ask."

"You have your secrets, I have mine," the warrior laughed, trying *not* to stare at a certain silver boss among the many that marched down the front of the other man's jacket. The same silver, in fact, as the silver arm that had given him his appellation: *Airgetlam*—Silverhand. His first name—his true name—he dared not think. The poet, whose name, safely enough, was John, did not know that Power rode with him most days, though the warrior imagined he was aware that the part always touched the whole, as far as some Workings went, and that connection between the once-joined was never entirely severed.

The poet—John—dug through the ashes, dragged out a hand-long block of hardened clay, and cracked it open, to reveal a feast of pearly, sweet-smelling flesh. He offered it to his visitor, who took it with a certain amount of trepidation.

"Sharing food and fire . . ." that one said.

". . . makes us friends," the other finished. "Thought we already were—much as your kind and mine can be."

The warrior ate without reply—odd how hungry he was, no doubt a function of the Power he had spent so profligately of late, spiriting close to fourscore mortals out of Tir-Nan-Og. Eventually he became aware of his companion's gaze upon him.

"Sooooo," John ventured. "Feel like tellin' me why you showed up here? Homage to Bobby Bruce it might be, but I doubt re-creating mortal history was your main concern. No spiders here," he added.

"I am no king in exile," the warrior retorted, flourishing his silver arm. "Nor can be, with this. But I suppose I *am* in exile, for the nonce."

John scowled, cleared his throat. "I'm not sure I'm entitled to speak for my folks," he began, "but I appreciate what you've done. You're the second most powerful person in Tir-Nan-Og, best I can figure. You chose to help my folks when the crap hit, 'stead of tryin' to save your own king."

"Which some would say brands me a traitor," the warrior observed. "And I would be one, had I not been following that king's commands."

John looked startled. "He had wind of it?"

"He has a seer—Oisin, of whom I imagine you've heard but doubt you've met. Oisin foresaw a threat but could not tell when or where. It was no real news to him. Tonight—the evacuation—was—I think the mortal word is *contingency*."

"One of several," John drawled back enigmatically, applying himself to a second fish.

The warrior's eyes flashed dangerously, but he fought down anger. This was no time for dissension. "Would I be correct in assuming you are concerned for the boy?"

A curt nod. "Got a debt to him. Blood debt. He lost close kin 'cause of me. Somebody got killed trying to connect with me, anyhow."

The warrior fumbled inside the neck of his tunic and retrieved a disk of oddly glimmering crystal framed in gold. "Would you see how he fares?" Without waiting for reply, he closed his eyes, called upon a trickle of Power and reached to a certain place, then to a certain *other*, and bound them together, then opened his eyes once more.

The disk caught fire as it twirled first between silver fingers, then on the sand between the men. And as it spun, it expanded into a sphere of light as wide as John's forearm was long. Images moved inside. John frowned in resignation and scooted forward.

And the two of them—mortal and immortal, poet and warrior, John Devlin and Nuada Airgetlam—both at the same time saw . . .

. . . *mountains: lumpy with age, now softened more with*

the summer-toned crowns of countless trees—conifers and hardwoods in equal riot . . . roads webbing them like scars of silver-gray; lakes splashed among them like melted mirrors . . .

. . . water everywhere: rainwater . . . *drowning the lowlands, ignoring the banks of streams, filling every hollow with silt scoured from those mountains like flesh flayed away to granite bone . . . washing every rooftop, sheening every leaf, plastering every hair on man or beast to the precise contour of skin and skull . . .*

. . . closer now, as though a bird flew there, or wide-ranging thoughts gained more focus . . .

. . . a wide road through bottomland, thick with corn and sorghum but framed by mountains to either side . . . a thinner road running off it, once gravel, now washed down to bedrock beneath a glaze of mud . . . a farmstead crouching on the mountains' knees . . . a church, a graveyard, an iron-ringed family cemetery . . .

. . . closer . . .

. . . a farmhouse on the road's southern side, its boards decayed, its roof retained by patches . . . its front porch in ruins, its back stoop scarcely better . . . glass in half the panes, and a chimney a yard shorter than it ought to be, from which thin smoke wheezes, before drowning beneath the ongoing storm . . .

. . . cedars in the yard; a house trailer on a knoll nearby . . . cars in the drive: a Dodge minivan, a brand-new Lincoln Town Car, a red '66 Mustang, an aging Mercury Monarch, a new Ford Explorer . . . a BMW touring motorcycle . . .

. . . and now inside . . .

. . . an old room, all but abandoned—but crammed to the rafters with people. A door opens onto the collapsing porch, a window gapes beside it. In the left-hand wall, a massive stone fireplace stands behind an imposing hearth. Opposite the entrance, another window overlooks a backyard. Doors to the right lead to bedroom and kitchen, with the remains of a sofa between. A man sits on the hearth, folded upon himself as though his shoulders bear a world's worth of pain. He is golden-haired, armored, and wears clothes not seen by mortal men in half a thousand years; his face bears the

same alien cast as Nuada's. John does not recognize him. Nor can he identify many of the others strewn about the room, save that he has seen them once before. Among those strangers are a slight, wiry fellow carrying bagpipes, and beside him an imposing black woman who, by the way she hovers about him, is clearly the wiry lad's lover.

There is a boy, fourteen or thereabouts, with a surly expression and waist-length jet-black hair.

There is a woman a little older than the rest, clean-featured, and with hair bound atop her head like a blond fountain. Her clothes—black minidress and tights—scream Gothic. Something in her face brands her an artist to her soul.

And there is a man in his late twenties, lanky, angular of jaw and chin, blond and worried-looking, as though guilt and fear wage some inner race to consume him.

The rest John knows.

There is Dale Sullivan, close to eighty, white hair worn in a tail; khaki-clad, hard as a fence post and nigh as gnarly-lean—and all but father to John's lost friend.

There is Calvin McIntosh: black-haired and rusty-dark, with features that proclaim, unmistakably, Cherokee Indian.

There is Sandy Fairfax of the waist-length light-brown hair, athlete's body, and scholar's mien.

There is Aikin Daniels: twentyish, brunet, compact, and furtive; clad in cammo and black; with a forestry degree all but completed.

There is Alec McLean: slender and blandly handsome, and even amid the surrounding chaos, somehow a trifle too neat.

There is Liz Hughes: a slight, pretty redhead, with more magic about her than she dreams.

And there is the one he knows best: David Sullivan. Mad Dave. David Kevin Sullivan, to give his whole name: the same as John's dead friend. He too is twenty-odd; a tad on the short side, and built like a wrestler or a gymnast. He has thick blond hair caught back in a tail, and a handsome, snub-nosed face. He is also the leader of this company, though clearly unhappy to be cast into that role.

And there are two other people in the room. Like the fair-haired man, neither of them is mortal.

One would be barely more than a boy—had he not also been immortal. He might be a younger version of Nuada; then again, all Daoine Sidhe tended to look alike.

The other is a woman: hair like black ice and perilously fair. She stands in the doorway between living room and kitchen, looking dazed, and with some odd garment clutched about her, as if she had donned it in haste . . .

Nuada looked surprised at her presence and leaned closer. John noted his interest and likewise attended. "What . . . ?" John wondered.

"The last time I saw that one," Nuada hissed, "she was a cat. And before that, an enfield."

John's eyes narrowed in confusion. "Like the rifle?"

"Like the beast—Lugh's pets—you would know them from heraldry." Nuada pointed once more toward the tableau. "It would seem that a discussion is about to commence that it would be wise for us both to attend."

John shook his head. "When . . . ?"

"A week, in your World, since you . . . left. Less than an hour, if that, for me. Now be silent, and let us see what we shall see."

PART ONE

Chapter I:
Ongoing Chaos

(Sullivan Cove, Georgia—
Friday, June 27—early morning)

"This ain't no natural storm," Big Billy Sullivan opined from the smaller of the two back porches that flanked the kitchen extension on the back of the north Georgia farmhouse he'd occupied for close to fifty years. He thumped the morning's third cup of coffee down on the porch rail and leaned against the post nearest the steps. The worn, faded wood groaned at the pressure: two hundred pounds was a lot to bring to bear on old construction. The yard was all but invisible, masked by slanting sheets of rain and rushing streams of mud-colored water that carried more of the driveway—and the mountain, on whose knees the house squatted—into the frothing river at its base that had once been Sullivan Cove Road. His lower lip stuck out in his standard scowl of disapproval. A chill breeze caught him—*damned* chilly for Georgia in June—and he shivered, hugging the brawny torso that strained beneath the plain white T-shirt he wore above worn jeans and bare feet.

"No natural storm," he repeated.

The initial response was from Tiberius, the ancient yellow tomcat, who made one quick pass against his legs, apparently sensed a kick impending, and fled to the sheltered corner where Little Billy's bedroom had been tacked on ten years back.

"You ever think it was?" someone snorted behind him, the tones so masked by the rattly timpani of what sounded

17

suspiciously like hail on the roof he couldn't tell if it was his wife or younger son who had spoken—save for the wording. Nor did he look around, as JoAnne, his spouse of twenty-three years, padded out to join him. The scent of breakfast came with her: coffee, corn bread, and bacon freshly fried. He felt her stop at his back, and reached around to draw her close. Warmth flowed across his shoulders as her arms enclosed his ribs. Hair brushed his neck where she laid her head against him. *Gettin' to her, too,* he thought. *Has to be, for her to be like this.*

"Hoped it might be," he replied in a pause between blasts of thunder. He squinted into space, gazing west: toward the lake, the mountain—Bloody Bald—and the farm that lay between his own and those two landmarks: Dale Sullivan's place, home of his single surviving uncle. It was dark as pitch over there, as if all the fury that had wracked the mountains for nigh onto a week had been distilled into one single vat of gloom that was rupturing out there, half a mile away.

"Men in this family do a lot of hopin'," JoAnne murmured through a shudder he knew she'd have masked if she could. "Me, I do most of my hopin' *about* the men in this family."

"Billy okay?"

A shrug. "Think so. He was up half the night, but once he's out, he could sleep through the Second Comin'."

Big Billy nodded toward the yard, the rain, and the road. "Might get his chance sooner'n we thought."

JoAnne eased around to flank him. "Wish it *was* that," she acknowledged. "That I'd understand. It's this stuff that comes from that *other* place I can't puzzle out. I've seen it and I still can't. Seen enough, anyway."

"Magic," Big Billy agreed. "Just ain't natural. Folks like us oughtn't to have nothin' to do with it."

JoAnne nodded solemnly. "Yeah, well you an' me both know that, but this ain't our world anymore. We got the kids, but this *sure* ain't their world now! Shoot, they know more now than we'll ever know. And David's just barely finished the first part of college, never mind Billy—I still say he's gonna beat 'em all, smart-wise."

Big Billy gestured at the yard with a stubby right hand,

while the left sought his abandoned coffee; he winced as a gust of wind whipped rain into his face. JoAnne edged behind him again. "Shit," he spat. "Reckon I oughta go check on Dale?"

"Might be a good idea. Phone was still out last time I tried. Comes and goes," she added, as her husband turned toward the house.

"Wish this fuckin' *rain'd* go!" Big Billy grumbled, aiming one final frown at the storm before retreating inside. "Guess I'd better walk; truck'd prob'ly flood out on the way."

As if in answer, thunder boomed again—louder and closer alike. A final gust of wind flailed at him, as though to hasten him away from things he did not understand.

It was just as well that the loudest thunderclap yet had that moment rattled what remained of Uncle Dale Sullivan's first-and-birthright house, because the noise hid a room's worth of startled exclamations; and the flare of lightning that followed hard on the thunder's heels—prelude to a clap that was even louder—gave the occupants something to gape at besides the figure that had just appeared in the doorway to the ruins of the collapsing farmhouse's kitchen.

A woman. A beautiful, dark-haired, exotic-looking woman. A *Faery* woman, who was clutching—barely—the remains of what looked suspiciously like a tablecloth around her like a threadbare sarong.

A woman who instants before had been a yellow cat named Eva and who twice a day, for a few moments at dusk and dawn, had worn a third, less likely, shape entirely. One patently *not* part of mundane reality.

Not that the woman David Sullivan saw now was either.

"Aife," he blurted into the silence that followed the last round of thunder. Silence, save the white noise cacophony on the roof.

The woman blinked at him as she slumped against the doorjamb—and kept on slumping, as though she were mortally tired. David lunged toward her, but Alec was there before him—and the other fifteen people in the crowded room—and eased the woman's descent as she sank down

atop a pile of dusty cushions between the worn-out sofa and
the floor. And went utterly mute, as though tongue-tied.

An eruption of voices followed: questions, cries of aston-
ishment, admonitions of caution, offerings of advice. David
ignored them all, save Alec, who had a vested interest. Yet
even he sat back on his haunches as the woman's face contorted, a mighty cough racked her, and she doubled over,
coughing twice more, before choking something dark into
her hand. He recognized it as she dried it against her sketchy
robe, and was reaching toward it even as she passed it up to
him with the merest ghost of a smile.

"Iron has its uses," she murmured in a voice soft and
oddly accented. "Especially iron that is overlaid with
Power—even when one wears the substance of this World."
She paused, dark eyes probing the room. David twisted
around to follow that gaze as it settled on the smallest person
present: a boy of about fourteen, slim and feral-looking, his
face pale with alarm beneath a belt-length flag of patently
dyed black hair. *Gothic elf* was how someone had described
him. It fit, as much as his name did—the name he went by
anyway: *Brock.*

Brock's eyes locked with David's, who countered with a
wary smile and an upward quirking brow, as one tiny mystery was clarified.

"Told you it was magic," the boy chuckled.

David regarded the object curiously. It was a medallion
the size of a half-dollar, wrought of black iron that still
showed a faint metallic sheen beneath the patina of ages.
Quite a few ages, to judge by the wear that had smoothed
the device raised on both sides. A wild boar: the ancient arms
of the Sullivans of Ireland, though Brock claimed to have
bought it from an old woman in an antiques store in York-
shire.

"What's that?" someone asked nearby. David started—
*God, but there were too many people in too small a space,
and too much was hitting him too fast, and he was having a
damned hard time sorting it out. And now one more thing!*

Finally he cleared his throat—no one else seemed able to
say anything coherent, including Alec, whom logic suggested
might have *some* comment, given that the woman to whom

he was ministering had once, in a fashion, been his lover. "Lady, is there anything we can do?"

Aife shook her head even as she accepted a cup of coffee from Liz Hughes, David's own sweetie. "That was a potent magic, and a strange one," she managed at last. "Or"—she paused, staring at the grimy window to her right, as though what she sought might somehow be visible there—"or perhaps it was not only the Power of the medallion but also the fact that he who bespelled me is no longer in touch with *his* Power."

Lugh, David thought through a chill, and scanned the room for reactions—or advice. Troubled faces stared back: his friends, and friends of friends, the latter mostly folks he knew through Myra Buchanan, the blond woman with the fountain of hair gathered atop her head. Folks like James Morrison Murphy (Piper, to his chums) and LaWanda Gilmore. Not to omit Myra's sometime-lover, sometime-basket-case, under-achiever, work-in-progress: Scott Gresham, who had more than a little to do with why they were all crammed in here.

Never mind the immortals. Besides Aife, there was rash young Fionchadd mac Ailill, David's closest friend among the Sidhe. And the newest arrival: the golden-haired man who sat slumped on the hearth with his inhumanly handsome face buried in his hands, while his tattered white surcoat steamed in the heat of the fire someone had (in spite of the season) had the sense to stoke up—for light as much as anything, given that the cabin's power had long been discon-nected. Shoot, he still didn't know that guy's name—or anything else, save that he'd been a guard to Lugh Samil-dinach, High King of the Daoine Sidhe in Tir-Nan-Og, and had just escaped that place with his life—and a warning.

Too many people, too much chaos. Too many stories that had to be told one at a time and debated.

And, if what the Faery had revealed scant seconds before Aife's arrival was true, quite possibly far too *little* time.

Somehow, too, he had found himself leader of the band—which was a laugh, given that he was barely twenty-two, not quite five-foot-eight, and was only now on the threshold of his first college degree—though he doubted, at this point, he'd physically graduate.

Twenty-two, and a veteran of nearly six years dealing with Faerie and the World Walls and those strange glowing roads that laced between them that were the Straight Tracks.

And now, he feared, he faced war between his own World—the Lands of Men—and Faerie.

Everyone was looking at him, too, dammit! Even Uncle Dale, who was well past seventy and had fought in more than one war himself. Never mind Aife, who'd been in Lugh's guard, and this still-unnamed stranger, who—until the last few hours—apparently still was. He had just opened his mouth to ask what their Faery guest's name might be when he heard the sodden thump of footsteps on what remained of the back porch stoop. He was already glancing frantically around for a makeshift weapon when he caught—muffled by rain and a room's worth of breathing—someone male grunting, "Oh, fuck! Shit!"

David relaxed even as he caught Alec's scowl. With Liz at his heels, he bolted for the door. "Pa!" he gasped as Big Billy Sullivan stomped through the kitchen door. Water puddled around his feet like the lake around the mountains, and his thinning red hair was plastered to his skull like a bathing cap. "I had a hat," he growled as he divested himself of a sodden slicker, "but the wind got hold of it. I—" He broke off, irritation replaced with anger, and then that wistful, disturbing confusion David had come to realize meant an adult had suddenly discovered he was in over his head—or thoroughly outgunned.

"Got company, Bill," Dale drawled smoothly, joining David and Liz in the tiny room. "And most of it the kind you don't wanta see."

Big Billy glared at him. "Right now all I want to see is something dry."

"What're you doin' here, anyway, Pa?" David ventured.

His father's gaze shifted toward him. "Checkin' on Dale. Phone didn't work, and the storm was so bad I got worried—trailers and storms don't mix. Saw all these cars down here, and lanterns burnin', and the chimney smokin', and figured something was goin' on I oughta know about."

David handed his father a towel. "*Lots* goin' on, Pa," he acknowledged wearily.

"Well, start at the beginnin'," Big Billy retorted. "I ain't got nothin' *but* time."

David took a deep breath and steered his father back into the larger room. "This is my pa," he explained. "He can figure out who's who as we go along—easier to keep folks straight that way." Big Billy looked seriously pissed—and a dozen other emotions all at the same time—but nodded a greeting and flopped down on the floor as close as he could get to Dale. He studiously avoided looking at any of the three Faeries—though his gaze did creep now and then toward Aife. Not that David blamed him.

David accepted a cup of coffee-an'-'shine from Liz (who promptly contrived another for his pa), then cleared his throat. "Okay, Pa," he began, "you know about the Worlds, right? How there's more than one . . . reality occupyin' the same space at the same time, but with different rules in some of those places than we count on here. And I know you've heard me talk about the World Walls—they're what separate these overlapping places from each other. Are you with me so far?"

Big Billy grunted assent, and David went on.

"Fine, so anyway, you know how a few years ago me—first—and then most of my friends, started runnin' into situations that took us to some of these other Worlds, to Faerie, mainly, but also to Galunlati, the World of Cherokee myth, if you want to think of it that way. And sometimes we took the Straight Tracks, which connect . . . everything just about, at some level; and sometimes we just went straight through the World Walls. Well, it turned out that wasn't good for the World Walls. And what's worse is that iron—plain old everyday iron and steel that's *everywhere* in our World—has different properties in some other places, and one of those differences is that iron in our World can actually eat through the World Walls and into places on the other side, like Faerie, and . . . basically dissolve 'em away."

He paused for a swig of coffee, then went on. "Another thing, though, is that as best I can tell"—he looked at Fionchadd for confirmation—"our World's the primary one that holds the others together, and Bloody Bald exists, in a way, in both Worlds. We see it as a mountain in a lake; you've seen how it looks in Faerie, 'cause I showed it to you. Lugh's king there, and any Faery king is joined to his realm by an almost physical bond, and the place that holds that bonding—the heart and center of Lugh's Kingdom—is also Bloody Bald.''

Big Billy coughed impatiently. ''Most of which I knew. You think you could get to the new stuff?''

David drowned a retort about how *little* his father actually knew in another slug of coffee. ''Okay, fine. So, do you know about the real estate developers?''

Big Billy's face flushed red—if that was possible, given his already ruddy complexion. ''Hell!'' he snapped. ''They been after me for weeks, but I didn't say nothin' to you 'cause I figured you'd blow sky-high—when they wasn't nothin' we could do anyway, 'cause we can't deny 'em access and we don't own the Cove no more.''

David fought down anger of his own—at his father for giving up so easily, and for limiting his options, and for a thousand thousand other things besides. ''So you know about the resort?''

''Know they're plannin' to build some stuff down at the Cove and a lodge in the mountain itself. *If* it ever stops rainin' '' he added with a snort.

''You better hope that's no time soon,'' David growled. ''That rain's savin' our asses right now.''

Big Billy's eyes narrowed; he glared at Dale accusingly. ''You're not sayin' this—that *you* guys made this rain.''

''Helped,'' Calvin and LaWanda grinned as one.

''Anyway,'' David went on, ''the bottom line is that Lugh got word of the developers' intent and . . . basically found his back up against the wall. Any construction that close to the center of his realm, with the iron beams and all it entails, would cause major damage to Tir-Nan-Og—and he's not gonna put up with it. Add to that the fact that the little folks there are all emigrating, and that the place is full of young hotheads who don't like mortals anyway, though they're cool to bop in here any time they feel like it and raise hell . . . and you've got a recipe for disaster.''

''Gettin' ahead of yourself, ain't you?'' Uncle Dale inserted.

David sighed. "So anyway, short form: 'bout a week ago Lugh invited what I presume to be every mortal he could get his hands on who's ever had dealings with the Sidhe to this grand council meeting in Tir-Nan-Og. And what he tells us is that if the resort is built—actually, the first time *any* iron bites into Bloody Bald—they're gonna flood this whole area. He gave us two weeks to come up with a solution, and we've still got a little time left, but not much. Anyway, we were attacked in the palace, fled here—and decided to go see what we could do solo."

Another pause for a drink, then: "Basically, we decided to split into three teams. One would go to another Faery realm and try to enlist the aid of some folks there who have come in and slapped Lugh's hand before—they're called the Powersmiths and Finno's kin to them. I was with that group, and to make a long story short, we ran into trouble on the way and got turned back at the border of the country we had to cross to get where we were going.

"Meanwhile, Aik and Sandy tried to find out what they could about all this stuff on the Internet—Aik also, uh, squirreled around with their computers, you might say. And a third group stayed here and made it rain." He eyed the ceiling dubiously.

"And then on top of it," Alec put in, "we'd just got back to Athens from our fools' errand in Faerie when we heard from Aikin that all hell had broke loose up here. So we hopped in our cars and here we are. Awful trip—got here in the middle of this storm—and right at the worst, this guy"— he indicated the despondent-looking Faery warrior—"came runnin' out of nowhere and tells us that Lugh's been deposed and that the Sons of Ailill are in control."

"One other thing, too," Scott chimed in with his soft Tennessee accent. "Somewhere in there I got offered a job doing survey work for the developers—Mystic Mountain Properties. I needed a job," he continued defensively. "They offered me one, and good money, and a chance to be outside a lot. I'd forgotten about Bloody Bald—it kinda does that to you. And then these folks showed up outta nowhere and told me I was workin' for the bad guys. Still am," he added.

"Covert operations, I guess: stall as long as I can before they figure out that I *am* stalling."

David took a deep breath and looked at his father. "That's the very short form. The long one would probably take all morning. The folks here didn't know until just now that our embassy to the Powersmiths failed. I know a little about what's gone on up here 'cause Aik told us on the way up, but there's still plenty we don't know."

"One thing we *have* decided," Myra inserted, "is that we've got to put Lugh back on his throne."

"But to do that, we have to know what happened in Tir-Nan-Og after we left—what was it? A week ago?" David wondered.

"By your time," the nameless Faery warrior volunteered. "Little time at all in our World, for time flows oddly between the two just now."

"Oddly indeed," Fionchadd agreed. "I was ordered from that fight a week gone by—in *this* World—yet you seem to have but lately come from there."

"Yes," Aife echoed from the corner. "It would seem, then, that we should have your story next, if we are to learn anything at all."

"Yeah," David acknowledged. "And I know it's rude to ask, but a name would be good, too, if you trust us enough to tell us yours."

The Faery regarded him curiously. "You *are* astute, for a mortal, so perhaps what I have heard of you is true. Too, you have trusted me with your names; therefore I will tell you mine. I am Elyyoth, of the house of Angus, of the first comers to Faerie out of the High Air, and I am a guardsman to Lugh Samildinach."

David gnawed his lip from impatience, though he knew that such an introduction—the full panoply—carried the force of ritual, which was a thing Faeries respected beyond almost everything.

"Former guardsman, I should say," Elyyoth amended. "For surely a man cannot claim that status when he has failed in his assigned task."

"You were *sent* here, as I recall," Fionchadd countered. "If you fled, obeying orders, you are no failure."

The Faery's face was grim. "Yet I failed."

David cleared his throat, impatience—and fatigue—having gotten the best of him. "The story . . ."

"Oh, aye. Very well, first of all, you should know that those who bear blame for this are many. Some—most—were the Sons of Ailill''—he paused to look at Dale and Big Billy—"a faction among the Sidhe who think your kind have encroached too closely on our World, whether in knowledge or in ignorance does not matter, and who decry what they claim is Lugh's too-tolerant attitude toward mortals.

"In any event, during the time since David here first learned of Tir-Nan-Og, this faction, plus most of the other disaffected in that land, made secret cabal with certain powerful folk in Erenn and Annwyn and even among the Powersmiths, and so they began to plot against the High King, with an eye toward deposing him and substituting one of their own thinking. This was no easy task, for Lugh is the most Powerful man in Tir-Nan-Og, and possibly in Erenn or Annwyn as well. There was much plotting, and—"

"How do you know this?" Scott broke in roughly. "Seems to me a refugee like you knows a little too much for me to feel good about this."

"A reasonable concern," Elyyoth replied amiably, "and one which shall be addressed anon. Now, as I was saying, Lugh, for all his knowledge, skill, and interest in mortal kind, does not truly know as much about how mortals think as he might. Or rather, he knows the minds of but one sort of mortal: the sort he brought to his council—the best and brightest. Mortals of the baser kind—the ignorant, the rough, the infirm, the violent or mad—he ignores. The Sons of Ailill did *not* ignore them. They were younger, rasher, more eager for excitement, and they took themselves into the Lands of Men—often. And there they learned much of the darker side of mortality—and used it to advantage. We have a saying among us—the guardsmen do—that a mortal who deserves our attention at all deserves our respect. The Sons took another tack. They saw mortals as resources to be exploited, not respected; and to make a long tale short, they assumed control over a number of mortal men."

"Why?" Alec wondered aloud, even as a very likely answer occurred to David.

"Iron!" Elyyoth spat. "Mortals can wield iron; Faeries cannot. Nor can a Faery assume the substance of the Mortal World while in Tir-Nan-Og, and thus wield it that way."

Fionchadd nodded his agreement "I should have thought as much. Still, Lugh is strong—"

"Lugh was distracted, and the attack came from unexpected quarters, for the Sons were wily indeed. First, they divided themselves into groups. One—in effect a suicide team, though you know that death is no final thing among the Sidhe—attacked you mortals who were guesting in Lugh's palace after his council. Nuada was able to forestall much of that attack, and with the help of certain others, spirited most of you away." He looked at David. "Nuada says to tell you that your friend John Devlin is well."

David exhaled his relief. "Go on."

A deep breath. "Aye . . . Well, it turned out that the attack was mostly a ploy. Yet it had the desired effect. Lugh was enraged—one of his flaws, I must say; for though he is slow to anger, when it does awake within him, he does not always think like the wise man he is. In any event, Lugh dispatched a third part of his guard to capture those who had had the temerity to attack his guests, and he sent a part of his Power with them, so that he might more quickly know how events transpired.

"Then, while Lugh was thus distracted, one of the Sons, who had infected even our own ranks and who had obtained a potent poison from the Lands of Men, took that poison and gave it to Lugh in a goblet of wine while he lay at ease in his bath."

"Poison!" Aikin blurted. "But I thought—"

"Some from your World act with amazing speed," Fionchadd informed him. "Most of those we make are slow to work. And while your bodies are not as our bodies, still, some things are the same. Thus, while a poison might not kill Lugh, its healing could easily consume an enormous amount of Power."

"Which is exactly what it did," Elyyoth confirmed. "The poison was timed precisely. It took the High King from consciousness, and—we think—he went inside himself so as to heal himself. And at that moment of vulnerability, the Sons of Ailill acted. They were already inside the palace. But they had ensorcelled men from this World and laid glamours on them so that they looked like familiar men of the Sidhe. They had also shifted their own shapes to small things, so that they might ride with those men and not be noted. Then, careful to avoid any of the more Powerful among Lugh's comrades, many of whom were still abroad seeking the decoy attackers, these traitors split into two groups."

Another pause for a sip of coffee, and the Faery went on. "Now keep in mind that mortal men are able to wield iron weapons, both in this World and in Faerie, and you see what valuable allies they might be. And as soon as Lugh's consciousness failed—not a hard thing to know, when one speaks from mind to mind—one group of bespelled mortals bearing ... *guns*, I think they are called, attacked the Throne Room while the other assailed Lugh's chambers, intent on capturing him while he was unconscious. The throne was but lightly guarded—most of these Lugh sent away were among those normally stationed there. The mortals used these guns, and shot Lugh's guards where they stood—not killing them, but wounding them nonetheless, for a shattered limb or a blind eye cannot be repaired immediately, and pain is pain regardless. That achieved, they entered the throne room and erected a cage of iron around the throne—"

Fionchadd's gasp cut him off. "The King is the Land!" the young Faery hissed. "The Land is the King. Lugh had put much of his Power into that throne; a shield of iron would cut him off from the bulk of his strength!"

Elyyoth nodded grimly. "And another portion of his Power was afield with the guardsmen chasing decoys."

"While the rest he used to heal himself of poison!" Fionchadd groaned.

Again Elyyoth nodded. "While the remainder of the englamoured mortals attacked Lugh's quarters, incapacitated most of my fellow guardsmen, and took the High King captive. Cowards' weapons," he added, wiping his mouth as though he had tasted something foul. "Guns ... that wreak havoc from afar."

"Like the Spear of Lugh," Fionchadd chided him. "Like the Horn of Annwyn."

"Weapons of war," Elyyoth countered. "Not for close combat."

Fionchadd looked very sad. "No, my friend, it *is* war. It was already going to be war with the Mortal World if this resort is built. Now it is war . . . everywhere."

David was about to explode from impatience. "So basically what you're saying is that a bunch of Faery traitors set it up so Lugh stretched his Power too thin and then contrived events so he'd have to divide it further, caught him at his weakest, and zapped him where he wasn't looking."

"Nuada tried to warn him," Fionchadd noted.

"Nuada," David echoed. "What *about* him?"

"He is the reason I am here," Elyyoth replied. "I was among those guarding Lugh's Throne Room, and I alone survived that attack—though it shames me—by playing dead. As soon as I could, however, I hastened to Lugh's chambers. I could hear the commotion within but could not reach him. Fortunately, most of the mortals had been abandoned by then, and wandered about dazed and aimless. Their traitor masters had apparently left them with some final orders to defend Lugh's quarters, and so they attacked me—with their bare hands, their guns apparently having few . . . charges. Nevertheless, I was forced to fight them—and no few of the Sons who heard the commotion and came at me with swords. And then Nuada was with me, and together he and I escaped. Along the way, we chanced upon one of the wounded Sons hiding among Lugh's halls and captured him. Nuada read his thoughts and there learned what I have told you. That, and their plans for Lugh: to sacrifice him on the feast of the Sun and set up a new king then—one who will brook *no* traffic at all with mortal kind. Nuada sent me here to warn you."

"That they'll flood the Cove regardless," David growled. "Sons of bitches."

Liz scowled thoughtfully. "So where's Nuada now?"

"Rallying those who would aid in Lugh's restoration, I imagine," Elyyoth replied. "Alas, many were away from court, and disaffection is more widespread than Lugh thinks, wily though he is. It may take a while.''

''A while we may not have,'' David sighed.

''Yeah, well, I don't know if this is an omen or not,'' Calvin observed ominously. ''But it's just stopped raining.''

Interlude I:
Travelers' Tales

I

(Erenn—high summer)

Finvarra mac Bobh's summer seat, in what mortal men called New Grange, was not notably warmer than his winter halls beneath the Hill of Knockma, west in County Galway. Certainly it held a chill this season that seemed to shadow him as he stalked restlessly along the endless corridors, wondering vaguely whether his brother monarch Lugh did not have the right of it: to build a palace level upon level, with towers, stairs, and turrets, in lieu of this nigh-onto-endless sprawl.

His robe—gray velvet edged with matching fur—swished along the polished agate floor behind him, and swished again as he turned a corner and entered his favorite place in all that enormous maze. The Hall of Time, he had named it. It was the newest room in the palace; indeed, it was incomplete at the far end, which represented *now*, for *now* was always ongoing.

This end, however—He took a step, and his pointed velvet shoe pressed down on an explosion of jewels that represented what in the Lands of Men was called the Big Bang. And as he trod the length of that hall, history passed beneath him: the history of life in the Lands of Men, at least, which was also that of life in Faerie. For Faerie *had* no history, not from the beginning like this. No one knew *whence* the stuff of which it was wrought had come, before the Tracks had claimed it (and where had *they* come from? made or natu-

32

ral?), no more than anyone knew how the Worlds had grown up around those nodes of Power, mass, and force—with the subtle great Powers that supported the Lands of Men reaching through to hold things steady here.

Windows gaped by on the left: high square panes set in slanted stone walls an arm's-length thick at their bases, the stone unfinished to better draw the gaze to the mosaic miracle underfoot. Beasts battled there now: dragons, of a kind (and surely these behemoths had begot dragons when they chanced into Faerie and mated with other creatures there in a way that was impossible in the Mortal World); and a few dozen strides farther on, a ball of flame crashed down from the sky in a sparkling explosion of yellow gold and crimson jewels, and when life resumed the dragons were no more and the beasts were furred. He wore the pelt of one now, as trim on his robe: a great cat with foot-long teeth that still dwelt in Erenn.

Yes, that floor was truly a wonder, and Finvarra marveled anew at it (not the least because it was mortal work; the Sidhe could not create such things and had long since left off trying). But a larger part of Finvarra's thought was turned to puzzling out what in all the nested Worlds had made him so anxious this morning. It was not the Tracks, whose unexplained and unpredictable resonances sometimes awoke him in the night, demanding he use his own Power. Nor was it the strange pull of the Seas Between, which had been oddly calm this season, though more Holes gaped among them than ever. The Land itself, then? Was the Land troubled? Surely not, for Erenn overlapped the Lands of Men at an earlier time than Lugh's Tir-Nan-Og overlay the continent to the west, and the things men wrought there of metal were not yet a problem here; though soon enough, as men numbered time, his own realm would find iron burning through. For now, however, the iron problem—and with it, the mortal situation—was Lugh's dilemma. Himself—best to watch, wait, and remember.

He had just recalled a certain mortal wench he had borrowed from a Leinster farm, and was already turning his steps that way, when a darkness flickered into the edge of his vision. He froze at that, blinking, off-guard, hand flashing for the dagger that always hung at his hip. Yet by the time he had found its hilt, eyes, mind, and senses subtle and obscure had identified the flicker as a vast raven gliding with uncanny ease just beneath the massive square stone beams that supported the roof a bare three times his height above his head.

And not merely a raven; one of *those* ravens, lately come across the Seas Between from Tir-Nan-Og.

The raven circled once before alighting—precisely in the center of the pavement, which perhaps not accidentally put it atop a rendering of an extinct flightless bird mortal men called a moa, executed in jet, black jade, onyx, and rutilated quartz.

"Hail, Messenger," Finvarra cried when the fowl had folded its wings and cocked a wary eye toward him. It was ritual politeness; one addressed such messengers as though they were their masters themselves—for sometimes they were. Lugh had been known to shapeshift, Ailill had done it constantly, and Nuada was a reluctant master. "Are you someone I ought to know?" Finvarra continued amiably.

"Raven," croaked the raven, preening itself.

"Who is your master?"

"No one—now!" the raven replied promptly.

Finvarra took a step back. "No one?"

"No one."

"Not the Morrigu?"

"Gone and not returned."

"Not Nuada?"

"Vanished away."

"Nor . . . High King Lugh . . . ?"

"King no longer—soon."

"Then who sent you?"

"When the ravens leave the White Tower in London Town in the Lands of Men, it is said that land will fall."

"And when they leave the twelve-towered palace of Lugh Samildinach?"

"They say that Land will fall, too. Or perhaps it has already."

Finvarra took a deep breath, feeling an odd flux of emotions ranging from fear through distrust to a vague, hopeful elation. "Lugh is Ard Rhi no longer? Then who rules Tir-Nan-Og?"

"No one," said the raven—and flew out the nearest window.

"No one," Finvarra echoed, staring back down the long trod of the Hall of Time—which might as easily be called the Hall of Extinction.

"No one reigns in Tir-Nan-Og," he mused again a short while later as he gazed with keen interest at the vast fleet anchored in his harbor.

II

(Annwyn—high summer)

It was hard to tell the departing ravens from the gloom that gathered in the sky. Black they were—all twelve, save the single white one that winged most clearly west. But black also were the clouds that hung above Annwyn's rocky coast: black as boiling pitch, as the tumbling stones in a dragon's craw, as kraken ink boiling in wine and brackish water.

But red showed there, too, reflected from foundry fires up and down the coast, for every forge in Annwyn was aflame. *War*, the word was—and Arawn it was who had proclaimed it. And so every smith and fletcher, bowman and weapon-wright in all his vast, dim land worked day and night, forging bronze and copper and those esoteric new metals whose secrets came from the Lands of Men into spears and swords, daggers, axes, and arrowheads. Shields too they crafted, each with its own device, the colors born of the very metal; and armor they likewise made; the fine mail that moved like a second skin upon the body and held no weight at all but would stop anything that did not carry with its substance more than a hint of wizardry.

Smiths were not the only ones occupied, however. Every magus, wizard, and sorcerer to be found was at work as well, laying spells of direction on those weapons as they were wrought, and spells of protection on shields and armor as soon as they were done. Annwyn might be poor and under-populated when compared to the lush, fecund splendor of Lugh's bright Tir-Nan-Og, but Annwyn still claimed mighty wizards, and its bare, shattered rock and tumbled mountains yielded up far more ore than Lugh's land, which was fit mostly to supply gaudy gems, strange beasts, and lavish vegetation.

Arawn sighed as he watched those birds depart. Many fled where one had entered, bearing a certain message. Of a throne emptied but not yet filled, of the mighty of an entire kingdom fled, of a rich realm ripe for picking. Those were temptations indeed, and Arawn had not been slow to heed them. Yet for a good while longer he lingered on the high rocky headland where he had released those ravens, each with a particular message for a particular other ear, which would be repeated in precisely his own words and tones. He stood until the last black tail had faded utterly, vanished both to eyes *and* mind—and yet he waited, rust-red hair blowing wild around his shoulders, the wayward locks at the end merging with the dags on his cloak like dried blood among torn and rattled feathers.

The messages were gone. A throne stood empty. In a hidden cove two leagues to the south an immense armada waited.

Arawn wondered if he was ready. A throne usurped was one thing, a throne vacant quite another. And if Lugh fell (and it was *time* someone fell in Faerie; affairs had been as they were millennia too long to be entertaining), it would be wise to have the goodwill of Tir-Nan-Og's new master (and his measure as well—assuming that master was not Arawn himself). And if Lugh had not fallen or regained his Power (which there was more than a little reason to expect), why then the forces a fellow monarch could muster to shore up a shaky throne might be much appreciated.

No matter how affairs resolved, Arawn would profit: a new alliance, a new throne, or a new debt. Each had possibilities.

Another sigh, as he turned from the view of the dark, frothy sea and toward the inner land. Two things alone gave him pause.

One was his seer—Taliesyn—who claimed to see nothing

at all ahead but a dense knot of change he could neither decipher nor comprehend.

The other was the ship of Powersmith make that had lately approached his coast, flying the sign of Fionchadd mac Ailill, which had been attacked by those whom Arawn chose to regard (with careful toleration) as refugees from Tir-Nan-Og (Lugh would have styled them rebels), and retreated— straight into a Hole in the Seas Between.

He shuddered at that. Ships did not enter Holes freely. Not even ships built by the Powersmiths. Not *even* ships commanded by high-minded, dare-anything fools like Fionchadd. There had been mortals on that ship, too, which was troubling. Then again, Fionchadd liked mortals, he had heard. But what could have brought them here? Desire for an audience with his own splendid self? Unlikely. But Fionchadd had Powersmith kin, and to reach them, one must pass through Annwyn. That the boy had turned tail and fled rather than proclaim his errand did not bode well. That he had fearlessly entered a Hole boded even worse. (He had given out that Fionchadd had been slain and his mortal crew had entered the Hole in confusion, but he and two others knew that was a lie.)

There had been a taint of Power riding that boat as well— mortal Power, and of more than one derivation, and mortals with Power was not a concept Arawn was eager to embrace or, really, understand.

But, he told himself again, he truly was ready. His only fear now was that he might not be the only one prepared.

Chapter II:
Muster

(Sullivan Cove, Georgia—
Friday, June 27—mid-morning)

The high, soft peals of Myra Buchanan's laughter tumbled around Big Billy Sullivan's den like a toy ball that had escaped its master and gone exploring on its own. It bounced off cheap paneling and expensive leather furniture (the funding for which had not come from this World), and would've been louder yet had it not been absorbed by thick brown shag carpeting and a room full of refugees lately come from Uncle Dale's house, which had simply become *too* crowded.

David looked up from the yellow legal pad on which he'd been scribbling notes on an hour's worth of preposterous revelations, and glared at her. "What's funny?"

She stifled another giggle into a smirk, then peered absently at the bottle of Miller beer Big Billy had provided to calm all those frazzled nerves.

"What?"

"I was just thinking," Myra murmured, "how screwy all this is. I mean, here we sit, for all practical purposes a Faery government in exile—if you can call three people who barely knew each other a government. But what's funny is that Tir-Nan-Og is so strange and perilous and . . . fucking aloof, and yet here's this bunch of college kids, flaky artists, and rural farmer types trying to save two Worlds, one of which would shaft us if it could. We're like George Washington trying to restore King George because he's the devil we know."

· "You noticed that, too?" Calvin chuckled, combing his still-damp hair.

"Noticed what?" Alec wondered, padding barefoot and shirtless from the adjoining kitchen. His hair was even wetter than Calvin's, legacy of the hot shower he'd been latest of that company to claim. That pissed David, too, though he tried not to let it. War was impending, after all, against which clean hair and fresh clothes paled out of consequence, screw what Liz had whispered in his ear about people being more cooperative and thinking more clearly when they were warm, well fed, and dry. David had acquiesced to her—but vowed to be last to bathe.

"So . . . is there a plan?" Alec asked more loudly, as he slid down beside Aife. She caught his hand as he hesitated, then looked around again.

David ruffled his notes. "Actually, we've just come to that."

Liz looked up from a notebook of her own. "The way I figure, we've got three problems. First: where, exactly, *is* Lugh, and if nobody knows, how do we find out? Second: how do we poor mortals spring somebody who's bound to be guarded to the hilt, both with people and magic from someplace strange enough to cut him off from his Power? And third: assuming we solve the first two, how do we get in and out?"

Silence filled the room, broken only by breathing, the rustle and creak of clothing against leather, and the occasional cough. And by Little Billy munching Frosted Flakes in the corner, before David's own mother, a weary/wary-looking JoAnne Sullivan, shushed him. She hated this, David knew. So did Big Billy. So, if he had his head on straight, did the kid. This was no place for this kind of conference, but the cabin was just too cramped and uncomfortable. That moving it here meant involving his folks—well, he supposed it was time for that.

"I know where he is," Aife announced abruptly, with absolute conviction.

David lifted an inquiring brow. "Where?"

"I thought I knew earlier, but so much was occurring then that the memory fled. Indeed, it was a memory I did not know I possessed, but with the breaking of Lugh's spell, others seem to have broken as well.''

David tapped his pencil against his pad . . . loudly.

Aife looked him straight in the eye as though daring him to command her to haste; some things rarely changed with Faery folk. ''The Iron Dungeon.''

David scowled. ''I've heard of an Iron *Road*. It's a secret route into the bowels of the palace Lugh had built to guard his treasure. There's also an Iron Stair.''

''Neither of which lie precisely in Tir-Nan-Og, else the iron would have eaten through,'' Aife continued coldly. ''But I speak of the dungeon Lugh's queen had built without his knowledge to house a rival.''

David started at that. ''Lugh's . . . queen?''

Aife regarded him levelly. ''Her name was Ainu. The Tracks sang to her one day and she . . . left. No one knows where she now resides—if she still lives. As I said, even Lugh does not know of the Iron Dungeon, but certain of Ainu's women do—among them, my mother. She confided that knowledge to me, and I, in my foolishness, relayed that secret to the Sons of Ailill when I allied myself with their number.''

''I knew it!'' Liz snapped. ''You had to be one of them!''

Aife shrugged, though her eyes flashed dangerously. ''That was when I thought Ailill hung the moon, kindled the stars, and enflamed the sun in the sky. Before I knew what true love was,'' she added, clutching Alec's hand tighter. ''I have learned better since, else I would not be here now.''

David cleared his throat. ''Okay, fine. But how can we be certain that Lugh's in this Iron Dungeon? I doubt we're gonna get a second chance to spring him.''

Aife's jaw tightened. ''When I was among the Sons, even then they discussed Lugh's dethronement. That was the plan they laid out at that time. From what Elyyoth said, it must still be their intent, or near it, for their plot involved looking where Lugh did not: to mortal men and iron. Their thinking would therefore already have been of iron.'' She paused for a sip of beer, wincing at the taste. ''Too, something must block Lugh's Power, or the spell that held me would not have failed, though in truth it did not slip away all at once.

Few things could block such Power, but a shell of iron might, which could only be the Iron Dungeon."

"Okay," Liz inserted cautiously. "Assuming Lugh *is* prisoner in this Iron Dungeon—I presume you know where it is?"

"Close enough. I know which Track it lies upon—leads to it, rather."

Liz cleared her throat. "Okay, then, next problem is how to get him out."

"The same way they got him in," Fionchadd replied. "They attacked Lugh where he had chosen to be blind; we attack them the same way."

LaWanda frowned. "What you mean, Faery boy?"

"That the Sons will be expecting any response to come from Nuada, the remains of Lugh's guard, and the old elite. They will not be expecting mortals any more than Lugh was. Certainly not mortal men with . . . iron."

"Guns," Scott crowed. "Of course!"

"And if Elyyoth's right," Myra mused, "they're faster than even Faery reflexes, never mind Faery weapons. And do more damage, of course."

A general muttering coalesced into a call for quiet from David. He looked first at Aife, then at Fionchadd. Gnawed his lip. "That means we'd have to . . . kill people?"

"The price of war," the Faery shrugged. "The Sons accept it. You should as well."

"The Sons are immortal!" Aikin flared. "We don't have that luxury."

"It is what you were designed for," Elyyoth countered, speaking for the first time. "Like mayflies."

"Okay," David growled. "We'll save that for later. Next question is: who is *we*? I mean, we can't all go."

"Right," Liz agreed, looking back at her notes. "Way I figure, we oughta send as small a group as we can: harder to detect, if nothing else. Given that, we need as wide a range of skills as possible. Which means mortals *and* Faeries. Aife, for starters, since she knows the way to the Iron Dungeon. And—"

"Me," Fionchadd broke in. "You have not decided how to get in and out, but I have an answer to that."

"The ship!" Brock yipped from where he'd been drowsing in the corner. "Of course!"

Fionchadd nodded ruefully, then noted the puzzled looks on more than one set of faces. "Suffice it to say I have a means to take us straight there and back, if affairs proceed optimally."

"You mean no overland treks, stealthing, and hiding?" From Aikin, who sounded at once disappointed and relieved.

"Aye." Then, to Liz, "Go on."

"Okay," she continued. "We send Finno and Aife, for Faery lore and magic. But it'd be good to send someone from another magic tradition, just in case."

David elbowed Calvin in the ribs. "You up for it, Red Man?"

Calvin started. "Actually . . . I've got an errand in Carolina—some folks I need to check on. And another potential ally—if that's okay."

David had started to ask who when Brock spoke up from his corner. "I'll go—and before you say no, remember who got you out of the Holes in the Seas!"

"Boy's got a point," Myra conceded. "We should be looking at skill and competency *only*, not species, sex, or age."

David rolled his eyes and almost gnawed his pencil in two, but went on. "In any event, the rest of the folks need to be our best fighters."

Aikin's eyes narrowed. "Fighters? Or marksmen?"

"Both, ideally." David surveyed the room. "Any volunteers?"

"Besides me and you?" Aikin shot back instantly.

"I'd love to go," Sandy said. "But with school and all, I absolutely can't. Not within your time frame."

"I . . . can," Myra hedged. "But I'd rather not."

"And you can forget about Piper," LaWanda snapped. "But I'll go."

David started. "You?"

"Can shoot with the best of 'em, white boy. 'Sides, I've got two or three dozen bones to pick over there. And," she added for effect, "don't forget my mojo."

"Whatever," David mumbled, blushing. "Alec, you don't

have to tell me this isn't your game. Liz . . . I know you want
to come, but maybe not this time."

Liz nudged Alec. "Actually, we've . . . uh . . . got graduation."

"Which you'd best attend," Dale agreed. "Dave's got a
good excuse, and we all know what it is. But your folks and
Alec's—well, this ain't the time to be explainin' to them
'bout Faerie and all. We'll cover for Davy if either of 'em
calls. Say he's sick or something."

"Makes sense," David agreed sadly. "But back to the
plan: it's me and Aik and LaWanda for armed support?
Brock, can you shoot at all?"

"A . . . little."

"I'll go," Dale volunteered.

"The hell you will!" JoAnne snapped. "What're you
thinkin' about, old man? I can shoot as good as you!"

"Hush, woman," Big Billy rumbled in turn. "But she's
right. More to the point, though, somebody who knows about
all this shit needs to stay here and keep an eye on the Cove."

JoAnne glared at him. "If you're thinkin' what I think
you're thinkin' . . ."

"I'm gonna go," Big Billy stated firmly. "I've let the boy
fight my fights too long, and this *is* my fight. I can shoot
good as anybody here—'cept Davy and Aikin, I reckon. And
I'm a-goin' to go!"

David took a deep, troubled breath and once more surveyed the room. "Looks like a good solid core. Anybody
else?"

Alec took a deep breath. "So what do the rest of us do?"

"Yeah," Little Billy chimed in. "What about me?"

"You stay here," David told him firmly. "And you watch
him like a hawk, Ma, 'cause this is just too dangerous to
have him chasin' around. Dale, I'd love to have you, but
Pa's right; you need to stay here and keep things coordinated.
Provide a bolt-hole like you've been doin'. Explain what you
can to . . . anybody who needs to know."

"I'll do 'er," Dale affirmed.

"And I *have* to stay here, dammit!" Scott spat. "Covert
operations against Mystic Mountain and all that. Damage in
the guise of damage control."

"As for me," Myra sighed, "much as I hate to say it, I have *got* to get back to Athens for a couple of days." She looked at Piper, who hadn't said a word throughout the entire discussion. *Poor guy,* David thought. *He hates this sort of thing even worse than Alec.* Still, this was a crisis situation; they needed people they could count on, not someone who'd curl up and go catatonic when the shit hit the famous fan.

David eyed Alec thoughtfully. "Uh, roomie, while you're in Athens, could you pick up a couple of things for me?"

"What?" Alec asked dumbly, even as Liz's face woke with recognition. "All the magic whatsis we've got left, right?"

David nodded. "From here on out, we'd better bring in the whole arsenal—every single thing any of us have that's come from some other place." He glanced at Calvin. "That means all your gear from Galunlati, too. Uktena scales, war clubs, everything."

"I'm way ahead of you," Cal laughed. "That's one of my reasons for headin' to Carolina."

David studied Myra thoughtfully. "Any chance you could get down there and back before we leave? Or—Crap!" He looked at Fionchadd. "What kind of time frame are we on, anyway?"

"We *must* conclude everything before the Feast of Lugh."

"Which is when?" LaWanda wondered.

"July 31," David supplied automatically. "Folks nowadays call it Lughnasadh, if they call it anything."

"A month and change, then," Sandy mused. "That should buy us a little time."

"If we don't lose a bunch swappin' Worlds," Calvin retorted. "Things seem to be really screwy here versus there."

"That variance is passing," Fionchadd assured him. "But do not forget the Sons may act against this place at any time. And never doubt that they *will* act."

"Speaking of which," Aikin broke in. "Exactly what kind of heat should we be packin'?"

"Shotguns," Big Billy offered instantly. "Better range, and you do maximum damage with minimum effort. Maybe some handguns for close-in stuff, plus they ain't as bulky.

Got a bunch of both,'' he added. "One of each kind for everybody in the family: eight right there."

"I've got a couple, too," Aikin confirmed. "Could probably scrounge up one-two more."

"Me, too," Dale chimed in. "Plus my old .45 and Hattie's derringer."

"So what about this?" David began. "Everybody carries *something*, whether they can shoot or not, and we try to bring the newbies up to speed in transit. Everybody who *can* shoot takes a shotgun and something smaller as a spare, and we take all the ammo we can physically carry."

"Knives, too," Fionchadd suggested. "Steel ones, just in case."

"What about clothes?"

"Faery garb would attract the least attention," the youth replied. "There should be enough on the ship. Or we could englamour you, but that would take Power we might need elsewhere, and would be detectable by the skilled among my folk. The best approach would be to try to pass as Sidhe with mortal prisoners until we reach our goal."

"How many guards you lookin' for?" Aikin wondered.

Aife shrugged. "Not many, if luck favors us, for the Sons of Ailill are not many, only very dedicated and organized. They will have more than one agenda afoot."

"What about the mortals they took over?"

Another shrug. "They *should* pose little trouble. Most will have been returned to this World or else have been ensorcelled, for it takes much Power to control another mind, even a mortal one."

"Thanks a lot!" Calvin muttered.

"Truth is truth," Aife shot back.

Silence ensued, as though everyone had chosen that moment to ponder the enormity of their undertaking. God knew David had little enough to say, in spite of the fact that he still had a day's worth of questions, contingencies, and stratagems to bring up. Never mind the fact that he was tired to the bone. When *had* he slept, anyway? Back on the boat, between their arrival in the seas of Faerie and their return to the Oconee at Whitehall: twelve hours, maybe? Plus a catnap on the way up from Athens. Shoot, he was barely back from one fool's errand and here he went on another! "Well," he yawned finally, rising, and realizing to his surprise that he was sore, "what I suggest is that everybody who's goin' to Faerie get fed, clean up, and grab some shut-eye if you can; and everybody else chase down as many bangy-things as they can and meet back here in . . . an hour." He glanced at Aikin. "That work for you?"

"Make it one-point-five," Aikin countered. "I have *gotta* get a shower, but I can do that over at the folks' place. Guns're over there anyway."

Calvin laid a hand on David's shoulder. "And, Dave, my man, I hate to say this, but now that the sun's out, might be a good time for me to make tracks—'less you want me to hang around."

"It's cool," David grunted, reaching over to give him a rough half-hug. "Just take care of yourself and give my regards to . . . whoever."

"Right," Calvin affirmed, then made the rest of his good-byes and departed.

"So we're basically lookin' at noon?" David asked Fionchadd.

"Aye," the Faery murmured, then stared at Elyyoth warily. "And what of you? What would you do in all this?"

The guardsman sighed wearily—like a mortal, David thought. "It is my duty to guard, to fight. But I am tired, so very tired . . ."

"Your strength will return soon enough," Fionchadd assured him. "And if your duty is to guard, then guard you shall. It is likely the Sons, or others of their ilk, know already what transpires here. There may be attacks on this house in our absence. Such protection as you can afford, by weapon or Power, you should provide these folk. I would put on the stuff of this World, however."

Elyyoth simply nodded.

David slumped down in the nearest chair. God, but he was fried! Too fried for any of this, frankly. He started to speak, but Fionchadd was already kneeling beside him. "Sorry, man," David mumbled. "Just need to grab some Zs."

"A bath," Liz corrected. "You're starting to smell a little ripe."

David sniffed an armpit. "And *then* a nap."

"There will be time to sleep on the journey," Fionchadd informed him curtly. "Of that you may be certain."

"Just hope we wake up again," Aikin called from the door, then suddenly looked alarmed. "Oh, crap, I don't have my car. Will somebody . . . ?"

"Take mine," JoAnne hollered, fishing in her pocket for the keys to her latest Crown Vic. "Not your style, but *some* of us got taste."

Aikin caught the keys on the fly and grinned. "And some of us got brains."

David giggled like a fool as his mother chased his buddy out the door, swearing like a sailor in mock anger as they fought the latest skirmish in the lesser but more tenured war between Ford and Chevy.

"Bath's clear," Alec prompted. "You go, then Brock."

"I'll chase down the guns and ammo," Big Billy rumbled.

"And I'll—" Little Billy began.

"—stay out of the way," his mother finished for him.

"Come . . . child," said Elyyoth the Faery. "I will show you a wonder."

David wondered whose smile was brighter: this odd silent refugee warrior, or his voluble younger brother.

"I'll call the rest of the Gang," Liz volunteered. "Figured they'd at least like to see you off. Plus, they really do need to know what's going on."

And then Alec dragged David to his feet, hustled him down the hall, stuffed him into the bathroom, and closed the door.

Chapter III:
Weapons Practice

(Sullivan Cove, Georgia—
Friday, June 27—noonish)

"So let me get this straight," JoAnne Sullivan said stiffly. "You really have *no* idea when you'll be back?" She was addressing David, but her eyes were averted, fixed firmly on the rocky shingle beside Langford Lake. Which meant she was having a hard time staving off tears and didn't want anyone to notice. David hated to see her this way. He wasn't a father—yet, and maybe never—but he'd seen people he cared about march knowingly into situations from which they had no guarantee they'd return. This was the same. The lapping of the waves against the shore made a counterpoint to her breathing, as though the world echoed her regret.

He reached out to give her a cursory hug, which she returned with surprising vigor. "No idea," he murmured. "Sorry. Time runs screwy over there. It *shouldn't* take long—you might get home and find us sittin' there—but there's no way to be sure." He paused, shifted his weight, looked around at his friends for support that didn't seem forthcoming. "Plus, if things go like they're supposed to, we'll have Lugh in tow, and there's no tellin' what he'll want to do once we spring him—whether he'll try to retake the palace then, and if so, whether he'll want us around for that, or whether he'll hie himself off somewhere to lick his wounds and regroup, or what." Another, more uneasy pause. "Shoot, there's even some chance we might have to bring

48

him back here. I hope not, and I'll try to keep his stay short if that happens—but be prepared.''

JoAnne ruffled Little Billy's hair. David snared his no-longer-so-little brother—he was a sturdy eleven and change—and embraced him roughly. "Take care of our ma," he admonished. "Dale's gonna be there, and Elyyoth, but *you're* the man of the house.''

Little Billy stood up straighter, which put him not far off eye level with David. "I'll fight for you, Dave," he said solemnly, but his blue eyes were bright with tears. "I'll fight for whatever I have to.''

"You and me both," David sighed.

Fionchadd cleared his throat. David grunted a reply and rejoined the group waiting with the Faery youth at the shore. And shivered. Not a week had passed since a similar crew had met here, a quarter mile south of the incipient construction at what he and his friends called B.A. Beach (in memory of a particularly embarrassing fall that had occurred there) to embark on what had proved to be a fruitless mission to enlist the aid of Fionchadd's Powersmith kin. And here he was again, on the vanguard of a similar mission, though to a far more accessible and familiar place, and he was scared all but shitless. Maybe it was the fact that there was a good chance there'd be fighting, a chance he or someone he knew—his father, even—could be killed. Or perhaps it was simply that Big Billy would be present: his first foray into Faerie.

David didn't know what he thought about that. His pa was about as earthbound as you could get: narrow-minded, almost a bigot. But he loved his family and his land. And he was proud of his children, David had no doubt. Still, the natural order of things made David defer to him—yet *he*, David Kevin Sullivan, was effectively in charge of this mission. Would they find themselves contesting control at some crucial juncture? Or defending kin at the expense of a higher goal?

No! He wouldn't think about that now. He'd think about how pretty this little out-of-the-way cove was, where the mountains pointed into the lake in pine-gloved fingers that made a vee around a quiet backwater where stone shelves

sat on the porch of the Enotah National Forest. He'd think
about how *this* was what he was fighting for: the land itself.
His land, and his family's, for nigh onto ten generations.

But it was Calvin's land, too, for far longer; and for a
moment he wished his Cherokee friend was here. The others—Liz's folks had been here a fair spell, and Scott was a
mountain boy, though from Tennessee. But Alec's parents
had moved here to teach at MacTyrie Junior College five
years after their son was born; and Aikin was also technically
an outlander, having arrived in MacTyrie at ten; while Darrell and Gary (who had joined them to see them off, with
the promise of a briefing from Myra afterward) had appeared
in their teens, when Myra was already in college. It wasn't
the same for any of them. As for Piper and LaWanda, they
were nice folks, but they were flatlanders.

Yet LaWanda was going anyway, and he had to admire
her for that: how a black woman from south Georgia would
put herself on the line for residents of what was essentially
an all-white county in a state that had made slaves of her
ancestors. "People gotta be free," she'd said. "Lugh's people, and he's gotta be free. You're people, and folks are
comin' down on you, and you gotta be free, too."

David blinked, having lapsed into one of those fits of
dazed reverie that caught him now and then. He was suddenly aware of eyes looking at him—many eyes: those who
were going, and those who'd stay behind. Calvin and Sandy
had already departed. Alec, Liz, Piper, and Myra were
packed and ready to hit the road. Dale and David's ma and
brother would watch to the end, as would Scott and Elyyoth—who looked god-awful strange in a set of David's
sweats that fit fairly well at waist and shoulders but were far
too short at the cuffs.

Another deep breath, and David joined the voyagers: Aife,
Fionchadd, Brock, Aikin, LaWanda, and Big Billy. Fionchadd wore the clothing he'd arrived in: tunic, cloak, hose,
and high leather boots that looked vaguely fifteenth century.
Aife (who was tall for a mortal woman, though not for one
of the Sidhe), wore Elyyoth's castoffs: armor, weapons, tattered surcoat; all of it. David had the armor and surcoat Fionchadd's mother had given him all those years back, which

blessedly still fit. Good fortune that: deciding that a suit of Faery mail was just too obvious a thing to go flashing around even in a town like Athens. The other four were in service-able black as far as possible, but Fionchadd had promised more suitable outfits once they were under way. Each carried weapons, too, which Dale and JoAnne had spent half the morning cleaning. As best David could recall, they had at least two guns apiece per mortal combatant: five handguns, notably an heirloom Colt .45 that had belonged to Uncle Dale, a pair of Ruger Blackhawks, and Aikin's brand-new Glock 22; four shotguns, and (in case they met *large* non-human opposition—like wyverns) a big-bore rifle.

Fionchadd cleared his throat again and gazed at the sky as though trying to read something unknowable in the angle of the sun and the thickness of the dispersing clouds. "Now," he said quietly—and reached down to retrieve that which he'd carried in a cardboard box full of Styrofoam pea-nuts all the way from their last landfall in Athens.

A toy boat—as Darrell had just blurted out.

"No," David whispered. "Watch."

Fionchadd held out the object for inspection, looking a tad too resignedly tolerant, David thought. It most closely resem-bled a standard issue Viking ship—save that it was no more than a foot long. Certainly it had the low, slim build, high carved prow and tail, and central mast of the typical Norse drakkar. But there was also a tiny cabin amidships, and cer-tain other details were not quite the same. And of course every seam, bolt, nail, peg, and rivet was absolutely perfectly made and installed with a precision that would've done Ro-lex proud.

Without saying a word, the Faery turned and marched with calm deliberation to where the lake whispered against the shore. He squatted there, his cloak a fan of gray around him, and set the vessel in the water. Then, in one deft motion, he extended his right hand. A ring gleamed there: twin serpents twisted around each other, one of silver, one of gold. A stroke to the golden head, and a tiny spark of flame shot from its mouth, just far enough to brush the crimson sail furled around the spars atop that pencil-thin mast. The boat caught fire at once, and there was more than one gasp of protest before those who didn't know what to expect realized what was occurring.

For the ship was expanding as it burned, arcane fires tearing atoms from the air and binding them into the vessel's substance. "It's like freeze-drying," David told the awestruck LaWanda. "'Cept they take out the fire—the energy, you could say—instead of water. This just puts it back."

"Whatever you say, White Boy," LaWanda growled, patting the Colt at her hip.

And then, all at once, the ship loomed higher in the water, and then higher again, and with a final whoosh of green-purple fire reached its full size and stood waiting in the lake, just far enough offshore to prevent its keel scraping bottom.

"This is it," David said, because somebody had to. And suddenly the sketchy shoreline was a confusion of hugs, kisses, and an endless series of "Best wishes" and "Take care of yourself" and "I love you" and "See you later, man." David felt lost in the muddle, but made time for his mother, brother, and uncle, and for Alec and, most especially, for Liz. He hated going without her, but sometimes you had to let logic rule.

When his crew seemed inclined to linger, Fionchadd uttered a sharp "Enough! Those who would accompany me, board the ship and do not look back."

David gave Liz a final kiss and turned. They had to wade through water up to their hips to reach the ladder that hung from the gunwale, but David had warned them about that, and everyone held their weapons and other gear clear. Climbing up was no problem; they were all young, supple, and in excellent condition—save Big Billy, who was huffing, puffing, and red in the face as he heaved himself over the rail. "Too much winter and too much rain," he gasped. "I ain't been out enough. Done lost my wind."

"Watch it, then," David cautioned as he helped him find his feet, leaning against the rail, with the line of decorative shields behind him. "Can't afford to lose you, too."

"I ain't *that* old!" Big Billy snorted.

"Yeah, but you've smoked for thirty years," David countered. Not adding that his pa also drank too much beer and would've eaten a hockey puck if it was deep-fried.

Fionchadd, meanwhile, had made a beeline for the bow, where the intricately carved curves, whorls, and spirals that marked the dragon prow loomed above their heads. David saw him there, busy with a scrap of fabric.

"What—" David began as he joined his friend in the vee behind the prow. But then he saw: torn white velvet stained with blood. "So that's how we're gettin' there," he murmured for Fionchadd's ear alone.

The Faery nodded. "I would prefer the secret of navigating this vessel did not become common knowledge, but alas, there is only one way to accomplish this."

David indicated the fabric. "Lugh's blood?"

Fionchadd shook his head. "Nuada's. I thought it wise to seek him first. He—"

David grabbed his arm. "What do you *mean*? I thought this was all decided—and here you go changin' the rules again! Whose side *are* you on, anyway? I haven't forgotten what your friend said back in Annwyn about you havin' tangled alliances everywhere."

"I am your friend," the Faery replied simply. "If I wanted to work harm to you or your kin, I could have done it ere now. As for my change in plans, it came to me while we were mustering our gear. I was telling Elyyoth that it would be useful to have something of Lugh's to use as a focus for a scrying, and he said that while he had nothing that belonged to him, Nuada might, and Nuada's blood was splattered along with that of many others on his surcoat. And Nuada, as you know, would be a valuable ally. Still," he went on acidly, "if it looks as though a side-quest to seek the second most powerful man in Faerie will lead us too far afield, I will abort that mission and seek the Iron Dungeon at once."

"Whatever," David spat, and strode away. God knew he had friends on board to whom all this was new and amazing, and those people needed him now. Still, he couldn't resist watching as Fionchadd uttered a certain *word*, whereupon the drakkar's carved neck curved around—and kept on turning until the vast wooden beak was barely above the Faery's head. Whereupon Fionchadd deftly inserted the strip of bloodstained fabric into the right-hand nostril. The head seemed to inhale, then slowly, with much creaking and groaning, returned to its former position.

Abruptly, they were moving. Big Billy staggered back a half step, but caught himself on the rail. Brock giggled at him—then had the tables turned as a lurch to the right upset the boy's perilous balance and set him on his backside. He scrambled to his feet at once, rubbing his butt dramatically.

And then they were moving in truth: out of the sunlit cove and into the light mist of fog that drifted like ghosts upon the larger body of the lake. Already David could feel his eyes tingling, as Power awoke. A Power that manifested an instant later as a glitter of golden reflections on the water. And then more gold, and the reflections rose above that surface, and his friends joined him as they pondered the way ahead. The sun was behind them, yet no true shadow lay before, and then the fog began to thicken, and the mountains to dim, and all at once they were surrounded by thick clammy white, save where an indistinct light in the sky wove pink highlights through it.

David held his breath—they all did. And in that sudden silence, they heard, faint but clear, voices from the shore calling out farewells. And James Morrison Murphy, who loved music and hated Faerie, playing on his new Uilleann pipes that had been made in that strange land a rousing chorus of "Brian Boru's March."

"Well," David whispered to nobody, "looks like we're on our way."

If David had thought this latest of his seemingly endless forays into Faerie would proceed without incident, he was mistaken. Barely had his companions taken their bearings when Aikin, of all people, cleared his throat and called everyone to join him in the stern. His face was grim—as serious as David had ever seen him. He stood close to the cabin and had spread a cloak on the planking of the deck. A round shield was propped up on a box just clear of the dragon tail at the aft end of the vessel; two feet across, its thick dark wood was carved in the semblance of a human figure in a style between traditional Viking zoomorphs and more realistic later styles.

"Okay," Aikin began. "This is your party, Dave, but we both know who the gun ace is, so if you don't mind, I'm gonna act on that suggestion you made earlier and give these folks a quickie tour through Shootin' Irons 101." He glanced at David for confirmation, then continued. "First thing, then, is for everybody to put whatever artillery you've got on this cloak so I can see what we're workin' with here. After that, I've got a few things to say, but mostly I just want us all on a level playin' field. We're gonna have to watch each others' backs, so we need to know our strengths and weaknesses."

A deep breath and he surveyed the group. They were all present, David noted with satisfaction. Even his father— taciturn, granted, but there. David caught his eye and mouthed a silent "Thanks" as Big Billy laid his trusty Stevens shotgun beside the other weapons. *Good soldier,* David conceded. *Knows when he's in over his head and how to take orders—for now, anyway.*

Aikin studied the array of armament with keen curiosity. "Looks good," he acknowledged. "Okay, first off: any questions?"

"One thing," LaWanda replied immediately. "What, exactly, can a gun do to a Faery? I know what Elyyoth said about the attack, but I'm lookin' for specifics here. Also, can't they, like, ward against it?"

Aikin raised a sheepish brow at David. "Uh, this one's yours, I guess."

David chuckled wryly and assumed his lecture tone. "A bullet can inconvenience *anybody*. A shattered joint or fucked-up eye's the same in the short term whether or not its owner can heal. Pain's pain, like somebody said earlier. As for this situation: if they aren't expectin' it, they'll be unlikely to ward against it." He glanced at Fionchadd. "Correct me if I'm wrong, Finno, but it takes a little warnin' to ward or cast a glamour, right?"

The Faery nodded curtly, in spite of his earlier suggestion, clearly ill at ease at the presence of so many steel-based weapons. "More or less. The more Powerful you are, the faster you can accomplish that sort of thing, but like any mental discipline, it requires concentration to activate properly. That applies to glamour, warding, *or* healing. It is difficult to concentrate while in pain," he added.

David nodded in turn. "And on that score, we've got an ace in the hole." He turned to Aikin, who was loading a clip for the Glock. "It was your idea, Aik; let 'em have it."

Aikin grinned self-consciously. "Y'all heard what Dave said earlier about the Sidhe and their, shall we say, allergy to iron. Well, it just so happens that Uncle Sam gave us a hand there—for a change." His grin expanded, all reticence vanished. "You folks know that most bullets, shot, or whatever are made out of lead, which might be fine for damage but still has certain limitations. Happily for us, however, it seems that waterfowl tend to mistake shotgun pellets for munchies. The feds therefore banned the use of lead shot for duck hunting, so when I'm floating the Oconee, I have to use some substitute—the cheapest of which is"—he paused for effect—"*steel* shot."

Both Sidhe promptly paled to their hairlines, their faces slack with horror and disgust, but Aikin continued obliviously. "*And*, boys and girls," he enthused, "it just so happens that I've got a couple boxes left over from last season."

Big Billy nodded sagely, favoring first Fionchadd, then Aife, with long appraising stares. "Shit, boy, you may make a soldier yet." But then his face clouded with thought that gave way to a scowl of realization. He looked at David and Aikin again. "You know, you boys are older'n I was when I went to 'Nam. My *sergeant* then was the same age you fellers are. Got us back alive, too, so I reckon I can count on you gettin' me back as well."

David slapped him on the back, and even Aikin beamed. "Fine," Aikin breathed eventually. "Any other questions?"

"Okay," David said a short while later as he eased up to stand beside Brock, who was studying the array of weapons with wary interest, "let me get this straight: you've never shot a pistol before? Right?"

Brock shook his head sheepishly.

"Guess we'll have to show you, then," David yawned. "I defer to Aik."

"Just as well," Big Billy mumbled through a smirk. "He can outshoot you anyway."

David spared his father a glare and wandered back to the cabin to watch. Aikin motioned the boy over to the weapon-covered cloak. "All right, let's get you started," he sighed. Brock promptly reached for the wicked-looking matte black Glock.

Aikin slapped his hand away. "Uh, uh," he chuckled. "You're startin' off with a revolver. You wanta throw lead, you use the automatic. You wanta *hit* what you're shootin' at, you start with the Blackhawk."

He picked up the large revolver. With a barrel that alone was over seven inches long, it was a lot more weapon than what David suspected the kid had seen in the old cop films that likely comprised his firearms database. The stainless steel gleamed in the eerie light; the grip was smooth, deep reddish-brown hardwood.

Aikin eased up beside the boy. "This is a Ruger Black-hawk. Fires six forty-five long rounds. It's a single action, which means you have to pull the hammer back before you shoot. You can't just pull the trigger. Got it?"

Brock nodded. Aikin turned away for a moment, and David caught the clink of rounds slipped, one by one, into the cylinder.

"Now, I'm assumin'," Aikin went on, when he'd turned back around, "that you know to treat this thing like it's loaded even if you know it's empty. That means makin' damned sure it only points at something you wouldn't mind puttin' holes in. You ever point that thing at *me*, I'll beat the snot out of you—with the butt of the gun."

Brock nodded meekly, and Aikin handed the pistol to his student. Brock hefted the weapon, then swung around, pointing it at the target shield.

Aikin studied him for a moment, then: "Okay, now; take a firm grip with your right hand and rest the butt in the palm of your left. Yeah, that's right—but don't lock your wrist too much, 'cause the gun'll jump up in your hand. You'll get the hang of it."

Brock scowled seriously and adjusted his grip. Aikin nodded in turn. "Okay, look down the barrel. The rear sight's a notch, the front's a post. Put the post in the notch and line the top of the post flush with the top of the notch. Now, set the target just on top of the post."

Brock did so, gnawing his lip unconsciously.

"Now ... pull the hammer back with your thumb ..."

Brock did. An audible *click* ensued.

"Take a deep breath, hold it, and squeeze the trigger."

Again, Brock did as instructed. David saw his eyes narrow, his finger tighten on the trigger, the anticipatory tension that filled the boy's slender body.

Snap.

"What the ... ?" Brock yipped. Aikin's lips curled in a smirk. David had to suppress a guffaw.

"First off," Aikin informed him, "you anticipated—and you flinched."

Brock's face was red with shame and taut with ill-suppressed fury David at once understood and held no sympathy for, having been there himself with a far less tolerant teacher. "Wasn't loaded!" Brock spat. "You tricked me!"

"Worked, too," Aikin retorted. "You flinched, so you'd have missed. Next time, relax. Don't anticipate the shot; just let it take you by surprise." And with that he retrieved the revolver, lifted and cocked it in one fluid motion, then took aim at the shield.

Snap. He cocked the handgun. *Click.*

"Just squeeeeze it off."

Snap. Click.

"Niiice and easy."

The pistol barked and bucked in Aikin's hands. David's ears rang with the report. A hole less than half an inch across pierced the bronze boss in the center of the shield. Aikin grinned. "Nothin' to it," he smirked, as he slipped another round into a chamber and spun the cylinder. "Try again."

The first live round startled the boy, and his shot hit high. "Not bad," Aikin conceded. "You'll get used to the kick. Hold firm, but allow some give or you'll hurt your wrist. And try to get closer to the center of the target. Remember, you don't aim at the deer, you aim for a specific spot on the deer—or whatever; otherwise, you'll miss."

Brock practiced with a dozen more shots, his aim improving steadily. Aikin plopped down nearby and began sawing methodically at the barrels of his shotgun, all the while continuing to advise his pupil.

LaWanda sauntered over to join him, then raised an eyebrow in alarm. "Is that *legal*?"

"Screw the law," Aikin snorted. "This is war!"

"Little melodramatic, aren't you?"

Aikin put down his saw and regarded her coldly. "You think I'm takin' this too seriously?" He gnawed his lip, then looked up at Brock again. "Yo, John Wayne, get your butt over here." Brock started as if he'd himself been shot, then padded over to stand at Aikin's booted feet. Aikin's gaze took in the two of them—and the rest of the company as well. "I probably don't need to tell *you* this, LaWanda, but even if I don't, it bears repeatin': this ain't *D & D*, boys and girls; ain't *Sands of Iwo Jima*. This is real. You shoot somebody with any of this stuff, it's gonna be messy."

"Blood," David added quietly. "Bone fragments. Severed tendons and nerves. Ruptured organs—and let me tell you, viscera stinks."

"Right," Aikin agreed. "But you freeze up, it's your ass *and* mine. I had a cousin fucked up in the Gulf, and an uncle who lost his sight in 'Nam. Dave had his favorite uncle in the whole wide world blown to shit and back with a hand grenade somebody was *playin'* with. Never mind John Devlin, who could sure as hell tell you a thing or two if he was here."

"Don't forget that Dale had front row center for World War Twice," Big Billy put in, clearly relieved to find familiar ground. "And I did a tour of 'Nam myself."

"Damned straight," Aikin affirmed. "Now, Brock-boy, you think the pointy-ears are gonna let you off with a warnin'?"

David rose from his seat, not alone at being taken aback by his friend's outburst. God knew Aik wasn't one to give speeches when a word would suffice. Only LaWanda spoke up in the boy's defense. "So what're *you* gonna do, hunter-boy?"

Aikin stared thoughtfully at his handiwork. Time passed. "I don't know," he admitted finally. "Reckon I'll do . . . what I have to. If it's a choice of us or them, that'll make it

easier.'' His gaze swept past David to settle on Fionchadd.
''But I'd sure as hell want to be sure about the rules of
engagement. Like, who *are* our enemies? How do we tell
'em from the good guys? Do we bluff, or do we shoot first
and let the god of their choice sort 'em out? If we shoot, do
we shoot to scare, disable, or . . . kill, given that we're dealin'
with iron now. What about it, Finno; any advice?''

Fionchadd met the mortal's hard stare evenly. ''Fine questions, young hunter, and to be sure, our code of war makes
no provisions for such arms as you wield. By rights, this
should fall under the Morrigu's province, yet she is with us
no longer. Still, our situation is desperate; we must therefore
act accordingly. First of all, any who oppose us should be
treated as enemies. If you wound a friend in ignorance, they
will likely recover, and there will be time for those mightier
than either of us to explain things later—assuming we succeed. Should our adversaries find us, however, they will be
on us swiftly. Unless I warn you otherwise, do not hesitate.
Strike hard, for to one of our kind a wound is easily dealt
with; death takes longer to overcome.''

'' 'Specially from steel shot,'' David noted dryly.

Fionchadd tensed. ''Yes . . . especially. But do not forget:
our foes commit treason against King and Land, and such
traitors deserve a traitor's death—the Death of Iron.''

David's glance strayed to Aife, who was staring silently
at the deck while Fionchadd went on obliviously. ''Those we
seek see mortals as mere nuisances, or at best as resources
to be exploited. Your arms will be a threat unexpected—and
such a deadly power as your new weapons wield may be
unheard of. The first blow they feel will be the sharpest. I
doubt not your skill in arms, Aikin, nor your mettle.''

Apparently mollified, Aikin resumed his work, and after a
flurry of strokes, a two-foot section of gun barrel clunked
onto the deck. He tried a few practice swings before declar-
ing it a success, then handed it to David, who likewise tested
the weapon: shouldering it and sweeping an arc across the
sea before centering it on the shield. His first shot, after loading, took half the top away.

For the next hour and a half (at a guess; watches always
misbehaved in other Worlds), everyone on board gave them-

selves over to target practice. Brock embraced it with the wholehearted passion of the young with some new toy, and wouldn't rest until he'd tried every last theme and variation of available ordnance. Big Billy worked silently and methodically—and with intense, if workmanlike, confidence. LaWanda was as easy and relaxed as with anything else. *Does nothing scare her?* David wondered, then answered his own question when he recalled her devotion to Piper. By and large he was encouraged about their competency, as far as armed combat was concerned—though, he admitted sourly, he'd never be Aikin's equal.

They even offered the weapons to their Faery companions, stressing that some had wooden stocks or handles and at least one had almost no steel content at all. Aife made a minimal effort, but shook her head and returned the pistol after one round of shots, saying sword and Power had served her for nigh on a thousand years and would suffice a little longer.

Fionchadd, however, seemed reasonably game—not surprising given that he was young indeed for a Faery—certainly young to have so much responsibility thrust upon him. David suspected it was a case of young male macho kicking in—the two races were not *that* dissimilar, and God knew he'd contended with his Faery friend before, when the stakes were higher. Fionchadd proved a competent shot, too, though not as good as David had expected—a function, he and Aikin surmised aloud, of the Faery's ingrained aversion to iron, which made it all but impossible to maintain a steady hand.

And then LaWanda yawned, and what passed for a sun grew too hot for anyone sane to remain on deck, and they all went inside for some much-needed repose. David's ears were ringing.

It had been high noon when the drakkar left Sullivan Cove, but somehow it had become morning again—or the Faerie equivalent thereof—when the ship glided out of the swirled and twining fog that had embraced it all the way from Sullivan Cove and into a reality that included more than variations on a theme of white. Certainly the light that enflamed the sheer rock wall ahead held the same pink-gold quality morning light evoked, though a backward glance showed no sun to cast the black shadows that etched those glittering cliffs like some obscure ancient ogham.

Cliffs they were, too, rising nigh out of sight above, like the Cliffs of Moher, on the west coast of Ireland, back in the Mortal World. A swatch of sky showed above them, cloudless and bright as blue glass overlying etched gold. Nor was the place entirely lifeless, for ferns, moss, vines, and other sturdy plants laced in and out of the cracks and crowned shelves and outcrops like a net of life cast across the petrified corpse of that which lived no longer.

There was also a trail, visible as the ship eased closer: a shelf in the rocks an armspan wide that rose and fell along the rock face until it vanished into a golden haze to the right that could only be a Track. To the left, the cliff continued a ways, then simply . . . *wasn't*, as though reality ended there. David looked away quickly, just as movement in the corner of his eye made him jump almost out of his skin. It was only Big Billy, who'd ambled silently up to stand beside him, a frown masking what David suspected was genuine fear.

"Ain't nothin' over there," Big Billy drawled. "I ain't never seen *nothin'*—not sure I like seein' it, either."

"Then don't look behind you," Aikin advised, joining them in the prow. The rest of their band followed, as the cliff face swept nearer. "Nothin' back there either. Ditto down below."

David risked a glance over his shoulder. His friend was right: there really was nothing there—the same nothing one "saw" inside a Hole, save that this bore a faint filigree of gold before it, as though the merest veil of substance staved off that insanity. They had come here by way of a Track (though the ship did not require one in order to navigate between the Worlds), but not *along* a Track, he didn't think.

They were somewhere now, though, and that was major comfort. "Is this what I think it is?" Brock wondered, stroking the handle of the Blackhawk he'd thrust into his belt.

David eyed him warily, relieved at not having to explain the unexplainable to his father. "I think so," he replied, wishing Fionchadd were here for confirmation instead of back at the tiller adjusting the trim of what seemed clearer by the moment was to be landfall, and nowhere near Lugh's palace. "It's a bubble universe, basically an accretion of matter built up along the Track."

"Or something that has split off from a larger World and drifted here," Aife countered. "That has occurred often in Tir-Nan-Og of late; I heard as much when Lugh kept me captive as an enfield. It is the result of happenings in your World. Iron eats through. Pieces . . . fall off. If they are connected to a Track, sometimes they float down its length like a bead upon a string." She studied the terrain critically. "This one, however—it is old, the rock is. Perhaps it has merely broken off the larger Land like the edge of a glacier wearing away in summer."

"And Nuada's here?" David ventured.

Aife shrugged. "It would be an odd place to find him."

"Maybe so," LaWanda observed, padding over to join them, "but dust me with flour and call me white if that don't look like him comin' out of that crevice there."

Aife glanced around sharply, and David recalled that she had once been placed under judgment by the powers here—including Nuada—and had not yet served out her sentence. Was it any wonder that she dreaded this encounter? Still, she held her head high as the ship turned to angle closer to a section of ledge fronting a darker fissure than most, in the shadows of which a tall blond figure was standing with that odd light raising highlights along the metal that comprised his right arm, so that it looked like a limb of flame.

David watched as the Faery raised that arm in greeting—or warning, for his other hand clutched the hilt of a wickedly gleaming sword.

"That's him sure enough," David acknowledged, jogging across the deck to stand behind the gunwale nearest him.

"Hail!" Nuada called as, without further protocol, he leapt lightly from the stone shelf to the oak boards that decked the vessel.

"Hail," David replied awkwardly, reaching out to steady his—he hoped—friend.

Introductions followed to those who had not formally met the Faery Lord before, notably Big Billy, for LaWanda and Brock had encountered him first at Lugh's council, then during their subsequent evacuation. Nuada murmured greetings as he took each hand in turn—a custom from the Mortal World at which he seemed perfectly adept. Only when he reached Aife did he pause. "Lady," he breathed at last, "the world we know would seem to be changing. I trust there is a story behind your presence here in the form in which I greet you, and that the one I heard is true. I trust, also, that these good folk can likewise trust you. Were it not for the presence of Fionchadd, I would take this meeting with very hard bread indeed."

Aife's chin went up. Her dark blue eyes were blazing. "Trust is a thing people have given me, then used against me, and a thing I too have abused. It did me no good and much ill. I have debts to pay on both sides of the World Walls. By coming here I hope to begin that payment . . . Lord." A pause, then, in a voice cold as ice: "Or *are* you lord of anything now? Beyond cliffs and vines?"

"There are things behind these cliffs few have seen," Nuada answered. "And things within everyone here few have seen as well. But," he added, "this is clearly no afternoon outing with young Fionchadd, or I do not know mortal weapons when I see them."

Fionchadd motioned toward the cabin. "Aye, Lord. But first, would you have some refreshment?"

The Faery shook his head. "Knowledge is all I require now, though some things I already knew before your coming."

David's brow wrinkled at that, before he noted the thin golden chain hanging around the Faery's neck: a chain he himself had given him. Once it had supported a hologram pendant: cheap in Athens, but in Tir-Nan-Og, a wonder. Nuada had valued it, studied it, and improved on it, and finally made a sort of spy crystal using some of the same technology. "You used that, didn't you?" he dared, not at all certain he liked the idea of *anyone* spying on his comings and goings.

"One uses what tools one may," Nuada gave back amiably, though his eyes flashed warning. "And what weapons. Is that not what you would make of me? A tool to your own devices? A weapon in your own plans?"

"To save your king, you mean?" David retorted.

"To save your Land, *you* mean!" Nuada snorted, but the tension that had ridden along his jaw had vanished.

"Doesn't matter," Aikin broke in. "We can divvy up the tab later. Right now we need to get in and out, and frankly, anybody who can help would be useful."

" 'Specially as we're still not sure where we're goin'," LaWanda noted sourly.

Nuada's face registered honest surprise. "You came here with no notion of where he whom you seek might be?"

David eyed him narrowly. "Obviously you didn't spy enough, or you'd know."

"My Power has limits," the Faery snapped. "I had other business—in *your* World, as it happens. I had but lately returned when you arrived."

David rolled his eyes at Fionchadd. "Good thing, or we'd have wound up farther from where we wanted to go 'stead of closer."

Fionchadd looked back at Nuada, nodding subtly at the chain. "I take it that you could use that to confirm Lugh's whereabouts?"

"Within limits."

"Time flies," Fionchadd prompted. "This vessel merely . . . hovers."

"Aye," Nuada sighed. "Well then, if you would find Lugh, let us all make ourselves comfortable, for this is best done without distractions."

"Circle up, folks," David said a moment later, motioning to the rug on which they had napped, which now lay spread upon the deck. His father, he noted, sat as far as civility allowed from the Faeries. Once they'd all arranged themselves, Nuada reached into the neck of his tunic and drew out a gold disk on a fine gold chain. A deft motion of his silver hand freed the disk; a tweak of those metal fingers set it spinning. A *word*, and it was glowing. Another woke images there.

Something was wrong, David realized instantly. For while he'd rarely seen one of these devices in action, he could tell by the creases that barred Nuada's brow that all was not well. Images *did* form—but they never clarified. It was like TV with interference. Once, David was certain, he caught a glimpse of Lugh's face: tense, wild-eyed, and contorted with pain. Once, too, he glimpsed the body of a naked man, with chains running off into some obscure distance, but it dispersed as he watched, as though fire had burned it away. Indeed, fire was the most pervasive image, and eventually there was nothing *but* fire: a sphere of the stuff, like a small sun, with a sense of something bubbling and seething nearby.

Nuada inhaled sharply, muttered another *word*, and the red glare vanished. The disk clinked to the deck, its glass totally dark.

Nuada's face was as grim as David had ever seen it. "I have not seen this place," he whispered. "But I *did* glimpse Lugh; the bonds of friendship between us are strong enough to pierce even the Power of iron to show him to me. But it must be as Aife said: he must be prisoned by iron, for only iron could block my Power so; and only iron would appear as a flame in the disk."

Fionchadd coughed—perhaps in relief, perhaps to draw their attention to himself. "There is a reason we sought you, Lord," he began, "beyond your Power, your advice, and your cunning, and that reason is this."

"Yes?"

Fionchadd took a deep breath. "In order to bring this vessel to Lugh, it must have something to direct it there: something that belonged to Lugh, or better yet, something that bears his very substance, as it was your own blood on a bit of fabric that brought us here. I ask, Lord, if you have such a thing."

Nuada gnawed his lip. "Of gifts from Lugh, or things that belonged to him, alas, I own many but brought none with me out of Faerie. But there is something else that might serve better, though it might cost us as well, and myself not the least."

David's brow furrowed, but before he could speak, Nuada had spread the silver gauntlet that comprised his right hand before Fionchadd's face. It gleamed in the ruddy light: a marvel of workmanship; the joints that articulated it all but invisible, the range of flexion easily that of a mortal hand. Yet it was metal, made by Diancecht, the Faery master healer, if he remembered his mythology right. David had always wondered about it, for it was the main reason Nuada was not himself king of the Tuatha de Danaan. Kings must perforce be physically perfect, and he was not. That Nuada had not died and been reborn with all his limbs intact was a subject he had never dared broach. Nor, he sensed, was this the time to venture into that.

Still . . . Nuada scowled and did something David couldn't catch with the little finger of the gauntleted hand—then raised his fleshly fingers for their inspection. Silver glittered there, and it took David a moment to realize it was the end joint of that metal digit: hollow, which surprised him. Nuada took it gingerly and upended it into his palm, as though to shake an object from a fabulously well made thimble. Something tumbled onto the metal: the merest crescent sliver of some pale material, like plastic.

Fingernail. It was a fragment of fingernail.

"When my arm was made," Nuada said quietly, "it worked perfectly; every curve, twist, and articulation I desired was part of its design—but I had not strength enough on my own to wield it fully. Yet Lugh was my friend and saw my anguish, and he took a knife and pared off the end of his nail—no more than that did he dare, for fear of rendering himself imperfect—and put some of his own Power into that remnant, and set it here, and so was my arm empowered. 'I may need this back, in time,' he said. And now, I suppose, that time has come." Nuada folded his fleshly fingers around the fragment and passed it to Fionchadd. "If this does not take us as close as this boat *can* come to my ancient comrade, nothing will."

"It will, Lord," Fionchadd assured him, already stalking toward the figurehead. David wondered if he was the only one who saw Nuada's silver hand tremble as he rose to join them in the prow. For already the dragon ship was turning.

Scott Gresham's Journal

(Friday, June 27)

Well, they're gone, and it's me and my friendly (?) neighborhood computer again—which I still don't like, even after the week I've had to get used to the thing. And boy do I wish that was my only problem!

Shoot, a week ago all I had to worry about was a dead-end but fairly interesting job at Barnett's Newsstand down in Athens and a PhD dissertation I had to finish this summer or start losing credits. Nothing major there—except that I knew about Faerie and all that, which played games with my head when I tried to balance it against the so-called hard science I'd been dealing with since I was a kid. Like, how do you reconcile the fact that you know there are Worlds that absolutely are *not* round with the fact that those Worlds also have gravity just like ours—and stratigraphy and stuff—only they've got the same relationship to our World that scraps of wet tissue thrown on a globe would have. Which I guess made me feel like dissertating on Geology was as phony as computing the age of the earth by adding up the ages of everyone in the Bible. *It just wasn't like that!*

And now everybody's gone off trying to play hero again, leaving Good Old Scott to mind the store and try very hard not to feel sorry for himself. I mean, if I look at it objectively, I *do* have an important job. All this shit hinges on preventing (optimally) or delaying (practically) the Mystic Mountain folks from driving anything iron into Bloody Bald, and otherwise stalling things here. Trouble is, the folks off in other places don't have to be responsible for what they do there. Ain't no extradition treaty with Faerie, and besides, the Faeries know we're here. If I blow up a generator, I gotta worry about the Enotah County Sheriff, or worse; I can't just say the Faeries made me do it. I gotta be careful, whereas those other folks don't, not in the same way.

And the thing is, while the very idea of going back to Faerie scares me shitless, I still feel like I've been left sucking hind tit here, 'cause part of me would absolutely love to see that place—any of it—again. It's like I've been told heroin is: one hit and you want it forever. And I'm a mountain boy, too, dammit, just like Sullivan. I've got a right to fight, not just have my head patted and be told that digging trenches is as important as shooting out of 'em.

So I guess I'm as trapped by corporate America as I was by academic America. Maybe I'll go off and see if Dale Sullivan wants to get drunk. Or Elyyoth. I could use a good drunk right now.

Chapter IV:
First Blood

(the Straight Tracks—high summer)

"We may have a problem," Fionchadd announced from the cabin door. He hung heavily against the jamb, eyes wide, face flushed, as though he'd stood too near a fire.

David shifted around from where he and the rest of the crew had been debating battle plans belowdecks, the better to avoid continued scrutiny of a landscape that some time back had simply become *too* disconcerting: too much change too fast, so that Worlds flashed by with the pace and force of a strobe light. "What kind?" he sighed, rising and giving his father a pat on the shoulder as he passed on his way to the flickering rectangle in which the Faery stood. Something about that light had changed, too; likely the same thing that had produced his friend's flush.

"Nothing you have not seen, but disturbing nonetheless," Fionchadd murmured from the foot of the short stairway that led on deck.

David knew before he'd taken two steps what awaited him—knew because he'd seen its like before, in the Lands of Fire, which lay beside Tir-Nan-Og much as his own World lay beneath it. "Your mother took me through here," he breathed, joining his friend topside. "She sent me through one of those, too," he continued, for sight had confirmed what the red light flaring around the stairwell had merely implied.

"Pillar of Fire," Brock gasped behind him.

David started, not having heard the boy approach. He wondered if his own face showed the same crimson glow that lit the boy's features. "Pillar of Fire," he acknowledged, at which point the dragon prow shifted and David saw indeed.

They were on a Track, the golden motes that comprised it so thick they looked solid. The landscape had stabilized, too; into the blasted white desert of the Lands of Fire. But straight ahead a vast blazing redness rose into a sky the color of dawn and sunset and midnight conflagration, and even as he gaped, the landscape blinked and they were closer. Less than a mile, perhaps, and the Pillar was a tower reaching to heaven: brilliant glowing red at its heart, but flickering with gold and yellow, orange and white—and an eerie bluish purple, as though impossible metals burned there.

"Neat!" Brock breathed.

"And perilous," Fionchadd warned. "Not a thing to experience while on deck."

"You said it might be a problem," David hedged.

"I expected its like, but not one so . . . huge. This vessel may not withstand it."

David looked at the Faery askance. "But we rode one out before in a boat like this."

"But not a Pillar this size. A boat may navigate rapids, yet come to pieces on a waterfall."

"I have faith," David managed weakly.

"So do I," Fionchadd acknowledged. "But faith is not always sufficient."

"I'm going below," Brock announced, not bothering to hide the tremor in his voice.

"Right behind you," David called.

Fionchadd said nothing at all, but his eyes spoke eloquently.

"If this don't stop *real* soon," LaWanda grumbled through a choking gasp, "I'm gonna puke out my guts all over this fancy rug." As if to punctuate her remark, she slapped a hand across her mouth and turned to face the cabin's corner. Its *back* corner, David noted, the one farthest from the door and what transpired without. He wouldn't have minded joining her, and would have had his father not been firmly ensconced in the opposite corner—facing outward but

with his eyes closed and his hand gripping the stock of his
old Stevens shotgun so hard his knuckles had turned stark
white.

This wasn't fun at all—not this screwy sensation in his
head, his gut, and his soul alike. Had it been this bad the
other time he'd assayed a Pillar in one of these absurd ships?
David didn't think so. At least that time both inner ears had
agreed on the signals they received, even if they hadn't liked
them; and his stomach had stayed fairly level—possibly a
result of something Morwyn had fed him before departure.
He wished he had something now—and had asked first Fionchadd then Aife for advice, but they'd merely shaken their
heads and informed him that they had enough to do keeping
the vessel together. God knew *that* was troubling, too: the
way the vessel creaked and groaned, bucked and snapped as
it navigated the inside of that monumental inferno.

As for Nuada—the second most Powerful man in Faerie
this side of the Seas Between: he did nothing at all. "There
are things I can do that Fionchadd and Aife cannot," he'd
said, "but Power is finite, the same as strength of limb. Were
I to spend it now, it might not be there later. Too, I have
come to rely on the Power of my friend Lugh to sustain me.
I did not know how much his strength was merged with
mine." And that was all.

David tried to distract himself by once again inspecting
his weapons. The Beretta 9mm automatic was fine, oiled and
gleaming; but a year spent in his closet had not been as kind
to his Winchester pump shotgun. In spite of his mother's
efforts, rust showed there, not enough to impair function but
irritating nonetheless. Scowling, he retrieved his cleaning kit
and set to work.

Tried to, anyway, for the queasy spinning in ears and gut
alike would *not* leave him alone, and he'd finally concluded
that LaWanda was right, he might have to empty his stomach, when, with absolutely no warning, the flames' pervasive
roar, which had become like white noise, ceased abruptly.
The boat popped, snapped, then went quiet, as its joints and
seams settled back to their familiar stresses. Fionchadd and
Aife exhaled as one, and he could see tension flow out of
their bodies. Fionchadd blinked like one newly awakened,

paused for a moment as though listening, then cautiously opened the door.

Air flowed in: moist, if very far from cold. And with that first sharp inhale, the sickness that assailed David dispersed, save a dull throbbing in his skull that could well be an ordinary headache.

"Are we—?" he began, but a frown from Fionchadd shushed him, as David rose from yet another inventory of his gear: mail, surcoat, boots, sword; shotgun, ammo pouch, and automatic. All there. Of course.

The Faery turned full to face him. "Yes," he mouthed, even as David heard the word echoed in his mind: a means of speech Fionchadd rarely employed, which meant something serious was up. Whereupon a flash of pure raw *thought* arced through his head, and he caught fleeting images of a vast boiling lake beneath a dome of rock. And, unmistakably, as though he shared not only Fionchadd's thoughts but his very soul and essence, what could only be the hard adrenaline thrill that presaged battle.

Silence! came that silent command. *Prepare for combat,* came another hard on its heels.

"What?" someone asked aloud. His father or Alkin, it sounded like.

On deck now, and see, came the Faery's voiceless whisper.

The cabin filled with grunts, gasps, and troubled glances as his comrades scrambled to their feet. *Lord Silverhand,* came Fionchadd's thought again, *you are Lugh's Warlord. We are in Lugh's service. It is your right to lead us.*

For now, Nuada agreed. *But I am not well versed in iron as an ally.*

The new plan, then? Until we have cause to change it?

Nuada nodded.

It was a flimsy ploy, David knew, as they filed toward the stairs; wouldn't stand any kind of scrutiny, but perhaps it would be enough.

Nuada, Aife, Fionchadd, and David himself wore Faery armor and clothing—and the glamour-wrought visages of known members of the rebels. Big Billy, Brock, Aikin, and LaWanda wore mundane togs and went bowed and stooped, with their well-armed hands held close behind them, as though they were prisoners to those Faery warriors, retrieved at last after the postcouncil attack from which Nuada had helped them escape. The Sons didn't necessarily know the particulars of that, after all, nor could they recognize every face among their sympathizers. If challenged, Aife would claim to be who she was: a former member of their ranks, newly freed from Lugh's glamour-wrapped imprisonment and eager to rejoin their ranks; with captives brought as proof of her commitment and competence.

It wouldn't stand long or close scrutiny, of course; iron made its presence known through smell, to the keen-nosed among the Sidhe—like metal newly forged, Aife had told them—and anyone with Power could sense a glamour. Still, the plan was for the Sons to see what they expected and relax their guard until it was too late. After that—who knew? It depended on too many things: surprise, Power, the effectiveness of mortal weapons in this World, Faery fear of iron, the sheer number of foes they would face, and the circumstances under which that battle was waged.

That last, at least, was answered when David finally got a clear view of the place into which the Pillar had delivered them.

True to the image he'd caught from Fionchadd's mind, they were inside a huge stone chamber, easily half a mile across. A perfect sphere, it appeared, the ceiling (limestone or granite?) smoothed to a uniform bowl but unpolished and lit by a quivering reddish glow that hinted at once of unseen external flame and those rocks' own inner heat, as though they'd stood long and long beside a forge. The air was hot, too, and vapors seethed across the decks to wrap them— vapors that rose from what David saw, as they eased into formation on the foredeck, was a solid sheet of boiling, frothing water that evidently filled the lower half of that cavern. The air *smelled* hot, too, and the vapors were foul-scented steam such as issued from hot springs back in his own World. Droplets of condensation fell like hot, sticky rain.

But there was no sign of anything manmade—nothing iron or even ironlike—nothing but that dripping ceiling, the steaming lake, and their own ship that had somehow been spat out of the Pillar of Fire that rose from the center of all that frothing turmoil to pierce the dome above with a spear of bloody light.

Which was strange in its own right, for though the Pillar glowed, it did not illuminate; as though it was not entirely present, or existed at one remove, like a perfect hologram of a flame.

But something *else* was certainly present, for David's eyes were burning, as they did in the presence of Power in active use. And by straining them in the wavering light, he was able to make out another vessel, near twin to this, but directly across the center of the bubbling lake and thereby masked by the eerie glare of the Pillar between.

Yet even as he watched, the vessel moved, its strange, limp sails filling with the force of some impossible wind as it glided slowly around the Pillar toward them.

"What?" LaWanda spat, then rounded on Fionchadd. "This ain't what you expected, is it, Faery boy?"

Fionchadd shook his head, and David caught a wash of confusion and anger aimed at once at the approaching vessel and at LaWanda—the latter clearly accompanying a warning that she *had* to appear submissive and that he and Aife would try to cloak all their thoughts, but it would be difficult if those thoughts were also spoken, fueled as they were by strong emotion.

"No," Nuada countered—aloud. "Perhaps tongue speech *is* best now, for the Sons dislike that mode—the province of mortals, they say—and so may not be attuned to it. In any event, this is not what we expected. Do you have any ideas, Fionchadd?"

"Only that this place is not precisely in Tir-Nan-Og. Indeed, I believe that may be a function of Lugh's imprisonment. He was the Land, and the Land cleaved to him. If he is cut off from the Land, his Power will not hold it—not those parts already tending to rebellion, such as this place, or that in which we found you."

"So the Sons may have—"

"Unleashed the whirlwind," Big Billy concluded. David wondered what his pa was thinking—he'd certainly *said* little enough since the shooting lesson. Then again, he wasn't one to talk when there was work to be done, and definitely not one to admit ignorance or fear in the face of a foe.

Nuada eyed Big Billy askance. "Aye . . . perhaps. Perhaps, indeed, when the time comes for them to set up their new king there will be nothing left for him to rule, whether we free Lugh or not."

"Who *is* their new king, anyway?" David asked abruptly.

"His name is Turinne," Nuada muttered. "He is young and rash, but very, very canny, or I would know more of him than I do, which is almost nothing."

David's hands were starting to sweat on the stock of his shotgun. "Would bullets do anything at all against that?" he murmured to anyone who would listen.

Iron will wreak little harm against Powersmith vessels, came the quick flash of Fionchadd's thought. *Save your strength for living foes.*

How many? David thought back at him, desperately hoping their conversation was masked.

Enough for this place—and more than we command.

And then David felt a dull, alien buzzing in his mind that was surely the approaching vessel bespeaking the Faeries that crewed their own. Other consciousnesses brushed his too, and he cringed, so full of contempt were they. "Don't think," he rasped to his mortal friends. "They're tryin' to read our minds."

At least Aife's ploy was working—maybe. But David's fingers were sweating more, and the cursed, pervasive heat was a constant distraction, given how liquid was starting to pool on his forehead, run into his eyes, and make tickling forays the length of his body. He prayed nobody had an itchy trigger finger.

And then the steam cleared enough for David to glimpse the insignia emblazoned upon that approaching sail. Lugh's device was *argent, a sun-in-splendor, Or*; or sometimes that sun on a field *murry, sable,* or *gules*. This was a parody of that: a golden field; a white sun impaled on a sword, the sun releasing a rain of scarlet drops across the lower half of the field—*goutee de sang*, in the jargon of heraldry.

Only then did he pause to wonder what device their own vessel bore. Earlier—last week—the sail had been crimson, displaying a silver American chameleon or anole, in reference to Fionchadd's Cherokee name, Dagantu. If that still billowed above them, they were in trouble.

Unable to resist, David looked around, but the sail was mercifully furled, a bound cigar of red fabric decorating the spar atop their mast.

But would that itself be read as a sign?

Closer now—the ship had covered half the distance between the two of them, and still no words had been spoken, though the troubling buzz half in his head, half in his ears was neither comforting nor intelligible, for it was entirely in the incredibly complex Faery ceremonial speech, which was distant kin to the most formal and highly inflected Gaelic.

Closer, and the dragon prows bobbed in the seething vapors, as though they too sought recognition.

Closer yet, and he saw their opponents clearly for the first time: tall, hard-faced men in golden surcoats ranged along the deck, with as many more of rougher shape, if not more roughly clad, among them, every other one, with a final Faery at the tiller.

David wondered if those mortals were there by choice and from what lands and places they hailed. He didn't want to *kill* them, but knew he would if pressed: his death or another's. But did these foes—the mortal ones—have family and friends who would mourn their loss with soul-wrenching regret? Or were they solos, soldiers of fortune recruited to a stranger war than any of them could ever have anticipated? Elyyoth hadn't known, and Nuada had only ventured guesses: that they were not all men of David's land or time. Aife had no idea at all; the utilization of mortals having come about after her departure from the Sons of Ailill.

Closer yet, and then, for the first time, David heard voices and the slow, heavy beat of some vast brazen drum.

Nuada's warning was like lightning through David's brain, and it took a moment to sort out the words. *Should you seek to board that vessel, be very sure of your footing, for if you fall into the cauldron beneath us, mortal flesh will die!*

And that was it. David's only recourse now was waiting.

A billow of steam washed between the vessels, and when it parted again, and he blinked the latest runnels of sweat from his eyes, the vessel was suddenly alongside, the shields along both gunwales not a dozen feet apart.

David's companions faced that other crew in two grim-eyed lines, one before the other. The back—Aife, himself, Fionchadd, and Nuada—wore the guise of Faerie, all in cloaks and mail. Nuada and Aife, at either end, sported bared swords; Fionchadd kept his hands hidden, as did David, who gripped his double-barrel in sweating fingers beneath a close-drawn cloak. Before them ranked the mortals in deliberately disarrayed mortal togs: Aikin in front of Aife, Brock ahead of David, Big Billy before Fionchadd, and LaWanda in Nuada's van. It was a deliberate arrangement: three of the most distinctive mortals from the Sons' attack on Lugh's guests displayed to the fore. If they were lucky, their opponents would focus their attention on them, not on their all-too-lightly-englamoured "captors."

If they were lucky.

More orders stabbed David's mind, quick and brutal with haste: a plan Nuada had clearly formulated on the spot and had no time to finesse into their minds, no time to debate or delay. For an instant, David's brain went utterly blank; the next, he was certain he'd been struck blind. Yet his body was already responding to commands his brain knew but could not express.

"Now!" Nuada roared. And battle was begun.

The four obvious mortals knelt as one, hands still behind them as though joined by chains in forced submission. But even as they stumbled onto their knees, even as eyes in the opposing vessel swung their way, hands that had *not* been bound swept around and four sets of gun barrels belched lead and steel, noise and pain.

Distraction. Maximum damage. First offensive. David flung his cloak aside and leveled his shotgun at the center-most rank of warriors, not ten yards across from him, fixed on a red-haired Faery man, took a deep breath, and squeezed the trigger. He felt the kick, but the report was lost within an explosion of other sounds: startled cries, some of them clearly of pain or surprise and *not* in English; a blast of alarm and rage in his head; the rapid rattle of small-arms fire as those in the front rank peppered their opponents with bullets and shot intended to shatter joints, blind eyes, and distract mortal and Faery alike with as much pain as possible.

David got off the requisite two shots and saw the red-haired Faery fall, clutching his belly, where an enormous red cavern gaped. His own stomach promptly revolted, but he fought it down as the mortal beside the redhead turned to gape at him, half dazed, half furious, hands diving to his waist, where a pair of pistols waited.

And then noise gave way to movement, as the bogus captives hurled themselves forward to crouch behind the gunwale: smart, given they wore no armor and had surprise alone on their side—not that David approved Nuada's plan. It was too hard on the mortal faction—like the British sacrificing the Aussies at Gallipoli.

Which burst of anger ate maybe half a second before David too lunged forward, aiming for the narrow gap that had opened between Big Billy and Brock. More movement caught his eye as he hit and rolled: Nuada, to his left, had raised his sword and swung it in a smooth arc before his body, and as he did, flame roared up before it to slash across the gunwale of the opposing vessel. Shields charred in its wake, and a whole vast section fell away, revealing the vessel's ribs, thereby depriving their opponents of half their cover. *So why didn't he sink it entirely?* David wondered as he fumbled frantically for ammo for the twelve-gauge.

Prisoners. Nuada's thought whipped into his own. He glanced that way reflexively, and felt his heart all but stop as Nuada charged screaming toward the railing, poised there a moment, then leapt across that boiling, seething rift to the other vessel. A hard pounding to his right was Aife likewise running—leaping—vanishing into steam, a coil of rope clutched beneath the arm that didn't wield a sword. David assumed she touched down, but Aikin's irate grunt reminded him that this was no time to gawk and ponder. For now his business was simple: reload as soon as possible, shoot as accurately as he could, and try to keep his own skin intact. For a bare instant all he knew was his father's face to his left, white as death; Aikin jumbling through his cache of ammo to his right; and Brock crunched up before him, unable to move at all.

Reflexively, he eased back—as a deadly rain of objects thunked into the deck. *Daggers*: the first weapons easily at hand to warriors who, for what was hopefully a crucial moment too long, had not expected attack. Somehow he managed to reload, swallowed hard, and thrust his head above the gunwale between two shields in hopes of getting off another pair of shots—only to jerk it down again as, with unbelievable speed, one of his foes flung a dagger that rang off the earpiece of his helmet. A fractioned second slower or faster for either of them and he'd be sporting a hand's length of metal in his eye.

More thunks. More shots—some coming *toward* them now—and more cries of every kind, and he had barely time to note that Nuada had engaged the vessel's captain one-on-one, and that Aife was doing likewise with a rangy mortal at the other end, all the while tugging hard on the rope to draw the vessels together. Too many things at once, though, and she hadn't noticed the helmsman sprinting toward her, sword upraised.

"Aik, there!" David yelled, pointing with his gun, feeling rather than seeing his friend twist around and fire, his position giving him better odds of missing the Faery woman.

A third round of thunks, more opposing fire, two more possible hits of his own, and then his blood turned to ice as he heard a strangled cry at far too close range. "Finno!" someone yelled—LaWanda? But he had no time to check, as a new hail of bullets sprayed across the deck inches behind his feet. He drew them up instantly, huddled into an awkward ball as random fire exploded and at least two bullets made it through the thick bronze shields. Shrapnel grazed his fingers, and he felt a wash of heat he suspected was Faery flame not unlike Nuada's being brought to bear on their vessel.

Two more reports, right beside him. "Got 'im!" Aikin crowed abruptly. "Go, Aife!" And then silence for an instant—and a hard, crunching thump as the vessels slammed together. The impact knocked David back from his shelter, as Nuada's command slashed his mind again.

"Over!"

What did Silverhand *mean*, "Over"? This wasn't part of the plan—

Nor was encountering our foes afloat, came Aife's terse reply.

"Over, you mortal fool!"

The command carried the force of compulsion, and before David knew what he was doing, he'd leapt to his feet and was hurling himself across the now-narrow gap between the vessels. Steam washed his face with a bath of wet agony, and he had a moment of horrible, frozen panic as he saw nothing below but churning, boiling water, and ahead, a sweep of charred deck littered with shards of wood, scraps of bronze, a splatter of blood, and the sprawling shapes of warriors scrambling to their feet.

Somehow he was on his feet as well, traction uncertain upon the slippery deck, shotgun—empty again—a dead weight in his hands.

"Dave! Look—" came Aikin's desperate shout. But before he could react, something heavy slammed into his back, flinging him hard across an inert body, to fetch up short against the raised metal boss at the base of the mast. He twisted as he hit, trying desperately to maintain any hold at all on the twelve-gauge, wondering if he ought not to forget it now and trust in sword or pistol.

Traitor! came his assailant's thought—Faery speech, yet intelligible—then: *Mortal scum!* as David's thrashings shook his helm aside, revealing his all-too-obvious features. He kicked savagely—all he could do—and continued twisting, and somehow found himself half upright, facing the largest Faery male he'd ever seen, scrambling toward him, sword upraised. David rolled as the sword arced down, but managed to knock the weapon from its goal with the shotgun swung one-handed. The stench of hot metal scorched the air; the sword flew from startled fingers—and then the man fell full upon him.

But not a man any longer: an enormous catlike creature, sleeker than a lion, black as a melanistic puma, fanged like a saber-toothed tiger. Twice his size, too, and easily thrice as heavy.

Thank God for mail!—as claws slashed his chest, rending his surcoat to ribbons and sending metal rings popping. Another like that, and—

There'd better not *be* another! And then his field of vision narrowed to a mouthful of teeth bearing down on his head. He batted at it desperately—and was appalled at the roar that ensued, and only then recalled that he still held the shotgun in one hand and had a pistol at his waist. The first was empty, the latter wasn't, but at these quarters, what you could wield most effectively was what mattered.

"Fuck you!" he snarled as he smashed the twelve-gauge down on the creature's back. The thick, acrid stench of burning hair filled the air, and the beast's growl became a scream as it leapt aside. He leapt after and managed to fumble the automatic free, even as he used the shotgun as a combination sword and cattle prod to force the beast farther away. A breath, a pause to check for impending assault from other quarters, and he thumbed off the Beretta's safety and fired point-blank into the cat-beast's maw. It screamed again and blood gushed forth. David got off another shot, this time in the chest. *You better have a heart in there!* he raged through a third. *Better not be able to fight with the fuckin' thing stopped!*

"Fool!" the beast snarled back, in dreadful parody of mortal speech.

"Who you callin' fool?" came LaWanda's shriek from somewhere behind, followed instantly by a shotgun blast.

The beast fell silent—possibly because it lacked a head. Yet even as David watched, that shape altered, reverting to the man-form that was its proper state. Already queasy, he gagged, turning hastily away, hand across his mouth, propped against the mast while he got his bearings, already seeking another foe. "Thanks, Wan—" he began, but his savior was gone.

Steam—or sweat—or simple shock—veiled his vision, and when he could see again, it was to gaze upon chaos. Aife was to his left, sword dancing as she fought one Faery, while the corpse of another—a woman—lay behind her. Aikin was wrestling frantically with a lavishly bleeding human twice his size. Brock was nowhere to be seen, though an occasional bark of gunfire from the other ship suggested that he alone had ignored Nuada's command to board. LaWanda was a dark blur darting here and there, hiding, and choosing her targets with clinical precision. Nuada was still engaged with the man he'd first assailed, but *that* encounter was difficult to see, and David suspected magicks went on there. Probably the man was the most Powerful among their foe, and as such, Nuada's natural nemesis.

As for Fionchadd—no sign, so probably his cry had heralded an injury.

And Big Billy—

Christ? Where was his pa? He'd been next to him at the gunwale, had been vaguely aware of him leaping beside him to this vessel. But now?

"Dave!" came Aikin's strangled gasp, and reflex sent David stumbling to his friend's aid, where he still struggled to subdue his human foe. Four yards and he was there, Beretta poised to end that battle. Only . . . they were moving too fast to risk it, with Aikin in the muddle, and no way Aik wouldn't have shot already, had he access to any of his artillery. For an instant he caught Aikin's gaze: hazel-eyed and furious. And then David grabbed the enemy by the shoulders and heaved him up and away. As if in response, the ship promptly tilted, and all three fell, and when David figured himself out again, he was sprawled atop that man. Fortunately, he was a decent wrestler for a little guy, and was able to pin the fellow's arms with his knees as he brought the shotgun down hard across his foe's unprotected throat.

"Kill 'im!" Aikin gasped behind him. "Shoot the bastard!"

"He's one of us," David hissed back. "I don't want—"

And then it didn't matter, because something cracked beneath David's fingers, and the man suddenly ripped free, to tear wild-eyed at his throat while he vented awful, gurgling sounds and flailed ineffectually for air. David stared at him incredulously, not believing what he'd done.

"Oh, fuck," he sobbed. "Oh, flyin' fuck!" Then, to Aikin, who had scrambled up beside him: "Oh, fuck, Aik; I crushed his windpipe and I didn't mean to!"

Aikin's eyes were cold. "People die," he spat, and gave David a handup as he likewise rose.

"I think we're . . . winnin'," David choked back. "I—"

He didn't finish his sentence, for the flurry of movement

in the prow that was Nuada and the Faery captain suddenly clarified, to reveal Nuada alone, standing slump-shouldered above a mass of *something* that presumably had been his foe. Victory showed on the Faery Lord's face for an instant—and then, to David's horror, abject concern.

"*Back!*" Nuada shouted, motioning wildly toward their own boat.

David started to yell a protest, but Aikin was already shoving him that way. Others rose to join him, thrusting aside foes who no longer struggled or gave token resistance at best. He saw Aikin—Aife—LaWanda—all leap toward their home vessel.

But where was his father?

Oh, *there* he was: shoving aside a bald guy who'd been trying to wrest away his shotgun.

And then they were at the ship's side, and leaping, and back on their own deck.

The first thing David saw was Fionchadd, sprawled across the boards, bleeding from a dagger wound in his side. Aife was already there, however, hands a blur as they probed the injury. Fionchadd's face was white as snow, but he smiled as David came up beside him. "We . . . I think we won."

"Maybe," came Nuada's voice behind him. "Or not. I—"

For the second time in far less than a minute, his words were cut off, this time by a rumbling explosion. Flames erupted from the vessel they had just abandoned, and a cloud of heat and stench and steam rolled over them. Already queasy, David vomited—and yet somehow managed to rouse himself in time to see one final figure come hurtling across the gap between the vessels.

"Pa!" he yelled, reaching to brace his father when he touched down.

"Shit!" Big Billy yelped back as David grabbed him. In spite of both their efforts, they fell. And then another explosion lit the air, and a dreadful shrapnel of wood, metal, flesh, and bone rained down upon them. Big Billy's face smoothed with a relief David was insanely glad to see, then contorted abruptly.

"Pa! What—?" David gasped, as his father slapped at his

back and collapsed, a foot long splinter of metal-bound oak lodged close beside his spine. Blood was everywhere.

David froze as though he'd himself been shot, then gazed about wild-eyed. "Aik!" he screamed. "Aife! Nuada!"

Aife was beside him instantly, leaving Nuada to tend Fionchadd. She touched his father's body but briefly, then looked David square in the eye. "He bleeds within," she said, "in a way I am not trained to heal."

"But can't you remove that?" David protested.

Aife shook her head. "I dare not. If I do—"

"He'll bleed to death," David finished for her, feeling oddly calm. Or numb.

"I'll be okay—" Big Billy gasped, trying in vain to roll over.

Aife touched his forehead and he went slack, though he didn't quite lose consciousness.

David rounded on her. "What do you think you're doin'?"

"Conserving his energy," the Faery woman snapped. "Blocking his pain. For now, as your kind would say, we have other fish to fry."

Nuada rose from where he'd been tending Fionchadd and strode over to join them. "What happened?" David demanded, because he had to say something and dared not think about his father. Not when their mission was still unfinished.

"Their captain was Powerful indeed," Nuada replied, removing his helm to reveal golden hair slicked to gloss with sweat. "As Powerful as I care to meet, weakened as I am. I fought him because no one else could have, and fortunate it is that we had the advantage of them for a crucial moment. It was enough to turn the tide in our favor, but the captain saw that, and would have destroyed both our ships had I not read that intention in his eyes and called retreat."

"But . . . why?" Aikin panted.

"Think, boy!" Nuada snorted. "If he survived or surrendered, we would have had prisoners, and so the Sons' cause would have been compromised, whether or not we succeed in freeing Lugh. If he died, we died with him, and others there surely are who can take his place guarding the Iron Dungeon.''

''Others,'' LaWanda mused, staring at the dome far above.

''There *will* be others,'' Aife emphasized. ''We must hurry.''

''Aye,'' Nuada sighed. ''For the last thing I sensed as the captain's soul fled his body was a warning to more of his clan who even now approach from without.''

''Shit!'' LaWanda groaned, wiping her brow.

''But my pa—!'' David cried.

''If we flee with him now he stands a chance of living,'' Nuada said coldly. ''If we free Lugh, his odds grow less. But consider, boy, the things that hang in the balance.''

David fixed the Faery Lord with a glare that could have flayed him. And then he looked at his father: barely conscious, but with his face—almost—at peace. ''I have no choice,'' he said grimly. ''There's more than just what I want at stake here. Assuming,'' he added savagely, ''there even *is* an Iron Dungeon!''

''Take heed . . . *mortal!*'' Nuada snarled back. ''You try my patience!''

Chapter V:
Prisoners of War

(the Iron Dungeon—high summer)

"... you try my patience!"

Nuada's warning hung in the air like the pervasive steam, the incessant drizzle, yet David barely heard it. For a long sick moment, he stood frozen: mouth open, arms hanging limp at his sides, shotgun dangling loose in half-numb fingers. Sweat slid into his eyes, indistinguishable from the tears starting there. A stray gust of whatever odd wind whirled about the spherical cavern that constituted present reality whipped the remnants of his surcoat against his legs.

And still he stood. Gazing at . . . nothing, really. And then, in spite of himself, back at his father, motionless on the deck, heavy body contracted into a fetal crescent, as though to shrink away from the splinter lodged in his back.

"Ma is gonna kill me," he said at last, to nobody. "She is gonna fucking *kill* me." What had he been thinking, anyway, to drag his pa into crap like this? And what had his pa been thinking?

"I knew the risk," Big Billy rasped through a sleepy cough. And with that, his body went limp.

For a moment—far *too* long, as though time itself held its breath—David thought his pa had died. But then he caught the swell of his ribs, the pulse of a vein where his surprisingly small ear met the rough auburn thatch of hair. Abruptly he was on his knees, weapons thrust roughly aside, oblivious to the confusion of voices around him: questions, answers, groans, and cries of jubilation—his companions trying to sort out the battle they had just, somehow, survived. A second

87

only it took to locate his cloak and roll it into a pad to slip beneath his father's head. Barely longer was required to rip away the tatters of his surcoat and, very gently, use it to wipe away the blood (What kind of blood? Human? Or Faery?) that ensanguined his father's face. Aikin joined him, silent, face a screwy mixture of elation and concern; and with the aid of his friend's trusty Gerber, David managed to cut the heavy khaki work shirt away from the wound. A strip from the surcoat made a makeshift dike against the steady seep of blood. Only when they'd finished did Aikin speak. "If that was war, I don't like it."

David merely nodded—and didn't look up until a shadow fell upon him. "You have done what you can," came Nuada's voice: a veil of silk across polished metal. "Now come; the sooner we complete our mission, the sooner we can attend his healing."

"No," David mumbled. "I don't have any fight left in me right now. No ideas. No feelings. Nothin'. Just . . . go away."

A hand brushed his shoulder: Nuada's living one. He flinched, tensed to fling it away, then felt the reality of it, and a sense of—not love, but honest concern that leapt the gap between their selves and their races alike. The Faery's anger, it seemed, had been short-lived.

Even so, David started to protest, but Big Billy opened his eyes. Funny how David had never noticed how startlingly blue they were. "Go on," his father whispered. "I can hang on. And if I don't . . . well, at least I've seen some things most folks ain't."

David nodded mutely, patted his father on the shoulder, and rose to join the others sprawling in a rough semicircle around Fionchadd, who, minus his tunic, was sitting up, looking very pale. David sought automatically for the wound in his side, but saw no more than a patch of red-stained skin surrounding an angry pucker that even as he watched grew smaller. "Would that all wounds were of such like," the Faery volunteered.

"Would," Aife agreed in a hard voice. "I—"

"So where's this Iron Dungeon?" Aikin broke in, already

breaking down his shotgun. "Second question: how long have we got to find it?"

Aife puffed her cheeks. "Look around you and recall what you know about the substance of Faerie, the nature of iron, and reaction between the two."

Aikin frowned, but Brock spoke up at once. "Iron's hot—in this World. And this water's boiling, which means—"

"That the Iron Dungeon is within the water," Aife finished for him. "Very good."

David's heart sank. "So we have to go . . . underwater?"

Aife shook her head. "The Iron Dungeon is the heart of this cavern, at once within it and not, as the Pillar is here and elsewhere. And the cavern is equal parts air and water, as its shell is earth, and fire pierces it, top to bottom. The Dungeon is exactly in the center of it all."

David craned his neck to peer over the gunwale toward the Pillar of Fire that had delivered them here, more than ever convinced it was not entirely present.

"It is not," Aife confirmed, as though she'd read his thought. "That is how we were able to pass through the Dungeon itself, before we were spat out here."

Brock shook his head in utter confusion. "I don't get it."

"You're not supposed to," David muttered. "I don't either."

Aikin, too, regarded the flame uneasily. "You said that the folks guardin' this place had sent out a call for help? So when'll they get here? More to the point, can we assume they'll also come through the Pillar?"

Aife shrugged. "Soon, probably, to the first. As to the latter, I would suppose so." She glanced at Fionchadd. "Do you think . . . ?"

"It would be my best guess."

"What about the Dungeon itself?" LaWanda wondered. "What, exactly, is it?"

"Different things at different times," Aife replied. "To some degree it conforms to the strengths and weaknesses of whomever it imprisons." She paused, fished in her belt pouch, and to David's surprise, withdrew an ordinary yellow pencil and a small pack of Post-it notes upon which she began to sketch. A sphere, divided at the equator, chains extending inward to support the body of a man spread-eagled by manacles at his extremities—all exquisitely rendered in about ten seconds, giving the lie to Faery infacility at art.

Aikin scowled at it. "Is this accurate?"

"An accurate guess. The chains support him so that his body does not actually touch the iron, yet its heat can—almost—destroy him."

The scowl deepened. "So I assume he's got an air supply?"

"His captors would not have him die of suffocation before they are ready for his death in truth."

"So why doesn't he just shapeshift and escape that way?"

"Because the pain of the iron makes it impossible for him to concentrate, and even one such as Lugh must exercise discipline in order to alter his form. Too, even if he did escape his manacles, he would fall to the bottom of the sphere, which would be his doom. Oh, he might hover in bird shape for a space of hours—days, maybe even years—but eventually he would tire. So, no, there is no escape from that place, for one of Faerie. Its designers knew that very well."

It was David's turn to look puzzled. "Still, whoever controls the Dungeon has to have some way to get prisoners in and out. You folks can't actually teleport, best I can tell, therefore there has to be an opening—hinges—*something*. The thing can't all be in one piece."

"Actually, it could," Aife countered, "but in this case, you are likely correct."

Brock squinted toward the fire. "It can't be very big or we could see it."

"Maybe thrice your height across," Aife supplied.

"So if we could get hold of it, could we, like, tie something to it and drag it to this ship, and then open it up here?"

"That was my thinking," Aife acknowledged.

"Mine as well," Fionchadd echoed. "The problem lies in reaching it. None of you mortals can bear the touch of those flames beyond the confines of this vessel. Yet no one who is Faery can handle iron. Which leaves—"

"Me," Nuada finished, flourishing his silver hand—which

he'd evidently "repowered" during the postbattle chaos.
"Watch!" And his shape began to shimmer.

God, I'm gettin' jaded, David thought, as he stared at the
elder Faery. He'd seen the Sidhe shapeshift before, of course,
but never truly watched it. As best he could tell, it was much
faster and far less bound to the limits of one's physical body
than what he and Aik and Cal had assayed with the aid of
uktena scales. Heat went with it, too, which he'd never noticed before. The bottom line was that one instant he was
looking at a tall, imposing, if slender-limbed, man; the next
he was gazing at a glowing blur of particles, and then,
abruptly, the particles solidified into another shape: low-
slung, four-legged, maybe six feet long, sleek in a reptilian
way, and patently not human.

"Lizard," he blurted, then squinted, realizing that the skin
was smooth, the nose blunt, the joints more splayed, and that
a filigree of gills erupted from the juncture of head and neck.
And that it was red and faintly glowing.

"Salamander," Brock corrected. "Saw 'em in a heraldry
book."

"Salamander, fuck!" Aikin snorted. "No salamander's
that big."

"Heraldry," Brock repeated. "Most of the critters I've
seen or heard of here exist in heraldry books, though not
always exactly the same."

"This one is," Aife informed him as the beast waddled
toward the rail. "And if you, young badger, know enough
to recognize such a creature, you also know why that shape
serves us now."

Brock's brow furrowed briefly, but then his face lit up.
"Fire!" he exclaimed. "Folks used to believe salamanders
lived in fire."

"Bullshit!" Aikin huffed again.

David elbowed him. "Not our World. Not our laws. Ben-
efit of the doubt."

Aikin elbowed him back. "Christ, he's goin' over!"

And so he was: the beast had reared up on its stubby hind
legs, laid its forelegs—one of which did not quite match the
others, and not merely because it was made of silver—on
the gunwale, and in one fluid movement thrust itself over-

board. Aife was behind it instantly, releasing the many-hooked anchor with its long coil of gleaming, gold-toned chain. David joined the other ambulatory members of the company at the rail, trying to pierce the incessant sweeps and veils of vapors to view the seething water. At first he couldn't find it, but then he saw: the salamander swimming strongly, the chain clutched between triangular jaws.

It was barely a hundred yards to the Pillar, which was maybe thrice that distance across. Presumably Nuada knew what he was doing: turning himself into a creature impervious to flame; locating the Dungeon, securing the chain, and then—what?

David didn't care. He'd caught sight of his father again, and all his angst—his raw *terror*—over his father's condition returned in force. Somehow, he realized, he'd made a decision. He did *not* have to lead, did not have to be party to every decision made that concerned affairs between the Mortal World and the realm of the Sidhe. Others there were who could think as well as he, who knew as many of the facts. Who were more levelheaded and rational. Let them figure it out. Himself—well, his pa was lying on the deck with a good-sized stick of kindling in his back! More to the point, his pa could easily die. This might be the last time they had together this side of the veil.

Steeling his face to as much calm as he could muster, he made his way to where he could sit down and shift his father's head to rest in his lap.

Aikin joined him—silent, as was his way, but his face full of concern. Funny how he'd never really appreciated Aik until now. Then again, when had the two of them weathered a crisis solo? There'd always been Alec, or Liz, or the rest of the Gang. And even when Aik had actually been present, the guy was so low-key you often forgot he was around—except when he was gaming, but that wasn't so much Aikin as his quasi-twin: the creative persona that masked the actual *him*.

"Thanks," David whispered, reaching out to pat his friend on the knee.

"No problem."

And then it returned to haunt him—*another* "it"—one of

those dreadful things he'd experienced but not yet processed, obscured, as it was, by his father's injury, their own precarious situation. "I killed a guy," he choked. "One of . . . us. I crushed his throat. He was as alive as I am; maybe had a family or friends or huntin' and drinkin' buddies. People who loved him. And all that's over—'cause of me. Somebody's gonna hate me forever 'cause I did something I thought was right."

Aikin nodded solemnly. "All my life I've wondered about this—about war: how it'd feel. About how our uncles and fathers and brothers dealt with 'Nam and stuff. How they felt then, how they slept at night after. Whether it followed 'em." A pause. "I know the answer now, yet I don't. See, on one level, it's the easiest thing in the world: twitch your finger, powder ignites, shot flies, somebody falls down dead. I did that: Faery guy. Hell, I think we were both surprised when the damned thing went off. Double whammy on me when he toppled." He looked away, to the horizon. "I knew what to expect—imagined it pretty good, anyway—but it didn't help. Ain't helpin' now, either."

David nodded in turn. "At least *they* don't stay dead—if they're strong. They come back—their souls do. But that guy I killed—"

"Who knows?" Aikin grunted. "But you're not the first guy who did something awful for a good reason—not the Cove, either, though I know that's important. But we're talkin' peace between the Worlds, here. And don't forget what Elyyoth said: the Sons recruited . . . not bad guys, maybe, but unconnected guys. Folks nobody would miss, whose lives were already messed up, or why didn't they have somebody to care about 'em or to care for?"

"Maybe," David conceded. "But I'm gonna feel that windpipe crack for—"

"As long as you live," Big Billy rasped, beside him. David looked down to see his father's eyes open again. "I did that once. I still hear it. Not much comfort there, but sometimes just knowin' you're not alone helps."

"Thanks, Pa," David whispered, and realized he was crying.

Aikin stirred beside him, clearly uncomfortable at his

proximity to so personal a moment, yet also, David suspected, glad to have had the chance to share. A shadow fell across them; soft footsteps came to a stop behind. David caught a whiff of LaWanda's strange herbal perfume, and wondered if she'd used any of her patented "juju" in the battle. She'd seemed to be an awfully good shot. Maybe too good. "We won," she murmured. "Doesn't help this, though. Sorry."

"What's goin' on?" David asked, not looking up.

"Can't see the Lizard-man no more—too much steam. Cat-woman's watchin'. Elf-boy is too—like he wasn't even stuck in the side. Kid's about to go crazy. I—"

Her words were cut off by an exultant shout from Brock. "I see 'im!" he yelped. "He's coming back."

David grimaced, and carefully removed his father's head from his lap before crossing to the rail. At first he saw nothing save the swirling steam, backlit by the Pillar of Fire. He searched the bubbling waters vainly. Then, bright red against the blood-dark hues around it, as though the heat had brightened his natural hue: Nuada, still in salamander form, swimming strongly back toward them.

Without the chain—which meant, David hoped, that he'd been successful.

Steam obscured his vision, almost scalding hot, forcing him to wipe his eyes and face, and when he could see again, Nuada was alongside and Aife was reaching down to help him aboard. David joined them, but had to retreat when he glimpsed what floated thick in the water around them: ship wrack, mostly, but also a spiraling eddy of what could only be intestines. Not until he heard the slick thump of Nuada slithering over the gunwale did he look that way again, to see the Faery lord already shifting shape.

David caught a fleeting glimpse of sleek bare flesh and silver metal before Nuada resumed his former form—clothes and all. "It was as we thought," the Faery announced, so quickly his words were slurred by his still-changing mouth and lips. "There were hooks all around—evidently it was made to be moved, which I did not know. I was able to attach the anchor securely and to determine that Lugh is within— and well, if not happy."

"But wait," Brock began, "if you're Faery, and the Dungeon's iron—"

Aikin elbowed him. "His hand's not iron though. Right?" he added, to Nuada.

"Yes and no. Iron devours everything of Faerie, but not at the same rate. My silver arm withstood it longer than my fleshly one might—and can be replaced. Still, much longer and I would have sported a melted stump." He flexed his fingers before them for emphasis. The metal joints of palm and finger were bubbled and distorted, as though a hand wrought of wax had been set too near a flame.

"Hopefully," Nuada went on, "when next we deal with it, it will be mortal hands that perform the labor."

"Speaking of which," Aife sighed, "do we free Lugh here, or flee first and release him at our leisure?"

"We secure his prison, then decide."

Aife returned to where Fionchadd was resting on the deck; in spite of the lack of outward sign, he was clearly not entirely recovered from his wound. Which made David wonder how functional any of the Faeries were. They had endurance in spades, but evidently didn't bounce back quickly. And Fionchadd had managed scant rest the last several days. Still, the Faery youth rose—stiffly—and joined Aife at the slot in the railing from which the anchor depended. A *word*—because it was his personal ship—and the chain began to retract. David watched it briefly, then turned back to the Pillar. For a moment, he saw nothing, but eventually he made out a humping darkness inside the burning shaft, that clarified as the flame washed around it (turning whatever fires touched it purple), then became much clearer as it pierced that veil and entered the boiling sea. It was fifty yards away, at a guess, but another *word* hastened its approach dramatically. A pair of breaths and it had covered half the distance. A dozen more and it was beside them, no more than ten feet out: a dark orb of rusty metal maybe twenty feet across, crusted with hooks and excrescences; it looked like nothing so much as an old-style water mine, save for the yard-wide strip of grating that circled its equator like the rings of Saturn. David wondered where the metal had come from. The makers of the Dungeon had used human wrights—among others. Had they pilfered wrecked vessels from his World as well? Or was the Dungeon too old for that?

"Perhaps I could open it," Nuada admitted. "But I have not the strength I once had, and have just spent much of what remained. It would better if you mortals—"

LaWanda's curt nod cut him off. "Any locks?"

Nuada stared at Aife pensively. "I noted none, but it makes no sense to imprison one such as Lugh without them—and spells to secure them, and more spells to bind those spells."

Aife's brow furrowed in turn. "But they imprisoned him in haste—in iron, which they can no more manipulate than can we, and against which spells bind but scantily. The way water will not adhere to some materials in your World," she added to a puzzled Brock. "Nor would wyvern skin have been sufficient; they must have used their human minions."

"And whatever spells *were* employed must be simple ones, if the Sons could set them in haste," Fionchadd observed.

David folded his arms, trying *not* to look at his father. "So what do we do?"

LaWanda rolled her eyes. "Look, folks, this *ain't* that big a deal, but we don't have time to jaw if more bad guys are on the way. We've got what we came for. No reason—"

"It's got hinges," Brock broke in excitedly, pointing to the far side of the sphere. "*A* hinge, anyway—and a counterspring, I think."

"Makes sense," David acknowledged. "Anything else they'd have to raise and lower, which would require touchin' iron, or something that could touch iron, or—"

"Power," Aife concluded. She strained up on tiptoes, eyes probing the bobbing Dungeon. "The boy is correct, too, and probably there is a catch on this side, for do not forget, Lugh's queen had this made. It is therefore likely it was built for one person to manage. Or very few servants."

Nuada gnawed his lip. "It could still be locked, warded, or otherwise bespelled." He eyed Aife and Fionchadd critically. "Neither of you is normally my match, and Fionchadd is injured; but I think if we merged our strength, we could counter whatever protections have been laid upon it."

In reply, Aife simply reached to her waist and unsheathed her dagger, which she then presented to the Faery Lord. Fionchadd did likewise. Wordlessly, they joined the taller warrior, one to a side. What happened next was obscured by Nuada's cloak—deliberately so, David suspected. But he did glimpse Aife locking fingers with Nuada, with the naked blade of the dagger between, so that their blood might mingle, and Fionchadd doing something similar with Nuada's metal hand. A brief gasp—pain was pain, regardless—and all three froze, barely breathing. David felt the hair on his body start to prickle, as though he stood in the presence of a strong electrical field. His eyes burned, too, as badly as they had in at least a year, so that he had no choice but to wipe them. Power was at work, in impressive amounts, in spite of Nuada's poor-mouthing.

"Shit!" Aikin breathed beside him, as his vision cleared enough to show the sphere enveloped in shimmering blue-green *something*, like a film of oil on water, and beneath that envelope: arabesques, swirls, spirals, and shapes that were not exactly letters set in linkages that were not precisely words, all wrought in gleaming white and silver. But as they watched, those patterns first brightened, then exploded into light, as flames of gold took hold and devoured them, so that silver became bright red, then furnace white, then dimmed to gray, and finally to flakes of black that slid away from rust and bare metal alike. A moment later only wet iron bobbed in the steaming water.

"Done," Nuada sighed heavily, as Fionchadd and Aife drew away, wiping daggers that gleamed red upon their cloaks. "Simple—were I fully myself. My thanks to you, young Lord and Lady."

"And to you, Lord," Fionchadd countered. "For such a sharing."

Nuada ignored them, intent as he was on staring at the sphere. Finally he indicated a series of gold-toned bosses not far from the nearside edge of the narrow band that encircled the object. Each bore an intricate design—what David would've called Celtic knotwork—graven deep within it, easily a finger wide. There were five in all, of different metals, all subtly distinct. "If you mortals will trace those with your fingers,'' Nuada advised, ''from center out, then back again, without pause or flinching away, I think the sphere will open.''

David grimaced sourly but shucked out of his mail and eased over the side, not daring to think of the water that seethed scant inches beneath his feet and occasionally sloshed onto that narrow ring. The heat was appalling, too, and—no surprise—the Dungeon itself was all but impossible to touch, for though iron was not hot to David's kind, the sphere had heated the water around it, which had then returned that heat to its source. Still, he persevered, claiming the right-hand two, as Aikin joined him to the left, with LaWanda beyond, also doing two. ''Begin when I say,'' Nuada commanded. ''And together, as much as you may.''

David steadied his hands atop the bosses—each maybe a foot across and slightly domed. He found the centers with no problem and rested his index fingers lightly beside the slots, ready to insert them.

''Now!'' Nuada cried.

David let his fingers slide home—and almost yanked them out again, for the slots were fiery hot, as though lined with molten metal. ''Pain is in the mind,'' Nuada advised, as Aikin gasped and LaWanda bared her teeth in a stubborn grimace. Jaws clamped hard together, David began to draw his fingers along the curves and twists of the patterns—first to the edges, then back again, in paths from which, he discovered to his dismay, there was neither release nor retreat. Abruptly—so suddenly he uttered a yip of surprise—the pain vanished, and he could remove his fingers. Aikin exhaled his relief. LaWanda didn't react at all.

David hesitated, uncertain whether to remain where he was or return to the vessel, when a harsh grating reached his ears, and the top half of the sphere—its edge scant inches from his hands—began to rise, hinged at a point directly opposite. He held his breath, then caught his first glimpse of what proved to be a length of chain anchored to the shell of the sphere just below him, stretching taut toward the center to where a slender bare foot was clamped in a manacle lined with a silvery leather he recognized as wyvern skin. In spite of that barrier, though, the flesh nearest those bonds was puffed and blistered. Blood welled up around it.

Lugh! My brother!

Nuada's relief flooded David's mind, threatening to drown him with emotions not his own. Fear followed, then a fury that could barely be believed—or endured. Not until that instant did he realize the strength of the bond between those Faery lords. As strong as that between himself and Alec. Or him and Liz.

No one spoke as the dome continued to rise, revealing ever more of he who hung within, bound at wrists, neck, and ankles, and with a shimmering sprinkle of something across his naked body from which blood and pus oozed constantly. *Iron filings!* David identified. Not enough to kill, but more than sufficient to sap strength and dull awareness with constant pain.

"What about the manacles?" he demanded, when the dome finally clanked to a stop. "How're we gonna unlock 'em and still keep him from touchin' the sphere?"

"Not the best way, I fear," Nuada shot back, gazing first at the Pillar, then at Aife. "Lady, you are the only one who can accomplish this, for now."

David caught a buzz of thought, but already Aife's shape was altering into a vast white eagle that winged skyward almost before that shifting was complete, to settle into a tight circle barely higher than the mast. Fionchadd, too, must have received some command, for he, along with Nuada, had joined the mortals on the rim, each with drawn sword in hand, boots smoking at even that brief contact with the perilous metal. A *thought*, and those blades swept down, one on the band that bound Lugh's right ankle, the other on that which stretched his left arm straight out from his body. A flash of light, a metallic *ping*, and the manacles parted, to clatter against the sphere's interior. Lugh's limbs sagged with them—not quite touching the metal. Again—Nuada's doing—and the collar that clamped Lugh's neck shattered in a spill of light.

The air promptly filled with the rush of wings as the eagle swooped down to clutch the tortured Faery in talons a foot across and drag him upward, while swords swung a third time and the last bindings parted. For a heart-stopping moment Aife struggled with Lugh's weight, which for all his slightness considerably exceeded her own. Yet somehow she got him aloft and managed to keep his dangling feet shy of his prison until David and Aikin could take that weight themselves and pass him up to LaWanda and Fionchadd, who were back on deck, extending arms down to receive that unconscious burden.

David joined them at once, his companions doing likewise, while Aife resumed her own shape (slapping at her feet), and Nuada shouldered everyone aside to kneel beside his sovereign and friend, boots stinking of burning leather.

Lugh looked awful—what parts David saw before Nuada flung a cloak across all but his head, pausing only to brush ineffectually at the iron dust that clung stubbornly to the High King's sweat-soaked skin, oblivious to the pain it must have cost him. "Bring water!" he shouted. "We must wash away this . . . *filth.*"

"I'm on it," LaWanda replied, already trotting for the cabin.

"Is he—?" David dared.

"Weak," Nuada snapped. "As weak as I have ever seen him—and cursed be those who have bled such a one of nine parts in ten of his blood so insidiously that he is but half alive, and to have wrapped him in so much pain he must hide within himself to escape."

"You mean—?"

"He will command no one today," Nuada gritted. "He is weaker than your sire."

"So, what do we do?" Aikin wondered.

Aife joined them, her face grim, nodding toward the Pillar. "We run," she spat. "We have company."

David's heart gave a sick twitch as he followed her gaze. Another vessel was issuing from that flaming shaft, its contours uncertain at first, then clarifying, as though it turned some impossible corner there. Fortunately, it was emerging at the farthest point from them—which might buy them time.

"Finno—" David warned.

But the youth was already making for the tiller, a *word* poised on his lips. And as that new vessel veered toward them, Fionchadd began to steer their own away, on a slow outward spiral that then shifted inward, toward the Pillar of Fire.

Thoughts buzzed in David's head, angry and uncertain.

"Do we fight?" Aikin murmured beside him. "Or do we flee?"

"We—" David began.

"Much as it pains me," Nuada broke in roughly, "with Lugh as he is, we flee."

Chapter VI:
Dropping In

(the Iron Dungeon—high summer)

"You!" Fionchadd snapped at David from the tiller of their ship. "Get your father below. Aikin, assist him. LaWanda, you and Brock take Lugh. You as well, Aife, if they cannot manage; then return here. What we face is best not confronted above decks."

David started to protest—an automatic response when being ordered about during a crisis—then thought better of it, as reason overruled emotion. Thank God *someone* was taking charge, because he flat wasn't up to it right now. Not with them up to their asses in injuries, chaos, and threat; that last from the ship that had just issued from the Pillar of Fire, almost certainly full to the brim with reinforcements come to aid their late comrades, who had so patently failed to forestall Lugh's rescue.

"You get his top half," Aikin panted, sweat and steam molding his dark hair to his skull like a lacquered helmet. David nodded mutely and hunkered down, finding it awkward as well as alarming to finesse his elbows into his father's armpits while avoiding the splinter lodged in his back. Still, he managed, insanely grateful that Big Billy seemed to have passed out for the nonce—he *hoped* that was all it was. But there was a pulse at his throat, his chest rose and fell . . .

"Now," Aikin grunted. "Slow and easy. Try not to twist him."

David bit back another retort—and followed that with a choking cough as the remnants of breakfast invaded his throat when he found his fingers sticky with blood. He looked away reflexively—had to. And wished he hadn't, for that revealed more chaos: LaWanda and Brock half carrying, half dragging the unconscious and iron-scabbed Lugh, whom they'd maneuvered onto a cloak that looked far too much like a shroud. And through the mist beyond them, the ship continued to approach, even as a bone-tired and barely healed Fionchadd alternately steered, coordinated, and uttered *words* whose purpose David had no desire at all to understand.

That ship was still far off—maybe the only good thing that had happened lately—but it was alive with activity. He could see the flash of weapons, hear cries in a language that had no reason to be English, and feel, increasingly, that sick, thick clogging in his mind that was Faery speech—or will—being directed at this very vessel.

"Any time," Aikin urged.

David shook himself, mumbled a curt apology, and moved as quickly as he dared toward the cabin, staggering beneath his father's considerable inert mass. Somehow they made it—right behind the lighter Lugh—and with help from Aife managed to get Big Billy down the stairs without incident. David promptly froze, torn between returning topside (on the theory that a death you saw coming was better than one you didn't) and tending his pa, which would be an exercise in futility if they didn't get him to a hospital pretty damned quick.

LaWanda thrust a plain clay pitcher of water into his hands, along with a cup. "Drink this and use the rest to clean your old man—or yourself. Better yet, get that crap off Lugh."

"Gimme that!" Aikin sighed, claiming the jug when David hesitated. Eventually curiosity got the better of him and he darted back on deck.

And wished he hadn't. Fionchadd's screwy evasions had clearly born fruit, and they were bearing down on the Pillar of Fire, no more than fifty yards away—so close that he could hear the flames that ripped and tore at the air and feel the odd painless heat that radiated from it as though it *still* was not entirely present. Straining on tiptoes, he turned to check pursuit—and saw, behind Fionchadd at the tiller, that the second vessel was close enough to reveal detail: notably that it was made of darker wood than its predecessor, that its crew were even more agitated than heretofore, that the carved dragon at its prow was two-headed, and that both those heads were slowly stretching forward as though they would nip at Fionchadd's drakkar's tail, though several hundred yards still lay between.

Or maybe not. For even as those heads strained forward, the ship itself drew back—and only then did David realize that Fionchadd hadn't freed the knobby sphere of the Iron Dungeon from the anchor, so that it swished along a few yards behind and a little to one side. More to the point, Nuada and Aife were leaning far across the gunwale, with Aife supporting the other, while green light dripped from their fingers, evidently trying to close the thing with Power alone.

Abruptly, that light went out, precisely as the Dungeon's lid snapped closed. Nuada wavered briefly, then sagged into Aife's arms. David was there in an instant, taking half of the Faery's weight, flinging the metal arm across his shoulders as they dragged him back to the cabin. Were Faeries always so hot to the touch? he wondered.

It was as well they went below, however, for the light and heat had become unbearable. David had just helped La-Wanda stretch the barely conscious warrior down beside his king when Aife, who'd surrendered her burden and returned topside, reappeared at the foot of the stairs, looking as disheveled as a Faery ever did. Her face was pale and slack, but her eyes blazed with command and challenge. Wordlessly, she slumped down against the wall just inside the door, then elbowed it closed it with a thump. "Brace yourselves," she gasped, reaching out to grasp David's shoulder.

"For what?" Brock began, just as his eyes went big as saucers. David imagined he was feeling—seeing—*sensing*—whatever it was that had just played a dozen tricks in a row with his semicircular canals while making his eyes burn like novas with the Sight and charging his whole body with a kind of *twitch*, as though it had reversed polarity.

"We are inside the Pillar," Aife informed them. "That was . . . turning the corner, though if you had watched, you would have seen no such thing."

Brock made a beeline for the door, but Aife stopped him

with a warning hand backed up with a glare that brooked no argument. "Best mortals do not see the fire that burns but does not consume, that is here yet not present, that rises to the skies yet sweeps before us like a river."

"Been there, done that," David snorted, sprawling beside his father and starting to divest himself of several layers of sodden, bloody clothing before recalling the water LaWanda had tried to foist on him. He found it—Aikin was wiping iron-sweat off Lugh with it—filled the cup he still had, and downed it in one gulp. It was the best water he'd ever tasted. "So," he asked Aife. "What gives?"

The Faery shrugged, but her face, if anything, was grimmer. "We reached the Pillar ahead of pursuit, which *should* permit us to elude them. But Fionchadd is tired and not fully healed, whatever he says. Nuada has done far more than he should for far longer, and Lugh can do nothing at all. I am . . . functional. And the rest of you?"

"I'm . . . okay," David sighed, gazing around as he re-filled his mug.

"I'll live," Aikin agreed.

"Okay," Brock grunted, though he didn't sound at all convinced.

"Been better, been worse," LaWanda concluded. "You need me to do something, ask."

Aife glanced over her shoulder. "Wait, for now. And that may be hardest of all."

"Figures," David muttered. And fell silent.

"Won't they follow us?" Brock asked warily from where he was building a nest of pillows in the corner—remarkably unconcerned, so it appeared, until David caught a glimpse of his eyes, which were as fearful as he'd ever seen.

Aife shrugged. "Likely they will. We still have the Iron Dungeon in tow, and they may not know we have freed Lugh, which is why we were in such haste to close it."

Brock scowled. "But won't towing it slow us down? And won't they assume Lugh's still in it and chase us harder?"

Aife dared a thin, hard smile. "You are astute, for a lad," she told him. "But the Pillars, even less than the Tracks, are not made for pursuit. They are like a"—she paused, brow wrinkled—"like a *helix*. Several helices, actually, all twined together so that two vessels could pass going opposite directions and never meet—or follow the same path yet not issue forth at the same point.''

"Like the stairway at Chambord," David observed absently. "The one Leonardo da Vinci's supposed to have designed for Francis I."

Aife cocked a brow. "Only more so."

"Too," LaWanda added, "I doubt it'd hurt to have iron between us if they do catch us. They'd only be able to get so close, right?"

"Uh, I hate to mention this," Aikin broke in. "But where, exactly, are we goin'? I mean, we gotta get Lugh *somewhere*. And we need to get Dave's dad to a doctor—a *real* doctor—no offense."

"Which sounds like we gotta get back to our World," LaWanda observed.

"Your place, Dave?" Aikin ventured.

"No fuckin' way!"

Aikin stared at him.

David countered with a glare. "You wanta bring these guys down on my folks? Think, man! We're a bunch of puny mortals, with *one* fully functional Faery around. Two *if* you count Finno."

"Best not," Aife advised.

"In any event, whether or not we manage to shake 'em in here, that's the first place any pursuit would look!"

The woman nodded agreement. "So it would seem."

"Then where?" David persisted. He was, he realized, stroking his father's forehead. Big Billy never moved.

"A hospital," LaWanda emphasized. "Preferably one near a Track—assuming we have to stay on Tracks with this thing."

"It helps," Nuada acknowledged from where he lay stretched on the floor, looking as if he'd been bled nearly dry of vitality—which perhaps he had.

"But it doesn't have to be?" David countered, suddenly alert.

"No," Nuada conceded, face brightening as he, with some effort, sat up. "And *that* may be our salvation!"

David's scowl deepened. "Huh?"

Nuada's face was alive with animation, in marked contrast to its dull pallor of instants before. "A vessel such as this can travel anywhere if the dragon has a scent to pursue. But suppose we could set a scent in our vessel's nostrils the other could not duplicate?"

"Couldn't they just follow us anyway?"

"Perhaps," Nuada conceded. "Or perhaps they will be busy with other things."

"You've got a place in mind, then? And a means to get us there?"

Nuada—almost—grinned. "I have, though I would rather not speak of it lest we be captured beforehand." And with that he rose stiffly to his feet and steered toward the door.

Aife rose up there, blocking him. "Lord, are you sure you have strength?"

A shrug. "I have strength for *some* things. Whether they be the right ones is not for me to know. For the first part of my task, however, yes, I have strength."

And with that, he pulled aside the door and staggered up the stairs. Light framed him as he paused for breath: flickering red-gold-orange, mixed with a duller red like congealed blood, as though he stood at the open door of a furnace. The air smelled hot and seemed to surge into the cabin to sear their lungs, so that more than one of them began coughing. David hoped Fionchadd was okay, up there in all that. And Nuada—there he went now . . .

"Wait!" David yelled, and then he too was dashing up the steps. Fortunately, Aife's warnings had sunk in, and he kept his gaze fixed firmly on the deck, where shadows danced and frenzied to the tune of competing brightnesses from everywhere. The heat was beyond fierce, so that he felt the skin start to tighten across his cheekbones as though he'd stayed in the sun too long.

Still, he had to know, and so swept his glance carefully upward and aft until he glimpsed Fionchadd's boots where his friend stood braced beside the tiller, garments whipped nigh to tatters by the force of a battering wind.

And Nuada? There he was, up by the figurehead, speaking a *word* aloud—likely one Fionchadd had passed him mind to mind.

However it was transferred, it seemed to be working, for the carved dragon was turning around, and Nuada was placing something in one gaping wooden nostril. David tried to see what it was, but the glare and the sweat running into his eyes made it impossible to make out more than that whatever it was glinted like metal and was small enough to fit inside an adult male hand.

By the time the head returned to its normal position, David could've sworn that they were moving faster, as though their vessel were some hound that had finally scented a long-sought quarry. As for Nuada, he had reeled, then fallen back, aided by Aife, who'd materialized from nowhere to support him. David waited to see if they would go or stay, and when it became apparent they intended to remain on deck, turned his attention elsewhere. He *should* go below, yet still he lingered, shielding his face with his hand from the glare ahead as he turned back toward the stern, whence whatever disaster might strike would issue.

Fionchadd still manned the tiller—likely because the buffeting inside the Pillar was sufficiently severe that constant adjustments were required to keep them on track—and, of course, to evade the pursuing vessel, which still hung grimly on their tail, closer, if anything, though with the bulk of the Dungeon between.

There was something weird about the light back there, too; it was ruddier than that ahead, for one thing, which tended ever so slightly toward violet. Which made no sense, unless it was due to the red shift: approaching light compacting into shorter wavelengths than that behind. Which said a lot about the nature of the Tracks and would've intrigued the hell out of Sandy. David made a mental note to tell her, assuming he survived the next few hours.

"Dave, you better get down here," Aikin called from the foot of the stairs. "It's your dad."

David's heart skipped a beat. Ignoring the swirling, flaming chaos above decks, he made his way back to the cabin.

LaWanda was wiping his father's brow with water poured onto a scrap of David's surcoat and singing softly. Or chanting. Big Billy was awake again. His face was tight with pain, but he seemed to relax when he caught sight of his son.

"How're you doin', big guy?" David murmured inanely, patting his father's shoulder.

"Been better," Big Billy whispered hoarsely. "Tell you what, boy; this thing hurts like hell—not so bad I can't handle it, but—"

"We're workin' on it," David promised helplessly.

"Better put 'er in overdrive, then," Big Billy retorted, with a cough that, to David's dismay, brought forth blood, likely from where the splinter had grazed a lung. What else it might've grazed, he had no idea. Liver, perhaps? Kidneys? Good thing his pa had back muscles like steel cables, so there was a fair bit of meat to fight through before you hit anything important.

"We're doin' the best we can," David assured him.

Big Billy patted his hand. "That's all you can do, then. But Davy—Dave. I don't wanta scare you or nothin', but I gotta tell you two things. One is that no matter how I've acted, I love you. I know there's stuff to you I don't understand, and maybe I ain't tried real hard, and that's a mistake I'll admit. But I still love you. But tell JoAnne and Little Billy, that I love 'em too, and not to be pissed at me for goin' off and leavin' 'em. Tell 'em we wouldn't be here in the first place if our folks way back yonder hadn't gone off and left folks they loved for whatever reasons. And tell 'em I'm doin' this so they *won't* have to go away from a place they love."

David took his father's hand and clutched it desperately. "I'll do it, Pa. I swear. But don't forget what Dale always said: we're hard to kill. Wars get more of us than anything, and even then—" He broke off, appalled at what he'd just blurted out.

"This *is* war," Big Billy said simply. "But there's one other thing I gotta tell you . . . in case."

"Anything, Pa," David whispered, distantly aware of Aikin's hand resting gently on his shoulder.

"Don't ever—" Big Billy began, before another round of coughs wracked him. "Don't ever," he tried again, "let your kids get smarter'n you. You watch 'em from the time they're born and read every word they read and watch every movie and TV show they watch, and *maybe* you can keep up with 'em. 'Cause that's the sad thing about all this: how I've raised you and *not* raised you, both; seen you go places I can't, and wished I could, but not took the time to even try. Folks always want their kids to avoid their mistakes, and then make others instead. That was the worst of mine. Don't you do it.''

"I promise," David vowed. " 'Course that's still a ways off, I hope."

"Maybe," Big Billy mumbled back. And closed his eyes once more.

"Good advice," LaWanda affirmed. "My granny told me the same."

"The juju woman?" Aikin ventured.

"Yep. She— *What th—?"*

The entire vessel suddenly jolted, as though something solid had struck it. *"Oh, shit!"* David groaned, already scrambling for the door, with Aikin and Brock right behind, leaving LaWanda to minister to Big Billy. For a moment he thought to stop his two friends, then dismissed such efforts as futile. "Try not to look above the rail," he cautioned, and once more started up the stairs. "Finno, what—?" he yelled at the top, praying his voice would carry above the thunder of flames.

Either the Faery youth heard him or he caught the urgency of David's thought out of the ether itself. "They are firing upon us: arrows tipped with poison!"

"Poison!"

"Not aimed at me," Fionchadd added, "aimed at this vessel. It is to some degree alive, and there are poisons that can affect it. You felt it shudder just now. It would be as if a wasp or bee stung you."

David rolled his eyes, as one mystery was revealed only to be replaced by another. "How dangerous?"

"More, the more bolts strike us."

As if to punctuate that remark, a series of dark spots materialized from the glare behind them—spots that thunked into the deck and became arrows. The ship twitched again, as though to shrug away that irritation, and David's heart sank, for they were also slowing. "Can we shoot back?"

"To no avail, for we have no such poison with us."

"What about guns?"

"Even your iron bullets would not harm their vessel sufficiently to slow it, and your odds of hitting a person are tiny. There is more between us than sight reveals; it would be like—like shooting underwater."

"So we either slow 'em down or make ourselves faster?"

Fionchadd risked another glance over his shoulder. "Correct."

"Then . . . couldn't you free the Iron Dungeon? It's gotta be holdin' us back. And what if all that iron were to impact those other guys?"

Fionchadd countered with a thoughtful pause. Whereupon David's mind rang with a *word*, a very particular and potent *word*, to judge by the way it clogged his brain. The world went briefly white as that silent command blocked out all his senses, yet with it came a wave of relief and desperate appreciation.

Forgetting his own admonitions, David raised his gaze above the railing, to where the vast, impossible curve of the Pillar of Fire enfolded them, around the inner arc of which they spiraled like a fly climbing the inside of a hollow pipe. Behind—closer, even, than he'd feared—came the other ship. But streaking toward it—rolling, bobbing, gyrating like a beach ball amidst wild surf—went the dark knobby clot of the Iron Dungeon. David held his breath as he traced its trajectory. Fortunately, the farther it went, the more it seemed to track true, and he watched in vast amazement as it bore down upon the pursuing vessel. Their prow twitched as their helmsman tried to steer around it, but such were the tides within the Pillar that evasion was all but impossible.

One moment—one blink of David's eyes—and Dungeon and ship were two entities. The next, they were one, as a twenty-foot sphere of heavy metal slammed into the prow of a wooden vessel, staving the entire front half to shards and splinters. Bodies—man-shaped, if not actually mortal—flew free, silhouetted against the ruddy glare. One or two seemed to hover there in the hot *between*, then shifted shape and winged away. The ship itself was ruined, likely as much from the Dungeon's mass as the fact that it had been made of iron. Already it was hard to see, such was their speed away, as their own vessel lurched forward, much the lighter.

"Congratulations," Fionchadd called. "We have clear sailing—"

"We do *not*!" Aife snapped back, shaking her head vigorously. For the warriors on the vanished vessel had evidently managed one final volley, of which the majority had just struck home. And with that, their vessel gave the strongest shudder yet and began to slow once more, losing all the momentum so lately gained.

"How—?" David gaped, at once aghast and fascinated.

"They entered the . . . bubble of our World that accompanies this vessel," she replied, gazing intently back they way they had come. "Do not forget that more than space lies between us and our pursuit. But enough of that." She shook her head as though to clear it. "Quick! If you must remain above, help me!"

Darting aft, she began jerking the arrows free of the planking. David joined her, desperately glad to find some task he could actually accomplish, in lieu of watching, or waiting for *that* to happen.

It was hard work, though, for the bolts were barbed and the planking very dense. More troubling was the fact that the barbs were coated with a thin, shimmery liquid which, if its effect on organic matter matched its stench, was damned potent poison indeed. Aife avoided touching it like the plague, and the boards where the older shafts had entered were already corroded. Those shafts alone came free easily. David collected a clumsy handful, but when he made for the gunwale to toss them over, a cry from Aife stopped him. "Dangerous they may be, but we would be more than fools to abandon potential weapons before Nuada has seen them."

David cast about for something in which to cache them, but Aife flung him part of her cloak. He wrapped the arrows carefully and had started to add Aife's to the stash when the boat shuddered again: the most violent yet. Fionchadd swore—or such was the sense of the word David caught only as a slash of Faery speech accompanied by a flood of frightened anger.

Oblivious to the preposterous surroundings, David ran back there, fighting hard to resist the notion that his footsteps sounded not on any horizontal surface but on a wall. Ruthlessly, he forced his gaze to the deck. And almost brained himself on the tiller before skidding to a halt.

"Finno? What's—?"

The Faery's face was hard with concentration, as though more than hands on the tiller steered them along their fantastic path. "The ship dies," he said through clenched teeth. "Already I must direct it as much with my mind as with this mechanism, and its pain is my pain. But it *is* dying. My only hope is that we can reach our destination before it succumbs."

"How much longer—farther, or whatever?"

"Not long, I hope. Now leave me. I have no time for this."

David started to voice another of the countless perfectly reasonable questions that had welled up in his mind, but before he could choose among them he felt hands on his shoulders, drawing him away. Aife—of course.

"What're you doin'?" he demanded. "Can't you see—"

"I can see that we are slowing and veering away from the Track, which means we must be nearing our goal."

Curiosity got the better of David. He dared a glance at the route ahead, noting that the flames beneath them were now the same familiar gold as the Tracks, but, more to the point, they were edging away from that flaming path onto one less well defined. Unless he was mistaken, too, the flames beneath them were thinner, neither as substantial as heretofore nor as hot.

Another jolt wracked the boat, and they left the Track entirely. For a moment, David thought he was about to fall, or slide across the deck, or simply go hurtling off into space; for up and down, in and out, and all such things briefly held no meaning—or all those meanings at once. Abruptly, like a swimmer's hand slicing into water, the vessel entered the flame in truth—or sank within it, or slid through.

David held his breath as the fires reached up to enwrap him; closed his eyes as he felt them brush his hair and face with molten fingers that miraculously did no damage.

Another jolt. Up and down shifted again, and profound

darkness replaced the light, and when David's eyes popped open, the Track was gone.

Wherever they'd emerged, there were stars overhead—*familiar* stars: the ancient constellations of summer in his World. "We're back," he gasped. Then, more doubtfully, "Aren't we?"

Aife nodded and started back toward the cabin. "Best we get below."

Instead of following, however, David dashed over to the nearest gunwale and studied the landscape passing beneath. *Beneath,* for they were easily several hundred feet above terrain that looked hauntingly familiar. The mountains were identical to those back home: worn-out old things wrapped in thick robes of forest as though to shut out the chill that came of being older than dinosaurs. Lakes quicksilvered the lowlands, and a network of roads slashed them, like sunlight on morning spiders' webs. There were lights, too: a town to the north, but not a big one. Smaller patches were freestanding businesses or such facilities as schools and . . . *hospitals!* His heart leapt at that, the first real hope that they might actually be able to save his father.

Again he hesitated, torn between seeing what evolved and going below to check on a parent who could as easily be dead, awake, or dying. Still, if anything were amiss, someone would summon him. Thus, he remained in place, gazing over the gunwale as the boat continued northwest, lower now, almost brushing the trees that crowned the nearer peaks. He hoped no one bothered to look up. *UFO* would be the most logical thing anyone would say. And with Silverhand below and largely out of commission, and Tir-Nan-Og in shambles, who knew when anyone would spin-doctor such things again.

Restless—or desperate—he stretched forward along the figurehead, in search of some surer clue as to their destination.

And almost fell overboard when something jarred the boat from beneath. It bucked like a shying horse, then continued its slow earthward glide.

Lower.

Something snapped: important-sounding, and aft. Another

of Fionchadd's curses followed on its heels. David glanced back to see the Faery's fists pounding what was clearly a broken tiller.

Another crash, another jolt, and David decided sitting might be wise, and managed to wedge himself into the vee behind the prow. He could still see enough to note that they'd entered the less populated end of whatever state this was— it looked like Georgia—and were shadowing a big north-south highway that resembled Georgia 129, which connected, among other things, Athens, Georgia, and Knoxville, Tennessee, by way of countless tourist traps.

Another jolt put them lower yet, and was he dreaming, or was the ship listing to port? Suddenly, all he cared about was finding something solid to hang on to and the waning hope that they might somehow crash (for surely that was about to occur) in the open, in lieu of the woods or one of those no-longer-so-friendly-looking peaks.

Treetops beat at their keel, each prompting the ship to lurch, and a few now rose higher than the gunwale. "Land ho!" Fionchadd cried right behind him, grabbing his arm as the ship cleared the last of what was probably national forest and sailed into the scanty airspace above a clearing on the knees of yet another mountain: maybe two acres of open land, vaguely tended and sprinkled with tumbledown out-buildings, centered around a worn-looking house he thought he might recognize if seen from the ground in daylight.

He was still trying to fit a name to this all-too-familiar stead when the hull jolted one last time, bounced, came down hard on its prow—and then kept on bouncing as, wood screaming across rocky earth, the ship heeled over—and stopped.

It took David a moment to get his bearings, and another to elbow a breathless Fionchadd off him so that he could take stock of surroundings that actually stayed put; didn't burn, make noise, smell bad, or make him sweat; but were instead a small, rather run-down farm tucked somewhere in his own north Georgia mountains.

Surrounded by moonlit darkness (there was no security light), it was hard to tell much about the house facing them roughly fifty yards away, save that it had been built mid-century at best and had more the look of a cabin erected on impulse than a purpose-designed dwelling. Briefly, it was one story, with a tin roof and faded vinyl siding that might once have been cream or white but which now more closely matched the dusty, ill-trimmed yard. Nor was there any real architecture to speak of, the structure's main claim to fame being a simple frame porch across two thirds of the front, with a set of concrete block steps leading up to it and a room flush with its forward edge on the right-hand side.

And then David noticed the details.

Old Harley Electraglide in a lean-to shed along one wall. A wind chime made of bones depending from the roof rail. Assorted herbs hanging along the porch in drying bundles. A pair of muddy military boots set neatly by the door. A dark brown bottle with no label that had likely held home-brewed beer.

And the lean, middle-height, dark-haired man who'd just eased the screen door open to stalk carefully into the yard, a double-barrel shotgun resting across his left forearm. Moonlight darkening the man's jeans to black, while washing all color from his bare feet and what torso showed beneath an unbuttoned flannel shirt.

And the stump of featureless flesh that terminated that man's left arm at the wrist.

Which could only mean one person.

"John!" David yelled. "Hey, man! It's me, David!"

The figure still looked wary as he squinted into what must strongly resemble an explosion in a sawmill with a crazy man trapped in the middle. Not until he'd come within speaking distance did he relax: comfortable country grace replacing the taut military precision he'd previously affected—which extremes pretty well defined him, if one threw poet into the mix.

"Interesting . . . entrance," John Devlin drawled carefully, then set the shotgun down and ambled over to where Aife had just flung the boarding ladder over the side. As it was, the gunwale was barely above the man's eye-level.

"I try," David retorted. "Hang on."

"Never mind. I'll come up."

"Without your h—" David began, then caught himself,

remembering something more important. "You got any medical trainin'?"

A curt nod. "Comes with the turf—went with it, anyway." David noted that Devlin had neither remarked on their presence nor on the means of their arrival.

"Nice ride—or was," Devlin observed when Fionchadd had helped David hoist the former Ranger onto the sharply listing deck. "Who's the patient?"

David nodded toward the cabin. "My pa. Down there. Major league stick in the back, courtesy of a little altercation. I think it's plugged things up enough to prevent much blood loss—outside. Inside? Who knows?"

"I will, in a minute."

"You don't look too surprised," David dared, when Devlin reached the top of the stairs.

"Figured you'd show up, just not right now."

"Bad time to ask?"

"Wouldn't argue with that."

The cabin door, which appeared to have been jammed, was almost literally ripped from David's grip by a worried-looking LaWanda. " 'Bout time," she told David. "It's your dad. He—" She paused, studying Devlin. "I've seen you before, haven't I? And am I to assume we've finally got somewhere?" she added to the tired-faced Fionchadd, behind them.

"Talk to her, Finno," David sighed—and ushered John Devlin into the cabin.

Fortunately, the various impacts of what had passed for a landing didn't seem to have wrought nearly as much damage to Big Billy as they had to the vessel. But as David scooted around so that Devlin could join him at his father's back, he realized at once what had caused LaWanda's consternation.

"*No!*" he shouted as Devlin reached out to touch the stake that lay so perilously close to Big Billy's spine.

Too late. Or was it? Devlin's hand had halted just shy of the splintered wood—which now evinced an odd sort of transparency, as though it were not entirely present. He stared at it critically. "You didn't pull this out 'cause you were afraid he might bleed to death, right? That was smart thinking. Unfortunately, it's . . . dissolving."

"Iron," Fionchadd spat, looking very puzzled. "Only iron could affect it so."

"There's iron in human blood," David gave back. "Hemoglobin. Carries oxygen to the brain."

"What about Faery blood?" Brock wondered.

"Doesn't matter," Devlin murmured, then looked up at David. "Right now, folks, we've got a problem."

Chapter VII:
Aftermath

*(near Clayton, Georgia—
Saturday, June 28—late)*

"This man needs a hospital *now*," John Devlin said flatly, not looking up from where he was gently probing the swelling around Big Billy's wound.

"Sorry," David grunted, offhand.

" 'Bout what?" Devlin shot back. "I doubt your dad volunteered to have a piece of kindlin' rammed into his tenderloin."

"Better call an ambulance," Aikin inserted. "Just point me to the phone."

Devlin shook his head. "Bad idea. One reason you're standin' on. The other is that it'll take time to get one down here—which he may not have."

David eyed him warily. "You got wheels, then? Besides the Harley, I mean?"

Devlin gestured toward the side of the house opposite that on which the bike was sheltered. By straining on tiptoes to peer through the door, David could just make out the front of a small pickup. Black, old and rusty: probably a Mazda. "Truck somebody gave me in trade for a ride to town when it blew a hose. Nothin' to write home about, but it'll get you to Clayton faster'n an ambulance can get here and back."

"Mind if I, uh, borrow it? Unless you wanta go."

"Don't mind, but it's not real smart for *you* to leave just now. Folks are after you, if this guy next to your dad's who he looks like. You've clearly lost 'em—for a while—and

119

comin' back this side's probably the best thing you could do in the short term 'cause folks like that don't like to draw attention to themselves, plus there's the Power thing. But a hospital's no place to draft battle plans, and you'd have to leave eventually. And''—the man hesitated briefly—''here you'd at least have *some* protection.''

''But my pa,'' David protested. ''I gotta be there—''

''No,'' Devlin countered firmly. ''He has to *get* there. You're part of bigger things.'' He glanced around, gaze finally settling on LaWanda. ''You drive a stick?''

''I can drive a bulldozer if I have to!'' she snorted. ''You get me directions, I'm your woman.''

''I'll go too,'' Aikin volunteered. Then, when David would have protested: ''No, think, Dave: You guys have things to figure out, but I know your dad better than anybody here except you, plus he knows me, plus . . . I'm a guy, and a man needs other men around for stuff like this.''

Again, David started to speak, then gave up. ''You're right—dammit! But please call as soon as you get there.''

''What about the stake?'' Brock wondered. ''It's vanishing. Won't that be a problem?''

''Not ours,'' David retorted, decisive again now that the crucial matter had been resolved for him.

''Well,'' Devlin concluded with a yawn, ''let's get him loaded and you folks on your way. There's others could stand some lookin' after.'' He eyed Lugh speculatively.

Five minutes later, David had helped Devlin, Aikin, and LaWanda carry his father from the cabin, lower him over the side (Brock and Aife assisted there), then hoist him into the back of the black pickup. Devlin supplied a foam pad and a pile of blankets, then ambled up to the cab to give LaWanda directions. The Faeries were tending their own, and Aikin had slipped behind the house to pee, so that David found himself alone with his dad.

Christ, he looks old!—as David stroked his father's brow in a gesture that would've embarrassed both of them had Big Billy been awake. He was sweating, too, as though his body fought an invisible battle against that wooden invader, but his breathing was slow and regular, which David assumed was good. He hadn't regained consciousness, though, which could mean anything.

Suppose he didn't! Suppose David had had his last conversation with the man who'd begot him, raised him, and sent him off to college. Suppose his mom (who must be worried sick by now) had had *her* last conversation, and her last dinner, and her last night making love to the man who'd given her two sons. Suppose Little Billy lost his father. Himself, he could handle it—he thought—being mostly on his own now. But the kid—a boy needed a dad, even one like Big Billy who only half understood him. It would, David concluded glumly, be a long night.

"I'll call your mom soon as we get there," Aikin vowed, behind him. David nearly jumped out of his skin, not having heard his friend approach. "No sense in *you* doin' it until we know something," Aikin went on. "You got other fish to fry, and you can bet I'll be back with the tartar sauce soon as I can. But right now—"

"I'm on it!" LaWanda called from the cab, and cranked the rattly engine. Aikin scrambled over the tailgate to join Big Billy in the back, pausing only to slide the rear window open so he and LaWanda could communicate.

"Take care!" David shouted. And didn't watch as the truck lurched down John Devlin's half-graveled drive toward civilization.

Devlin accompanied him as they headed back toward the shattered ship, and only then did David comprehend how badly damaged it was. The front third had taken the brunt of the impact, mainly below decks, leaving the superstructure intact and everything below the gunwale a mess of splintered wood. Most of the shields along the sides had fallen off, and the mast had cracked halfway up and now leaned at a crazy angle, the sail unfurled in places like a flag of warning.

Devlin chuckled dryly. "Never figured I'd have the King of the Faeries as a houseguest."

"*A* king of the Faeries," David corrected. "There's a bunch of 'em." A pause. "Guess you knew that, though."

Devlin didn't reply.

"How much *do* you know?"

"More than we've got time to discuss right now," Devlin

gave back tersely but not unkindly. "That's gotta wait until we get the rest of those folks settled, and I can—" He didn't finish, for Fionchadd had leapt from the deck in front of them and was studying the ship critically. "If this was a horse, I would have to kill it," the Faery youth announced. "As it is—I do not know. It is not wise to leave it here. Still—" He pondered his serpent ring, then looked up at Aife. "Are the others—?"

"Nuada is tired beyond belief, but if we can get the King inside . . ."

David reached for the ladder.

Ten minutes later, Lugh Samildinach, High King of the Sidhe in Tir-Nan-Og, was lying on a thrift store sofa in front of John Devlin's fireplace with an heirloom quilt tucked under his chin. Though his face was pocked with open sores and he hadn't awakened even once, he still looked relatively peaceful, considering his ordeal. David sat on the hearth watching him. A mug of coffee steamed in his hands, barely tasted. Nuada and Aife slumped to either side, seemingly as wasted as David. It was damned disconcerting, too, to see such imposing figures brought low. Was it pure fatigue, David wondered, or being away from Tir-Nan-Og, or the fact that their ruler—their friend, in Nuada's case—was himself so altered as to seem a stranger? *Immortals, all of them, yet no one was truly immortal.* Even Faeries could die the Death of Iron, which did major damage to their souls. And souls could die or be devoured, as Ailill's had been, all those years gone by.

But that way lay guilt, of which bitter draught he'd drunk deep that night already. Idly, he scanned the environs: a living room-cum-library, with a minimum of simple furniture, plain paneled walls, sanded pine floors, and shelves everywhere bearing an even mix of books and what could only be described as "stuff." A door straight ahead opened onto a narrow hall that connected the front door to an extension out back that contained the kitchen, the tiny bath, and another room that was discreetly but purposefully locked.

As for Devlin himself—he'd shifted from take-charge Ranger to gracious host, all in a minute's time, and had made coffee, offered drinks (spring water, juice, beer, and wine—

but no soda, to Brock's dismay), and pointed out the 'fridge. "Anything that looks edible, eat," he'd announced, then vanished into the locked back room. At some point, he'd also acquired a left hand: a gloved prosthesis that covered the stump where flesh and blood had been shot away.

Brock had found a comfortable-looking armchair and was fast asleep, apparently his approach to stressful situations. Fionchadd had seen Lugh settled, then ducked outside, to return a short while later clutching what looked like a bird's nest. It took David a moment to determine that it was actually the remains of his boat. "It work?" he asked stupidly.

Fionchadd regarded the object sadly. "Whether it will *expand* again—that depends on whether that which empowers it still lives, and that I can neither predict nor alter."

"I don't want to know," David yawned. "Sorry."

Fionchadd merely shrugged and wandered off in search of food, though he studiously avoided the refrigerator, it being made of steel.

The telephone rang twice before David figured out what it was, hesitated briefly, then rose to answer it. "John Devlin's residence . . ."

"Dave," Aikin shot back breathlessly. "We're here. He's mostly okay—stabilized, anyway. Stick fell out in the parkin' lot, so we didn't have to worry about that. I went ahead and called your mom."

"She take it okay?"

"Dunno. I got Dale. He said not to worry, he'd been doctorin' her coffee all day and she didn't care about much of anything. They're on their way over, though, all three of 'em. Elyyoth's holdin' down the fort, I think with Scott."

"Best place for 'em—if we can keep 'em away from here."

"Dale's the only one who knows anything, and he knows when to keep his mouth shut."

"Good point."

A long pause. Then: "So, you need me here or there?"

"Juju Woman makin' it okay?"

"Cool as a cucumber. She eats RNs for breakfast."

"Cooked or raw?"

"On toast, but you're not answerin' my question."

David shifted his weight restlessly, noting that Devlin had emerged from the mysterious back room, now clad in black and with an equally mysterious black box tucked under his arm. "Protection," he offered in transit—and vanished into the night.

"Dave?" Aikin prompted.

"Oh, hell," David sighed. "Let's see: if Wannie's got her head on straight, you're not really needed there. Dale can keep Mom from goin' ballistic, and Little B'll just think it's an adventure. Which I guess means get your butt back down here and help me stress out for a while."

"Catch you, then. I—Oops! They're wantin' me to sign something. I told 'em I was you, if that's okay. Gotta go." Aikin hung up the phone. It was just past midnight, and now Sunday: a day and change since their departure.

David blinked into the sudden silence, the first he'd experienced in what seemed like centuries. Still, he'd made a decision, and while it was a crime to disturb that peace with more talk, one did what one had to. A deep breath, and he punched in his and Alec's number back in Athens. No answer—not that he'd expected one. But when he checked for messages, there was one from Alec, sounding harried, wired, and furtive. "Dave, just in case: the deed is done. Parents disposed of. Got the stuff. Folks wanted to feed everybody in Athens, and wondered why you weren't here. Bottom line: we're runnin' *very* late. At least we've slept. Catch you . . . whenever. Leave word where."

David did, then tried Liz, got the same result, and left the same reply.

Calvin and Sandy's place, then—where there was no response at all, which could mean anything. Cal was pretty canny, though, and it wasn't like he didn't have contacts.

"So basically," he sighed to the empty room. "I cool my heels and wait."

Not on an empty stomach, however. He'd just contrived a roast beef sandwich, and was debating chasing down Devlin or else phoning his folks' place, in case they hadn't left, when footsteps sounded on the porch. He tensed—*Lord, he was jumpy!*—but at least he still had the Beretta. Just in case.

It was only Devlin: tight-faced and tired-eyed, as he slung

off his black leather jacket and strode straight to the room in the back. David started to follow, but the man was gone. David heard the lock snap.

Seeing no other option, he finished his sandwich, claimed the one vacant chair that looked halfway comfortable. And dozed.

When he awoke half an hour later, Devlin was shaking his shoulder—with his real hand, to David's relief; he'd never got used to the other, though the glove was better than the stump. "Guess we better talk," the man said, dragging another chair over to join him. He was drinking coffee. Good stuff, too. It smelled heavenly.

"Might oughta," David agreed with a tired smile, followed at once by a yawn.

Devlin puffed his cheeks. "Okay then, how 'bout giving me the short form, minus the council at the palace, the attack on us mortals, the coup, and most of the politics. Contacts," he added cryptically. "Don't ask. Start with when you got on the Faery lad's ship."

"Fionchadd," David supplied a little angrily.

"Whatever."

David sighed, and for the next fifteen minutes gave an account of Lugh's rescue and their subsequent pursuit.

"*Somebody's* lookin' out for you," Devlin observed when he'd finished. "No way a plan like that should've succeeded."

David studied his mug. "Hey, it was the best we could do under the circumstances! And don't forget we had three of the Sidhe, and they all agreed that the only way we had a ghost of a chance was to play to the rebels' blind sides. They're used to underratin' us mortals, and most of 'em don't seem to know much about us, 'cept those guys they've got workin' for 'em, who aren't the best examples, from what I hear."

Devlin didn't reply.

David shifted in his chair. "So what about you and Silverhand?"

Silence. Then, eventually: "Didn't know who he was when we met. 'Course you don't generally expect to meet a demigod on the street in Beirut—or your daddy's back forty,

I guess. He'd heard about me through that business with your uncle. Thought I was ... intriguing. Then he discovered I knew a bit about some other traditions—there're strange folk in the world a whole lot closer than Faerie, in case you didn't know. Anyway, he told me a little and I told him a little. Mostly, we talked about history.''

David lifted a brow.

''Yeah, well, see, there's only four or five kingdoms over there, and they're all basically one people, not countin' the little guys. Our politics are incredibly complex to them: all those countries, kingdoms risin' and fallin'. Death that's real, so that good folks stay gone forever. Poverty, starvation, weather: all those are problems they don't really have. It makes 'em naïve, frankly. They're brilliant, but they haven't had to live hard and fast, so we're often better planners than they are. It's not really a fair trade, if you think about it.''

David frowned. ''So, how'd you know we were in transit?''

''Logic, mostly. I ... knew you'd left, and figured if you succeeded you'd be pursued, and since you had at least two Faeries with you, they'd be thinkin' in terms of bolt-holes, and I'd already told Silverhand he could use this as one, if he had to.''

David regarded Devlin askance. ''You got this place ... warded?''

A cryptic smile. ''Let's just say that if anything unpleasant comes around, I'll know. Might not be able to keep it out, but I'll know.''

''It could go either way,'' Nuada inserted quietly, joining them. Devlin studied him for a moment, then rose, retrieved a bottle of Guinness from the refrigerator, opened it, and passed to the Faery, who nodded thanks before drinking. Fionchadd joined them a moment later, and Aife. Brock slept on, untroubled.

''Time we talked,'' Nuada announced. ''I am rested—a little. There is nothing I can do for Lugh now. He hides within himself, but I can feel him stirring. Still, his suffering has been unimaginable.''

''Evidently,'' David acknowledged. ''No offense, but I had no idea you guys were so fragile.''

Nuada glared at him. "Best we talk," he insisted. "The more we decide now, the better it will be. Time may be in short supply."

Devlin nodded sagely, if a little warily. "Fine. You're senior fighting man. What's your read?"

Nuada took a long draught and cleared his throat. "Very well. The first thing we must consider is our danger of attack. This is difficult to assess, for we know not the full strength of the rebels, save that there are more than we supposed. What say you, Fionchadd?"

"*Many* more, evidently, though how loyal they might be is hard to say. Most are younger even than I, and many have allied with the Sons more from boredom than conviction. They may not be reliable."

"Still, there are enough to crew at least three vessels."

David scowled. "Three?"

"The one we first encountered would not have destroyed itself had there not been a backup. Nor is it likely that one would have risked subsequent pursuit in anything as perilous as a Pillar had there not been more backup in turn. Clearly they regarded the cause as greater than themselves."

"Odd, for our kind," Aife mused. "Perhaps contact with mortals has affected them more than they know."

"Perhaps," Nuada agreed. "In any event, it will take time for the Sons to determine that Lugh is free. It will take longer to locate him, and longer again to make their way here. And if we can endure until dawn—"

"Why dawn?" David broke in.

"The chance of observation is greater in daylight; I doubt they will risk it."

David's scowl deepened. "But what about glamour? Couldn't they just hide themselves?"

"You forget that not all the Sidhe are as skilled in the use of Power as those of us you know best. And any time one divides one's Power, usage becomes more difficult. To attack with anything beyond ordinary weapons and yet maintain a glamour would be almost impossible—as well as foolish, given the amount of iron you command. In effect, to attack with Power would require that they drop whatever glamour shields them, which would render them vulnerable to your eyes and therefore your weapons."

David gnawed his lips. "So what you're sayin' is that—"

"Any attack now would be mostly diversion, simply because it is unlikely they can rally their full force in an effort to retake Lugh so quickly. It will be designed to frighten rather than to harm—and do not forget that while I am weary, many of them fear me. Nor is it likely they know Lugh's condition, and to stand against him, even naked as he is, would require much courage indeed—or foolhardiness."

"So basically," Devlin summarized, "you think there'll be a diversion to scare us, after which we're safe during daylight, and then tonight they bring in the big guns."

Nuada nodded. "That is how I would plan such a thing, and I know your strengths and weaknesses better than the Sons, which gives us some advantage."

"And the intent of this battle," Devlin went on, "would be to recapture Lugh?"

"Primarily," Nuada acknowledged. "Though I would also make an excellent prisoner, and Fionchadd, being kin to the houses of Annwyn and the Powersmiths alike, would surely be taken hostage as well. As for Aife—"

"Death," she said flatly. "I have betrayed them. They will not forgive."

"You seem to require a lot of that," David growled, and immediately regretted it.

Nuada glared at him.

Devlin indicated the figure on the sofa. "And if he were conscious?"

Nuada's face was hard. "A moot point, for now. He could return at any time, but I can think of nothing in your World that would equate with what was done to him, in terms of pain. A mortal so tortured would have died. Do not forget that he was covered with iron dust, yet even the Sidhe must breathe. It follows he breathed some of that dust. We have cleaned the worst from his body, but that which is within— He must dispose of it and heal the damage alike."

"Or shift into the substance of this World!" David countered suddenly.

Nuada shook his head. "That would require that he be conscious, and likewise render him all but Powerless, certainly no stronger than the lesser Sons."

"Which means we need to get him back to Faerie!" David gave back. "To reconnect him with the Land, I mean."

Again Nuada shook his head. "Alas, no. Oh, you are correct in that he could draw strength from the Land, were he there. But how do we accomplish that? The ship is beyond repair. There are no Tracks hereabout, and even so, it would take time to reach Tir-Nan-Og, and surely the Sons now guard all access in and out."

David took a deep breath. "So what you're sayin' is that he needs a place where he can take whatever time he needs to recover?"

Nuada looked puzzled. "Do you *know* of such a place?"

"Galunlati," Brock supplied from his chair, not moving, though he'd opened his eyes a crack. He yawned and stretched languidly like a cat, then wandered over to join them. "I've not been sleeping as much as thinking."

Fionchadd raised a brow quizzically. "Galunlati?"

Brock shrugged. "Think, guys. If Lugh stays here, they'll eventually attack in force and retake him, which won't be good for the home team—*unless* he has time to heal, but he can't get that here or in Faerie. Therefore, he has to do it somewhere else, and the only somewhere else that makes sense is Galunlati. At least we've got allies there."

"True," David conceded. "But we don't have a way to get there."

"*Yet*," Brock corrected. "Cal could do it, I bet."

"And if he can't?"

Brock shrugged sheepishly. "I, uh . . . I haven't figured that part out yet."

Nuada scratched his chin. "Still, it is worth considering."

David frowned. "But isn't there some deal about not bein' able to go to a World more than one World away from one's home World?"

"Or what?" the boy yawned.

"Or you will go mad," Fionchadd replied. "Though like

most things to do with the Worlds, the rules vary from one to the next." He paused, looking guilty. "Actually, that could have been a problem when we made our embassy to the Powersmiths." He stared sheepishly at David. "But I knew we would be there but briefly, and the distancing is not so great in that case, for the Land of the Powersmiths both is and is not of Faerie."

Brock scowled. "But Galunlati touches the Land of the Powersmiths, and you've got Powersmith blood, right?" The scowl deepened. "But Lugh—"

"Has Powersmith blood as well," Nuada confided. "It is the source of much of his strength, though I alone now living know that, and that knowledge is not to leave the circle of our allies."

"Fine," David agreed. "And it just so happens that there *is* a healing lake in Galunlati. If we could get Lugh some of that water—" He broke off, face ashen. "Oh my God!" he breathed. "We could . . . we could've used *that* to heal my dad!"

Fionchadd shook his head. "We still have no way to get there, and he would have died ere now had we waited—from blood loss when the splinter . . . faded. His wound is not mortal, I do not think—no more than if it was wood from your World that had pierced him. He will heal."

"I'd still like to try it," David insisted.

"That is what we will do," Nuada concluded in a tone that brooked no argument. "I have heard of this lake, and the Sons will have no way to reach him there while he regains his strength."

"It's not quite that simple," David noted irritably, democracy having yielded to dictatorship all in a space of seconds. "And of course it assumes Cal can actually get us there."

"I have faith," Nuada said. "You should too. Or—"

Tires crunched in the yard, followed by the squeak of badly adjusted brakes applied too hard. An unmuffled motor grumbled unhappily, and a door slammed with a tinny thunk. Footsteps pounded on the porch; the knob rattled frantically. "Let me in!" Aikin shouted. "Let me the fuck—"

Devlin had acquiesced by then, slamming the door shut

behind the young man who dashed inside, pale-faced and far too out of breath for a bit of yard, a pair of steps, and a porch to account for.

"We got company!" Aikin panted, turning to face the night. "Came out of the sky, like birds and bats, then turned into people. They tried to block me as I turned in, but I ran 'em down."

David exchanged glances with Nuada and with Devlin. "Some escaped the ship in bird form," Fionchadd mused. "Perhaps—"

"Likely," Nuada agreed ominously, rising. "And if that is the case, we may be in for trouble, for anyone who could shift *and* survive the Pillar to arrive here must be far stronger than I expected."

"But few," Fionchadd offered. "I hope."

Aikin nodded. "Maybe six, if they all came together. I—"

His comment was consumed by the rumble of thunder from a sky that had been clear the last time David had looked. Another clap, and a bolt of lightning lanced into the yard. "I doubt any wards will prevail against the like of that," Nuada spat when the noise had abated. "It is a natural thing, and born of *this* World. Your wards, I would guess, are set against intrusion by *beings* from another."

Devlin could only nod sadly. David said nothing at all. Nor did Aikin.

"Well," Brock suggested far too brightly, "any reason we can't just *shoot* 'em?"

Devlin stared at him and scratched his chin.

Chapter VIII:
Divide and Conquer

(near Clayton, Georgia—
Sunday, June 29—the wee hours)

"Shoot 'em?" David choked, though the suggestion was not without merit.

Aikin rounded on him. "You got a problem with that?"

"I . . . shouldn't," David hedged. "But now that we're back home—well, it's just different, I guess. Reckon I'm afraid the Rabun County sheriff'll drop by and tote us off to the slammer, or whatever."

"For killing people who can't die," Devlin snorted.

"Their bodies would not endure long after death," Nuada acknowledged. "Not in this World, at any rate. But correct me if I am in error, but do not . . . guns function better in daylight?"

" 'Less you got a night scope," Aikin replied slyly.

Devlin favored him with a sharp look; the things were illegal, after all. "Got a heavy-duty 'lectric torch," he countered. "And I'm willin' to go out sniping if I have to, but I'd rather—"

Another blast of lightning stabbed the yard, close enough to turn the room stark white. When normality returned, Devlin made a point of unplugging certain crucial bits of electronics. "Lots of storms up here," he grinned. "Lots of lightnin' rods too—which I hope those folks don't know. But if they start foolin' with the wind—"

"Do not even think such things," Nuada cautioned. "They should not be able to touch your mind here, because of all the steel hereabout, if not because of your wards. Still . . ."

"Makes no difference," David grumbled. "We were just talkin' about attackin' them. If they can pick up one, they can pick up the other."

"True," Aife agreed.

"This is to frighten," Nuada emphasized. "Random energy—random *anger*—directed at the clouds and carelessly funneled. But if they merge their skills . . ."

Fionchadd had been staring intently out the front door. "I think they are."

David joined him—they all did. Little was visible, beyond vague movement near the entrance to the compound, where the flimsy wire fence that encircled Devlin's property terminated at a pair of posts on either side of the drive. Still, by straining his eyes and calling upon the Sight, David could barely make out a number of shapes clustered there. And as he watched, more lightning lanced into the yard. A tree was struck, then another. A third bolt surely found the house but was diverted. The air smelled of ozone. Every hair on David's body stood on end—and kept on standing, for the flashes were increasing in intensity, becoming nearly constant, though the bulk of them were now focused beyond the fence. Nor were they mere rapid jags of light any longer; rather, they were coalescing into an actual *shape*: a vast manform that flickered against the dark woods, tall as the smaller trees.

"I could disperse that easily in Tir-Nan-Og," Nuada sighed. "Fionchadd, Aife, and I could dissolve it with a puff of joined thought. But here, we are weak. Our foes are barely stronger, but can afford to spend strength where we cannot."

"What about the wards?" Aikin wondered. Then: "Shit! Where'd it go?" For the flickering lightning man had vanished into the woods that encircled Devlin's compound, save where the driveway cut through at the entrance.

"I'm on it," the Ranger announced, striding toward the double-locked door. He paused with the key in the lower lock and stared at David. "Somebody better see this."

"See what?" David asked edgily, joining him.

"Early-warning system. In case I'm . . . incapacitated."

And with that, he turned the first key, then inserted the second.

David held his peace as he followed Devlin into what proved to be a windowless room no more than ten feet square, with a low, sloping ceiling not much higher than the medium-height Ranger's head. The walls were bare wood, as was the floor, and the boards showed evidence of frequent scrubbings through the wisps of smoke that issued from four thick pillar candles fixed at the precise quarters of a chalk circle inscribed on the floor. Devlin paused at the threshold to remove his boots, motioning David to do the same, then stepped deftly over the chalk line. It was then that David saw the rest of the regalia, hidden as it had been by the glare of the nearest candle and the smoke. Not much really: merely a small chest like a jewelry box, with an elaborately embroidered cloth atop it, upon which a brass brazier sat, containing the ashes of a tiny scroll of expensive, possibly handmade, paper or parchment, to judge by others stacked neatly to one side. The other side held a flat soapstone dish full of dark red liquid, a quill pen, and a silver-colored dagger no longer than his hand, its blade obviously exquisitely sharp.

"Questions aren't wise here," Devlin cautioned. "But briefly: the circle represents the borders of my land. The candles mark the quarters and have counterparts of a less obvious kind outside. Should anything with bad intentions start gettin' pushy, the candle on that side will flare. If someone will watch, we can at least know which way to look."

"One suggestion," David dared.

"What?"

"Brock. Let him watch. He needs something to do. He also knows about ceremonial magic, Cherokee, in fact. And I'm afraid his trigger finger's a little itchy just now. He froze during the fight, though he thinks nobody noticed. I'm scared he may try to compensate."

Devlin gnawed his lip, then nodded. "Get him."

David nodded in turn and slipped out of the room, motioning Brock to join him. "Devlin wants you. Not a flash job, but important."

Brock looked as though he might protest, but then squared

his shoulders and complied. David followed. "You need me?" he asked from the hall, wondering if the westernmost candle wasn't a bit brighter than the rest, and recalling that he'd last seen the lightning-thing moving that way.

The answer came immediately, for the candle in question promptly sparked and flickered, then wavered as though blown by some unseen wind, before stabilizing at half again its former luminosity. Simultaneously, a low-pitched rumble that was not *quite* thunder reached them, along with what sounded disturbingly like wood splintering or a tree crashing to earth.

"Won't hurt the wards," Devlin offered, to David's unasked query.

"I'll leave you to it," David sighed, and returned to the living room.

And waited, as thunder continued to clash and clatter around the mountainside, while lightning stabbed the environs (but never the house) almost constantly, every now and then revealing a rush of movement among the trees or an explosion of sparks that reminded him of nothing so much as the invisible monster from the id in *Forbidden Planet*.

"Car's comin'!" Aikin warned from the hall, where he'd stationed himself for the better angle it allowed on what passed for a drive. "Might be Wannie; she said she'd beg a ride, or else call. But—"

"Two cars," David noted. "Not Dale, then—I hope."

"Athens folks?"

David didn't need to reply, for by then the vehicles had reached the house, though the lead one had to swerve right to avoid a bolt that destroyed Devlin's clothesline. And those two vehicles—a dark green Ford Explorer and a burgundy '66 Thunderbird—could only contain three people.

Without pause, he wrenched the door open and met them on the porch. "Cal, Sandy, and . . . *Kirkwood!*" he yelped. "Get in here! Things are—"

"We saw!" Calvin broke in, standing aside to let his lady enter, along with his older cousin.

Sandy rolled her eyes, clearly shaken. "If you mean a bunch of guys blocking the drive."

"Pretendin' to be werewolves, or sasquatches, or something,'' their companion concluded. "We called their friggin' bluff!''

"Good old American steel,'' Sandy chortled. "Big wheel just kept on turning.''

"Remind me never to buy a 'Vette,'' Calvin chuckled in turn, divesting himself of far more layers of serviceable-looking clothing than the season required, plus a backpack that was crammed to bursting. At which point he did several double takes in a row as he took in the company in the room.

Sandy dropped her duffel to the floor. "Good thing we saw the light show and decided to check it out.''

"Good thing we know our Spock-eared little buddies like to play games with the weather,'' Calvin shot back, staring at David pointedly. "Otherwise we'd be on our way to Sullivan Cove. You know: last known agreed-upon rendezvous?''

David sighed wearily. "Then you don't know?''

Sandy was gazing intently around the room, missing nothing. "I assume there's a reason your dad and LaWanda aren't here. Hope it's not bad news. I also assume the sickly lad zoned out on the sofa means you managed *some* of what you intended.''

David had just started to explain the gist of their adventure when the door to the "workroom'' opened and Devlin stepped out. He did a double take of his own and reached instantly for his hip—probably an old reflex—then relaxed when he recognized not only Calvin and Sandy, but also Calvin's cousin Kirkwood. The latter looked, as Calvin was fond of saying, "like an Irishman with an Indian paint job.'' In fact, he was local Cherokee, from the reservation an hour up the road. David had met him once of significance, and another time or two in passing, and recalled that he was a few years older than Calvin, a professional archaeologist by trade, and knew a hell of a lot about what he'd come to call "Power Traditions.'' In short, a good man to have on your side in a fight. Especially *this* kind of fight. Devlin knew him, too, which was odd. Or maybe he was one of the Ranger's mysterious "contacts.''

In any event, Kirkwood hesitated but briefly at the sight

of Nuada, Aife, and Fionchadd, his only comment being, "So all that stuff's true!"

"And more," Nuada replied drolly. Only then did anyone notice that the thunder had, for the nonce, abated.

"Guess we blew their concentration barreling in like that," Calvin laughed, a little giddily.

David laughed, too, but looked at Devlin uneasily. "Uh, what about—?"

"They only serve against foes; these folks aren't."

"*What* only serves?" Calvin began, then realization dawned. "Oh, I see! Uh, anything *I* can do? Along those lines, I mean?"

"If you're up for it," Devlin conceded. "Double-ring defense never hurts."

"Churchy's got the stuff in the car," Calvin assured him. " 'Course, it wouldn't hurt for somebody to stand around with some heat."

"I will," Aikin volunteered before David could either voice the same or stop him. "John," Aikin continued, "you said something 'bout a heavy-duty torch? I wouldn't mind borrowin' that if you don't mind lendin'."

David regarded his friend uneasily. "You go, somebody better watch *your* back!"

"And if nobody minds," Sandy snorted, "it'd be great if somebody brought me up-to-date. I don't have a *clue* what's goin' on."

"I'll tell you what I know," Devlin sighed, eyeing David warily. "Since I 'spect young Mr. Sullivan here's sick of it. Nuada can fill in the gaps."

Aikin cleared his throat. "About that torch . . ."

Devlin scowled and disappeared into his bedroom, to reappear with a potent-looking electric torch, complete with body pack. He hesitated briefly, then passed it to Aikin, who accepted it with solemn grace. Another pause, and Devlin slapped a box of shells into his hand. "Not unless you have to. And don't ever let it be easy."

"Never will," Aikin affirmed, retrieving his Remington before following Calvin, Kirkwood, and David (who'd reclaimed his Winchester) out the door.

In spite of the danger, David was glad to be outside. Oh,

he liked John Devlin fine, and found his home a place of instant comfort, rather like he'd imagined Tom Bombadil's house might be. But with three very out-of-place Faeries ensconced within and another unconscious on the sofa—well, some things were just *too* weird.

Outside was still the outside, after all, and he, Aik, and Cal were used to bumming around outdoors, plus Kirkwood was one of those guys with whom you were instant friends. They were all in good shape, too, and decent at self defense, from hand-to-hand on up. More security there.

Kirkwood made a bee line for his Thunderbird and popped the trunk. David was torn between watching him and keeping an eye on the clump of half-shapes he could just make out on the fringe of the woods to the right of the drive. He thought he could hear singing too—humming—something— and would've sent a round of shot their way if not for the distance. As for the big electric guy, he seemed to have dispersed. Probably it took a lot to conjure such a being, and Calvin's timely arrival had disrupted whatever concentration had kept it viable.

Meanwhile, Kirkwood had rummaged in the trunk for what seemed like forever and finally produced a bundle wrapped in supple, gold-toned leather David recognized (by the smoky scent as much as anything) as brain-tanned buckskin. Staves of wood protruded from either end. A small pouch clinked at his hip, hinting of ceramics within. "Which way?" he asked, as he slammed the trunk.

Calvin gnawed his lip. "Our troublesome friends are to the south, and I'd as soon they didn't know what we were up to until we don't have any choice. So I'd say start with the east, which is the direction of victory anyway, then work counterclockwise. If we're lucky, they won't notice, since we don't have to go as far out as John did. The closer the better, in fact; ten yards out, max."

David followed the other three as they ducked into the shadows beside the house. Devlin had no porch light, and they were all dressed in black, David having changed into spare garb he'd stored in the ship. They were all dark-haired, too, save him, but an olive-drab boonie hat obscured most of his blond mane.

Still, they stuck to the shadows, slinking low as they turned the corner by the bedroom to skirt the lean-to shed before entering the darker region where the kitchen elled off the back. Calvin studied the terrain, then set his mouth and trotted to a point that was as close to due east as possible. Kirkwood joined him and passed him a stick.

"Wood from a lightning-blasted tree," David informed Aikin. "Stained with blood, since red's the color of the east." Aikin merely motioned David out to the scanty shelter of a maple before claiming the southeast corner, alert as ever he was when hunting: checking constantly toward the east, then north, then back toward the driveway and the road. At least their enemies couldn't shoot back, not if they'd fled the boat by shapeshifting. On the other hand, clothing and other accouterments sometimes went with you and sometimes didn't when one shifted Faery-style; it depended on the strength and intention of whoever worked the spell. These guys were fairly strong, Nuada had said. But they'd also had to shift with no notice, so maybe they'd arrived in just their skins.

As if it mattered! David scanned the yard, the woods beyond, the yard again; straining his eyes in quest of anything untoward: eyeshine (did Faeries *have* eyeshine, and if so, was it different from mortal norm?), movement, light . . . And why wasn't Aik using that torch he'd made such a fuss about? (*Probably so he won't attract attention,* he answered himself right back.)

As for Calvin—he'd stripped off his black sweatshirt and was squatted on the ground behind the stick he'd jammed into the earth. He was chanting, too, with Kirkwood joining in. Invoking the protection of the ruling agencies of the east, probably: the red dog, perhaps, or the red bird, or even Uki's counterpart there: Asgaya Gigagei, the Red Man of the Lightning.

But if *their* side invoked the lightning, would their enemies be able to counter with yet more electrical manifestations of their own? Now *that* bore thinking about.

But not now, for the night was disrupted by the crunching roar of at least two more cars hurtling into the drive, then applying brakes with force, followed by the harsh blatt of a horn. "Dave! Now!" Aikin called from the corner, motioning David farther out while he disappeared into the shadows by the bedroom. David swallowed hard as he launched into the darkness, working his way toward a burst of light flickering through the trees at the entrance to the yard.

Headlights: two sets, both on high beam, and one pair augmented by fiercely bright driving lights under the bumper and on top as well. Which could only be Liz's Ford Ranger. David breathed a sigh of relief, even as his heart flip-flopped. They'd clearly encountered the same problem Sandy's crew had, but unlike them, seemed to be meeting resistance. Either that, or Liz, who was in the lead, was finding it impossible to bear down on what appeared, at the moment, to be people.

Aikin wasn't—as a shotgun blast ripped into the air.

Another shot. "Floorboard it!" David yelled. "Fuck those guys, Liz, just floorboard it!"

As if she had any chance of hearing above the cacophony that had erupted down there. Abruptly, David was running, with Aikin arrowing in to the right. Lights blinded him, as they were intended to blind the clump of rebels who'd been interrupted at their mischief: evidently something in the drive to forestall entrance.

If only he had a clear shot! But with the vehicles directly behind the targets, he didn't, and neither did Aik. Okay then, in that case—

He swerved left, describing a wide curve he hoped would give him a clear line of fire.

Had one! As part of the group backed up a fraction. A little more and . . . *now!*

He held his breath, squinting toward the shapes cut out in the headlights' glare—shapes armed with simple clubs. Another breath, and he took aim—and fired.

Some fell. Others looked his way. "Nice one!" Aikin yelled.

Another shot, at one who had risen.

"Floor it, Liz!" he shrieked desperately.

She heard, or found the nerve. The engine roared. The Ranger lunged forward. Bodies scattered of their own will, or were flung aside, as the small pickup shot through the unseen wall of John Devlin's warding and bounced into his front yard. Myra was right behind in her Dodge Caravan, with someone riding shotgun: wiry male, dark curly hair . . . *Piper!*

Piper—James Morrison Murphy—the sweetest, flakiest guy David knew. Also the best musician—and the person who feared dealing with Faerie more than anyone else in the world. He'd just finished one adventure, to the detriment of his peace of mind. David hadn't expected to find him near any of this stuff again.

Finally, the last of their crew—save LaWanda—had won their way into the yard, leaving him close enough to the confused attackers to manage two more shots into their midst, aided by the torch Aikin was fanning across their foes' last known location. He raised the Winchester for one final volley, then paused and lowered it again. He *hated* this, he realized: the ease with which he pulled the trigger, reloaded, and shot again. Immortal their adversaries might be, yet they were sentient as well, and not even evil in their essence, merely with priorities at odds to his own. And here he was wreaking mayhem in their midst like the most callous terrorist!

All at once he was staring numbly at the shells already in his hand, ready to be inserted into barrels he'd just broken open to receive them. And crying.

"No!" he said, to nobody. And it didn't matter anyway, because no one in that mass of Faery fallen was rising. Moaning, yes; and cursing in a tongue he didn't know. But not rising.

One remained upright, however, but then Aikin's shotgun sounded and that one fell, clutching what were likely shattered knees.

David turned back to the house, back to his girlfriend and his best buddy and people who'd understand what he'd just done—help *him* understand, anyway. Who'd tell him it was okay, or maybe even give him the dressing-down he both desired and deserved.

He met Aikin at the porch. His friend's shoulders slumped, but his eyes glittered. "I hate this!" Aikin spat.

"Yeah," David choked. "I do too."

* * *

Dawn arrived not a second too soon for David, who'd zoned out around three (he suspected Aife's collusion there), awakened a little *too* refreshed around five, and spent every spare minute since gazing distrustfully toward the end of Devlin's drive—when he wasn't pacing around to check other windows. That in spite of the fact that Brock was still maintaining scrupulous watch in what they'd taken to calling the war room.

For the rest, everyone had been debriefed (*before* David's impromptu nap). Which is to say Aikin had given a clipped but accurate account of their voyage to Faerie, their meeting with Nuada, and their rescue of Lugh and subsequent escape. Calvin had filled them in on his activities, which was basically that Sandy had refused to stay home, but had brought every weapon in her place, and that he'd recruited his cousin Kirkwood because, as Kirkwood himself had put it, "Two crazy Indians'll put the wind up anybody, mortal or otherwise."

And then Liz had quickly summarized what should also have been David's graduation—essentially that it had happened—and the parental chaos that had ensued, which had consumed massive amounts of time they hadn't known was all that critical. Happily, they'd also fulfilled their quest, as evidenced by the array of odd artifacts scattered on Devlin's coffee table. Bows, swords, war clubs—*atasi* was the proper term—and a few uktena scales.

"Got more of those," Calvin confided, to David's great relief. "Figured we might need to get the hell out of Dodge on the fly, as it were."

Meanwhile, the Faeries had focused most of their attention on the unconscious Lugh, washing his body repeatedly to remove ever more of the insidious iron dust, including that which had made festering lumps of his ears. He did look better, David conceded. Flesh that heretofore had been blistered and red was now utterly unblemished, without freckle, mole, or misplaced hair.

He was healing himself, Nuada had said. Slowly, from the inside. Quite possibly from the brain out. Maybe the Faeries were helping, though what good the two males could accomplish, David had no idea. Fionchadd had been no great shakes when the voyage had begun, and Nuada had pushed himself to exhaustion. David wondered whether he too might have some link beyond mere birth to the Land of Tir-Nan-Og.

Somewhere in the wee hours, too, Uncle Dale had arrived with LaWanda and news of the rest of the clan. Short form: Big Billy was stable but neither improving nor reliably conscious, which his doctor opined was shock: how else to explain the things he'd babbled when flirting with awareness. In spite of evidence to the contrary, no major organs had been compromised, though a couple of third-string arteries had taken significant hits. They'd X-rayed everything in sight, probed what the 'rays had missed, tested him for everything under the sun, irrigated his wound three times, and stitched him up. Oh, and added four units of blood to replace what had oozed away. JoAnne was planning to camp out there, along with Little Billy. Dale might make a run back to the Cove come daylight. Nor did he remain at Devlin's compound long, since they'd thoughtlessly brought only one car, which JoAnne would need in Clayton.

Thank God for Dale, too; running interference like he was, and keeping David informed on the one hand, JoAnne calm on the other, while laying down considerable law about how this wasn't over yet, that it was far bigger than she dared think, and that David was doing what he had to, with his father's full blessings.

As for the slain: Nuada, Fionchadd, and Aife had gone out there to check, along with himself, Cal, Kirkwood, Aikin, and Devlin. There was blood aplenty, but no bodies.

Whether that meant the enemy had gone into hiding, returned to Tir-Nan-Og, or simply dispersed (as Nuada had hinted they might), David had no idea. Nor cared, now that it was daylight and they could breathe easier. Tonight—that was what they were debating now, sitting on Devlin's porch, drinking coffee, orange juice, and herbal tea, and eating breakfast biscuits and omelets contrived from groceries Myra had provided.

"So you think tonight's attack will be worse?" Sandy was saying through a mouthful of ham and cheese.

Nuada shrugged. "That would be my intent if I knew

where my opponent lay and that he had valuable personages with him who were so injured he dared not move them far, nor could, with ease.''

"And if I had tested his defenses," Aife added.

"But dared not let my own actions be closely observed," Fionchadd concluded, "lest the tide be turned once more."

"Bottom line," LaWanda said. "We gotta hurry."

"Where? And to what end?" Sandy wondered.

David took a deep breath and slapped Calvin on the thigh. "Fargo, my friend"—he grinned—"we think we should get Lugh to Galunlati."

"Galunlati!" Calvin cried, genuinely surprised, which surprised David in turn.

"Galunlati," David affirmed. "I figured you'd already considered that, else why bring all those scales?"

Calvin shook his head. "Yeah, well, I thought somebody might want to zip off there, maybe chase down some help or something. But I never thought that Lugh—"

"Yeah, well, listen," David broke in. And told him about their plan.

"There's also the healing lake," Aikin reminded them, at which point Alec perked up, but Liz looked unhappy. "We used to have some water from there," she said, glaring at Aife. "Used to, but no longer."

"Another debt I acknowledge," Aife murmured back. "Another reason I am here instead of plotting your destruction."

David slapped his knees. "So we're agreed, then? We get Lugh to Galunlati—today, if possible."

"Possible," Calvin acknowledged. "Difficult and a pain, but possible."

Liz continued to look troubled. "But what about John? He's the one who'll have to deal with this attack if it comes, whether or not Lugh's here. I mean, think, folks; the enemy won't know Lugh's gone if they can't read through all the steel around here."

"They can read that much," Nuada corrected. "Power such as Lugh commands, whether directed inward or without, would shine from this house like a beacon."

"So there'll be no attack?"

"Shouldn't be," Devlin mused. "Then again, there're things like anger, retaliation, senseless slaughter. Down and dirty *meanness*. This is *war*, folks. In war there are no rules except win, and these folks we're fightin' here never heard of the UN. Our ancestors took heads, don't forget—those of us with Celt blood in our veins, which is most of us. *These* folks still take heads!"

David nodded grimly. "I've seen 'em do it."

"So, what about you, then?" Alec ventured.

"I stay," Devlin replied. "With Lugh gone, I'm a lesser target, whatever else happens. I've got protections of my own, and more I can call up if I have to, and . . . other eyes to watch."

Aikin cleared his throat. "I take it that we're plannin' to split up again?"

David looked at Devlin and Nuada, the two seasoned warriors present. "Your call, guys."

"I don't have enough scales for all of us," Calvin stated flatly. "As it is, I'll have to finagle some stuff."

"How many *do* you have?" Liz asked.

"Seven—that I can use." He fingered the one on his neck thong meaningfully.

"Well, that settles one thing," David sighed. "We know how to save the King. Now all we gotta do is figure out how to save what that King thinks is the enemy country."

Silence.

"Any ideas?" he prompted. "Anything at all?"

Silence.

"Aw, c'mon, folks. How many degrees we got in this room? How many SAT points? How much cumulative IQ? How many years of experience, you Faerie folk? Doesn't that count for something? Imagination? Passion? Dammit, why doesn't somebody just *think*, so I don't have to!" And with that David rose and began to pace.

"Lateral thinking," Liz murmured at last.

Most of the company looked puzzled, but David scowled thoughtfully. "You wanta explain that?"

Liz did: it was simply looking at a problem from a different direction, or at the literal, rather than implicit, meaning of words. "Like a knight on a quest for a virgin," she suggested. "He meets all these people and asks where he might find a young and virtuous lady, not realizing that, as stated, he could as well find a dried-up old crone or even a man."

Kirkwood frowned thoughtfully. "Okay, then, how 'bout this?" He paused for a sip of coffee, then leaned back against a porch post and folded his arms. "First off, best I can tell, the problem is that whatever separates Faerie and this World is being eaten away by iron on our side, which does the other side no good. The more basic problem is that Faerie depends on our world for existence, only ours doesn't have to be inhabited, it simply has to exist. But the *root* cause of all this—what's brought matters to a head—is the fact that some real estate developers are gonna put up a lot of ironwork on the one place in this World that Faerie is linked with most strongly."

Calvin elbowed him in the ribs. "What're you gettin' at, Churchy?"

"What I'm gettin' at is—well, what do most people do when one thing intrudes too much on another? You *destroy* one of those things. Or you—"

"Move 'em!" Liz cried. "Of course!"

"Yeah," Alec echoed sourly. "*Of course!* Liz, what're you thinking about? You can't separate our World and Faerie!"

"Can't you?" Calvin retorted. "Maybe you can't separate those two, but something like that *has* been done. My people speak of it as myth, but half the people here have been to Galunlati and met Uki, and we know for a fact that it was moved seven times before they got it right, and then, much later, moved again—away from us."

"And if Galunlati can be moved, no reason Tir-Nan-Og can't be."

Nuada stroked his chin. "An audacious plan, but not one I would dismiss out of hand. *Either* hand," he added, flourishing his own. Sunlight struck both, but one glittered metallically, the other gleamed with healthy flesh. Slowly he brought them together. "Two hands. Two Worlds. Air between." Then he drew them apart. "Two hands. Two

Worlds. The same relationship to one another, save one thing: more air between.''

David's mouth popped open. ''You mean—''

Nuada dropped his hands. ''If moving Worlds is possible, then we should look into moving Worlds. It is certainly better than war, for either side.''

''Won't argue that,'' Devlin murmured.

Myra cleared her throat. ''In that case, I know of at least one other case of moving Worlds—Worlds like we're talking about.''

''Oh, shit!'' LaWanda gasped. ''Girl, you don't mean—''

Myra nodded mutely. ''That place we wound up after that crap went down at Scarboro Faire all those years ago, that fucked Scott up so bad he's still not over it.''

Calvin shook his head. ''Don't know about that, not much.''

''Too much to tell in a hurry,'' LaWanda growled. ''Basically, some magic dude from one of these Faery countries discovers Tracks that are silver, not gold, and not only that, he finds out he can control 'em and use 'em to steal little bits of other places and build a country—a World, I guess— of his own. Well, we fucked up his plans and he was destroyed, and his country got shook up some, but might still be there. Even if it isn't, the Tracks might be. And if they can move little bits of Worlds, I figure they could just as easy move big ones.''

Nuada's brow furrowed thoughtfully. ''I know this tale, but had forgotten it—which I should not, just as I should not have forgotten Alberon of Alban, whose realm we visit but seldom and who sits and sulks and keeps his own council these days, even more so than Arawn and Finvarra.''

''Finvarra knows about them, though,'' Fionchadd supplied. ''I was imprisoned in a place with a view of them, and Finvarra sent me there. Whether he has studied them, however . . .''

Nuada shrugged in turn. ''Do not forget that as time runs differently between your World and Faerie, sometimes, too, it runs differently between the realms of Faerie. Time runs slow in Alberon's realm indeed, and less time will have passed there than in this World. I doubt he has had time to learn much at all. And Finvarra little more.''

"So we go ask some Faery king to tell us everything he knows about some Tracks that almost fucked up his own Land?'' Alec snorted. "I don't think so.''

"No time to get there, anyway,'' Nuada agreed. "Still, if Colin's realm—for such was the name of the druid who wrought that realm—yet survives, perhaps some clue remains there that might explain how he was able to manipulate the Silver Tracks.''

"He had books,'' Piper volunteered, speaking for the first time. "Lots of books. I saw 'em in his tower.''

"Which was destroyed,'' Myra countered. "The land may well have been.''

Nuada shook his head. "Not all. We watched these things. We should have investigated and did not. We thought we had all the time we needed.''

"So the records may still be there?'' Myra whispered. "Oh, Jesus!''

"Yeah,'' LaWanda grumbled. "And I got three guesses who's gonna have to try and find 'em.''

Myra reached over to squeeze her friend's hand. "You and me, girl, together again.''

"And me,'' Piper sighed. "I don't think you can get there otherwise.''

David frowned. "It was a cold place, surrounded by water. If it's the tower Finno was locked up in.''

"It was not,'' Nuada said. "There were two towers, one greater, one lesser. The one you visited was the lesser. The one your friends visited, the greater. When Colin died, his land fragmented. Parts drifted away.''

David eyed him dubiously. "If you say so.''

No one spoke.

"Well,'' Sandy said decisively into that lull, "now that's all decided, I guess the next thing we figure out is who goes where.''

"And stays,'' Nuada amended. "Some of us ought to. Some of us may have to.''

Calvin checked his watch. "Well, if Lugh's goin' anywhere before dark, we'd better get to talkin'.''

"Or rolling dice," Aikin put in, a trifle giddily. "Might be just as effective."

"No," Sandy assured him with a smile. "I've been thinking."

PART TWO

Scott Gresham's Journal

(Sunday, June 29—morning)

This is really great! Just fucking ducky! First of all, here I sat actually doing what's *almost* real work on Mr. Laptop here—for a change—and then all of a sudden I get this phone call from Myra wondering if just maybe, perhaps, might I kinda, from the goodness of my heart, being as how I'm a really nice guy and all, want to dump everything here and bop down to Athens so I can hare off to Faerie with a bunch of 'em looking for some kind of fucking magic book that may not exist.

And yeah, I know they've got a real and true important job to do (Myra caught me up on that, and old man Dale's kept me posted fairly well, so maybe I'm only sucking next-to-hind tit now), but I just can't seem to get it through anybody's head that while, yeah, a lot of really important things hinge on what they do in all those places, I've still got to function in the real world, and they've mostly been piss-poor at helping me cope. I mean, I *finally*, at the absolute eleventh hour dissertation-wise, finally get this really neat, good-paying job doing stuff I don't mind doing, and all of a sudden at the eleventh-and-a-half hour I find out it's completely at odds with all my friends' wild romantic notions of what I ought to do.

And the trouble is, they're right. And they've promised to help me keep my head on straight after this, but you know, Mr. Laptop, it's gonna be *me* having to list Mystic Mountain Properties on every job application I ever fill out from here on out, and something tells me I'm not gonna get an A-one recommendation. "Oh, right, you worked for that group that fucked up the mountains." Yeah, sure.

So I told Myra no. I told her I'd like to help 'em out on this Faerie-thing (which is true). But I told her I also had to cover my ass, and had (as they'd said) an important job to do here, so that I can maybe keep my nose clean. I . . .

Fuck it! Just fuck it! (They oughta call these rant machines.) Just goddam mother fuck it! I keep trying to do the right thing and I just can't seem to make it happen. Oh well. Elyyoth says he knows some kind of spell that might make it hard for them to get heavy equipment in here. Well, except that he also says it may not work on iron. In any event, he's a pretty cool dude, so maybe I'll get one good thing out of this.

And I guess, if I really want to be objective, the folks did promise to help me out money-wise, but I'm not sure if I want 'em to do that. Even fuck-ups like me got pride.

End of rant. Gotta call the guys back home, and see how my ferret's doing.

Chapter IX:
Swimming Upstream

(near Clayton, Georgia—
Sunday, June 29—late morning)

"I don't feel real," David grumbled to Liz in the first private moments they'd managed since she and Alec had arrived the previous night. They'd wandered out to the end of John Devlin's drive, ostensibly to case the place for artifacts the Sidhe might have left behind—or bloodstains, or any other tokens that might supply insight into their adversaries' strengths and weaknesses. None were forthcoming. What few footprints had survived three sets of invading vehicles plus Dale's Lincoln Town Car were bare, and all showing aberrations that evoked avian, canine, and feline alike; not unreasonable, for shapeshifters. David kicked at a patch of gravel. "Not real," he repeated, more loudly.

"I don't either," Liz sighed. "And I'm not exactly sure why. I mean, look at all this; every sense we've got's being stimulated to the max: clean air, cooking smells, pine trees, earth, birdsong, bugs in the woods, our friends chattering up at the house, warm wind, sunlight on skin, blue sky, mountains that're purple-gray-green. Trees in a dozen shapes. Cars in all kinds of colors. Those are the realest things there are!"

David scowled. "And then there's the war. It's real, but it's also remote. Like, there's a part of me that thinks I'm just goin' through the motions, that if I'll only go back to Athens and keep on takin' classes and hangin' out in clubs and readin' and listenin' to music and goin' to movies, folks won't really come out of Faerie after Lugh. They won't really build that resort back home. The Sidhe won't really flood Sullivan Cove if they do. Pa won't really be in the hospital. It's like—like I feel after a movie. Total immersion for a while, and then heightened senses, but it's all illusion.''

Liz gazed at him askance and reached over to take his hand. The wind ruffled her hair; the sunlight woke highlights in it: bright flame against darker, but still glowing, embers. ''I know one thing that'd make us feel real,'' she murmured, nodding toward the nearest patch of woods, which was conveniently screened by a stand of rhododendron. ''Looks pretty mossy in there.''

David grinned at her. ''And what use would we have for moss?''

Liz's eyes twinkled with mischief. ''Softer to lie on than leaves.''

David's grin widened. ''I don't have any . . .''

Liz regarded him levelly. ''This time I think it'd be okay to risk it. I think it'd be more real.''

''Yeah,'' David agreed a little shakily. ''I think it would.''

David wasn't certain if it was sunlight in his eyes, some subtle shift in Liz's breathing, or the sound of voices talking deliberately loud that woke him from a drowse he'd neither sought out nor intended. In any event, it took but an instant to realize that he wasn't exactly in the safest place in the world, that he was naked as the day he was born (as was Liz, beside him), and that decisions were being made even now with which, just possibly, he ought to be involved.

''Liz,'' he hissed, ''we got company.'' And with that he fumbled through his clothes and whipped a sweatshirt over her more interesting bits, where she curled on a nest of moss in his shadow. That accomplished, he found his skivvies, skinned them on, and was just buttoning his fatigues when the voices reached the point where he had no choice but to dash out of the bushes and yell ''Whoa!''

Aikin and Alec looked amused, if not startled, and shot him sympathetic grins. ''Sorry, man,'' Aikin muttered. ''Folks are leavin'.''

David donned his T-shirt. ''Thanks. I, uh—well, basically, we didn't mean to—''

"What?" Alec inquired archly.

"Nothing you wouldn't do yourself, if you had the chance," David retorted, glancing back at Liz and finding her . . . progressing.

Alec's face clouded. "Yeah, well, that's kind of the problem, isn't it? Not that she hasn't suggested it," he added hastily. "But it's been so long, and there's so much going on. And you know me; I'd as soon do it right, if I'm gonna do it."

David rolled his eyes at Aikin. "That's our buddy: ever the romantic."

" 'Least I won't get leaves in my butt crack!' "

"Depends on who's on top," David shot back sweetly. And ducked back into the thicket. "So," he continued, when he returned with clothes in hand and a barefoot Liz in tow. "What's the deal?" They sat down to deal with socks and shoes.

"The deal," Aikin replied patiently, "is that the Silver Track crew are leavin'."

David lifted a brow. "They're not gonna cross over straight from here?"

Alec shook his head. "And technically, it's not a *they*."

David's eyes narrowed. "What do you mean?"

Aikin shifted his weight and looked a trifle guilty. "I mean—that is, uh, me and Mach-One here are goin' too."

David shrugged a bit too nonchalantly as he attacked his second sneaker. "Whatever. I got tired of hearin' pros and cons of this person and that. I know where I have to go, for balance, if nothing else. The rest—it'd be good people anyway."

"I hope so," Aikin muttered, looking apprehensively back toward the cabin.

"So what's the final tally?" David asked. He snugged his last lace and rose, slapping leaves off his backside in the process.

Alec counted on his fingers. "John stays here—obviously. So does Brock, because it's the least risky proposition, plus he's got some background in Cherokee mojo, and Cal and Churchy thought it'd be best if we had as many traditions represented here as possible. And since Cal pretty much has to go to Galunlati, Churchy's got a vested interest in goin', and Sandy's in no mood to argue, that only leaves the kid.''

"So someone from Faerie's stayin' here too?''

"Silverhand,'' Alec acknowledged. "Finno's been to Galunlati, so it makes sense for him to return. Aife, being a traitor to the Sons, feels like she'd be better off if she wasn't so close to hand, plus she's an added attraction to anyone who might happen to attack, so she's going Tracking. Silverhand's an even bigger draw, of course, but he's also bigger mojo. And now that he's rested, he swears he feels as good as new.''

"What about LaWanda?'' Liz broke in. "She's from yet *another* magic tradition.''

"And a damned fine fighter,'' David added. "But she's also friends with Myra, who has to look for the Silver Tracks; as, apparently, does Piper.''

"Right,'' Aikin agreed. "Which is why McLean and me decided to go with 'em. They've got native guides. They got a Faery. They *might* have Scott if Myra convinces him to cut work for a day. But they need somebody who knows how all this stuff fits together.''

"And who's spent enough time away from his girlfriend,'' Alec appended.

"And of course they need someone tireless, resourceful, and decent with weapons, even if they don't expect to fight,'' Aikin finished with a smug grin, glancing at his watch, then at the sky, then back at the cabin. "And now, if you guys don't mind . . .''

David gave Liz a hand up. "We gotta get movin' too.''

A minute later, they were standing beside Myra's van. The owner was fidgeting with her keys and looking antsy. Piper wasn't doing anything at all, having withdrawn into that quiet place he went when fear, desire, and responsibility—and his love for LaWanda—resumed their invisible war.

Aife and Nuada were on the porch, talking animatedly, and only partly with their mouths, as the *clogging* in David's head testified. As best he could tell, Aife was debating whether to remain in the Faery substance she'd adopted upon leaving the Cove, in which form she'd have easier access to Power; or to put on the substance of the Mortal World, in

which guise she'd be better equipped to weather the proximity to iron riding in the van would entail.

Aikin, who'd also caught the conversation, settled the matter abruptly. " 'Less somebody's willin' to lend a pickup
with a bedliner, I don't see how she's got much choice." He
gazed at Liz speculatively, then at Devlin.

"Mine won't make it," Devlin said.

"And we may need mine," Liz added. "When we get
back from Galunlati."

"Gee," Alec sighed, crestfallen. "And I was hoping we
could ride in the back." Then, to David, with a wink: "Ain't
no *moss* in a pickup."

"Just pryin' eyes."

A shrug. "That's what cover's for."

"Abstinence," Myra drawled, "makes the heart grow
fonder."

"Heart, or—?"

David elbowed his friend and giggled. A man could only
take so much that was stern and grim and . . . *significant*,
after all, before he had to get punchy or go insane.

Myra jingled her keys meaningfully and opened her door.
Piper was already inside. Alec was moving that way as well,
propelled by Devlin. No argument there, David noted. No
endless discussion. Merely simple, direct action. He wished
everything was that simple.

But where was LaWanda?

"Sorry," the woman called, as if in answer. "Figured I
oughta have one last go at a for-real potty, seein' how I may
not have access to one for a while." And as LaWanda jogged
around to the van's passenger side, Myra Jane Buchanan
closed the door and cranked the engine.

Alec gave David one final hug, as did Aikin, which surprised him, and then they too climbed in the vehicle. Aife,
very white-faced, came last.

The air resounded with good-byes, or inanities uttered in
lieu of real emotion. And then, for almost half a minute, John
Devlin's yard filled up with silence.

Ten years ago, David concluded wryly, he'd have given
anything he owned, might own, or would ever have consid-

ered owning, to be doing what he was right now. If you considered *right now* to mean helping the King of the Faeries evade rebels by spiriting him to another World, anyway. Yeah, his twelve-year-old self would've thought that was pretty cool. Little Billy still thought it was pretty cool and was jealous as hell that David got to have adventures he only heard about, and that under penalty of worse punishments than he could imagine if he told anyone else! Of course, the kid hid most of that jealousy—and pride and anger—under a thickening veneer of attitude David didn't recall ever having. But he'd still have thought it was pretty damned cool.

David, age twenty-two, was royally tired of it. Even worse, as Liz said, there was no end in sight. At least the logistics were nowhere near as complicated as they would once have been, not with Calvin having custody of a sufficiency of uktena scales—scales from a serpentlike monster that dwelt in Galunlati, one incarnation of which he, Alec, Calvin, and Fionchadd had long ago helped to slay.

Yep, those scales had proven mighty useful more than once; and trouble, of course, as well. Shoot, the plain, un-adulterated items could help a man shapeshift. All you had to do was hold one in your hand, close your eyes, and think of what you wanted to become, then squeeze until the scale's sharp edges brought blood. And presto-chango: instant 'possum, or whatever.

Actually, it wasn't that easy. It hurt like hell, for one thing. And you had to have eaten the critter in question—which wasn't a problem for country-boy-woodsy types like him and Calvin, or forestry jocks like Aikin. It was also wise to shift to something roughly one's own mass; cougars, deer, small bears, wolves, and alligators were ideal.

Nor was that all uktena scales were good for. Another function was about to be utilized right soon. David wondered if he was ready—beyond being packed, fed, and sporting his *atasi*, the war club Asgaya Sakani had given him at his naming ceremony, three years back. Trouble was, as he'd already warned Sandy, Liz, and Kirkwood, this application *also* hurt like the devil. Fionchadd had said it didn't matter, and Lugh was still out of it, though looking better all the time. Still, he dreaded it.

He wouldn't be dreading much longer. Cal had suggested they wait until noon, which was a *between* time, since between times were auspicious for working with what the Sidhe would have called Power.

David wondered if he was ready. He'd spent most of the morning since the departure of the Silver Tracks crew helping Calvin, Kirkwood, and Sandy contrive a travois-litter-thing on which to transport Lugh, in case cross-country travel was required. The finished apparatus consisted of twin eight-foot staves of rattan wrapped with foam and duct tape at all four ends to form padded handles, and joined by a surplus army blanket stitched around the poles.

Fionchadd and Nuada were easing the King down on it now, both apparently in much better shape than heretofore, though both sets of eyes were tired beyond belief. Himself, he was on his second—or third—or fourth—wind, but the time couldn't be far off when he'd do a serious crash-and-burn.

He hoped nothing was competing for attention then.

Like survival.

Galunlati wasn't Faerie, after all; wasn't even halfway civilized. It was more like pre-Columbian North America, with a dash of Pleistocene flora and fauna thrown in.

He was still staring numbly at the unconscious Faery king and trying not to think about why Kirkwood was building a fire in the fireplace in the high heat of June, when Liz slipped up behind him and handed him a cup of iced coffee. "Kick, but no heat," she purred.

He took it, kissed her absently. "This'd be easier if we had the ulunsuti."

"Ulunsuti?" Devlin echoed, joining them. "Jewel from the head of the uktena, right? Cherokee shamans use 'em. Supposed to have oracular powers."

"Does, too."

"Somehow I missed that you guys have one."

"*Had* one," David corrected. "Uki gave Alec one the first time we went to Galunlati. Caused him a lot of grief, too, though it's also helped a couple of times, like when we've needed to check up on other places. Anyway, it's gone now. See, you can do certain things to 'em and use 'em to create gates between the Worlds. That's what caused part of the problem with Faerie, actually.''

Devlin nodded thoughtfully. "I knew they'd had trouble with what they called the gating stone, but didn't know they meant an ulunsuti.''

David shrugged

"So you could've used it to make a gate now?''

" 'Fraid so.''

At which point Calvin wandered back inside from where he'd been reinforcing his wards and instructing Brock on the maintenance of same. He ruffled the boy's long hair affectionately. "Gotta get you a war name, kiddo.''

Brock beamed.

David raised a brow at Calvin and shouldered his bag of gear.

Calvin gave him a weary nod and retrieved his own bag. "Head 'em up; move 'em out,'' he called.

Silently, they gathered round: those who would remain behind—Devlin, Brock, and Nuada—and those who would venture into Galunlati—David, Liz, and Sandy, who were all New World Celts; Calvin McIntosh and Kirkwood O'Connor, who were Cherokee-Irish mix; Fionchadd Mac-Ailill, who was part Faerie and part Powersmith; and Lugh Samildinach, High King of the Sidhe in Tir-Nan-Og. *Seven,* David realized. Which *could* be a lucky number.

Calvin checked his watch, then led his crew to the area they'd cleared in front of Devlin's fireplace—they'd moved the sofa back halfway across the room to make space for themselves, and at that, it was still rather crowded.

"Closer,'' Calvin insisted, urging them closer again, so that David felt the fireplace heat wash up into his face, reminding him unpleasantly of the Pillar of Fire back . . . wherever. "Take care, everybody,'' he called, a sentiment echoed by the others, though it was a more sober leave-taking than the earlier one, possibly because neither Devlin nor Nuada were demonstrative types and Brock had decided to be cool again.

Calvin squeezed through to kneel before the fire. David

was certain its heat flared hotter than ever. "Ten, nine, eight . . ." Sandy counted. And then Calvin reached into a white leather pouch at his waist, drew out seven examples of what looked like vitreous fish scales, milky-clear at the tips, blood red at the roots. A pause for a breath and a half-heard invocation in Cherokee, and Calvin tossed all seven scales into the fire.

Smoke.

"Hyuntikwala Usunhi!" Calvin yelled.

The fire blazed up immediately; the smoke thickened: *up* first, then *out*—enfolding them all in heat beyond heat, pain beyond pain, as though every cell in their bodies was being charred to ash one by one, and each had its own separate and exquisitely sensitive nerve. Someone gasped. Someone else cried out. A rush of wind; flame and pain found David's eyes, and the World simply disappeared.

As white light was in truth all colors merged into one all-consuming whole, what followed was the same thing rendered in pain. A pain so pure it almost was *not* pain. And then it *was* again, and was diminishing, as though his cells reasserted themselves one by one.

Wind on his face, the smell of growing things, and David opened his eyes.

"Well," Kirkwood breathed beside him. "So this is Galunlati."

"Looks like it," Calvin gasped. For his part, David was knuckling his eyes, wiping away the residual smoke that was making them tear like crazy. Eventually, his vision clarified, and he took stock of his surroundings. It was Galunlati, all right; not even Tir-Nan-Og had this primal freshness. The air was what air ought to be, what it was *designed* to be. And the landscape . . . ! He inhaled deeply and looked around—they all did, returnees and newcomers alike. Newcomer, rather; Kirkwood was the only complete neophyte save the unconscious Lugh.

God, but this place was beautiful! They stood at the edge of a good-sized river that bisected a narrow valley framed with mountains to either side, mountains that could have been his own native Appalachians a million years ago, before erosion—and *Homo sapiens*—had worked their will upon them. More rounded than the Rockies, they were, and forested to their peaks. Sure, those peaks were taller than the ones back in Enotah County, or the taller, craggier ones up in the Smokies, like those in *The Last of the Mohicans*. But the subtle softness was the same, a softness wrought at once by the underlying shapes and the growth that covered them: hardwoods mostly, conifers here and there, with laurel and rhododendron filling the spaces between.

And the trees closer in! Hundreds of feet high, they were, straight trunked, yet not unnaturally perfect, for limbs looped and whorled and twisted where they would in a riot of joyous growth.

The sky was clear, save straight ahead, where a paler smudge rose from a screen of pines to bleach it. A familiar stain, too. *"Hyuntikwalayi,"* Calvin murmured. "Where-It-Made-A-Noise-As-Of-Thunder."

"I know that name," Kirkwood whispered. "It's the old name for Tallulah Gorge."

"Which this both is and isn't," Calvin acknowledged. "Now listen."

As one they held their breaths—and felt as much as heard the steady, almost infrasound, rumble of water that fell so far and hard the rocks around it forever resonated.

"I take it," Liz observed, "that you guys have been here before?"

David and Calvin nodded as one. "Cave in the rocks below. That's where Uki lives."

"So where is he, then?" Sandy wondered. "I mean, that *was* his name Cal shouted, right? Shouldn't it have brought us to him?"

"*Should* have," Calvin emphasized. "It doesn't always—quite. I—"

A groan silenced him. Lugh. Lying as he'd lain in the Lands of Men: shrouded in a bedsheet, then wrapped to the neck in an army blanket, and resting on the ground between them.

One thing had changed immediately, David noted. Instead of being utterly comatose, the King of the Faeries was writhing and thrashing, twisting within his bonds, though whether to free himself from restraint or from pain he couldn't tell.

He was grunting and groaning, too, and had actually managed to work one hand free, though his eyelids were tightly closed.

He looked better, though: healthier, anyway; less abraded than before, with fewer pustules, far less angry red. A healthier glow suffusing what was always ghost-pale skin. His face was also fuller: his cheeks less hollow, the pouches under his eyes not as obvious. His hair, however, was still as wet as it had been: slicked to his skull with sweat and the water they'd used to rinse it free of iron dust. Not successfully, either, to judge by the oozing scalp. Only that—and his mouth—still looked tortured, likely a result of the dust they'd been unable to remove from his sweeping mustache, which Nuada had dared anyone to trim lest they face Lugh's wrath indeed.

And then Lugh's writhing redoubled.

"Is he having a *fit*?" Liz gasped, staring intently at Fionchadd.

The Faery was equally amazed, and more amazed a moment later when, amidst the worst writhing yet, Lugh's eyes popped open. They were a startling dark blue: the blue of sapphires and deepsea water. And wild—with fear, pain, or utter madness, David had no idea.

More writhing, and the blanket began to slip free. "Hold him!" Calvin snapped, but Fionchadd grabbed his shoulders and held him back.

"Finno? What—?" Calvin began hotly.

"I am not certain," the Faery hissed. "I caught a shred of thought unshadowed by insanity. I—I think he has a plan."

And then, with a groan and the ripping of fabric, the writhing, thrashing King broke free. He rose—slowly, awkwardly, yet graceful for all that uncertainty—and stood swaying for a moment, white and naked and mostly intact, with his black hair hanging halfway down a back that reblistered as they watched.

Before anyone could stop him, he uttered a long wild shriek and dashed toward the juncture of the river and the screen of trees that masked the source of all that liquid thunder.

Reflex had already set David running, with Cal, Liz, and Fionchadd close behind; all in pursuit of the fleeing Faery, who was already forcing his way through the low-lying, riverside brush.

They lost sight of him briefly, the foliage was so thick, but then daylight stabbed their eyes again. David blinked and had to rein himself in to keep from plunging over the edge of the precipitous cliff barely two yards ahead of him.

David had already opened his mouth to call Lugh's name, to summon him back from the brink, when the Faery uttered one final ecstatic shout—and flung himself into the river, not five feet from where it leapt over what was easily two hundred feet of ancient granite.

He lost sight of him, then, amidst the ensuing fountain of spray, but glimpsed him one final time before he disappeared over the cliff.

"Damn!" Kirkwood panted, jogging up to where he, Calvin, and Liz all stood gaping, with Fionchadd oddly silent at the absolute brink.

David joined the Faery, and could only stare down the long white plume of thundering water. Stare, and wonder, and try not to give himself over to despair.

Chapter X:
Second Gate

(US 129—Sunday, June 29—late morning)

"So," Aikin murmured, easing back in the Caravan's right front captain's chair, which had defaulted to him, "let me get this straight: you, Scott, Piper, and LaWanda have all been to this World before?"

Myra, who was driving (it was, after all, her van), nodded absently and ran a hand through her topknot of wheat-colored hair. She did that when she was antsy, Aikin noticed, as she had been ever since they'd got stuck behind a convoy of semis—packed with carnival rides, interestingly enough.

"Might as well give him the lowdown, gal," LaWanda called from the rearmost bench, where she and Piper were ensconced, leaving Aife and Alec to share the mid-range, to their chagrin. "Don't think Aife knows the whole tale either."

Myra sighed wearily. "Well, the basic story is that a few years back Piper and a friend of ours named Jay Madison happened on the manuscript of an unknown medieval mystery play down at the UGA library. Naturally, there was a big to-do about producing the thing, with Jay's asshole brother getting the right to direct it. They were gonna—"

"Get to the point," LaWanda urged.

Myra aimed a glare at her through the rearview mirror, then paused again to pass the rearmost of the semis before proceeding. "Right—so what nobody knew was that the manuscript also contained a spell which, if the play was performed under certain circumstances, would take whoever read it to another World."

"Gettin' ahead of yourself, now," LaWanda muttered.

Myra's jaw tensed, but she went on anyway. "Whatever. So shift to Faerie, or one of its adjuncts. A minor wizard there named Colin discovered these Silver Tracks, which have the ability to carry matter from one World to another—kind of the opposite of the gold ones we use, which help us move but don't move themselves. Anyway, Colin also discovered a way to use them to deposit material where *he* wanted, and eventually built his own little mini-kingdom using material stolen, I think, from Alban, which is the Faery realm in Scotland. It was pretty neat actually; apparently he could take every third grain of sand on one hand and entire mountains on the other. However it worked, he had a tower in the middle of it, and a maze of mirrors around it, and stocked it with all kinds of critters, notably gryphons, which are semisapient, and which he effectively enslaved."

There was much more of course, and though Myra was oddly reticent about the details, Aikin eventually got a satisfactorily complete story. Piper helped occasionally, and Aife ventured the odd speculation, as did Alec, who'd heard most of the tale from David, to whom Myra had once related the entire saga.

"So the reason we're going to Athens," Aikin summarized, "is that the last time anybody looked, that place *overlapped* Athens—okay, Myra: *Bogart*—and that that while it's sort of in Faerie, the Faerie we know and—uh—love also overlaps the same place."

"Basically," LaWanda acknowledged. "See, we don't know how big the place is, and the way we're plannin' on gettin' there . . . we basically gotta *be* there."

"Let's hope," Alec grunted. "Those little countries tend to float around a lot. Best I can figure, long as they're attached to a Track, they can move up and down it at—well, not at will, but by whatever screwy physics runs things over there."

"In any event," Myra concluded, "Athens seems like the best place from which to enter. And before anybody says anything about damaging the World Walls, remember that we really don't have any choice. Besides, we weren't the ones who started this."

Aikin yawned. *God, he was sleepy!* Then again, he hadn't slept since . . . when? Back on the ship sometime? Another yawn (best to close his eyes anyway, given how close Myra was to the back of that Aeromax) and before he knew it, he was dreaming.

"Wakey, wakey!" LaWanda teased, dragging Aikin up from far too deep a slumber by tugging on his ear. Aikin blinked groggily and knuckled his eyes, aware that not only had he slept, but that it had been very deep sleep indeed, and that he was having God's own trouble freeing himself from it. "What time—?"

"Just past noon," Alec supplied, thrusting a bag in his direction. "You zoned through the lunch-and-potty break up in Commerce, plus the run by Myra's place to retrieve a certain manuscript."

Aikin snared the bag and peered within: McDonald's Quarterpounder, big fries—and water: his standard order, courtesy of Alec. And then he looked outside.

He didn't immediately recognize the place, though he knew enough from his two forays into other Worlds to iden- tify their own home turf: good old Lands-of-Men, or what- ever. *How* he knew he had no idea: sounds, maybe; or the smell of the air? What was important was that Myra had parked at the side of a freshly graveled road not far from a set of railroad tracks, over which they might have jolted hard enough to rouse him, though he doubted it; and that they were effectively screened on all sides but one by the scrubby pine woods ubiquitous to middle Georgia. The other side— it looked like a castle gate but wasn't, unless castles were made of cinder blocks and painted plywood, and had signs over their portcullises proclaiming, in large Gothic script, "SCARBORO FAIRE: East Georgia's Own Renaissance Festival."

"We're in luck," Myra announced, peering through the windshield as the others disembarked. "Doesn't look like anyone's around."

"Didn't figure there would be," LaWanda snorted as she thrust Piper out ahead of her. "They closed last weekend."

"Unless somebody's rented the place for a banquet or

something," Myra shot back. "But to judge by how empty the parking lot is . . ." She gestured ahead and to the left, through a break in the trees.

"No time like the present," LaWanda prompted as Myra trotted around back to unload gear. Piper accompanied her, looking at once eager, expectant, and scared out of his mind.

Aikin could think of nothing useful to say. A yawn and a handful of fries, and he joined Myra in divesting the cargo bay of their equipment, including the shotgun he had no intention of letting out of his sight. He checked the sawed-off double-barrel automatically, though he'd cleaned it once that day already, then passed a Ruger to Alec. "Brock was totin' this, but I co-opted it, since Devlin's bound to have something he can use if he needs a shootin' iron. Best you go armed, though."

Alec rolled his eyes. " 'Least it's not that heavy old Enfield you're always sticking me with."

Aikin rolled his eyes in turn, then jumped half out of his skin as a preposterous noise shattered the peace of the forested roadside. A screech, it sounded like, and a wail, and a mournful, ripping cry, which finally coalesced into Piper tuning up the fine new set of Uilleann pipes Fionchadd had brought him out of Faerie a week and a lifetime gone by.

Myra checked her watch again. "Reckon we oughta wait until sunset, now that we've missed noon?"

LaWanda shook her head. "We're burnin' daylight. Try now, and if it don't fly, try again later."

For her part, Aife looked pensive, almost morose. Aikin wondered if it was some carryover from riding in a steel vehicle, though that shouldn't have been a problem, given that she'd succumbed to good sense before their departure and put on the substance of the Mortal World. She thought no one had noticed the actual transition, and indeed the change had been subtle: just a sort of head-to-toe shimmer-twitch, as though every atom in her body simply rotated ninety degrees, emitting a flash of light as it did. Which could well be the case for all he knew. In any event, Aikin *had* noticed, and was damned proud of himself for having done so.

"Okay, let's do it," Alec said with atypical decisiveness,

as the last backpack was retrieved and Myra secured the vehicle with the remote lock. Aikin followed the rest, moving instinctively to the open space beneath the gate. "Boy-girl-boy-girl, I think," Myra mused, shouldering an impressive-looking knapsack and reaching out to catch Alec's hand with her right and Aikin's with the other.

"Sounds reasonable," Aife affirmed as she claimed Alec's other hand. LaWanda promptly snared Aikin's left and extended the remaining one to Piper, before realizing that he needed both of his free to accomplish what he must. She settled for clamping one strong black hand down on his right shoulder, motioning Aife to follow suit.

As for Piper, he looked soulful and distressed, a condition not alleviated by his black jeans, boots, and trademark linen shirt (*handmade* by LaWanda, as she'd noted more than once), the latter also black in lieu of the traditional white, and capped by a black leather jacket with silver-studded pockets.

Nevertheless, his expression softened to mere resigned dismay as he checked the bellows under his right arm, massaged its twin beneath his left, and commenced playing—a soft, slow air to begin with. "To soothe you guys," he explained with a wry smile.

And then that other. Low notes at first, eerie yet almost bouncy, to establish an otherworldly ambiance, followed by a jauntier tune, possibly a reel, if Aikin knew his Irish music right. And then the whole played faster. Aikin had recognized the piece from the first bars, of course: the frantic fiddle tune called "The King of the Fairies."

"Close your eyes," Myra hissed. "Picture a tall, Celt-style tower, only with crenelations around the crown and the whole thing stuck in a plain of glittery gray sand. Might not hurt to add the Silver Tracks either: just bands a couple of yards wide radiating from the base of the tower."

Aikin did as instructed, and found it surprisingly easy to conjure the requisite image, possibly because Myra had once painted the same vista, then sold it to a Virginia art collector. And with his eyes closed, it really was easier to focus on the way the music kind of drew you out of yourself. As a final adjunct, Myra began to read from the mysterious manuscript she'd retrieved from her apartment, the dog-eared paper vying for contact with Alec in her right hand. *"I am called Satan, I'm Lord of this World . . . !"*

Which were the first lines of that long-lost mystery play in which Colin had hidden the formula that awakened his country.

For a moment, nothing happened save loud music and Myra's firm, if slightly flat, recitation. But then Aikin noted that he was growing warmer and that the breeze had shifted and was stirring his pant-legs quite forcefully, as though he stood in the midst of a tiny whirlwind. And when the chorus came around again and Piper began to pickup the tempo, the tempo of the whirling increased as well.

Aikin was mightily tempted to open his eyes, but dared not. And then it didn't matter, because, with a wrench and a jolt of not-unexpected pain, he lost command of his senses entirely for about ten seconds, and when he recovered them, it was to find soft moss beneath one boot and silver sand beneath the other, and to see, at maybe half a mile's remove, the fractured but still-imposing shaft of what could only be Colin's tower.

"We're ba-ack," LaWanda giggled, though she'd already shifted her machete to her hand.

"So it appears," Myra acknowledged. "Frankly, I'm surprised to find it so intact. I mean, when we were here last, the whole place was either falling into ruin or dissolving away as the Tracks passed by."

"Appears you were wrong, then," LaWanda retorted, looking at Myra appraisingly, then at Aife. "So which of you ladies wants to take the lead?"

She did not, Aikin noted, even consider Alec, himself, or Piper, though hopefully that was a function of age. Myra and LaWanda ranked him and Alec by easily eight years, and Aife ranked everyone by . . . centuries. Too, while Alec was smart aplenty, he didn't think well on his feet; and LaWanda didn't know his own sly self well enough to trust him. Piper had let himself out. He was at least as old as Myra, but, to quote the musician's own words, "I do not lead—*ever*. I do not take charge—*ever*. I pipe—*when*ever I can."

"Flip you for it," Myra chuckled, eyeing Aife speculatively.

Aife shook her head. "I was once a warrior. Best it is that I take charge."

Aikin simply stepped up beside her in the ranks they were forming, with Alec claiming her other side.

Poor Alec! To have loved someone in vain for so long, then have that person live with him for a couple of years, but only as a cat—except when she was an enfield, which was another of those heraldic beasts Brock was always talking about, this one essentially a fox with an eagle's talons in lieu of forepaws.

Like the gryphons hereabouts, he supposed, except that they were supposed to have a lion's body and an eagle's wings and head. And except that instead of wings, the males sported thin, flexible plates like softened rhino hide, from between the joints of which shafts of light shone when they moved.

Poor Alec, hell! he reminded himself an instant later. *Poor them!*

For it was *hot* in this fucking place: hot as a desert. Hot as the Iron Dungeon, and there'd been a *reason* for all that heat. Here nothing at all hung in a sky that though deep purple seemed at the same time as well lit as the clearest summer day.

Alec cleared his throat. "Uh, just to be on the safe side, folks; I was in a deserty place like this before, and there were some little folks that came up out of the sand and attacked me. Don't know about here, but we might oughta be real careful."

"Already am," LaWanda replied flatly. "All day, every day."

"God," Alec muttered back. "What've *you* got to be afraid of?"

LaWanda's snort could've been heard for miles. "You can tell you ain't never been black, white boy!"

"Sorry!"

And with that, Aife stepped from moss to sand.

Dust rose up immediately, and Aikin found himself coughing at once, not surprising, given his allergies. There was something odd about that dust, too: a certain sharpness, as though the particles retained the razor-sharp edges they'd possessed when they were sheets of glass. Idly, he scooped up a handful, and flinched at the wash of pain across his knuckles.

"So much for that!" he grumbled, and returned to the matters at hand: keeping a close eye on the tower lest it somehow slip away, and a closer eye on their environs.

And on they trekked: alert, wary, ever on guard for the appearance of foes.

They saw none. Nothing at all, save the undulating ripples and flourishes of the sand, some of which looked disconcertingly like Celtic knotwork.

"Perhaps it is," Aife replied when Myra commented on that fact. "We know that the Power of the Silver Tracks passed over this place, for otherwise the maze would not have been blasted so, though I believe Alberon had a hand in that as well. And I know that these shapes, when properly constructed, hoard and amplify Power, yet at the same time are shaped by it, where there is dust or sand."

"Well, *that's* interesting," Myra murmured, and fell silent.

It wasn't a bad trek, actually, though Aikin would've been happier if they'd left footprints, since the dust filled in their tracks as quickly as they formed. *Oh, well,* he reminded himself philosophically, he was pretty damned good at dead reckoning.

Somehow, too, they reached the tower before anyone truly expected it, and stepped into the welcomed coolness of a shadow that shouldn't exist in a place that had no obvious sun. In any event, the relative freedom from the pervasive heat was a welcomed respite, as was the ragged sward of moss that ringed the rough-stone shaft. "Drink!" Aife ordered, "those of you who will. And then we go inside."

Aikin needed no second prompting and chugged at least a third of the canteen of mountain spring water he'd brought down from Devlin's. That accomplished, he helped himself to the rest of his burger, then joined Alec before the tower's only obvious entrance: a thick, if rather squatty, oak door set deep into the nearby wall; the whole held together by the most intricate wrought-metal strapwork Aikin had ever seen. Alec had just reached out to touch the grinning imp's face that comprised the latch when Aife stepped in front of him, knocking his hand away. "You may be my lover," she snapped. "But that does not excuse you from being a reckless fool!"

Alec started to bite back; that much was clear to Aikin, standing right beside him, and in fact he caught the sharp, inhaled hiss, followed by grinding teeth, as a very wired Alec McLean fought to hold his peace.

"If everyone is ready," Aife continued coolly, in a voice that brooked no dissent, "we will go in."

"Hmmm," Myra mused, as she joined the Faery woman before the massive door. "Somehow I figured there'd be a guard."

Aife's reply was to close her eyes (*casing the place with Power*, Aikin assumed), then scowl uneasily, flip the latch, and slowly push the panel inward. It moved smartly for a short distance, then fetched up short against some obstruction: not unreasonable, given that the place had been on the verge of collapse when Myra's previous invasion force had fled. Or so LaWanda had described in graphic detail on the journey down.

Aikin had his shotgun loaded and ready when he followed Aife inside. Not surprisingly, it was fairly dark in there, with no windows at all on the level they'd entered, and only a few impressive-looking cracks in the high stone walls to remind him there'd ever been light. What illumination did find its way in seemed focused on the single enormous tapestry that still hung upright beneath an upward-curving stair, which hanging featured an even mix of preposterous animals (mostly gryphons) and gaudily garbed bards.

"Where's the library?" Alec asked edgily, crowding between Aikin and Aife, who in turn moved forward to admit the rest of their crew.

"Upon the second level," someone replied. It took Aikin half a dozen heartbeats to realize that the voice belonged to no one in their party. And that many more to determine that it echoed from all around them.

"Who speaks?" Aife demanded, in the sharpest tones

Aikin had ever heard from her. For an instant, he fancied that she glowed.

"You are the stranger here," that voice growled back in what certainly wasn't English, in spite of the fact that the words made perfect sense. "It is for you to say first."

"Names have Power," Alec called abruptly. "If you need something to call me, you could call me . . . Mach One."

"Hush!" Aife hissed.

"Mahkwuhn," the other replied bemusedly. "This means nothing to me."

"Nor do Faery names—to me!" Alec countered.

"We are not in Faerie!"

"Then where are we?" Aife challenged.

"You are in Colin's Land," that other supplied. "Or you might style it as it is styled by Alberon of Alban: Tir-Gat, the Stolen Country."

"Who are you?" Aife repeated. "I come in the name of Lugh Samildinach, High King of the Daoine Sidhe in Tir-Nan-Og."

"Who is not *my* lord!"

"Enough of this!" Aife spat. "Show yourself."

Silence.

"Show yourself!"

More silence.

"By your Name, I call you forth," Aife shouted. "By my Name, I swear that if you do not reply in ten breaths' time, I will tear down this tower stone by stone to find you!"

"Which is not why you are here," came that other.

"Perhaps not, but—"

Before she could finish, one of the dusty, fantastically dressed huntsmen in the tapestry suddenly shook himself and stepped lightly to the ground: grim-faced, blunter of feature, more muscular, and with far redder hair than any Faery male Aikin had ever seen.

Somewhere, too, in the transition between fabric and floor, the man managed to unsheathe an eerily thin sword. It glittered balefully as he ran a finger along one gleaming edge. "Very well," he purred with ritual formality. "Since you call me out, *Aife* of Tir-Arvann, I will give you my name as well. It is Yd."

"Yd?" Alec blurted.

"Yd," the warrior (for so he appeared, now he'd swept away the bright dagged cloak that gave him the air of a minstrel) affirmed. "I am Alberon's guardian here," he added. "That should be sufficient."

"And we thank you for it," Aife acknowledged with strained civility.

"Alas," Yd replied sadly, "it is too late for fair words now. For if I am not mistaken, I believe I just heard a challenge."

Silence, for ten heartbeats, and Aikin could count each one. Then, distinct in the mirror-dusted air of that shattered tower, the voice of LaWanda Gilmore, from the swamps of Savannah, Georgia, uttering a very audible and precisely pronounced *"Damn!"*

Interlude II:
Catching Up

(near Clayton, Georgia—
Sunday, June 29—just past noon)

"Anytime . . ." John Devlin grumbled into the telephone. He shifted it to his other ear and regarded his yard, which two days ago had been *only* his yard but now resembled a collision between a used car lot and a war zone. Lord knew he could recognize that last, too: war had taken his hand and left him a prosthesis. It had stolen one career and provided another. It had edited a couple of years from his life he could neither account for nor wanted to. And now he was on its border again, and the trouble was, it was friends—or friends of friends—who were in it, and John Devlin was nothing if not honorable. And since it involved the Worlds, there was no way to abdicate involvement. So far no one had asked more than advice, a little finessing of Powers, and a bolt-hole. But he doubted that would last past nightfall, when the Sons of Ailill might once again come calling.

At least whatever shit hit the fan would start flying somewhere else, probably Sullivan Cove, if the current power structure in Tir-Nan-Og lived up to their threat and tried to flood the place, and every other where this World underlay the Faery one. In that case—well, this really would become his battle, because this place as well as Sullivan Cove touched Faerie.

Now, if Scott Gresham would just answer his blessed phone!

One more ring and he'd chuck it, and check on Dave Sullivan's dad up in Clayton. He wondered if he was doomed to be party to the deaths of all that clan.

" 'Lo," a voice grunted abruptly.

"Scott Gresham?"

"Yep."

"You don't know me, but my name's John Devlin, and I'm a . . . friend of David Sullivan. He wanted me to brief you on some stuff, and find out what I could about how things stand over there."

"How do I know you're for real?"

"You don't. But I know what your lady was wearing when she left here a couple of hours ago."

Scott hesitated before replying. Not that Devlin blamed him; caution was good, even wise—when you weren't on the receiving end. "Okay," Scott said finally. "Shoot."

"How 'bout you catch me up first."

"Fuck," Scott grunted. Then: "Okay, okay. I guess the main thing you want is what's up with Mystic Mountain, right?"

"If that's their name."

Scott cleared his throat. "Well, they're antsy as hell 'cause of the rain. They're antsy *and* angry 'cause of a couple of recent cases of industrial espionage."

"Paint in the computers, huh? I heard about that."

"Didn't hear about sugar in a couple of gas tanks, though, did you? Caddy Seville and brand-new Dodge Ram."

"Ah!"

"And a fuel leak in a certain generator that accidentally caught a spark and fired itself *and* the tool shed sittin' right beside it?"

"Can't say I have."

"What about a bit of selective tree spiking?"

"Nope."

"Well, let's just say me and a certain Dale Sullivan have been right busy."

"So the bottom line is . . . ?"

"That they're behind. That they're tryin' to interest the local law, but the local law doesn't want to be interested, on account of they're afraid of the Sullivans. That lots of money's being thrown around to *make* people interested.

That the lake's still dangerously high but startin' to go down. That they *say* they'll have a new generator in later today and start diggin' holes on the shoreline then. And yeah, I *know* it's Sunday.''

"Thought a certain person sabotaged the blueprints.''

"Just the mountain lodge, apparently. The marina was an older design, and they'd already backed it up.''

"I see.''

"So . . . any other suggestions?''

"Keep your nose clean and lay low. I think things are comin' to a head.''

"Oh yeah?''

Devlin took a deep breath and told him.

"What about Sullivan's dad? Heard he wasn't doin' too well.''

"Depends on how you take a stake in the back. It's a routine fix, just hurts like hell and takes a long time to heal, assuming—Never mind.''

"What?''

"Let's just say I wouldn't be surprised if there wasn't something extra involved. Poison—magic—whatever.''

"What makes you say that?''

Devlin shifted the phone again and watched Nuada stride by on his latest patrol of his perimeter. And almost laughed at the notion of a fidgety Faery Lord. "Because,'' he replied, "Dave's mom called here just now to tell him she was worried about his dad, 'cause he didn't seem to be recovering as quick as he should. Apparently his blood's not clotting.''

"I see.''

"Wish I did,'' Devlin snorted. "Anyway, gotta go. I'm not much on small talk with strangers. Plus frankly, I don't trust this line, or yours.''

"Uh, well, keep me posted.''

"You got it.''

And with that, John Devlin hung up the phone. Just as well. It was time to check the wards.

Chapter XI:
Something Fishy

(Galunlati—high summer)

"Has he . . . ?" Liz cried desperately, edging as far forward as she dared, to peer down the the rocky escarpment over which Lugh had just flung himself. The vapor made it hard to see—Calvin could make out little, and he was standing right beside her. But at least the pain-crazed Faery had angled left before he'd leapt into the river and thence over the waterfall. Still, it was an awful end (and gut-wrenchingly *abrupt* on top of it) to one of the quests that had brought them here. And without Lugh, was there really any way to stop the rebels who'd unseated him from setting up their own king? Lugh had to die to fully ratify his successor, right? But wasn't Lugh lost—or dead—in Galunlati just as useful for that end?

"He shifted," Fionchadd announced before Calvin's despair had truly had a chance to sink in. "I glimpsed him through the vapor and felt the surge of Power."

Calvin stared at him. "But how—? Why—?"

A shrug. "I do not know. But I *think* he became a fish. A salmon, likely."

"A . . . salmon?" Calvin began. Then froze.

Where the notion originated, he had no idea, save that one moment he was standing on the cliff gazing down, the next he was poised on the riverbank, right hand closing around the uktena scale he wore on a thong around his neck, his strangely calm mind focused on one thing alone. *Scales! Slick . . . sleek . . . no legs . . . tail at the base of his spine . . . fins . . . wide, staring eyes . . . gills . . .*

And then pain and odd restrictions and a final frantic plea to whoever stood nearest that began with, "Get outta . . ." but didn't quite finish ". . . clothes."

Fortunately, Kirkwood grasped his intent, so that by the time the transformation was complete, Calvin was having trouble breathing, and strange, panicked instincts were assaulting his higher mind. Somehow, he was on the ground, half wriggling, half leaping down the bank and impacting water, abruptly all poetry and grace.

—Until the current snared him, and he was grateful indeed that he was a fish as he began that long, slow fall.

Longer and longer he fell. Perhaps he'd died in truth and would *never* reach the continuation of the river at the base of the cataract. Or maybe he'd *already* hit, but the pool below was bottomless and he'd be swimming down and down forever. And then he *did* hit the foaming water.

Disorientation ensued, during which he determined that yeah, color sense *was* supposed to work like that, and that you breathed through gills *that* way (and it wasn't as though he'd never been a fish before, and not that long ago, either), and then he was swimming.

—And looking for Lugh, and trying to keep firmly in mind that this was *not* his natural state, though his physical brain was closer to its primal prototype than any he'd dared essay before, so that it was harder than it had ever been to recall that he was human.

What kind of fish was he, anyway?—as he made his effortless way to the clearer waters downstream. *Trout, maybe? Since he'd both eaten and "hunted" them.* Not that it mattered. What *mattered* was locating Lugh and getting him back to someone—most likely Fionchadd—who could return the Faery King to man-shape once again.

Why had Lugh done it, though? What would revive a Faery Lord so suddenly, then prompt such precipitous action? And where *was* he? How did fish locate other fish? By smell? By sight? By this screwy sensation filtering in from along both sides that involved what were called lateral lines?

Or simply this *feeling* in his brain that *might* be Power in use nearby—or Faery thought in progress, or something else entirely—that drew him steadily onward and to the left, and which told him, to his great relief, that the one he sought was not as far ahead as he'd feared, and seemed not to be fleeing at all but slowly circling, as though he'd been a fish all his life and was merely taking his morning constitutional.

Closer, and Lugh was no more than five times his own length ahead, there where the water was clearest, where the sun beat down most steadily, where another of those obscure senses spoke of delicious cold depths where the riverbed spiraled down to darkness indeed. *Lugh?* he tried to think. *Your Majesty? Lugh Samildinach? Lugh the Many-skilled?*

Silence, at first; in the water and his mind alike.

And then confusion, anger, fear, and something that felt like relief, and then anger again—and challenge. *Who profanes my presence? Who questions my will? Who dares approach in my time of pain?*

Calvin didn't bother to respond, occupied as he was with trying to recall how to do something he'd only managed a few times before, which was to change back to his own form *without* feeding blood and pain to the scale. For he'd just that moment realized that now he'd found Lugh, he had no way to retrieve him.

In the absence of other options, he swam forward and down, trying to think *Comfort . . . calm . . . apology . . . freedom from pain.* Whether he succeeded, he had no idea, but the force of those other thoughts abated, and he finally got close enough to determine that that fine big salmon there was turned to face upstream, mouth agape, gills flapping like silver fans.

Yet Calvin continued on: down, then up again, so that he nudged the salmon's belly. It resisted, turned to snap at him, then relented and let itself be eased higher, though it didn't change its orientation.

Closer to the surface (*What then?*), and closer yet, and the water around them was clear as glass, and he felt the sunlight hot on his back as his dorsal fin broke through. Lugh was beside him, neither aiding his efforts nor complicating them, simply letting himself be nudged shoreward, where Calvin might find something sharp enough to summon sufficient pain to regain his own form without the scale.

But while his gaze sought anxiously for some stick or

stone, pain found him from another source entirely.

One moment he was floating lazily, half drifting, half paddling, with Lugh between him and the shore so as to minimize his chance of escape; the next, pain had stabbed into both sides (in five places, so those sensitive lateral lines supplied)—and he was yanked aloft.

His first impression, stupidly enough, was how there ought to be noise and wasn't. His next was that he'd lost Lugh again. But then he caught a burst of panic from that other mind that some sense informed him was close by, and then the fish took over with floppings and thrashings, forcing Calvin's *self* deep into the darkness that surrounded that ascendant primal brain. *Fight/flight.* It shrieked. *Caught. Fly-thing. Claws. Beat. Eat. No-spawn. High. Fall. Pain. Claws. Bird. Beak. Claws. Bird . . .* Bird—*Bird. No, some* kind *of bird. Peregrine? Hawk? Eagle? No,* osprey. *No,* erne: *sea-eagle!*

Sea eagle! Came another thought, neither his nor Lugh's, but soothing, comforting, as he'd sought to comfort Lugh.

Suddenly he was mostly Calvin again, and aware that he'd been snatched from the water by some kind of raptor, and that Lugh was with him, and that the bird *might* be more than a bird, but that wasn't to be expected (so said the fish), and maybe he ought to try to escape again anyway, just in case.

In any event, the decision might soon be taken from him, for the erne was clearly not equipped to lug two substantial fish and fly at the same time, and seemed to be having trouble gaining much altitude at all. The only comfort was that they were heading back toward the cliff and the waterfall, which was also toward his friends.

Calvin's heart skipped a beat. This was no safe situation, and Lugh likewise seemed to divine the same as the erne winged closer to a narrow ledge set back from the sheerer slope at the top, most likely to deposit them, then shift back to some more useful form, or perhaps even change them back.

But no; it was simply flying onward, wingbeats faltering more with every flap.

Lower, and it might not make the ledge at all, or might

drop them (and hadn't he just felt one of those claws slip, where they jabbed into his side?).

Lower again, but closer to the ledge. And then another shape was arrowing out of the nearby shadows, faster than anything animate had right to be: dashing, leaping, pouncing—slamming the erne from the air. Claws raked his sides, and he was flung free.

Panic found him; the fish reasserted; and when he was himself once more, he'd thumped down on hard rocks, with something much larger and darker than the eagle looming over him. Something with green eyes and a mouth full of sharp teeth at the end of a snarling feline muzzle.

Cougar, something supplied. And the fish came back.

He might just let it drive for a while. After all, if he was going to be eaten alive, it would be better experienced at maximum mental remove.

Yet the jaws that gripped him were lifting, not chowing down, and all at once he was being carried in long, fluid lopes up the near-vertical face of the cliff. It jolted, but not as much as he would've expected, though it was still damned disconcerting. And maybe there was enough pain now, if he concentrated.

Forgetting everything else, he reached within, to that place where he remembered Calvin. Remembered having arms and legs, fingers and toes, all of which were deft and strong and nimble; remembered having smooth bronze skin, thick black hair, and clear-cut brows; strong cheekbones and jaw, and a nose too short for any proper Indian, with a tattoo on his right buttock that had all but faded away from so many prior shiftings, and with nothing anywhere else that wasn't Calvin-as-designed.

Heat washed him and awakened hope, but then he heard—in his mind alone but heard nevertheless—his companion in adversity start to panic. And as that panic struck him, his own awakened, and for a long dark moment, fear consumed him.

Fear! Fear! Fear! Fear! Fear!

He was aware of being carried, of raw rocks close beneath him, of his tail slapping them painfully, and of increasing darkness in his mind as his gills dried, making it harder and harder to breathe.

He had just steeled himself for one final go at regaining his own shape when that wild upward surge gave way to a loping dash along smooth, dark, *damp* stone, with water splattering in from one side. And then a closer, more comforting darkness enclosed him entirely: stone passages and an all-encompassing unheard roar that he connected with the waterfall and another, more intense memory from back when he'd been Calvin. And then the jaws released him and he fell *splash* into a shallow, star-shaped pool. For a moment he gave the fish rein again and gloried in being wet all over and able to breathe.

A splash beside him was Lugh. A flood of relief like unto his own surged out to brush his mind, which helped keep his human aspect awake. And now he worked at it, he saw that they were enclosed by a vast rocky chamber that was almost certainly inside the cliffs behind the waterfall, that a matched set of sleek black cougars sat primly on the sandy shore just out of reach, and that a taller shape he recognized as truly human was striding up between the cats and reaching down to swish something leafy through the water while murmuring words he had no way of hearing.

Yet he *did* hear, sort of, and realized at the same time that he was stretching upward, out of the water, returning to his own shape with startling rapidity, without the rush of pain that usually accompanied it.

Too fast, though, so that by the time he had feet under him, he was balanced wrong to stand upright, and so made his reentrance into his own right form sprawling forward on hands and knees in the sand.

Laughter tickled his ears: female first, then . . . feline. Calvin blinked, coughed, sluiced hair from his face and water from his eyes, and finally managed to scramble to his feet and take stock of his surroundings.

He was in a cave all right, pale limestone of irregular height, the walls and crevices of which writhed with coiling, sliding life: snakes of every species, including some foreign to Georgia. Yet he noted that peripherally, for his attention was focused on the woman who sat before him clad in a buckskin skirt that left her bare above the waist, exposing fine round breasts, their upper curves brushed by waves of thick hair, black as his own. And the eyes: green and wicked-looking, almost cat eyes—he couldn't tear his gaze from them. The woman smiled. Calvin blinked once more, having finally sorted his memories enough to recognize her. *"Oka-cha!"* he blurted through a grin, rushing forward, then checking himself at the last moment, having realized first that he was wet, second that he was naked, and finally, that this woman, whom he'd helped send here in the first place, commanded a fair bit of authority hereabouts.

"Edahi!" she laughed, giving him his birthname in Cherokee. *"Siyu!* Welcome to Galunlati!"

"Uh, yeah," Calvin choked, recalling a jumble of things at once, one of which was the mission that had brought him here; another, that he had friends somewhere about; and finally, that no less a personage than the King of the Faeries had been his companion of late. He twisted around abruptly, gazing at the pool, and saw only a large salmon swimming angrily in tight, jerky circles while a pair of handsome young cougars looked on with languid interest.

"It's not for me to free him," Okacha chuckled. "And I'll probably hear words I won't like for having freed you, but you did me a favor once and I've never been one to claim the easy road."

Calvin nodded, looked around for something to wear, then shrugged and sat on the rock nearest the woman, taking care to confirm that it *was* a rock and not a turtle, which such seats had been known to be.

"Your friends will be here shortly," Okacha continued. "My husband's gone to fetch them."

Calvin eyed the pair of gleaming felines. "And the . . . boys?"

She lifted a brow at the cats. "They've grown, haven't they? I'm not surprised you didn't recognize them, though perhaps your brain was feeling . . . crowded at the time." She clapped her hands. "Lads . . . ?"

One cougar yawned and stretched, then kept on stretching in odd places, shedding hair as it did, so that a moment later a boy sat there: early teens, naked, more pretty than handsome, and feral-looking in a feline way.

Which was to be expected when his father was a demigod connected with thunder, and his mother the last survivor of a long-ago mating between a proto-Cherokee woman and a race of werecougars who lived, by choice, underwater. And which were also gifted magicians, Calvin recalled, especially when it came to weather-type things and shapeshifting.

Okacha sighed dramatically and shook her head as the boy acknowledged Calvin with a silent, wary bow. "His brother, I fear, is not so obedient and prefers four legs to two. I wonder what a psychologist would make of that."

Calvin laughed amiably, amazed at how relaxed he was now that *some* order had been restored to his life. "This is a very strange conversation."

"And a very strange visit."

"And strange hospitality," a third voice echoed from the rough arch of the entrance. Calvin looked around to see Fionchadd standing there, bare as himself and the cougar-boy, and no more concerned about it than the other. The Faery looked angry, though; as angry as Calvin had ever seen him. *"You!"* he demanded, leveling a finger at Okacha. "What was that you did? You and your pets! You could have injured me! You could have killed one who is your better. You could—"

"Show more courtesy to my wife, Dagantu!" yet another voice thundered, almost literally. To Calvin's vast surprise and amusement, Fionchadd jumped straight up, nearly braining himself on the low roof there.

Which brought more laughter from the passage behind him, some of it human and recognizable.

Fionchadd recovered quickly, and ever the courtier (even stark naked) managed to execute a formal and very contrite bow as he stepped aside to admit the true master of the cavern and the land around it.

Hyuntikwala Usunhi. Uki, for short. The man—demigod, or whatever—was well past six feet tall and sported black braids to his knees, but though his face clearly displayed Native American features, his skin, of which a great deal was visible (for he wore only a sketchy loincloth), was so white it almost glowed. Calvin had first met him years ago, when he, David, Alec, and Fionchadd had entered his realm in search of a back route to the Land of the Powersmiths. One had been found, and Fionchadd had left them there. But the highlight of that adventure had been the uktena hunt they'd undertaken, which had earned them all Uki's great respect, and himself a mentor.

"*Siyu, adewehiyu,*" Calvin murmured in ritual greeting. *Greetings, very great magician.*

"*Siyu,* Edahi," Uki acknowledged, his face sterner than Calvin would've liked, nor did he miss the omission of his war name. Without further comment, Uki strode forward. Snakes slithered from his path as he approached. Okacha rose, as did her human son. The other cougar likewise found its feet, but made no other obeisance. Calvin felt a pang of apprehension, which was only slightly relieved when the rest of their band filed in; Liz first, then David, followed by Sandy (carrying Calvin's discarded clothes) with cousin Kirkwood bringing up the rear, sharp eyes darting everywhere. He could practically hear Churchy scribbling mental notes as he found himself entering what was, to him, a childhood myth. For their part, Sandy and Liz looked remarkably smug, though perhaps that was because half the men in the room were handsome, well-built, and nude, while another wasn't all that modestly draped either.

"Okacha," Uki snapped. "Bring food. Bring clothes. Then we will talk."

Calvin scowled at that, wondering how such orders would fly with someone as independent as the cougar-woman, never mind the cultural norm. Yet she heeded those commands. He watched her go; it was impossible not to, the way she moved—and jumped half out of his skin when soft fur brushed his legs to either side: the cougars, both on four feet again.

Uki had paused a short way off and was studying him curiously, then frowned and continued his approach. "Gather 'round the pool," he told his guests, motioning them forward. "You, Edahi," he continued, "what am I to do with you? I knew of your coming. And truly I am glad to see you. But to arrive so, and then act so irresponsibly."

Calvin bit his tongue as anger surged within him. "How so?"

Uki's eyes flashed fire. "Have I not warned you about shifting shape without good reason? And did you not just do that very thing?"

"I had reason!"

"Did you think I would allow an envoy such as yours to enter unescorted?" Uki retorted. "Or permit an ailing visitor to escape without effort made to recover him? Do you forget that I also am a shape-shifter, that my wife is, and that her sons likewise can choose some forms at will? And," he added, eyeing Fionchadd speculatively, "that Dagantu here could also have effected that pursuit without the risk you take every time you change, about which I have warned you more than once."

"I've found a way to keep track of changes," Calvin challenged.

"Have you?" Uki snapped back. "But are you certain it is reliable here, or in other Worlds, with so much else awry? Power flows strangely these days, both within Worlds and between them."

Calvin gazed at him steadily, neither admitting guilt nor denying it.

Uki's brow furrowed. "Still, your rashness was well intended," he sighed, "and perhaps you did act in ignorance. I suppose, too, that I punished you enough, for it was I who denied you your own shape when you would have resumed it earlier. Here!" He reached to a pouch at his waist to retrieve the uktena scale necklace Calvin had abandoned with his clothes. Calvin caught it on the fly. "Now you are better dressed."

"I like him that way," Okacha purred, rejoining them with a pile of leather clothing, the top item of which she presented to Calvin. It proved to be a deerskin breechclout. Calvin hesitated as he shook it out. "I've got my own clothes," he dared.

"You do," Uki acknowledged. "But they are better suited to your Land than this, and to action, not reflection."

Calvin shrugged and donned the garment. He was just doing up the ties and wondering whether Uki had his companions so cowed they were afraid to speak (unlikely, since only Kirkwood had never met him), or if they were acting under orders, or were simply deferring to him as de facto leader, when a sharp splash from the pool reminded him that one matter remained unresolved, though if what Uki had just said was true, that *he* regulated shapeshifting in his realm, he had an idea why.

"Adewehi," he began again. "If I may be so bold—"

"You have been bold enough for one day," Uki rumbled, gazing curiously down at the pool, where an irate salmon swam in ever more agitated circles.

Uki grimaced dramatically and squatted by the edge of the pool, extending one hand toward it. Calvin wondered if he intended to tickle the King of the Faeries into his grasp. He also wondered whether, given the volatile politics bouncing about just now, that might not also be construed as an insult, thereby precipitating another war, with the Lands of Men caught not so innocently between.

Instead, Uki merely clapped his hands. A tiny bolt of lightning exploded from that juncture, flashing down to strike the water before continuing on to smite the salmon. Steam hissed into the cool, clammy air. The air stank of ozone and, ever so slightly, of cooking fish.

Nor did the steam show any sign of abating. Instead, it swirled higher, grew thicker, acquired a man-sized darkness in its heart; which clarified a moment later, when Lugh Samildinach, magnificently and unconcernedly naked, and with anger in his eyes like black ice, rose from the pool. Calvin scanned that smooth, firm flesh in search of the angry weals that had marred it. And found none.

"Nor will you, Red Man," Lugh spat gracelessly. "Why thought you I changed my shape? Here, in this Land, I could draw on Power as I could not in your rude World. I used what I could to adopt a form that had no hair, thereby disposing of the last of the iron caught within it; a form that likewise had gills, so that the iron I had inhaled could be washed from my lungs. I am free of pain, now. Free to be myself."

"Free to offer thanks to one who freed you," Uki added dangerously.

Christ, what a screwy situation, Calvin thought. Sun-god and thunder-god, facing off inside a cave behind a waterfall.

David cleared his throat.

Uki's gaze never wavered, nor did Lugh's.

"Thank you," Lugh growled at last, inclining his head minutely. "Never let it be said that courtesy is absent among the many skills I claim."

Uki merely extended a hand to help Lugh onshore. Calvin was struck by how alike they were, not only in having pale skin, dark hair, and sleek but efficient muscles, but also in the way they carried themselves and their eyes flashed and sparked at every thought, word, and idea. "Many-skilled," Uki mused. "In my tongue that would be—"

"Samildinach," Lugh finished. "I would not seek to rename you in my realm, Thunder Lord. Respect me as much in yours."

Uki raised a brow, then motioned Okacha forward with another deerskin loincloth, which Lugh proceeded to don. A fabulous, floor-length cloak of iridescent feathers followed, fit for a king of any World.

Calvin eased aside to watch, exchanging occasional glances with David and Sandy, who seemed as overawed as he. Clearly, Uki and Lugh—and maybe Okacha—were the big guns here. And equally clearly, each had a separate agenda.

"Welcome to Galunlati," Uki said at last. "I have sent for food."

"I would welcome it," Lugh replied with an easy smile, which made them all relax. "First, however, oh Chief of Walhala, I would withdraw for a time to compose myself. My mind has been much confused of late, and my body in constant torment. A moment of silence, of peace, of the coolness that lies without, would render me better company."

Uki smiled tolerantly. "Of course. The opening by which we entered leads outside. I have often found peace there, with the earth to my back and water pouring before me, while the sun beams through to color both water and air."

"Exactly what I sought," Lugh affirmed. "By your leave?"

Uki stepped aside as Lugh made his way among the

stones, shells, and other excrescenses that littered Uki's chamber as artfully as rocks in a Japanese garden. He paused at the cavern's entrance to sketch a bow and murmur, "Thanks to mortal and Faery alike," then disappeared into the moist darkness there.

It was almost an hour later, with the feast Okacha had spread before them growing cold upon the sand, that Liz first raised the notion that perhaps Lugh was not returning.

"No," Fionchadd informed them a moment later, having scoured the land about with his mind. "Nor is he anywhere close at hand."

Chapter XII:
Tossing the Dice

(Tir-Gat—high summer)

"A challenge," Aife mused, rolling the word around her tongue as though it were the most savory of morsels. "I have not been challenged in a very long time indeed."

LaWanda, who'd been observing with keen (if nervous) interest, felt her adrenaline fix kick up another level. Which might be just as well. She'd been walking a ragged edge for a while, poised between the cool common sense she prided herself on and the hard edge of take-charge, you're-gonna-wind-up-fighting-anyway-so-why-not-get-it-over-with force-fulness. The same determination that empowered her music when she really got going. Shoot, she'd already fought one battle in the last two days and had done herself proud in it too. There'd almost been another last night, and her main regret there was that she'd missed it, otherwise she'd have been out there in the yard with David and Aikin, beating Faery butt.

But now another challenge had been called.

Yd shifted his weight, which made his sword gleam wickedly without his flourishing it, which subtlety LaWanda noted even as he inclined his head in acknowledgment and spoke once more. "You have challenged, I have accepted, you have confirmed your intent. But though the rules that bind such things give choice of weapon to the challenged, I defer that choice to you, Lady Aife."

Aife bowed in turn, her face, though beautiful, at the same time hard and grim. LaWanda was vastly proud to have such a woman on her side. Perhaps even as a friend—*if* they survived. Warily, she eyed her comrades. Myra was very still, which could mean anything, though her artist aspect was certainly filing away images for future reference. Alec was tense as a bowstring, sweating and swallowing hard, and Aikin beside him wasn't much better, though he disguised it. And Piper—Aife wasn't the only one with a strange, sweet, non-assertive lover.

Aife cleared her throat. "Very well, Lord Yd, I accept the challenge. I also accept the choice you have set me. But tell me: is that not the lilt of Annwyn in your voice?"

Yd's eyes twinkled. "Aye, Lady. I was born of that land and fostered at the court of Annwyn's king."

"And is it not true that in Annwyn, as in Cymru, which that land overlaps in the Mortal World, things that come in threes hold significance and Power?"

Yd nodded. "It is. Do not forget that even the Trial of Heroes has as its base three trials: one of knowledge, one of courage, one of strength."

"I have not forgotten," Aife informed him. "What say you then to three challenges in lieu of one, each with a different weapon, wielded"—she paused for effect—"by a different warrior?"

LaWanda's heart skipped a beat. Not at the notion of fighting, but that Aife would so casually commit the rest of them to something they neither desired nor might survive. It was Faery conditioning, she supposed: mortals—any mortals, even de facto friends—were ultimately expendable, like lab animals or pets. Still, it was an intriguing concept. She shifted her weight in turn, letting the uncertain light inside the blasted tower glimmer along her own blade: her trusty heirloom machete. And then she grinned ominously, straight at Yd, fingers moving slyly in a charm of intimidation.

Fortunately, Aife missed her machinations, yet it was clear the woman had been thinking fast and hard, and without caprice at all.

"So be it," Yd murmured with a lifted brow and a quirky smile. "Lady, name your weapons and the warriors who will wield them."

Aife drew herself up very straight, one hand on the hilt of the sword at her waist. "Hear me, Yd of Tir-Gat, and heed my voice. Three challenges you have accepted, and three weapons I have in mind. Yet if you will, Lord, I would name both weapons and warriors one at a time."

"So it will be," Yd acknowledged. "Declare your first."

"Very well," Aife replied with what had to be pride. "I name first of weapons, the blade. I name as wielder . . . LaWanda Gilmore."

It was all LaWanda could do to retain a straight face, though from fear or relief, she had no idea. Part of her was crazy-eager to burn off a week's worth of angst and kick some serious ass. Another part realized that it *was* serious ass, and more than her own fine black skin rode on the outcome. Like her friends' lives. Like the fate of Sullivan Cove. Like the fate of the whole Mortal World, if worse came to worst. Still, it wasn't like folks hadn't confronted similar pressure before. Besides, Aife had turned toward her, and no way she could be less than all she was before a woman like that. She pointedly avoided catching Piper's eyes, however; though she could hear him softly reciting, "No, no, no, no . . ."

"Yes!" she answered, as much to Piper as to Aife or Yd. Then: "I accept. But I don't have a sword."

"I said *blade*, not *sword*—and you have a . . . machete, is it?" Aife retorted. "It rides in your hand as easily as a Damascus blade, is longer than some, and made of steel. Yd, I am certain, would prefer both a fair fight and a well-matched one. He has experience and skill. You have a weapon he does not know, and steel."

"Fine," LaWanda snapped. "Let's do it!"

It was Yd's turn to clear his throat. "There is still one inequality here," he observed. "You have matched our weapons somewhat, but what of armor? The lady has none; I have enough to challenge Lugh himself on the tourney field." He turned to face LaWanda. "Would you have armor, Lady; or would you have me fight with none?"

Well, that's easy enough! LaWanda thought. "I'm not used to armor," she replied civilly, "and if you've practiced as much as I suspect you have to have got where you are, I imagine you're used to doin' without. So no armor."

"So be it, then," Yd agreed, already reaching for the complex penannular brooch that confined his cloak, just to the right of his chin.

"Well," Aikin muttered to LaWanda, "I guess we're in it now. So thank you, good luck, and whatever you do, *don't break a leg.*"

"Hadn't planned to."

"I'm counting on you, Juju Woman," Alec added.

LaWanda glared at him. "That stuff won't help here. Takes time to set up, then works slow and subtle. Don't help in a fight when you've gotta work fast, 'less you've done stuff by yourself beforehand. Whatever happens here's just gonna be me." And with that, she sat down on a chunk of fallen column and calmly removed her boots.

However long it took to ready themselves for combat, it was way too long for LaWanda, with far too much discussion of picky things which nevertheless had boiled down to two: locale and rules.

Locale was simple: the more brightly lit side of the mossy greensward outside, which was maybe fifty feet across at the widest. Rules were more complex, but amounted to determining fair target zones and what would constitute victory. Yd, reasonably enough for a Faery, wanted to fight to the death, until Aife pointed out that death was one thing for him, another for LaWanda, but if it *was* death he was talking about, it was the Death of Iron for him, because that was what LaWanda wielded. He'd blanched at that and settled on third blooding. Which suited LaWanda fine. She'd done a bit of fencing and fooled around with the Society for Creative Anachronism, and while a machete was neither an epee nor a rattan sword, she doubted Yd had had much contact with the nuances of either form, if what Myra had said about Alban and Annwyn being "behind" the Mortal World in time was true.

In any event, she was ready. There was no out-of-bounds save the tower itself and the mirror-sand. To contact one or step into the other meant a restart equidistant between. Per agreement, LaWanda had wasted no time stripping down to her jeans and red tank top. The rest, jewelry and all, was piled neatly on the surviving table inside. The moss felt great against her bare feet: soft and tingly. It released a faint spicy scent when trod upon.

As for Yd, true to LaWanda's admonition, he'd replaced his bronze armor with a pair of what looked like sweat pants made of checked wool, purple and gray. He was barefoot and bare-chested, and had tied his hair back in a tail. And when he'd removed his tunic, his body had proved to be covered with intricate knotwork tattoos rendered in a brown that was scarcely darker than his golden skin. The effect was between vellum and damask, and not at all unattractive. Or maybe that was the body beneath: as fine a piece of manflesh as LaWanda had ever seen. Not that Lugh and Finno were hard to look at bare, nor David, Calvin, or Aikin—or even skinny little Piper. But this guy was more filled out than the best of them yet still as sleek, representing as close to her aesthetic ideal as she'd ever encountered.

An ideal it was her duty to despoil.

"At your pleasure," Yd declared abruptly, gazing at Aife, who would act as marshal. Just as well he'd spoken first, too; LaWanda had feared that to do so herself would betray an apprehension she didn't want revealed.

"Ready!" she called in reply.

Aife motioned them to where a single flat paving stone carved with a rising sun marked what passed in Tir-Gat for east. Which, she recalled from talking to Calvin, was the direction of victory. She wondered if Yd knew that.

Not that it mattered when she was standing a yard away from a far larger, more experienced warrior bent on doing her harm, with only a wooden staff Aife had found inside and proclaimed a marshal's baton thrust between. Yd was a lefty, she noted.

Aife regarded them levelly, her eyes hard as LaWanda's well-used steel. "My lord, my lady; you know the rules. For honor and glory"—and here she stepped back and withdrew the baton abruptly—"lay on!"

LaWanda shifted back instinctively, tried to assume a standard fencing guard, then quickly changed her mind when she saw Yd's more aggressive stance. *What then?* as she tried to recall the blocks and blows Scott had taught her in his days in the SCA. *Perhaps a feint . . . Whang!* As Yd's blade slashed in from her right, and she met it—barely. The blow made her arm vibrate and her hand hurt, never mind her wrist, which she'd had to twist to an unreasonable angle in order to block him. His sword smoked.

Whang! Again. Blind reflex that time. Scent of hot metal.

She danced away, let the recoil carry her blade around and down, aiming at Yd's sword arm. He met it, of course, but the force of her blow bent his blade so far back that one final twist nicked his forearm just below the elbow.

"First blood!" Aife called.

"Well done," Yd conceded.

Alec and Aikin applauded. Piper was nowhere to be seen.

A pause for breath and to reposition themselves above the stone, and Aife withdrew her baton. "Lay on!"

The second round was over almost before it began. Yd feinted left, then up, as though to cleave her head in twain, then low again, on LaWanda's unshielded side. She tried to swerve away, but the blow caught her hip—fortunately, with the flat of the blade. She felt the cut as a clear edge of agony and knew from the warmth trickling down her leg that her opponent had succeeded.

"Blood!" Aife cried again, motioning them back toward the center. Then, once more: "Lay on!"

This round lasted longer. Both parties had hardened to their tasks, and now that blood had been drawn from either side, the reality of the situation had sunk in, resulting in cold, grim determination from both of them not to yield. Or that's how LaWanda felt, what she read in Yd's gold-brown eyes.

Blows flew. Blows were blocked. Blows were evaded. Once Yd jumped straight up above a low one LaWanda was certain would take out his ankles. Once she ducked just in time to avoid one that could've bisected her nose. The follow-up *did* sever a pair of her bead-tipped braids, but she never faltered as they fell to the mossy sward.

Still, they were far more evenly matched than she'd expected, perhaps due to Yd's ingrained aversion to iron. Or would've been, had her injured leg not started to assert itself. Not that she couldn't endure, but it was a distraction nonetheless, and more to the point, enough of a hindrance that she kept favoring it, which did screwy things to her balance and made her play to the right more than she liked. That was Yd's sword side, after all, and he could block most effectively there.

Which, she realized grimly, had been his plan from the start. Especially when blows began to rain fast and thick on her off side, forcing her back, which stressed her injured limb.

And when a particularly vicious blow sent her staggering, it buckled. She fell backward. There being no rules to prevent it, Yd was on her at once. His first blow blooded her other hip at the same time her own caught him in the thigh. His next swept the machete from her hand. The follow-through nicked her throat with exquisite delicacy just above her jugular.

"Hold!" Aife yelled furiously. "Blood, and blood again, and Dana's blood on you, Yd, if you do not hold at once!"

"The time for a hold was after my first blow," Yd replied amiably. "She struck her next out of form and thereby granted me right to the same."

LaWanda could practically see steam seething out of Aife's eyes. "Aye," she spat. "You have the right of it, though I would have expected better of you!"

LaWanda sat up, one hand on her neck, which came away red. Aikin, bless him, returned her weapon. "But—" she began. "We'd only . . . started!"

Aife shook her head. "Rules are rules," she growled. "And the rules of combat are sacred." She eyed Yd angrily. "I had hoped for chivalry. But, as I have heard said more than once of late: there is chivalry and there is war."

"And there's a woman needs tending right now," Myra finished, as she helped LaWanda to her feet, already undoing her jeans, the better to access the wounds. LaWanda let her, stupidly glad to have on clean black panties. Blood gleamed against dark skin, the opened flesh nigh as bright where it showed in inch-long gashes on either thigh, both weeping freely but neither displaying more than superficial damage. "I can heal most of that," Aife offered. "When this is done."

Yd was calmly cleaning his blade. Neither of his wounds had vanished, LaWanda noted with smug satisfaction, and in fact seemed to be growing larger and festering besides. She wondered if that would put paid to the other challenges.

Evidently not, she discovered a short while later, when, thirst freshly slaked with water from an earthenware jug, the Faery warrior strode boldly up to Aife and said, quite calmly, " I believe there was to be a second trial."

Aife glared at him, then set her jaw. "Very well, if haste you desire, haste you shall have. The next challenge will be more subtle."

LaWanda wasn't certain, but it seemed to her that Yd's face darkened at that, as though he were not assured of victory. Yet still his voice was calm when he replied. "Very well, Lady, name your weapon and name your challenger."

"The weapon will be the hand itself," Aife shot back sweetly. "The challenger will be Myra Buchanan."

Myra nearly strangled on the cup of water she'd been drinking when she heard her name pronounced. "I'm no warrior," she choked, then realized what Aife had actually said. "The hand? You mean . . . literally?"

"A contest of art," Aife affirmed, glaring hard at Yd. "You, Annwyn-man, should hold one in as high regard as the other."

"For all we are none of us as skilled as mortal men," Yd added with more than a touch of sarcasm.

"Which seemed not to concern you at all in matters of arms," Aife retorted.

"She had steel."

"You had immortality and experience."

"And this time?"

"She has talent; you have had centuries in which to learn."

"Very well," Yd conceded. "Set the terms."

Aife's brow furrowed, nor did she reply at once. For her part, Myra's head was awhirl as she sought on one hand to tend her injured best friend and on the other to puzzle out what Aife might possibly have in mind. In the meantime, she tried not to think about the price of defeat, as she and Aikin masked LaWanda's wounds with spiderwebs and spit before binding them with surgical tape, Piper massaged his lady's temples solicitously, and Alec alternately offered water, stared at the surrounding waste, and paced. Likely he'd figured out that one challenge remained, and that it would devolve on himself, Piper, or Aikin. Which didn't bode well if either of the first were called.

"The problem," Aife announced eventually, "is determining who is to judge. Were I to give you pen and paper and ask you to prepare a drawing of this tower, then who is unbiased enough to name the better when everyone present has seen Myra's skill and knows her style? And since there must be some element of equality, what I have decided is this. I shall take water and the earth beneath us, and from them you shall both sculpt heads in my likeness. Neither Alec, Aikin, nor Piper shall witness this making. When you have done, they shall join us and chose whose work is the truer image, for with three judges, there is no chance of a tie. LaWanda, you may stand as witness."

"Sounds fair," LaWanda agreed. Myra had no choice but to concur. Aife had been clever, too, for she surely knew that while Myra was facile indeed with pencil and paper, paint and brush, she hadn't nearly so much experience working 3-D. As for Yd—she'd soon find out.

In far too short a while, they were ready.

True to her word, Aife had contrived the medium: water from the pitchers, claylike earth from beneath the mossy sward, mixed to a plastic soup Myra realized early on was like the best china clay she'd ever seen, so white and fine it was. Whatever else transpired, working with this material would be a joy.

"Half of one hour you have," Aife informed them, flourishing Aikin's watch as she motioned the judges inside. Myra felt a pang of regret at that; a cheering section would've been nice. God knew Wannie had had one. At least she *had* Wannie, though her friend was forbidden to speak, her role that of not-so-neutral observer.

Aife had chosen a place equidistant between the two, with the light falling full in her face so as to give neither contestant the advantage of heightened shadows. "Ten, nine, eight," she counted, her Faery accent adding a musical lilt to the words Myra found almost too soothing. She shook herself roughly, wondered briefly if blood had proved thicker than friendship, and Aife was about to betray them, as once she'd betrayed Alec. And then Aife whispered, "Begin," and reality narrowed to Aife's face and Myra's fingers.

Not once did she look aside to gauge Yd's progress, nor to LaWanda for support. She merely stared at Aife, analyzed each element of her face with the same calm deliberation she utilized when executing a commissioned portrait, then let her fingers do the rest. It was easier than painting, actually, because mistakes were more easily rectified; whereas a blob of red or white in the wrong place—well, you'd live with that a long time, unless you were working with acrylics, which she loathed. Or unless you wanted to negate good work with the bad by swabbing with turpentine.

And it wasn't as if Aife was difficult to look at, though she discovered early on that one could in fact be too perfect, so that she found herself longing for some mole, scar, or asymmetry to give that cool, vaguely Latin beauty genuine character.

As usually happened when she was working, she lost all sense of time, and so was more than a little startled when Aife called out that only five minutes remained. And then that time was up.

Myra blinked up from her work, amazed to find anything still existing beyond clay, her fingers, and Aife's too-faultless features. Color itself was a surprise, for surely the sky had not been so intensely purple, Wannie's skin such an iridescent brownish black. "Leave now," Aife commanded, including all present in her gaze. "I would have no stray gesture influence the judging."

Myra grunted her assent, wiping her filthy hands on her thighs as she rose. What difference did clean clothes make, after all, when the fate of Worlds rode in the balance? A moment later, she was helping LaWanda, who was limping slightly but trying not to show it, inside. An instant after that, the judges had been summoned.

The waiting seemed to take forever, and she passed it inspecting the tapestry in which Yd had hidden, trying neither to acknowledge nor ignore to the point of insult that strange new adversary, who, though overtly their foe, seemed in fact to bear them no real rancor. "The library," she said eventually, not looking at him.

"What about it?"

"Are you its guardian?"

"I guard everything in Tir-Gat."

"So that nothing can be taken away?"

"That is correct."

"Not even knowledge?"

"That depends on the knowledge."

She'd already started to frame her next query when the door opened and Aife eased in, with Piper at her heels. Piper's grin told the story.

"It was not so easy a contest as you imagined, Myra," Aife cautioned. "Though you have talent, Yd has the sharper eye and, for all he is a warrior, the softer fingers. Your victory was not unanimous."

"Thank you," Myra murmured. "I know it was hard to orchestrate that. You did your best to ensure that it was fair."

"Aye, you did," Yd acknowledged, though his face showed far less certainty. "You should know, incidentally, that though you call me warrior, and I *am* the guardian here, I would style myself more a scholar."

Aife's eyes narrowed. "You say you are a scholar, Yd of Tir-Gat, Alban, and Annwyn? Are you then a druid? Or might you be a bard? Such is the way they call scholars in both those latter lands."

"I have studied both styles," Yd admitted. "I have, as yet, completed neither."

"Then you have skill with music?"

"With dulcimer, harp, and pipes."

"Pipes . . ." Aife repeated, with calculated calm. "Very well, you named the weapon, I did not. Pipes it is! And to contest with you, I name our own master musician: James Morrison Murphy!"

To his very great surprise, Piper didn't bolt when he heard his name announced. Or perhaps it was simply that LaWanda was holding his hand with an iron grip that would've done a bear trap proud. In any event, he tried to fight down the fear he not only felt, and that had already set his heart to racing, but which had just poured a bitter taste into his mouth, so that he had to concentrate to understand what was said.

And then he looked at LaWanda and knew that however strong she was, he had to be her match. He was taller, after all, and his muscles—his actual *strength*—were equal to hers. He was decently fast when he had to run, and had a fine set of lungs from playing pennywhistle and Highland pipes, and decent shoulders from pumping the bellows of the Uilleann pipes he wore now. And Wannie had faced up to that big guy and all but spat in his face when she knew he'd be swinging a sword at her. This was only a test of piping, of which, so people kept telling him, he was master. What did *he* have to fear?

Losing, for one thing. The tally stood one-and-one; the outcome of their quest therefore rested on him. What would happen should he lose, no one had dared ask, but from what he recalled from hanging out with Myra's younger pals, these Faery guys were culturally, if not genetically, Celts. And Celts took heads, especially the less urbane variations, such as this fellow, with all those tattoos, seemed to represent.

On the other hand, no less a person than Nuada Silverhand had praised his piping. And the King of the Faeries—Lugh, he thought, though he'd never seen the man's face that awful time ago—had asked him to play as though his life depended on it. But he'd also enjoyed that playing, else he'd have demanded it end.

"I will!" he said abruptly. "And may God have mercy on my soul."

LaWanda regarded him sharply, and he knew that she knew he took this very seriously indeed, to thus invoke the Deity. He was a good Catholic boy, after all; in his heart. And good Catholic boys did such things.

Yd lifted an eyebrow. "I have no pipes."

Aife raised one in turn. "Nor do you need them, if Piper will lend his. There is no way for musicians to contest at once, save by volume of noise. You will therefore have to vie separately. We will all go outside, leaving the two of you within. You will chose which of you will go first, and you will each perform a lament, a jig, and a reel. I have heard neither of you perform, not even when I was a cat, for my memories of that time already grow dim. Therefore, I alone will judge. Is this acceptable to you?''

"I guess so," Piper mumbled.

"It is!" Yd boomed, with what Piper read as forced bluster.

"We will leave you to it, then," Aife sighed, and ushered them all from the tower.

Piper found himself alone with Yd, who'd drifted forward to stand opposite. "I don't like this," Piper told him. "I want you to know that."

"Nor I standing guard in this lonely place," Yd replied, his voice tinged with such genuine regret Piper felt his eyes misting.

"How do we decide?"

Yd flashed an alarmingly mortal grin. "We flip a coin, if you have one. After all, we are more alike than different, in our souls."

"Maybe," Piper grunted, fishing in his pocket to discover a single dime, which he placed on the table beside him. "You flip, I'll call."

"Do you not fear that I might charm it?"

Piper shrugged.

Yd flashed an even wider grin, then slapped his hand on the coin and flipped it high into the air.

"Heads," Piper called at the apex of that flight.

The coin landed. The hand came down. "Heads it is. The stage is yours."

"Thanks," Piper whispered, and watched silently as Yd walked to the stairs and followed them up and out of sight. And then he closed his eyes, settled his pipes in his lap, and began to fill the bellows. A lament, a jig, and a reel, was it? *Okay, then,* he breathed, *here goes!*

And with that James Morrison Murphy, who'd been named after another James Morrison, who was also a musician, began to play.

He faltered once, torn between two tunes, then settled into something new that simply came to him, with elements borrowed from "Brian Boru's March," for the martial undertone that ought to underlie what he was about, and with echoes of the two saddest songs he knew: "Willie Mac-Bride," which was also called "Green Fields of France," and "Foggy Dew." For good measure he threw in one of those tunes Fionchadd had taught him on that strange, timeless voyage to the Land of the Powersmiths.

Would he always bargain with music? he wondered, as he began a variation. Fionchadd had bribed him then with a new song in exchange for that other one he was still so loath to play, though he'd played it often of late. Music was his one great love, older than his love of rain, and far older than his very real love for LaWanda. But would he ever be able to play again, without recalling these two weeks? It was sad, is what it was: sad enough to deserve its own lament. And so, without conscious volition, he wove that sadness into his tune.

He had no idea how long he played, save that he did four variations. As he began a fifth and final, he heard footsteps approaching. Fear gripped his heart, and more than fear, for though he played with both eyes shut, his practiced ear recognized Yd's tread.

"Open your eyes, James Morrison Murphy," Yd said gently. Then, more forcefully: *"Open your eyes!"*

Piper did, from the reflex of command. And missed a pair of beats, for Yd was kneeling at his feet, sword extended before him. "There is no way in any World, were I to practice a thousand years," Yd whispered, "that I would ever be able to best you."

"You mean—?" Piper gaped.

"Aye," Yd acknowledged. "I am conceding."

"Well," Piper said with a wry, sad smile. "I guess somebody ought to tell the others."

Yd rose and resheathed his sword. "I will walk through that door and relay my intent to those without, and then I will keep on walking, for I am no fit guardian of this place or any other." He turned at that, swept his dagged cloak off the floor, but did not don it, nor any of his armor. Instead, barefoot and bare-chested, he strode toward the heavy oak panel. Almost there, he twisted 'round and pointed up the stairs. ''The library lies there—what remains of it. I hope you find what you need.''

Piper's final glimpse of him stayed with him forever: a black man-shape cut out against an arch of light.

''Well, lads,'' he informed his pipes, ''we did it.''

Interlude III:
Candlelight Afternoon

(near Clayton, Georgia—
Sunday, June 29—mid-afternoon)

Adventure, Brock decided, midway through the afternoon, wasn't all it was cracked up to be. Nor was magic. Certainly neither was anything to write home about when you weren't actively involved in 'em. Except that wasn't true either, because the one time lately he *had* been actively involved, namely the attack on the ship, hadn't been fun at all, because he'd been scared absolutely shitless.

True, he'd been pumped, right up to the point Nuada yelled "Go!" But somehow that neat tableau had gone all to hell, and all of sudden it was all heat and noise and pain and stench and yelling and *chaos*; and when that dagger had ripped through his jacket inches from his side (which he'd not bothered to mention, and hoped no one had noticed)— well, he'd basically gone catatonic and spent the rest of the fight crouching behind the gunwale on the pretext of awaiting a clear shot he'd never intended to make.

And then there'd been the daring escape, which really *had* been neat, until the crash landing, whereupon he'd found himself as useful as last year's calendar, without even a pinup to justify saving him.

Which brought him to here and now: sitting on the hard wooden floor of John Devlin's "secret room" watching four candles slowly burn down to nothing, and trying to be alert for any unusual flicker or flare. Which on the one hand was worthwhile because it freed the big guns to do . . . big gun things, but still pissed him because it wasn't like he was a complete novice with this stuff either. Shoot, hadn't Cal suggested he go to Faerie to start with because he thought that crew needed somebody learned in another magic tradition? And in spite of what he'd said, Cal could've accomplished most of what he'd done by telephone, and gone himself.

But however young and naïve he was, he was old enough to know how fruitless such speculations could be, and that playing "what if" mainly served to frustrate you if it didn't simply piss you off. So here he was, trying to be cool and conscientious, and to maybe pick up something about this mysterious "tradition" John was supposed to be party to or practitioner of. And maybe what his mysterious "other protection" might be.

He thought he'd figured *that* out, though, from a half-finished poem he'd noticed on John's desk during one of his off-duty phases. "To the Family Banshee" had been the title, and he knew from talking to Cal that at least one family banshee was real, namely David's. But John's clan was Irish, too, so it made sense for him to have one of those . . . whatever they were hanging around as well.

At which point footsteps sounded outside, rousing him from what had become a dangerous reverie. He sat up straighter, twisted his neck to hear it crack, snapped every knuckle in turn. And tried to determine who'd just passed by his tread. John, most likely; the shoes had sounded heavier than those soft boots Silverhand wore, though the two probably massed about the same. But then he heard the toilet flush and that decided him. Try as he would, he couldn't imagine a lord of the Sidhe using a porcelain loo, or excreting at all, for that matter. They *did* have fairly efficient metabolisms, and that was a fact.

So maybe good old Johnny D. was gonna ease in and relieve him, though he still had thirty minutes (by the timer rings on yet another candle) on his shift.

Alas, such was not the case, and so he sat and stared first at the candle of the north, then at its twin to the south, then to the east, then to the west, and then the whole thing backwards, and finally, at the bare floor between to rest his eyes from the glare.

North, south, east, west . . .

. . . east, south, north, south, east, west . . .

. . . east . . .

East!

East had just flared, which meant Power was being brought to bear there! His hackles began to rise, for north had flared as well . . . and west! And finally south.

"John!" he yelled as he bolted for the door, while chill after chill raced across his body. "You'd better look at this right now!"

Chapter XIII:
Absent Friends, Absent Foes

(Galunlati—high summer)

If Sandy had retained any doubts about whether Uki was in fact a weather elemental, his reaction to Fionchadd's confirmation of Lugh's disappearance dispelled them. From his place across the smooth soapstone slab on which Okacha had spread an excellent feast of wild game and barely tamed vegetables, Uki rose with a grim, slow steadiness so full of latent tension it was like the air before a summer thunderstorm. His eyes flashed with sparks not born of biology; every muscle on his body quivered like leaves enduring rain; his long braids seemed to stir of their own volition.

Faster than any mortal could have moved, or any Faery she'd ever met, Uki swept both arms straight out, then over his head, pointed at the cavern's ceiling, fifty feet above— and shouted.

Or *was* it a shout? The word merged into the crack of palms impacting, which became a true blast of thunder, as lightning—the genuine, electrical article—snapped from Uki's hands in a blinding white pillar of raw energy that struck the roof and splattered across the ceiling and down the walls to the floor. Stones rained down, fortunately not many, though she had to duck her head and David, beside her, yipped in alarm as the air went so thick with the stench of ozone she gagged. Snakes hissed. Those near the walls writhed and died. The pool in which Calvin and Lugh had swum an hour past bubbled and steamed, while the air went hot as a forge. Every hair on her body stood absolutely straight out on end.

"Liar!" Uki shouted, his voice barely lower than the brassy thunder that rang around the cavern as though trapped there, echoing, making her bones thrum, awakening a headache behind her eyes that would be long abating.

"Liar!" Uki spat again, lowering his arms to glare at them. "Why should I not blast you all, who call such a liar friend?"

Another blast cracked from his hands, scarcely less violent than the first, save that it wrought ball lightning that bounced and smashed dangerously near the company. More snakes died. The cougars spat and loped through a low arch into an adjoining chamber. Sandy closed her eyes.

Thunder: like drums exploding.

Another flash: more ball lightning. But that crackling died away abruptly, as though sucked into a vacuum.

"Enough!" Calvin yelled through the echoes. Sandy blinked up to see her lover on his feet, facing his mentor across the soapstone slab, both hands gripping the atasi one of Uki's fellow demigods had given him: upraised now, as though to block a blow aimed at his head. An atasi which had apparently just absorbed a cavern's worth of galvanic pyrotechnics.

"Enough," Calvin repeated more softly, swallowing hard, lowering the atasi to waist level, though the anger in his eyes had not abated. Sandy was sorry for him. Cal hated confrontation, yet he was the obvious counter here; though she doubted he relished the role of lightning rod in a storm-god's citadel. "Not friend so much as ally," he managed at last. "War sometimes makes strange bedfellows. A week ago, Lugh was our enemy. He threatened my home World and David's—Yanu-degahnehiha's, I mean. Then someone threatened Lugh *and* our World, and *that* threat was worse than Lugh's, and he became the lesser foe: someone who might have cause to bargain."

Uki's eyes narrowed. The tension that crackled through his body diminished minutely. "I see."

Calvin took another breath. "Sometimes, Adewehiyu, it is best to address business before formality. We are on the edge of war, and war rarely waits for breakfast."

"I will hear this tale," Uki declared coldly.

Sandy cleared her throat into the ensuing silence. "Perhaps," she ventured, "it would be best to find out where Lugh *is* first. He's been under tremendous pressure, after all; was barely recovered, in fact. We've no proof he was in his right mind when he left, but whether he's crazy or sane, he's powerful. He's also a rogue element."

Uki glared at her so vehemently Sandy was certain she was about to receive her own personal thunderbolt, and was already steeling herself for whatever came when Uki uttered a terse "So be it!" and reached down to snare an enormous diamondback rattler that happened to be coiling by. One breath, and he stared the serpent straight in its beady black eyes. The next, he'd shifted his grip behind the heavy jowls of the ugly triangular head. Whether by force, magic, or the snake's own outraged ire, its jaws popped open, revealing inch-long fangs—

—that pierced Uki's impressive pecs to the bone when he slapped that head against his chest. Blood oozed from between those needle-teeth as Uki's features knotted in pain, though he held the serpent there for a long, still moment of frozen time.

Abruptly, Uki flung the reptile to the ground, where it lay quiescent—whether sated, stunned, or dead, Sandy had no time to determine. For Uki had crossed the two paces between them and the pool and stepped into its center. Blood dripped into that pristine water.

It spread outward at once, sheening the surface with a film of glowing red. Uki scowled at it briefly; muttered a certain *word*; reached to a waist-pouch to retrieve a handful of corn, which he flung into the gleaming water; then eased back to crouch on the pool's rim. A deeper scowl, and he clapped his hands once more, prompting a tiny bolt of lightning which flared out across the surface like flaming oil. "You may watch," he grunted, and continued to stare.

Sandy wasn't sure she *wanted* to watch. Then again, any knowledge was better than none, so she rose gracefully and padded barefoot to squat beside Calvin, who'd claimed the place to Uki's right. At first she saw nothing, though the stench—ozone and burned blood—made her want to gag all over again, but then the pool began to ripple and stir and she lost herself in wonder.

At first, all she saw was red: water dancing and swirling as though lit by sunset fire. But those ripples gradually rose and stabilized into miniature mountains, while the swirls flowed in between them and fixed themselves into streams, lakes, and rivers, and some of the shadows took on green highlights like burning copper, so that she found herself gazing down on an eerie relief map of a strange, wild country that had to be Walhala. The limits went vague at the west, drifting into a black that had nothing to do with shadows. The east seemed brighter, and a thread of red-gold beach gleamed there, edge of an unknown sea. The north was bluish, the mountains there higher, where they merged with the pool's stone frame. A lake sparkled there, too: ruby against red velvet.

And south: White like forge fire. Like Uki's anger. Like his skin, or Lugh's.

Uki's hands crept sideways, to where Lugh's footprints were graven in the sand, and snared a fistful of grains. Another *word*, and he sprinkled them into the water, at the same time reciting a version of the formula for finding Sandy had heard both Cal and Brock use a score of times before.

For a moment nothing happened, but then motes began to drift to the surface, thickest at the tiny waterfall in the northern point of the southernmost quadrant, which she was certain marked this very cave. A hard clot of golden light formed there, moved infinitesimally toward the minute cataract, then pulsed bright and vanished, but not before a strip of gold had blazed across the miniature landscape like a meteor. And then the light winked out.

"Gone," Uki grunted, rising with what seemed like genuine weariness, or perhaps that was some aftereffect of all that rattlesnake poison.

"He called a Track, I think," Fionchadd dared, barely breathing. "Or rent the World Walls themselves and went elsewhere."

"But why?" Sandy ventured in turn. "And where'd he go in such an all-fired hurry?"

Fionchadd cleared his throat. "The haste is likely due to

the way time runs between the Worlds. The rest—who can say? Lugh came here and the Power of this Land awoke his own Power enough to restore his thought and memory, and to enable him to take on that form which would most easily free him from the iron that tormented him. That accomplished, he . . . left. He has lost a kingdom, do not forget. He would surely seek to reclaim it, which is not easily done from here. Still, he would have had to enter your World first; there would have been no alternative to that. Given that, he would likely seek out Nuada, whom he would know at once was there.''

Liz eyed him narrowly. ''You're sure he's not just gone crazy? Think what he's been through, Finno: a coup, torture, sickness—or whatever you guys get. Do you have any proof that iron dust didn't get into his brain and rot it?''

''God, I hope not!'' David gasped. ''But my guess is that Lugh's been around the block enough to know his own body *and* his own mind. I think he could fight madness.''

''He didn't fight the poison that took him out,'' Liz countered.

''He didn't know *to* fight it,'' David shot back. ''Whatever happened here was premeditated.''

Uki scratched his chin, the edge of his anger having faded, though there was a raw harshness in his voice. ''Were I a chief who had been deposed and exiled,'' he mused, ''I would seek the most powerful allies I could find. I would also seek anyone loyal to me who would see me regain my throne.''

''Yep,'' Kirkwood agreed from his silent, watchful corner. ''Which is why he'd chase down Silverhand. Lugh hears the clock ticking. He *might* find allies here, but he'd have to do some convincin', and he doesn't know how many warriors, if any, he could count on. His captain's in our World, though, and back in Faerie, he's got a ready-made army—assumin' he can collect 'em.''

Fionchadd nodded sagely. ''Wisely said—for someone who relies on reports and rumors.''

''And history and human nature,'' Kirkwood appended.

''I think you are right, too,'' the Faery went on. ''Most of Lugh's guard are loyal, though without any true leader, and most of the mighty in Tir-Nan-Og would support him, assuming he could be found. He would therefore seek to rally his troops.''

Sandy eyed the oracular pool speculatively. ''I agree. But it still seems to me that what we do here depends on what Lugh does . . . wherever. Which means we really do need to try to find him.''

Calvin gazed her askance. ''Which means . . . ?''

A deep breath. ''Well, basically, I was just wondering whether that pool can look at any other World besides this one?''

The silence that ensued was as loud as the previous thunder.

Uki's face was grim, though whether from residual anger, ongoing pain from his still-oozing wound, or newfound concern, Sandy was uncertain. For a time he stared at the pool, then gazed pensively at Okacha, who'd silently claimed his other side. ''To spy upon your World *here* requires blood of your World. And that blood must be born of pain.'' He fixed Sandy with a challenging glare. ''Are you ready to dare that pain?''

Calvin coughed. ''Does it have to be her?''

''*I'm* willing,'' David chimed in, though he looked pretty uncertain—with reason, given what he'd been through lately. It was easy to forget that his father had been wounded and might well die. She doubted *he'd* forgotten, though; how else explain that stony expression, or why her lover's best friend was no longer in the thick of things. She wondered when he'd bring up the healing water.

Uki shook his head. ''You are warriors. You bear war names. You know pain. Yet woman's Power is stronger than ours at times. A woman's blood it must be.''

Sandy exchanged glances with a pensive-looking Liz. ''I'll do it,'' she declared. ''It's necessary. It won't kill me—I hope. And a year from now I'll remember the results, not . . . whatever.''

Uki nodded gravely, drummed a certain cadence in the sand, and promptly snared the copperhead that responded to that unheard call, then offered it to Sandy.

She swallowed hard, but received the serpent with steady

hands. A country girl herself, she had no fear of snakes per se, but poisonous ones were another matter. Calvin reached up reflexively to stop her, then withdrew his hand. "You damned better take care of her when this is over," he growled at Uki.

Uki shot him a sharp glare, then returned his attention to Sandy. "Perhaps I will; perhaps I will not! Uncertainty will strengthen the summoning."

Sandy swallowed again. "Does it matter where?"

"Closest to your heart."

"I was afraid of that!" A deep breath, and Sandy closed her eyes, keenly aware of the snake's weight where she supported its body in her other hand. It was cool but not cold, and she could feel its blood race, the long slow pulse of its heart. Her own was going ninety beats a second.

A final breath; she shifted her grip—and thrust the snake down her shirt and into the vee between her breasts, angling its head toward the left one. Muscles twitched beneath her fingers and the jaws sprang open. Its breath was unexpectedly hot.

She didn't actually feel the prick of the fangs, but the flood of fire-hot poison that accompanied them roared through her like molten lava. For an instant she was certain her breast was about to explode. *It's only pain,* she told herself as agony pulsed in strong, sick waves. *Pain is only a warning. It is no danger by itself. It is chemicals. Electricity. It—*

It hurts like a son of a bitch!—as tears sprang shamelessly into her eyes. Yet still she pressed the snake there, through endless microseconds during which hot blood began to slide down her flesh. Her stomach knotted. Sweat soaked her body. Reality vanished and returned.

Hands brushed her: male, but surprisingly soft and gentle, and from the wrong quarter to be Calvin. The snake was withdrawn. But it was her own hands that unbuttoned her shirt, baring her chest so the blood could drip upon the water into which she even now was wading.

It was cold as ice! She gasped, opened her eyes, glanced down, saw the two tiny holes closer to the nipple than she'd expected, and the rivulets of blood that slid down the milky skin like the rivers on the landscape already forming below.

She reeled. "Back," Uki murmured. To which she was only too glad to assent. Reality whirled again.

A *word;* more corn, more lightning; and a strange new vista clarified. Even so, it took a moment to identify the familiar contours of her native Southeast, partly because she was gazing at it from an odd angle, and partly because it was defined without artificial boundaries, with mountains and rivers in their natural shapes and colors, ornamented with numerous tiny bright jewels that had to be towns and cities. Atlanta was the brightest, the largest and most prickly. But Asheville was present as well, almost home, and beyond it what was probably Charlotte. And there were Chattanooga and Knoxville, and farther south in Georgia: Savannah, and a thin blue crescent of the coast. West vanished at the rocks, but she had no idea how far Faerie went that way, for surely she was only seeing those parts of her World that were also of concern to Lugh.

A blink, and she could make out the remnants of the map of Walhala lying below the brighter, clearer one her blood had wrought, like a reflection in cold, still water. Ripples appeared abruptly, born of sand Uki tossed across that phantom landscape. And where those ripples touched and mingled, patterns slowly took form, like tiny bolts of electricity tracing the intricacies of a complex printed circuit.

For easily a minute they meandered aimlessly, but then those motes slowly joined, clarifying into a brighter focus centered near the tiny silver splatter that was Langford Lake, which bordered Sullivan Cove.

She stared at it, fascinated, and actually cried aloud when a slap of Uki's hands sent another lightning bolt spearing the heart of that brightness. The image shattered, then reformed as suddenly into something more recognizable, viewed at closer range.

Lugh: clad as they'd last seen him, in breechclout and feather cloak, and sprawled facedown across a rough, lichen-crusted boulder the size of Sandy's Explorer. Shadows dappled him from unseen sunlit trees, and wind stirred the pine limbs that framed her field of view. A blink, and she gazed not across Lugh's shoulder but through his very eyes, and saw with the Faery King's seeing.

It was the lake at the end of Sullivan Cove. There was the cone-shaped mountain offshore that was called, perhaps too aptly, Bloody Bald. And there was the sweep of wooded strand, the storm-swollen water still high enough to mask the rocky shelves that lined it, though that water was receding. Closer in was a spear of peninsula, where a campsite was all but flattened, tent and utensils strewn about like shrapnel.

And very close indeed were two vans, each bearing the logo of Mystic Mountain Properties. Men stood about, anxiously watching the road that threaded through Sullivan Cove, sole link to the outside world. An instant later, she saw the cause of their concern when a flatbed truck rumbled in, followed by another truck pulling a small house trailer made up to be an on-site office. The flatbeds bore a generator *and* a backhoe: bright yellow and brand-new. Scott was right: Mystic Mountain didn't cut corners.

Speaking of Scott, where was he? By rights he ought to be smack in the thick of things. *Oh, there he was!* Talking to a fat man she recognized from a photo Scott had shown her as Ralph Mims, the moving force behind this development. By the way Scott was gesticulating, he was clearly pissed as hell. Intrigued, she strained her hearing and caught the end of a conversation.

"Can't wait any longer," Mims was saying. "You don't have to finish A before you start on B, and there've been too many delays already."

Scott's shoulders slumped. "Yeah, well, it's just that I wasn't done yet, and I really wanted to do a *good* job, and all this fuckin' rain's played hell—"

"No reason you've gotta stop," Mims broke in. "Continue your survey. Look for gemstones. Check the stratigraphy. But we've got enough here to go on."

Scott studied the sky apprehensively, then checked his watch. "So what's your timetable?"

Mims fairly beamed. "Tomorrow we bring in the Porta Pottis. By noon, we oughta be placing stakes and stringing guidelines. Backhoe'll be digging by three."

"Stakes," Scott managed weakly. "What kind of stakes? You're dealin' with rock 'round here."

"Steel spikes," Mims enthused. "If they won't go in easy, we'll use a jackhammer on 'em."

Sandy blinked—or Lugh did. The Faery looked up apprehensively, peered over his shoulder, shook himself like a nervous animal, then checked behind again, and frowned. Words whispered into the air, and Sandy no longer shared his senses, though she was aware of him rising and calling on Power as he whipped the cloak around him. Somehow, too, there was a sense of a door being opened, but she never saw what lay beyond, for something twitched between her brain and her eyes, and she was wrenched away. She gasped, saw nothing, blinked again, and when vision cleared it was to gaze into Calvin's worried brown eyes.

"What'd you see?" he demanded. "Best I can tell, the rest of us saw the map of our World, and then it all went to sparkles."

She took a deep breath—and told them.

"Well," Fionchadd mused when she'd finished. "That is very interesting indeed. It makes sense, too, that he would spy out your home place first, for that will tell him something of how much time he has in which to act, which he would then have to hand when he meets Nuada—if he is Lugh's next goal."

"But wouldn't the map show that?" Liz wondered, peering at it intently.

"No," Uki replied flatly. "One scrying is all one bite can purchase."

"Bite," Sandy echoed, gazing down at the bloody holes marring her creamy white flesh. They hurt like hell, and there was already some swelling, but she could handle it. For a while. She thought. God knew she'd endured as much before. Okacha evidently observed her discomfort, however, and fetched a clay pot full of sweet-smelling unguent. Sandy dabbed it with a finger, then smeared it across her wounds. Coolness and healing flowed in at once, and the distant pang of nausea that had haunted her since the first whiff of ozone departed as well.

Which was just as well, because Fionchadd was speaking once more. "Blood and pain," he muttered, looking at Uki. "You said it took blood and pain to do such a scrying as we just witnessed. I wonder, though, could we not scry out Tir-Nan-Og as well, either to see how things fare with Lugh, if he is there, or with those who would unthrone him?''

Uki's brow darkened into a scowl. ''I do not like that idea, yet I do not know why I do not like it, save that it troubles my scaly servants. Very well . . . you may make the attempt. Be warned, though: to look two Worlds away is very difficult. It would be impossible unless *you* supply the blood.''

''At your leave,'' Fionchadd replied formally.

By the time Uki had summoned a third serpent—two, actually: a pair of the less venomous cottonmouths—Sandy was feeling considerably better, but Fionchadd was looking anxious. Clad only in the breechclout Uki had lent him upon arrival (though he had other clothing to hand), it was a simple matter for him to seize each serpent behind the head and press them both to his smooth, pale chest. Sandy assumed he had a higher pain threshold than her fellow mortals; still, it had to hurt, and she wasn't surprised to hear him gasp and see his jaw tighten as he fought for control.

Another gasp, and he let the serpents fall. They slithered away harmlessly into a hole beside Liz's foot, evoking a sharp cry from her, born more of reflex than fear. Liz was as tough as they came, but instinct was instinct, regardless.

Meanwhile, Fionchadd was bending over in the center of the pool, so that the blood that dripped from his chest fell clear into the water. Both previous landscapes still ghosted there, like layers of glass beneath each other, but a third now manifested atop them, aided by a thunderclap from Uki that sent Fionchadd, who'd been gaping as though ensorcelled, scurrying back to shore.

The first thing that formed was a complex, three-dimensional webwork of golden lines that had to represent Tracks and Pillars. And around them, slowly, more concrete shapes coalesced. This landscape was smaller than the Mortal World, however, and more tenuous, especially to the north and west. But Bloody Bald's Faery analog was preposterously easy to pick out, while the haven at the coast also showed brightly.

More troubling were what at first looked like glowing embers: spots of red-edged black strewn here and there across the land like a sprinkling of burning pepper. "Holes," David gasped. "Those are Holes, aren't they? Those black things?"

"Likely," Fionchadd murmured distantly. "Touch me now, if you would watch."

Sandy did—and suddenly found herself zooming in on the glittering white cone of the surrogate Bloody Bald, watching towers rise and point, while arches and windows, walls and gardens clarified, all wrapped around that impossibly perilous peak.

One garden in particular caught her eye: small, and entirely surrounded by the black-glass and wrought-silver walls of one of the lesser towers that wasn't numbered among the twelve that gave the palace its most common appellation. It was actually a rather plain garden, almost austere, and Sandy quickly determined that the silver designs inset into the black glass were meant to be winter-blasted trees, and that the paving stone was the same glass but unpolished, across which wrought-silver roots sprawled, rising above the surface and imbedded within it. An irregular, car-sized pool occupied the center, not unlike the one she and her companions contemplated. And around that pool, an assortment of figures were ranged.

Every one was Faery, and most looked very young; younger than Fionchadd, even, or Aife. More were men than women by a wide margin, though the women looked little different, clad as they all were in smooth black leather and a coarser hide of silvery hue Sandy thought might be the wyvern skin she'd heard so much about. They looked tired, too; and not as clean as was typical for the Sidhe. A few sported hair that had been hacked off roughly, and more showed wounds and blisters that looked strange indeed against all that fair, smooth flesh; possibly, she suspected, proof of encounters with iron during a certain recent altercation. All were beautiful, of course, but most faces were hard with anger, hatred, and maybe fear, rather than stern with pride or authority. Something, she reckoned, was rotten in Denmark.

A discussion was in process, too, in the strange tongue of the Sidhe, of which the only words she could make out were *Lugh* and *Turinne*. And with two sets of World Walls between, no thought rode with those words to translate them in her brain. It was, in short, a meaningless, frustrating muddle. By the attentive look on his face, however, it was a great deal more to Fionchadd.

For a fair while that debate continued, only breaking off when a door opened in what she'd taken to be the cast-silver trunk of an enormous tree, and a pair of soldiers entered, with an old man stumbling between them. An old *mortal,* by the look of him: white-haired and clad in a tattered robe that might once have been the silver-blue-gold of bright moonlight. His hands were manacled behind him, and his head bowed with what looked like resignation or outright despair, so that Sandy didn't immediately get a look at his face. But when she did, she gasped, for it was a young face and an old face at once; beautiful beyond mortal longing, yet clearly that of a mortal man. The eyes, when she finally glimpsed them, were featureless orbs of cold, dark silver. *Blind!* she knew. *Stone blind!*

At a word from the red-haired youth who was leader of that cadre (Turinne? Was that his name?), the soldiers flung the old man forward on his knees, where he remained unmoving. More discussion followed, and then one of them chanced to look up, as though he were a doll who'd just discovered that someone larger was observing his machinations, and the contact dissolved. The pool rippled, then skimmed over with featureless dull red. A final bolt from Uki, and the red dissolved like fractured glass, leaving eight exceedingly puzzled people.

"Well, Finno," David prompted. "What was all that Faery mumbo jumbo?"

Fionchadd took a deep, shuddering breath. "Many things, but four in particular. First, that was the rebels' ruling council, with Turinne at its head, and they have vowed that they *will* find Lugh. The second is that they still intend to flood those parts of the Lands of Men that lie beneath Tir-Nan-Og, commencing with Sullivan Cove. The third is that they plan to start tomorrow."

Calvin scowled uncertainly. "Our time or—?"

"I corrected for the change," Fionchadd snapped.

"And the fourth thing?" David persisted, a nervous edge

on his voice, as though he already knew but needed confirmation to validate that fear.

"You saw the old man?"

David nodded. "Oisin. Lugh's mortal seer. He's kind of a friend."

Fionchadd regarded him solemnly. "It will not go well with him. Being mortal, he will not be able to resist certain things. Being Lugh's seer, he will also know many things."

"Including *us*?" Liz dared.

"If they know how to ask about you. Oisin is wily; he knows how to answer such questions as they will pose. He will betray no more than he must. He—"

"Enough!" Uki broke in. "We have spied on three Worlds today, and I have heard every one of you speak of war, and war it is I see brewing, yet no one has related the tale that brought you here, though much I have divined already." He stared at Calvin meaningfully.

"Aye, adewehi," Calvin sighed. "Maybe you oughta sit down, though, and have some black drink, 'cause this is gonna be a long one."

"I have time," Uki said solemnly, stalking back to the soapstone table.

"I'm not so sure that *we* do," Calvin countered. "Not if they're gonna do the Cove in the morning. In the meantime, this is how it goes . . ."

He spoke for almost an hour, by guess; since Sandy's watch—no surprise—wasn't working. (Watches often didn't in places like this, though their failures were as inconsistent as they were inexplicable.) Throughout the narrative, Uki said little, but his face grew more and more troubled.

". . . and here we are," Calvin finished, leaning back and shaking his head before helping himself to a cup of bitter black drink.

"Here we *all* are," Uki echoed ominously, rising to his feet. For a moment Sandy thought he was going to storm the cavern again. Instead, he strode to a raised terrace, wrought of the cavern's natural stone, and climbed atop it.

"*Yanu-degahnehiha*," he called to David: He-wrestles-bears, which was his warname in Cherokee; "*Utlunta-dehi*"—to Calvin; it meant He-killed-Spearfinger—"and your kinsman: Kirkwood, as I recall. You will join me.'' A pause, a scowl. Then: "These words have vexed me greatly, so that I cannot plot proper action alone. Come, warriors, I must construct a Power Wheel.''

Calvin started. "But, you've already got one!''

Uki nodded stonily. "*Outside*, to reach which takes time. And any time saved now may save all of us in turn.''

Calvin didn't reply. All Sandy could do was gnaw her lips in anguished perplexity at what could so disturb someone like Uki. And for a moment, all anyone heard was the waterfall's heartbeat thunder.

Chapter XIV:
Relics

(Tir-Gat—high summer)

It was just as well he was sitting on soft, cushiony moss, Alec thought wryly, else they'd have heard his chin drop all the way to the other side of this screwy little pocket universe. But what other reaction was possible—when, right in the middle of their last and most crucial trial, with Piper playing the best he ever had: a tune so sad and full of pain it even had a tough broad like LaWanda going all soft and misty; and then—*bang*—he just stops? Whereupon the door opens and out walks Yd, wild-eyed and grim-faced, with his britches bagging around his hips and that preposterous cloak flapping in the breeze like the wings of a dozen birds of paradise?

And keeps right on walking into the sand as though the rest of them weren't even there, whereupon he turns and says, without expression, "I concede. I wish you joy of what you seek."

And keeps walking.

Alec watched spellbound—they all did—as the former guardian of Tir-Gat dwindled to a dark point against the silky glare of the mirror-sands. And then was gone.

"Did he—?" Myra choked. "That is . . ."

Aife shrugged. "He arrived here somehow; perhaps that is the way he returns, though I would not be him when I came to face my King. Or perhaps this World simply ends out there and he stepped off."

"Or through." Myra shivered. "This place isn't all that stable, as I recall."

"It is farther away from your World than it was then, however," Aife observed.

Myra had just opened her mouth to ask *how* far when Piper appeared in the tower's open doorway. He was drenched with sweat, had his shirt open all the way down, and wore the bellows for his pipes still fastened around his waist like panniers. But the smug, shy, uncertain grin he was flashing would've lit up a small country. "I . . . won!" he mumbled, half dazed. "I . . . actually . . . won!"

"Figured," LaWanda snorted, then grinned even wider than her lover and rushed forward to sweep him off his feet and spin him around, only stopping when her wounds made her stagger.

That broke whatever emotional logjam had been in effect, however, and they besieged their wiry, tousle-haired friend. Backs got thumped, hugs were given, kisses exchanged without discrimination. Only Aife looked troubled. "A strange man, that: a guardian, yet his heart was not in it. Such a one should be fierce, should give no quarter, should . . ."

"Maybe it was like you said," Myra mused. "Maybe his heart really wasn't in it. Maybe it was a punishment or something."

"Yeah," Alec agreed. "Seems to me like folks over here tend to exile the weird ones to out-of-the-way places."

"Beats killin' 'em," Aikin muttered. "Killin' doesn't really matter when you can come back sooner or later."

"Whatever," Alec sighed. "What say we grab something to eat and go plunder that library?"

As Yd had reminded Piper upon departure, Colin of Tir-Gat's library occupied the tower's second level, which was accessed by a wide, freestanding stone stair that curved around the inside of the ground-floor room. Nor was reaching it difficult, though the footing was somewhat problematical, what with a few loose treads and one place where two steps had fallen away entirely, so that they had to step across a two-foot gap. Fortunately enough of the carved stone railing remained to make even that passage relatively easy.

Myra giggled. "Going up at your own speed sure beats

running down in the middle of an earthquake, with a bunch of crazy men in tow!''

LaWanda smirked back. ''That's for sure!''

Myra eyed her male companions. ''Well, one thing hasn't changed.''

And then they reached the second level.

If navigating the stairs had been uncomplicated, what awaited them at their terminus was not. Though the room itself occupied the entire floor and was mostly open to the sky, chaos was everywhere, courtesy of the next two levels' having collapsed atop it, leaving a hollow shell that continued several levels higher. There'd been fire up there, too, but it hadn't reached this low—fortunate, if you were looking for fragile artifacts. Still, blackened timbers and fallen blocks of masonry, both carved and plain, and much of it inlaid with malachite and lapis-lazuli, were everywhere and had to be stepped over or steered around, all the while keeping watch for unstable portions of floor and rotten timbers. Some of the latter bore disturbing marks, too: as though they'd been gnawed—or clawed—by something larger than Alec wanted to contemplate.

But this really was the library, Alec knew right off, because the far quadrant of wall was still lined floor-to-ceiling with rough wooden bookcases, many of which retained their precious cargo.

''Oh, wow,'' Myra gasped, clearly in awe, as she got her first good view. ''Oh, fucking *wow*!''

''You read . . . Sidheish?'' Aikin chided, though Alec could tell his friend, who was a serious bibliophile, was also wildly impressed.

Alec froze in place. ''Good point,'' he said seriously. ''We're here, but how do we know what we're looking for? I mean, I hate to say this, folks, but we haven't really thought this through very well. We've mostly been going on hunches, guesses, and dead reckoning.''

''Which seem to work pretty well,'' Myra shot back. ''Besides, you're supposed to be the logical one: you and Hunter-boy. I, sir, am an artist, as is Wannie.''

''And we're women and therefore more intuitive,''

LaWanda added sarcastically. "We don't fight. We don't do nothin'."

" 'Cept fret about birthin' babies," Aikin teased.

LaWanda threw a chunk of charcoal at him and reached for another.

"No!" Piper said flatly. And to Alec's amazement, she stopped.

"Sorry."

Alec simply stared.

Aife had eased into the lead, eyes narrowed intently as she scanned not only the shelves but the shattered detritus of equipment and furniture. Alec followed her gaze, realizing belatedly that this had not only been a library but also a lab. The proverbial sorcerer's den, in fact. "I assume we oughta ask before we touch anything, right?" he murmured, trying not to stare too long at a particularly well-wrought sculpture of a pair of naked lovers cast in pure gold, though smudged with black and partly obscured beneath a block of masonry that itself was inlaid with a hunting scene in copper cloisonné and precious stones.

"It would be wise," Aife agreed, pausing to regard Myra curiously. "You were here before, were you not? When this place was intact? You climbed the stairs to the roof. Would you have seen this room as it was then?"

"Yep," Myra affirmed, with an uncertain gleam in her eye.

"Good," Aife retorted. "If you will grant me leave, I can enter your mind and share your memories of that time. Perhaps I will see something that will aid our search."

"But do we even know what we're lookin' for?" Aikin broke in. "A book, or . . . what? I mean, are we even certain this Colin guy wrote this stuff down? Wasn't he a druid? And didn't they rely on memory?"

"Aye," Aife acknowledged. "But he was old, even for one of the Sidhe, and when one is immortal . . . eventually one's mind cannot encompass everything. Since Colin created Tir-Gat late in his life, it is to be hoped that he was forced to record the spells he used to control the Silver Tracks. My only hope is that we can understand whatever tongue or cipher he employed."

"And we still have to find it," Aikin persisted, looking meaningfully at Myra.

Myra grimaced, shrugged, and sat down on a conveniently chair-sized fragment of sculpture. The stone contained fossils, Alec realized, wondering if it would be safe to make away with some of them.

Maybe later—for Aife had eased around behind Myra to grasp her temples with both hands. "Close your eyes," she breathed. "Think back to that day. Forget your emotions, recall only with those eyes that serve you so well. Think of what you saw—and now of what you *see*!"

Myra flinched ever so slightly, and Aife's eyes too slipped closed. For more than a minute they simply sat there, immobile. Alec wondered if he'd ever feel comfortable with Aife again. True, she'd said she loved him as recently as an hour ago, and had been acting as though that were so in their few unstressed moments together since her return. But might she not be playing another role? God knew she'd been acting when first they'd met: pretending to be some lost mortal foreigner in order to win her way into—to be blunt—his pants, since she'd needed his seed to effect certain controls over him. But she'd been one of Lugh's guard then, though also secretly allied with the Sons of Ailill—more acting there. And then there was the enfield episode, which had certainly served her own ends in spite of its also being punishment, never mind the cat variation that had come after. And now, all of a sudden, she was this high and haughty stranger: by turns judge and jury, but always manipulator.

So which was the real Aife? And what was her true agenda?

Nuada trusted her—kind of. But Lugh had as well, and look what had happened to him. Besides, in the last analysis, it was like David said: there really were other, more accessible but equally accomplished women. And it *was* a seller's market.

Which was a damned fool thing to be pondering when you were about to go rummaging through the ruins of a wizard's lab.

"Oh . . . !" Myra's yip startled him from his reverie. He looked up with a jerk, to see that Aife had backed away from

Myra and that Myra's eyes and mouth were open in amazement.

"It exists," Aife said without preamble. "Something with the appropriate characteristics exists, at any rate; for such a book would be written in a certain style and bound in a particular way. And though there are many variations and possibilities around us here, recall that he did not expect to die that day, that death caught up with him; he would therefore have had no cause to hide it. In any event, we seek a book with a gold leather cover emblazoned with silver solar rays. Do not open it if you find it, but call me at once. It would be somewhere near the middle of the room," she added. "For that is where Myra saw it long ago, all unknowing."

"Great," Aikin grunted. "Right where all those beams fell."

"Well," Myra sighed philosophically. "We won't find it standing here gawking."

It was Alec who actually located it, and that by accident. He'd been moving a pile of dusty square stones stacked like shattered dominoes upon a likely-looking volume—and one of the stones had felt too light, and had proven, upon being wiped off, to be no stone at all but a book. *The* book, as he announced when he realized what he had. It fit the description perfectly, though he hadn't expected it to be so large: maybe twelve by eighteen inches, and studded here and there with silver-toned bands and knobby excrescences, some of them sporting jewel-crusted arcane symbols or monsters wrought in brilliant cloisonné.

He surrendered it to Aife without comment.

She gnawed her lip, brow furrowed pensively as she scrubbed at the cover with a fragment of tattered tapestry. The silver rays gleamed forth. Another pause, during which she closed her eyes, nodded absently, then flipped the metal clasps that bound its fore edge. A final breath (*Was she actually frightened?*), and she opened it.

Even seeing it upside down at a yard's remove, Alec couldn't suppress a gasp at the beauty that lay within. He'd seen the world's great books, of course, in photographs; and part of the greatest—*The Book of Kells*—when it was displayed at the Smithsonian. But beside this—well, *Kells* and *The Book of Durrow* and *The Lindisfarne Gospel* together couldn't compare with the incredible wealth of intricate detail that blazed forth from just the first page.

"Oh, Jesus Christ!" Myra gasped, actually staggering, so that Aikin had to brace her to keep her from falling. "Oh, my God—Jesus *Christ*!"

"Mighty fine," LaWanda agreed. "Mighty fine. Question is, does it have what we need, or does it just look good?"

"Does it matter?" Aikin breathed. "One page of that, you could buy a country."

"Over my dead body!" Myra snapped back, glaring at him. "Anyone damages that book for *any* reason deserves to die."

"They used to put *The Book of Kells* in cow troughs to cure diseases," Aikin retorted.

"Silence!" Aife spat, alone of that company unimpressed with such preposterous intricacy and beauty. "I *think* this is what we sought, but this script—for there *is* script—is damnably difficult to read." And with that, she effectively shut them out, eyes darting from side to side, but otherwise not moving save when, with great reverence, she now and then turned a page.

The rest of them spent the time variously. Myra rebandaged LaWanda's wounds. Piper cleaned his pipes and tried to nap; like Brock he tended to do that when he was stressed. Alec and Aikin explored the rest of the library. A few books they examined, and a few scrolls, but none could compare with the one they'd just located, though many bore illustrations of fabulous beasts or buildings, or strangely delineated maps that seemed to rise up to engulf them if they gazed at them too long. More than a few, too, fell away to dust upon being shifted, and one literally shocked the hell out of Aikin when he accidentally brushed it with a finger.

After that, they contented themselves with scouring the floor for interesting detritus: stray jewels, bits of enamel, general odd lots that could fit into pockets and packs. "Christmas shopping," Aikin grinned, scooping up a wooden box through the crystal lid of which the board and pieces of an incredibly delicate chess set gleamed, wrought of opal and hematite, with accents of silver and gold. "This stays with me."

"Assuming Aife lets you keep it," Alec cautioned, ambling back to where his troublesome lady was still turning pages in the center of the room. "Find anything?" he ventured, after watching her read a good minute longer. The script, he noted idly, was like nothing he'd ever seen, though Arabic calligraphy came closest. "He can't have really written that," he added, when Aife still didn't reply. "You people can't do art, remember?"

Aife slowly raised her gaze to him. "Nor could many men duplicate those books you so admire. But like every possible endeavor, there is always someone who is best. And at calligraphy, Colin of Tir-Gat excelled."

"In both Worlds," Myra acknowledged.

"Maybe," Alec gave back. "But don't forget how much stuff we've lost: burned, and whatever. We lost the Alexandrine Library, and all those Greek plays; like, we'll have one or two masterpieces by somebody like Aeschylus, but they might've written fifty or more. And don't forget how much the Vikings liked sacking monasteries. Shoot, they were *full* of things like the Ardagh Chalice, but they just wanted 'em for the gold and precious stones."

"Don't forget the Spaniards in the New World, either," LaWanda broke in. "What was it? A room full of gold ornaments melted down to ransom the Inca, and they killed him anyway? And those incredible illuminated codices they burned in Mexico just 'cause they were pagan."

"Which is all very interesting," Myra sighed, looking at Aife intently. "But what, exactly, does it say?"

"I . . . *cannot* say," Aife replied sadly. "That is, something forbids me. I know the words when I see them, but they sink into my brain before I can comprehend them. Perhaps I might know them if I actually tried to command the Silver Tracks, but that I dare not do, not now, now here."

Alec gnawed his lip. "So you haven't learned anything we can actually *use*?"

Aife shrugged. "I have learned how to locate one of these Tracks when in another World, or at least how Colin did it while in Faerie, which this is not. And more importantly, I learned that to work them, Colin utilized a well that once occupied the top of this tower. Beyond that, I am not certain if I do *not* know, or if I read and can no longer recall.''

''Either might be the case,'' a harsh voice answered, the tones wild and fierce and feral. ''But what I would like to know is who, exactly, you are and what business it is that brings you here.''

Alec jumped half out of his skin, but before he could locate the source of that voice, Aikin identified it for him.

''Oh, my God!'' Aikin cried. ''It's a gryphon!''

Interlude IV:
Dish

*(near Clayton, Georgia—
Sunday, June 29—mid-afternoon)*

Faeries didn't make good houseguests, John Devlin decided wearily, as he pondered the piles of dirty dishes that had transformed his stainless steel sink into a collection of mini pagodas made of china by way of Wal-Mart. Oh, sure they (Nuada, rather, him being the only Faery presently present) were tidy in their own way, brilliant conversationalists, and not at all hard to look at (and he was *straight*, for God's sake). Still, when one was immortal quasi-royalty and not that far from godhood, one probably got accustomed to having servants around to attend things like cleaning. And to be fair, steel *was* steel, even when it was stainless; and chrome, such as ornamented his various faucets, was actually worse than ferrous metal as far as the Fair Folk were concerned, so he supposed that also conferred them some grace when it came to washing up. But could Silverhand maybe use the *same* glass more than once?

Or was he simply so fried he was being petty?

This *was* war, after all; it just didn't look like one—yet. And while that neat bunch of folks who were trying to run things (and doing a damned fine job of it, actually) acknowledged that, and a few of them had even managed to get themselves sufficiently bloodied to skin the romance off the concept right fast, he still wasn't convinced that the cold *reality* of the thing had sunk in.

He wondered, too, what part he ought to be playing. He

was mortal, the Mortal World was under attack, and he was nothing if not loyal to whatever causes honor demanded. A batch of these folks were on the ragged edge of being friends, too (and that didn't count Nuada), but the particulars of this were not his battle.

Except, dammit, if the incumbent regime in Faerie lived up to their threat and flooded *every* place Tir-Nan-Og overlaid this land—well, he might just find himself with beachfront property, or worse. The thing to do, then, was to afford what aid he could but volunteer nothing—and wait—

—Not long, apparently, because the kid in the wardroom was all of a sudden raising holy hell for him to get back there.

Sighing, John dismissed the dishes (perhaps Silverhand had a cleaning spell) and strode back to see what had got the kid's boxers in a wad.

One look at the flaring candles told him. An instant later, shotgun in hand and boy in far-too-eager tow, he was marching across what remained of his yard to where Nuada was busily engaged with someone (he hoped it was some*one* and not some*thing*) at the border.

He couldn't help but grin when he saw what three traditions worth of wards (his own, Calvin's, and Nuada's) had wrought: a sort of invisible cage that admitted certain beings with certain qualities for a certain distance but denied them retreat, while certain other Powers fenced . . . *whatever* in from either side.

This captive proved to be a woman: Faery, a Son (so to speak, and judging by the black-and-silver livery) of Ailill, and pissed as hell—as evidenced by the way she kept shapeshifting and yelling things the wards conveniently kept unheard.

Nuada seemed to be mightily amused, which put John on guard at once. Usually when Fair Folk got tickled, it meant their egos were acting up and they were getting cocky. His experience said to *never* underestimate an enemy.

"Caught one, did you?" he inquired more amiably than he felt when he came into hailing range.

Nuada shifted his gaze minutely and nodded. "I am uncertain, however, whether she is a spy or bait."

"Or a test," John appended, folding his arms and regarding the woman (who was growing black and orange scales) with a disapproving scowl. "Kamikaze, maybe? Sent to get as close as she could at whatever cost?"

"Aye," Nuada acknowledged. "Immortality makes for easy heroics."

"Wrote a poem about that once: 'Easy Heroes.' "

"I know. I read it."

John lifted a brow in genuine surprise, then peered at the woman. "Interrogation might be worthwhile. A hostage is a hostage."

Nuada shook his head. "Not when the hostage can build new bodies at will."

"What about iron?" Brock blurted out, wide-eyed.

Nuada shuddered, which shocked the hell out of John. "That *could* be done, but it is *not* done by the ethical; the same way your folk *could* torture criminals but do not."

John puffed his cheeks. "She could also be a plant. I'd verify anything she told me before I acted on it."

Nuada tweaked his scrying pendant. "Aye. And this, by the way, is something they do not have. Good for verification."

"For which we may all be grateful, though I bet they've got something just as good."

"I could strip her mind," Nuada mused, his words aimed at the woman as much as John. "Even so, I would have no proof it was *her* mind I stripped and not merely thoughts stored there in place of a mind already stripped by others. Do not forget that mind does not *have* to connect to body for us."

"Reckon we oughta hear what she's saying?"

"I already have," Nuada admitted. "Few of the Sons choose to speak with tongues, which they feel a mortal affectation, and the wards damp down her thoughts, so I doubt that you have sensed them. But rest assured I have 'heard' every taunt she has hurled at me, and some are quite remarkable." He grinned wickedly at the woman.

John had started to frame another query when his attention was drawn by a flare of light beyond the warding. Gold rolled through the pines there like a strip of filmy carpet, and light blazed at the point it drew nearest. He knew what it was too and, for all his experience, gasped, for he'd never seen a Track activated, not in his own World at any rate. Nor had this Track been there until that moment. Whoever commanded it had *moved* it there, which meant he was Powerful indeed.

Which proved to be the truth, for the glow grew strong enough to illuminate his whole place more brightly than the waning afternoon sun, and an instant later, Lugh Samildinach himself stepped off, clad only in a white leather breechclout and a fabulous cloak of feathers. He looked perfectly at home in the ensemble, as though it were no more remarkable than John's worn blue jeans.

A wave of Lugh's hand, and the woman collapsed with a whimper, regaining her own shape as she fell. "Best she not think for, oh, a thousand years," Lugh spat offhand. "My thanks to you, John Devlin," he added tersely, nodding absent acknowledgment to John and Brock. "Now, by your leave or without it, I must reclaim my friend and warlord, for I have a kingdom to regain." And with that, he marched straight through all three sets of wards to enfold Nuada in a hearty warriors' embrace.

Nuada merely nodded as the Faeries strode toward the cabin, ignoring their host completely. John caught a few words of their final conversation—a few of their more cogent thoughts, at any rate—and prominent among them were two word-images: a lichen-covered monolith and a spear that gleamed like the sun.

Perhaps, he concluded, it was time to do the dishes.

Chapter XV:
Power in the Land

(Galunlati—high summer)

Kirkwood O'Connor, anthropologist extraordinaire, had heard of Power Wheels, of course, and knew from endless all-nighters that his quirky cousin Cal had considerable hands-on with them; but he'd never seen one in operation, much less helped construct one in a cavern in another World. Still, he had a vested interest in such things; and so viewed the process as a learning experience, to use a term his profs had been too fond of tossing around back at the University of Georgia.

It wasn't that hard, actually, else dear old cuz wouldn't be whipping 'em up right and left. First thing: using pine-bough brooms, they smoothed the sand that covered the top of the stone terrace to which Uki had summoned him and Cal and Dave. That accomplished, they used the old string-and-peg method to define a circle maybe four yards across, which Uki then deepened with a flaked obsidian dagger. Crossbars followed, delineating the quarters, and likewise marked with Uki's knife. Then came the fine-tuning. Colored sand from stone jugs was poured into the markings, further differentiating them from the surrounding white. And finally, staves of stained or painted wood were set to mark the cardinal directions exactly as Cal had done to set wards back at John Devlin's place. All that accomplished, a small fire pit was dug in the center and filled with kindling. And then Uki called everyone but the Cougar Boys to retrieve their gear and join them.

Once asembled, they ranged themselves in a circle, with

Uki in the south and Cal, Dave, and himself occupying the remaining directions, using some obscure symbolism Kirkwood didn't recognize. The rest—Sandy, Liz, Fionchadd, and Okacha—filled the spaces between. And there they sat and waited, staring fixedly, a little nervously, at the unlit pyre in the center of the Wheel.

Until Uki clapped his hands and lightning flashed down to ignite that cone of kindling. It burned brightly—*too* brightly for normal flame—but at least Kirkwood didn't jump half out of his skin this time. As soon as the fire was burning steadily, Uki began to chant in what sounded like archaic Cherokee, of which Kirkwood could make out about five words. To his chagrin, Cal joined in (he'd have to drag the text out of the lad one day), and that chanting continued until Uki clapped his hands again, and it began to rain— *inside*: huge, slow, sloppy drops that soaked him through in seconds. The fire sputtered but didn't go out, though steam began to rise, so that pretty soon the entire area was as thick with the stuff as the inside of a sauna. At which point he recalled that one of the key tenets of Cherokee mojo was that *between* things had Power. And what was steam but a substance *between* water and air? Fog was, too, but while Cal could summon fog and had once done so to prove it, this in all likelihood had more esoteric significance. Grist for yet another all-nighter.

No, dammit! He was supposed to be keeping his mind blank and centering on his breathing. And had just found a rhythm that suited him when Uki clapped up another bolt of lightning and reality turned over.

It wasn't much fun, Kirkwood decided, this teleportation thing. But at least this iteration was nowise as ball-busting painful as the journey here had been. This was merely sick disorientation and a bubbly-prickly sensation from the inside out, with no external impression at all—

—and then warmth and light and more sand beneath his bottom. Whereupon Kirkwood exhaled a breath he didn't know he'd been holding and opened his eyes. And opened them wider still as he took stock of his surroundings.

Cal had told him about this place, but that hadn't prepared him for what was to all intents time travel. Shoot, this might as well be the ceremonial complex in one of the pre-Columbian chiefdoms, reconstructions of which he'd seen in places as diverse as Town Creek, North Carolina, and Moundville, Alabama. Certainly it had all the requisite features: four enormous earthen mounds maybe fifty yards to a side and half that high marking the quarters, each topped with a wattle-and-daub, thatch-roofed sanctuary approached by a flight of split-log steps; the whole mess centered on another Power Wheel, this one much more finely constructed than the one they'd left, and focused in turn on a fifteen-foot pole topped with what looked alarmingly like a cave bear's skull. Or at least something beside your basic *Ursus americanus*.

Too bad he didn't have time for a closer inspection, but Uki had arisen, and Cal and Dave were taking their cues from him and doing likewise, whereupon the rest of the company (all quite dry) followed suit. He yawned, stretched, and shook his head to clear it. Uki, to his relief, was grinning, having evidently worked through that snit that had possessed him earlier. There was a disquietingly expectant glint in his eyes, though, and he kept peering at first one sanctuary, then another.

Lightning again, from a cloudless blue sky. Three bolts stabbing down, striking the sanctuaries of the east, north, and west, respectively. The air went white.

Thunder followed, though Kirkwood only noted it subliminally, intent as he was on determining if he'd just had his eyeballs seared beyond redemption. Shapes reappeared, however: dim at first, like sun-bleached photographs, then clarifying. As it happened, he was following Uki's lead and looking east, and so was first to see the figure who strode from the temple there. Not unlike Uki, he was, in general size, build, and features, save that his skin was deep, rich red. "Asgaya Gigagei," Cal confided. "The Red Man of the East, Lord of Lightning."

Kirkwood didn't pause to watch the man join them, because a nudge from Cal had drawn his attention north, where another figure had appeared, near-twin to the others, save that his skin was the blue of deep, cold water. "Let me guess,"

Kirkwood whispered. "Asgaya Sakani, the Blue Man of the North."

"Catchin' on," Cal chuckled, by which time a fourth man was emerging from the dark, roiling smoke that shrouded the sanctuary to the west. This one needed no introduction, for it was Asgaya Gunnagei, the Black Man of the West, whom Kirkwood had encountered before, when Cal had journeyed to the fringe of the Black Man's realm to rescue a boy who didn't belong there. The same journey on which Cal had encountered Okacha, and he'd first met Dave, Liz, Brock, and other members of their odd confederation.

"Asgaya Unega," the Blue Man cried, addressing Uki by one of his alternate names as he stepped from the stair to level ground. "Why do you call us here?"

"Why indeed?" the Black Man echoed, his voice ominously hollow, like James Earl Jones in a cave.

"I assume it is important," the Red Man concluded, likewise drawing near. Whereupon Kirkwood realized to his distress that they were effectively surrounded. Still, Cal had dealt with these guys before, and though formidable, they were also fair-minded and would at least grant them a hearing.

Which raised the question of why Uki *had* summoned these obviously powerful dudes—his analogs in the other three quarters—and which of their own band would take the lead in pleading their case.

Cal solved that last by stepping forward, greeting each in turn (with David in reluctant tow, since he too had met these beings), and finally looking Uki straight in the eye and saying, "By your leave, adewehiyu, Yanu-degahnehiha is best suited to tell this tale. If anything is unclear, please ask, and one of us will try to answer."

Uki inclined his head, but raised a hand to halt David before he could speak. One at a time he surveyed the other Chiefs. "I have summoned you, kinsmen; nor do I do so lightly, though I myself know little of what we are about to hear. Still, weighty matters are afoot; matters that, though they primarily affect the Lying World and that place that lies beyond it, may nevertheless cast shadows here. Too, some of those here are friends. Hear them with open ears, open hearts, and open minds, as I shall hear them with mine." A pause, while he surveyed the environs. "I have lingered indoors enough today. This seems as good a place as any to speak of war and Power."

David raised a brow in wordless confirmation that it was indeed time to begin, then motioned them all to sit, though he himself remained standing. *"Siyu,"* he began formally. "I greet you, oh great Chieftains, in the name of myself and my friends, and in behest of many thousand thousand people you neither know nor have cause to love, who dwell in what you call the Lying World and in Tir-Nan-Og, in the greater realm of Faerie, which lies above it as does Galunlati, save on what I have heard described as the 'other side'." He paused for breath, then continued in a more relaxed manner. "Great Chiefs, some of what I have to say you probably know already and some you don't, but bear with me if you've heard some of this before . . ."

And so he continued, describing first the various realms of Faerie and how they related to his own World in space and time, then something of those realms' respective rulers, and finally of the complex situation in which they had found themselves embroiled.

There was a fair bit of discussion of the gating problem, and a certain amount of doubt concerning the vulnerability of Faery substance to iron, until Fionchadd bravely demonstrated by touching his palm with a blade from Kirkwood's Swiss Army knife. The seared, smoking flesh that ensued proved more than sufficient to dispel any doubts about iron's intrinsic threat, so that David was free to continue.

His second harangue was more difficult, and he was constantly interrupted—sometimes politely, sometimes not—by questions. The gist of his tale centered around the relationship between Bloody Bald and the mountain that lay atop it in Tir-Nan-Og that Lugh had made the literal heart of his realm, and how the plan by certain developers (a notion which *really* took some explaining) to place a resort there threatened to precipitate a war between the two Worlds, with dire results on both sides.

War, the Chiefs understood well enough, but the problem lay in clarifying how the folk of Faerie and Galunlati knew of the Lands of Men and what went on there, but few indeed in that Land knew of (or believed in) either Faerie or Galunlati, which fact would render aid from the political powers in the Lying World unlikely until it was too late.

Which brought him to the reason for their embassy: the possibility of having Tir-Nan-Og *moved*, as Galunlati had been, more than once. And, almost as an apologetic afterthought, the fact that David's father was very ill and that water from Atagahi might be useful.

All these arguments the Chiefs heard, but the one that drew their attention most forcefully was the loss of ancestral land. Kirkwood couldn't help but be amused by the irony of that: a purebred white boy explaining to the gods of a people his kinsmen had dispossessed how he *would* retain his ancestral soil or die. Eventually, however, Cal pointed out that while it was true David's kin were guilty of de facto genocide, his clan had likewise been dispossessed from Ireland two hundred years before, and from their central European homeland a millennium before that.

That sunk in. And as best Kirkwood could tell, the Chiefs were not overtly hostile, if not obviously sympathetic, to the notion of providing aid, especially when Cal pointed out that said assistance would reduce the likelihood of congress with the Lying World. Once the mortal rank and file learned of Faerie, David emphasized, it was no leap at all to wondering if other Worlds existed, of which the nearest, as far as anyone could tell, was Galunlati.

All in all, Kirkwood concluded, it was a damned well-stated delineation of the problem.

". . . and that's all I can think of," David finished wearily. And sat down.

Silence ensued, but eventually the Black Man spoke. "I know that Land," he rumbled. "And I know war. War has peopled my Land countless times and continues to do so, though not as once it did. Still, I think the wisest course would be to see for ourselves how affairs fall in these other Lands. Therefore, before we take further counsel I would urge that we spy out what happens there."

Uki nodded sagely; they all did: the other two Chiefs, and Cal and Dave as well.

Kirkwood badly wanted to ask how this particular scrying was to be accomplished; whether they'd retreat to Uki's pool, use an ulunsuti, which he was certain someone here had, or what. But before he could ask, the Red Man rose. "Wait here. I have means to achieve this seeing quickly." Without further comment, he strode up the steps to the sanctuary of the east, returning a moment later with a large wooden box carved all over with stylized bears. This he sat in his quarter of their circle, then opened. It contained masks: made of wood and carved with the faces of bears, the eye holes filled with transparent mica. "I made these the *last* time mortals troubled us, so that many might gaze into that World at once." There was one less than required, but Sandy volunteered to do without on the theory that she knew least about the intricacies of the situation. Kirkwood hesitated, then slipped one over his face, noting how surprisingly clear the mica lenses were.

The Red Man donned his as well, then reached into the chest once more and retrieved a pair of sticks, with which he smote the pole that bore the bear skull. "This pole," he explained, "has roots in more Lands than this, including a tenuous one in the Lands of Men, and a single tendril that touches that Land you call Faerie. What the pole touches, the skull, when awake, can see. This is not without danger, however, for the skull sometimes desires to be fed, and what it demands, it must get, else it will slay us all. *All*," he repeated for emphasis. "It is a gamble, you see, and a risk. Will you all dare it?"

"Aye," Cal said at once. "Sure," David responded as quickly. Liz seconded him, followed by Kirkwood, Fionchadd, and finally the various Chiefs, who had the most to lose.

"Very well," the Red Man affirmed. "I will wake the bear and we shall see what we shall see." And with that he began to chant in a tongue that was *not* the one Uki had spoken earlier, and while he chanted, he kept time by striking the pole with his staff. Kirkwood followed his progress for a time, aware that not only was the chanting damned hypnotic but that it was either getting late or the mask's mica lenses were darkening.

Darker and darker they grew, and then utterly black, then light again, but revealing a completely different vista than he'd seen before.

It was the rebels, and one or two seemed familiar: notably the red-haired man he'd assumed was Turinne and the two lads who'd guarded the old man—Oisin, or whoever. What was the story there? Something about a mortal man favored by the Sidhe and granted eternal youth in exchange for remaining in Faerie, lest all the age he'd escaped fall on him at once. Legend said that had happened; Dave and Cal vowed it had not, for they'd met Oisin, and it was clear from what they now witnessed that that most ancient of mortals still lived.

But not much longer, if what Fionchadd had hinted was true.

"Oh, shit," he heard David gasp, and looked closer.

The rebels had exchanged the palace for a wood: a thick, dark, eerie-looking place that would've given him serious heebie-jeebies back in his own World. The Sidhe seemed unconcerned, however, as did Oisin (who couldn't see anyway), but what had evidently elicited David's reaction was what lay at that party's feet.

If you could call something that was nothing *what*. For what lay there—gaped there—sprawled there—*opened* there, was simply a splash of *nothing*. "A Hole," Fionchadd muttered. "I do not like—"

He didn't finish, for with no more ceremony than an unheard word from the red-haired leader and an outstretched, thumbs-down hand, the guards thrust the old man to the very brink of the Hole. He balanced there an instant, spinning half around as though he might make a break for it. But it was only an effort at catching himself, and then he stepped back one step too far and fell.

Into nothing.

"Oh, God, no!" Liz shrieked. "Oh . . . goddamn, motherfuck, *damn* them!"

"Damned they may well be," Fionchadd groaned, sounding half in shock, "but Oisin is surely dead. Either the Hole consumed him itself or he touched the Lands of Men and succumbed to old age there."

"But . . ." David managed, sounding close to tears, "that shouldn't matter! I saw him in our World! I've *met* him there."

"Not exactly," Fionchadd countered. "Sometimes he only sent a shadow of himself. Others, he was careful not to let his bare feet touch the earth of your World. This time, he was barefoot, or did you not notice?"

"I'll kill 'em *all*!" David roared—and fell silent.

They watched until it became clear that the Sons had concluded their business at the Hole and were preparing to leave. "I think that says enough," Cal announced. "It reveals what the rebels fear, and it shows what they are willing to do in order to achieve their ends."

"Kill their enemies," the Black Man snorted nonchalantly. "People die."

"Aye," Uki replied. "It is what they are designed for. But places should not die."

"Would you see more?" the Red Man demanded. "The Ancient of Bears is tired."

"Enough," Liz agreed at once. "I'm not sure I needed to see that much."

"Enough," someone echoed, probably David.

"Enough, then," the Red Man finished. "You may remove your masks."

Kirkwood did, and spent the next minute taking deep, appreciative whiffs of air that didn't smell of wood smoke, cedar oil, and his own, none-too-fragrant breath.

The Red Man cleared his throat. "I knew that old man," he growled. "He journeyed here once. We exchanged gifts and names and tokens, though the name he gave me was not the one you spoke. I would have my vengeance upon these who worked his doom."

"Then you'll *help* us?" Dave blurted out, eager as a boy. Like the rest of them, he was running on empty and letting emotion drive. Which might be good or might not.

The Blue Man shook his head. "Moving Worlds is difficult, though we know that art from having wrought such a working before. But to move a World, one must enter an adjoining World, and that we can no longer do easily, and maybe not at all."

"And Tir-Nan-Og?" Sandy ventured.

"We could not go there. You all know the Rule: one cannot enter a World more than one World from one's own unless blood of that World runs in one's veins."

"Or what?" David challenged.

A shrug. "One might go mad. One might simply be pulled apart. One thing is certain: one would never be the same."

"Or simply never be," the Black Man concluded ominously.

"But you'll help?" David persisted. "I mean, I hate to put it this way, Great Chiefs, but we need a yes or no."

"I will help," the Red Man affirmed. "And there may be war in Walhala if any of my kinsmen here say me nay. But we cannot go to Tir-Nan-Og. We may not be able to enter the Lying World, and if we do, it will be only for a brief while."

"I enter it quite often," the Black Man countered. "I met more than one of these folks there."

"You had business, too," the Blue Man shot back.

"I expect to have more anon!"

Calvin eyed them narrowly. "So what've we figured out here? You guys—"

"We will come to your Land and do what we can," the Red Man snapped. "We must consult among ourselves to determine the best plan both for ourselves and for this place we have been given to protect. *That* is our prime concern. But yes, Utlunta-Dehi, we will come. *In our own good time*, we will come."

"To move Tir-Nan-Og?" David dared.

"To move *something*, if that is what must be," the Red Man retorted. "But be warned. The price of such a working will be very high indeed."

"H-how high?" Liz demanded. "I'd appreciate a straight answer, too."

The Red Man glared at her—likely because she was female and had spoken out of turn.

"Death," the Black Man said flatly, breaking the tension Kirkwood could already feel building. "There *may* be a death. Almost certainly there *will* be one. The working requires it."

"Whose death?" Cal asked carefully.

"The working itself will decide. Death will be of the Power's own need and choosing."

"People die," Liz muttered dully, staring into the air. Her face was calm, but her eyes were bright and her voice trembled.

"People die," David echoed. "Lands die too. But if it comes to that, I'm ready."

"David!" Liz choked. "I don't need this!"

"Nor do I! But think, Liz: we've met folks who've come back from the dead. We know that soul can survive the body. I know there's *something* afterward, or I wouldn't have been able to square things with David-the-Elder that time. And we know that trip was real because Alec lost the ulunsuti, and because the Morrigu . . . died."

"And hasn't returned!" Liz flared.

"*Yet!*" David gave back. "Jesus Christ, Liz, what do you—" He caught himself, flushed, and shook his head, gazing at Calvin for guidance.

"You must leave," the Red Man said flatly. "Do what you can, and we will come. Never doubt we will be watching."

"But," David began, "what about—"

He didn't finish, because the Red Man made a sign Kirkwood doubted anyone but him noticed, and the four Chiefs clapped their hands.

And all Kirkwood felt, knew, remembered, or *was* for a very long time was the long, slow, painfully empty pause between the lightning and the thunder.

Chapter XVI:
Talking to Gryphons

(Tir-Gat—high summer)

Aikin stared at the creature that had just ambled up the stairs of Colin's Tower and now sat calm as any cat at the top, conveniently blocking the only exit. It was an eyeful, too, and had his background in forestry not made him blasé about megafauna, he might well have acted on the urge he felt to bolt in the face of a creature roughly the size, shape, and color of a healthy African lion but covered in flexible, plush-furred plates; sporting the front claws of an eagle; and bearing—this was most troubling—a head that closely resembled the reconstructions he'd seen of the extinct killer bird *Titanus*.

"No wings," Alec breathed, beside him.

"Males don't have 'em," Myra hissed from the other side. "Watch when he moves."

Aikin hoped this guy *didn't* move for a while, not until he finished sorting information. Like how Myra knew so much. (Oh, right; she and LaWanda had once confronted one of these things.) Like why males didn't have wings. (No idea, though it made as much sense as a creature that was overtly mammalian *having* them. He didn't want to ponder the skeleton, though, never mind the muscle articulation.) And, most importantly, how this one could speak when they were supposed to be but semisentient, never mind how a beast with no lips could manage words that required them.

Or *had* it spoken? The Sidhe could talk mind-to-mind, though the ones he knew usually didn't around mortals. But it really had sounded—

The gryphon yawned hugely, revealing a blackish purple tongue more feline than avian. It blinked yellow eyes that would've suited either cat or raptor. And rose, to amble toward them. At which point he understood Myra's admonition, for every time it moved, light pulsed from the affected joints: soft flickers with more the aspect of flame or bioluminescence than electric light. Chemical reaction, perhaps, or static electricity between those plush-furred plates, and likely designed to attract mates, since it would make quite a show in the dark.

Aife cleared her throat angrily, set aside Colin's journal-cum-grimoire, and eased in front of Aikin, who stood nearest the beast. "I have heard," she observed carefully, "that your kind do not speak."

"I have heard," the gryphon gave back, "that the Sidhe do not consort with mortals, and certainly not at mortals' choosing, and that the guardian of this place was a man named Yd, not a woman whose name and lineage I do not know."

"Nor will you, until I know yours," Aife retorted. "Such knowledge can be dangerous."

"Maybe he's a shape-shifter," Alec muttered. "That'd explain how he can talk."

The gryphon cocked his feathered head. "I speak because of who I am."

"And we will speak of that anon," Aife assured him, hand resting lightly on her sword. "What I would know at present is whether you are friend or foe."

"That depends upon your business here."

"I was given to believe that this tower was abandoned and that anything that remained was free for the picking."

"It is under the sovereignty of Alberon of Alban," the gryphon replied. "Since it was mostly made of matter from that Land."

"Yet it is far and far from Alban."

"Far and far," the gryphon agreed.

Aife took a deep breath. "Our business is our own, until you give us cause to trust you. Suffice to say that upon our success hangs the fate of two Worlds much larger, older, and more populous than Tir-Gat."

"Faerie and the Lands of Men, perhaps?" the gryphon hinted, taking another step closer, then plopping down like a cat, but with his head upraised attentively.

"Perhaps."

"Fish and fowl," the gryphon murmured. "Unlike Tir-Gat, which is neither, being made up of bits of one thing and another."

"Moveable bits," Aife dared.

"Fish and fowl," the gryphon mused, as though he hadn't heard. "Or lion and eagle, and one more thing besides."

Aife raised a brow. "Would this other thing explain your speech and intellect?"

"Fish and fowl. Lion and eagle. Gryphon and man."

"You are a—" Aife began.

"Half-breed," the gryphon finished heavily. "My mother was a gryphon from birth. My father was Colin of Tir-Gat. He was lonely here, for he dared not reveal the existence of this place to others of his kind. Yet he *was* lonely. He had needs. He could shift shape. The rest you see before you."

"Did he know of you?" Aife shot back suspiciously. "I found no mention of you in his grimoire."

The gryphon shook his head. "My dam knew I was different and hid me, but I broke free. I was careful to attract no attention to myself. But Father loved gryphons and always had many around; whereas Lugh, so he said, merely kept enfields. Still, Mother hated Father for having given her a child she could not easily raise. And I hated him for making me neither man nor gryphon."

"With the best of both," Aife countered. "Strength, beauty, and intellect."

"With no one to spend it on. Oh, Yd and I spoke now and then, but he was as frustrated as I."

"How so?" Myra broke in, curiosity having gotten the better of her.

The gryphon regarded her levelly. "Look at this place and recall what you knew of Yd. He was a warrior, aye, but also a scholar. Then think: would a scholar leave this library untouched? All this knowledge unpilfered?"

"No," Aikin blurted. "He wouldn't."

"What does that tell you, then?"

Myra scowled. "That he either feared the knowledge here or couldn't access it."

The gryphon nodded. "Colin laid a ban on this place that no one of Faery blood could touch aught here without his consent. He did not consider that mortals would ever come here, and since such spells are very specific, that ban did not include them. And of course once a mortal touches something like Colin's grimoire, the spell on it disperses."

"There're other spells, though," Aikin grumbled, nursing a hand that was still sore from being shocked.

Silence.

"So what brings you here?" the gryphon asked eventually. "I saw Yd leave, and must assume he did so of his own free will; that as far as he is concerned you have freedom of this place."

"You watched us before you revealed yourself, didn't you?" LaWanda challenged before Aife could frame a reply.

"I did."

"Then you know already."

"I know you seek knowledge in Colin's grimoire. But even I have heard of Aife of Tir-Arvann. I know that she is a lady not unlearned."

"You know more than that, then," Aife snapped, hand returning to her sword. "Enough of this, beast! We converse while the fate of Worlds runs out. Either you will leave us to our work or contest with us. There are more of us than you, and we wield steel, and more than one form of it. You might kill some of us, but we would kill you in turn. Would you be the first of your kind to know the Death of Iron?"

"I would not be," the gryphon countered easily. "And in reply, I tell you this: my name is Deffon."

Aikin nodded mutely. The critter had given his name; therefore he was giving them power over him.

"Friend, then," Aife conceded.

"Let us rather say 'not foe.' "

"Sufficient for now. Now go or stay. We have work to do."

The gryphon coughed, cleared his throat, or whatever such beasts did. "There is more to this tale that I do not know than otherwise, if you would enlighten me—"

Myra looked at Aife, who looked at Alec, who looked in turn at Aikin, who looked at LaWanda. Nobody looked at Piper, who was quietly cleaning his pipes in an enormous, thronelike chair of greenish wood inset with mother-of-pearl and tigereye.

"You know the most," LaWanda said, glaring at Myra. "You do it."

Myra did.

"So you need to move Tir-Nan-Og?" Deffon mused when she had finished.

"Or the Lands of Men," Aife countered. "But Tir-Nan-Og, being smaller, would be the simpler task."

"Maybe not," Deffon gave back. "It may be smaller, but there is far more Power there than in the Mortal World. Such Power may be needed."

Aife shook her head. "Much of that Power maintains the land and feeds those who dwell there. And without the *rightful* king, such a working has no chance of success. Besides, anyone seeking to prepare for such a thing there would surely attract the attention of the Sons of Ailill, who would do all they could to forestall it."

"Even though it would aid their cause, should Tir-Nan-Og be moved?"

"Even so—now."

More silence. Aikin got a strong sense, however, that the gryphon was weighing options. Finally the creature spoke. "The secret of the Silver Tracks is indeed to be found within that volume, though I do not know where and believe that information to have been coded. I know this," he added, "because I watched in secret. I learned much, though Father did not suspect it. But there is one thing I must tell you now, for the longer you ponder it, the less likely you will be to act in error."

Aife eyed him warily. "And what might that be?"

Deffon rose and marched solemnly toward them, then sat back on his haunches, looking very heraldic. "The Silver Tracks require blood to manipulate. If mortals choose to attempt this, it will require a great deal indeed."

Aife's eyes narrowed. "Blood . . . or Power?"

"The Power in the blood. No more can I say, for more than this I do not know."

Aife studied the rest of her companions. "It occurs to me that now we have Colin's grimoire, our business here is finished. I can study it as easily in your World as this, and Nuada may also want to examine it. Perhaps he can make suggestions."

"Wish we knew what was going on back there," Alec grumbled, kicking at a clump of half-burned wood.

The gryphon perked up at that. "You do?"

Alec glared at him. "Wouldn't you?"

"Colin once owned a scrying stone with which he would sometimes study other Worlds, though he did so infrequently lest he be detected."

Alec raised a brow. "You know where this stone is?"

Deffon extending a gleaming talon toward where Piper sat. "In that chair."

Piper looked startled. "Here?"

"Not where thieves would look first," the gryphon chuckled, "yet easily accessible. You might want to check beneath."

Piper blanched, but put down his pipes. For a moment, he fumbled around under the chair. When he withdrew his hand, he held something fist-sized and milky-clear that flashed glassily in the eerie light. Aikin squinted at it, then got the shock of his life when he noticed that the object was bifurcated by a septum of ruby-red.

Alec noticed it too.

"Oh, my God!" they cried in unison, "that's an *ulunsuti*!"

"What—?" LaWanda began, but Myra drew her aside to explain, while Alec and Aikin rushed forward.

"What the fuck is one of *those* doing here?" Alec burst out.

Aikin snickered. "Thought you were well rid of that thing, McLean."

Alec rolled his eyes, though he consciously slowed his approach. "Sometimes you change your mind."

"You have to feed it—" Deffon began helpfully.

"I know, I know. The blood of a large animal, or it'll go

insane. Wonder how long since this one's been fed," Alec
added, peering meaningfully at the gryphon.

Piper looked as though he held either a skunk or a flaming
coal, and was all too eager to relinquish the object.

"Think we should?" Myra asked the company in general.

"Won't hurt," LaWanda acknowledged.

"What I want to know," Alec announced, having claimed
the object, "is what one is doing *here*."

Deffon shrugged. "Obviously Father either brought it here
or had it brought here by the Tracks."

Aikin's mouth popped open. "They can reach that far?"

"No reason not to," Deffon answered amiably. "And I
believe that he acquired it in his youth. He traveled much
before coming here."

"Never mind that," LaWanda snorted. "What can it show
us?"

"Whatever you want," Alec retorted, a little protectively.
"You have to prime it with blood—just a little will do—
and then—Actually, the best thing is to just sort of worry at
it." He eyed Aikin speculatively. "Probably ought to use
my blood, though."

"Allow me," the gryphon rasped, and before anyone
could stop him, the beast lashed out with one of those claws
and laid open the side of Alec's hand in the most delicately
finessed maneuver Aikin had ever seen, to have been executed so fast.

Alec blinked, then blanched as his blood oozed out along
a thin, sharp line. Fortunately, he rallied and raised the hand
above the ulunsuti, which he held in his lap, so that the blood
could drip upon it. "Best you not touch it with the wound
itself," he cautioned. "These things'll suck you dry if you're
not careful."

"So would the well Colin used to empower the Tracks,"
Deffon observed absently. "Alas, it exists no longer."

Alec glared at him, then at the rest of his companions.
"Well, folks," he muttered, "since this guy's been activated,
I reckon we oughta do something with it. So unless somebody's got a better idea, let's join hands and close our eyes
and . . . hang on. Just think about what's going on back

home. And hope. I mean, if that makes sense to you, Aife,"
he appended apologetically.

The Faery woman shrugged distantly as she joined their
circle, but was careful, Aikin noted, to sit next to Alec. Myra
claimed his other side, and Aikin took her hand, offering the
other to LaWanda, who grasped Piper, to bind themselves
into the traditional boy-girl circle that seemed to work so
well. A deep breath, and Aikin closed his eyes.

For a moment it was impossible to think, or rather, he was
thinking so hard *about* thinking that his thoughts had gone
to war. Too, there was the small matter of what had happened
the last time he'd used one of these things. It had shown him
the way to the Track in Athens, sure, but that had opened
another kettle of fish he'd still not consumed to the bottom.
When you got down to it, though, that one foray into Faerie,
born of jealousy as it had been, had been more trouble than
it was worth. Did he want to risk that again? Or would
maybe, finally—as Dave had long desired, and he was starting to agree—this whole mess of inter-World politics finally
end?

But how?

How, indeed?

A deep breath, and he opened his eyes, and stared at the
ulunsuti's blood-red septum.

Stared at first; but all at once it was as though the stone
stared back, then reached out some strange unfocused consciousness and grabbed him. For an instant, he was floating,
but then vision clarified, and he was high in the air, as though
in bird shape, and gazing down at the ocean.

It was a strange ocean, too, for its waters were oddly dark,
as was the sky; as though those waves leaped and frothed in
a place of perpetual twilight. Certain there was no visible
sun, and now he looked at it, that ocean seemed to go thin
in spots, as if it were a film of gauze stretched over a more
solid reality he could almost but not quite see. In other places
golden strips overlaid it, like ribbons of tenuous light.
Straight Tracks—and Pillars of Fire.

There were also places were the ocean simply *wasn't*,
which must be the Holes everyone was so concerned about:
places where their World had not only burned through Faerie
but through other Worlds besides.

And finally, so small he didn't note them at first, there were ships.

He wished a closer look, and got one. And stared, from no more than thirty yards up, upon at least a hundred vessels, very like Fionchadd's or those that had pursued them earlier, each with a black sail bearing a crimson eagle. And each crammed to the gunwales with Faery warriors.

A gasp, a blink, and *more* ships! Another fleet as large as the first, but with a different device upon its golden sails, this one more complex than the others he had seen. He squinted. Had it! A scarlet anvil surrounded by a ring of white skulls.

A third gasp—not his own this time—and whatever Power had commanded him let go, and he looked once more on red and milky-clear. Tears stung his eyes, and when he could see clearly again, Aife's face was grim as death.

"I pray that we look on *now*," she whispered, "and not on the past, for I dare not hope for the future."

"What . . . ?" Alec asked, peering at her anxiously. Aikin hoped they'd all had the same vision. Otherwise—well, if they'd all seen different things, they might be in even deeper trouble than they were already.

"Two fleets," Aife said tersely. "*Two* fleets," she repeated. "One bore the arms of Finvarra of Erenn. The other the sigil of Arawn of Annwyn. Both smell an empty throne. Both, I am certain, sail this way."

The gryphon, who'd taken no part in their impromptu séance, rose and padded over to join them. "War indeed," he mused in a low, thoughtful voice full of regret. "I did not share your visioning, yet I could not help gazing at the stone. I saw many endings and some beginnings. More to the point, I saw important things. Things worth saving and things worth changing. Therefore, if you have need of me, sound the horn you will find in that cupboard there, and I will come."

All eyes swiveled toward the single cupboard that yet retained its doors, but Aikin was first to leap to his feet. "No," he warned when Alec made to follow. "Everyone else has done something worthwhile here; I've been like tits on a bull. This is mine. Not my horn," he added, "my responsibility."

"Go to it," Alec sighed, likewise rising. "I've gotta find

something to store this in." He flourished the ulunsuti. "Ceramic jars are nice," he added hopefully.

Aikin left him to it, made his way to the cupboard in question, twisted the latch (in the shape of a leering demon's head), and opened it. The horn was the first thing he saw: as long as his arm and gently curved, like a hunting horn. He started to reach for it, then hesitated, squinting at it uncertainly. What was it made of, anyway? Ivory, maybe. Or bone. Except that it was red, and he didn't think it was dyed, stained, or painted. It was carved, too: four separate bands of marching gryphons, interspersed with delicate interlace. And there were ties attached to it: cords of crimson silk ending in matching tassels.

Steeling himself, for he recalled Deffon's reference to protections, he reached out gingerly and touched it. Nothing happened. Another breath, and he took it in his hand. "Hail to you, Aikin Daniels," Deffon said quietly, at his side, though he hadn't heard the beast approach. "Hail to you, Mighty Hunter: for this time and place, and the times that come after, the Lord of the Gryphons."

It took a moment for those words to register. Then: "What? *Me?*"

The gryphon nodded sagely. "Colin used that to summon us so he could then enslave us. Yet a threat to your World is a threat to ours, and in this World, at least, we are free. Only a mortal or one of Faery kind can wield that horn, but by your kind alone may it be destroyed. Think of that when such seems good to you."

"Thanks," Aikin replied solemnly, gazing into the beast's vast sad eyes. "I will."

"Hey, Aik!" Alec called. "Get your butt over here. Women folk say it's time to travel."

"Thanks," Aikin whispered again, then turned to retrieve his shotgun. Aife had a firm hand on Colin's grimoire. Piper was already tuning up his pipes.

"Until—" the gryphon whispered in turn, and in three swift bounds had vanished down the stair.

"Until . . ." Aikin murmured back, one hand on his sawed-off shotgun, the other on a Faery-wrought hunting horn.

Interlude V:
Time and Tide

I

(Sullivan Cove, Georgia—
Sunday, June 29—early evening)

Scott Gresham, who alone of the shaky fellowship bent on saving Sullivan Cove had actually *remained* there, kicked a discarded beer can and wished it were Ralph Mims's head. Not that total decapitation of Mims and his cronies would do much good now, nor dismemberment and displaying the quarters at the mountain passes by which the tourists the assholes hoped to attract found their way here. *That* wouldn't help at all, not with the on-site office all but installed, the backhoe primed to start excavating, and bulldozers on the way. Mystic had a foreman now; there'd be a dozen men on-site tomorrow, a dozen more two days later. Too many to stop single-handed, too many prying eyes. Never mind the matched set of rent-a-cops that'd be staking out the place from here on.

Only magic could save the Cove now—or divine intervention. He hoped David and his clan would forgive him for failing to stall these guys. For that matter, he hoped he'd forgive himself. Maybe it was time to take the considerable stash of ill-gotten gains he'd already accumulated and hit the high road for Alaska. Presuming there were no Faeries there. Or other troublesome realms.

Sighing, he kicked the can again and tried to go through the motions of being busy, which meant marching smartly, measuring, and looking intense while jotting down random figures in a notebook.

God, what a waste this was! To despoil such a lovely place! He felt like a goddam rapist.

"Yo, Scott!" someone called amiably from the huddle of men crowded around the front of the office. "Get your ass over here, boy!"

Scott was tempted to ignore them. Mystic's hired hands weren't bad lads (the ones he'd met, anyway), nor was Mims intrinsically evil. But he wanted no part of them. He was just flat out tired of faking.

"Scott! C'mon! You don't want to miss this!"

"I'm on it!" Scott yelled back, because he had no choice. But he took his own time ambling down the rise on which he'd pitched his tent back before Cal and LaWanda's home-made deluge had flooded it, and into what remained of the broomsedged acre that marked both the terminus of the Sullivan Cove road and ground zero for Mystic Mountain Properties' unstoppable resort.

A pause to check the sky (it was getting on toward sunset, which meant Mystic was paying double weekend overtime for folks to be out this late), and Scott joined the rest of the crew. It was nearly an even split: half in khaki work togs, half in expensive suits; but every pair of shoes, wingtips and hobnails alike, was caked to the ankles with mud. Which made Scott grin.

"'Bout time," Mims snorted as Scott panted up beside him.

"What's the deal?" Scott inquired with calculated nonchalance.

Mims pointed to a small folding table on which rested a shiny new iron spike marked with bright red paint. An equally pristine sledgehammer lay beside it. The man was all but glowing. "Well, Scott, my boy; I can't tell you why, but I just had this hunch it'd be lucky if we drove the first spike on Sunday night. You know, so we can hit the ground running tomorrow."

"I . . . see," Scott managed, feeling as though someone had kicked him in the gut.

"Yep," Mims went on enthusiastically. "Figured I'd drive that sucker in right at sundown."

"Right," Scott said again, staring west, where the sun sat

right atop the mountains. But the mountain he saw was much closer, and the sheer quartz cliffs atop it glowed red as burning blood.

II

(Clayton, Georgia—
Sunday, June 29—near sunset)

JoAnne Sullivan smoothed no-longer-so-Little Billy's white-blond hair for the thousandth time that day and wondered for the ten-thousandth what in the world was going on with her husband, who'd been recovering just fine when she and Dale and the boy had arrived last night, but now seemed to be going steadily downhill.

The waiting room at Rabun Regional was deserted save her clan. The rest—two old men, one old woman, and a teenage girl with a baby she looked too young to have—had departed just after seven, likely in quest of dinner. As for Bill—her husband had been whisked away half an hour ago for another round of tomfool tests.

Tomfool because she knew what was wrong with him: something insidious that had entered his body with that stick of wood and now gnawed away at him, invisible to mortal detection. "Shit!" she spat abruptly, fumbling in her purse for a cigarette.

Little Billy glared at her. "Wish you wouldn't smoke."

She glared right back. "Gotta do *something* when things get like this. Can't drink, don't feel like eatin', too wired to sleep."

Dale put down the outdated issue of *Southern Living* he'd allegedly been reading since noon and ambled over to join her. If he was tired, he didn't look it. If he was worried (as was likely), he was keeping it to himself. If he had anything to say, he'd already said it: "Don't worry." "He'll be okay." "If they can't fix 'im here, we'll find somebody who can."

She didn't know if she could stand to hear those things again.

"Goin' for a burger," Dale muttered instead, looking at Little Billy. "Anybody wants to tag along can."

JoAnne almost accepted his invitation. "Better not," she sighed. "No tellin' when they'll bring Bill back. I promised that Devlin man I'd call as soon as I knew anything, even if it was nothin'." A pause, as her eyes misted and she almost broke down. "God, Dale," she choked into her hand. "I wish David was here! I wish this hadn't happened. I wish . . . I wish poor Bill was *well*!"

"We all do," Dale murmured, patting her arm, then giving her a fierce, hard hug. "Some things are bigger'n we are, though."

"Right," Little Billy agreed. "I—" He broke off, cocked his head as if listening to something outside.

"What?" JoAnne prompted. "What is it?"

Little Billy shrugged and managed a very forced smile. "Nothin'—not really. I just thought I heard a woman cryin'."

Dale's face went pale as the bone-white walls.

JoAnne could only look at her menfolks and shudder.

III

(Tir-Nan-Og—high summer)

Turinne mac Angus mac Offai stared first at the spreading bloodstain that ensanguined the pearl-white marble floor, then at the headless corpse of the latest of Lugh's former guard to be ferreted out and dispatched (he thought this one's name was Froech), and finally at the gridwork of iron that caged Lugh's throne, there on the dais in the audience hall at the heart of Tir-Nan-Og. "Careful, lads," he cautioned. "There may be more, but they will think twice before they waste their lives, now that they know they face the Death of Iron."

"Aye, Lord," Ciarran, his warlord-to-be, acknowledged; watching with absent, smug interest as Turinne flung a pouch of gold (the real stuff, not the usual englamoured surrogate) to his human executioner, who was even now wiping his steel-bladed sword on his ill-fitting livery. The man grinned wickedly and stared at Turinne's throat, as though he'd cheerfully add it to the considerable tally he'd already amassed that day, in the Sons' final sweep of the palace before freeing Lugh's throne from its iron tomb. They'd use mortals for that, of course, and then get rid of them. Unless Lugh showed up, or Silverhand, or other of the deposed Ard Rhi's clan, household, and kin.

But since Lugh was *dead*, as far as any seer they had could determine—well, there was no longer any point in waiting until Lughnasadh to bind Turinne to the Land in truth. He would be king—a good one, he hoped—and Tir-Nan-Og would prosper, as she had not since the World Walls (he'd tend to them first) had begun to fade and wear and rupture.

Oh, iron would still be a factor, but there'd be no *more* iron, because the Mortal Lands that so disrupted Tir-Nan-Og would all be underwater, and eventually the Land would heal. And after a longer space of years (though not so long to one who was immortal), the iron already present would rust away, there in its watery grave.

And then—

Turinne froze—they all did, everyone in that whole vast chamber, down to the brain-numb mortals.

It was a sound, yet not a sound. A thrum, like a harp string snapped, but not the thrum the Tracks made when unsourced Power pulsed along them. Yet he heard it: like a gong, like a chime, like a bell; so high and clear and pure he almost *didn't* hear it, but with roots that reached straight to the roots of the mountain.

Indeed, Turinne realized, it *was* the mountain. The rock itself was ringing. Shuddering, rather, as though something tiny but infinitely sharp had pierced it to the root and set every atom in the whole stone pile to shaking.

Which could only mean one thing.

"The gauntlet has been thrown," he told Ciarran. "That which we have awaited has occurred in the Lands of Men. War, my friends, has awakened."

PART THREE

Scott Gresham's Journal

(Sunday, June 29—late afternoon)

Well, fuck. I shouldn't even bother doing this, but Dale's gone, and Elyyoth's a nice enough guy, but he can't really relate to this stuff—probably because he's trying to relate to all the stuff in the Sullivans' house, most of which has some iron content, so he's probably, at some level, freaked all the time.

Only I seem to have got used to ranting on this thing, so stay tuned, boys and girls, for Scotto's latest self-indulgent tirade.

The shit, as it were, has hit the famous fan. I knew it was coming, but it just didn't seem real. Actually, a lot of this doesn't seem real, and I'm not just talking about the obvious stuff. No, it's like this is all stuff we're fighting really hard, but the folks from Mystic Mountain may want it just as bad, and I have to try to see their side, too: that maybe some resort like this is something Ralph Mims has wanted all his life. Maybe it's something he doodled designs for in the margins of his high school notebooks. Maybe he's mortgaged everything he's got so he can throw money at me like it was Mardi Gras beads or something. Maybe he's got a wife who's just the neatest person in the world and a kid who'd be my best friend if I met him, and here I'm trying to completely ruin him forever. I mean, the Faerie thing makes sense, too, in a Medieval History 101 kind of way, but . . .

Fuck, I've got away from myself, and I've just realized that if I'd spent as much time dissertating as I have working out my angst on this fucking computer, I'd have the fucker done by now. But anyway, back to where I was trying to be:

this doesn't seem real. All that stuff I bragged to Devlin about, that me and Dale did. I was proud of it, but I wasn't the guy whose expensive car wouldn't start, or the mechanic who'll have to figure out how to fix it, or the perfectly innocent person on some production line somewhere who decided to make that one fuel pump the best fuel pump he'd ever made just to see if he could, and I went and fucked it up. It was real to him then. The sugar was a game.

Fucking up all that computer gear was a game to me, but the stuff that got wasted might well have been pretty damned real. And now they've driven that spike, and that wasn't real either, only I've gotta feeling it's gonna be, 'cause the air already feels like rain.

I think I'm gonna go hang out with Elyyoth some more and see what he thinks is real these days. Like people maybe. Like ants are real to us. Fuck, it's raining!

Chapter XVII:
Return to Sender

*(near Clayton, Georgia—
Sunday, June 29—sunset)*

... heat ...
    ... light ...
    ... pain ...
    ... heat ... light ... pain ...
    ... heatlightpain ...
    ... heatlight ...

Light ... that was not that which suffused Galunlati: softer, less stark, less focused. Or maybe merely less clear.

Heat that was quickly fading.

Pain that was not the impossible agony that had characterized their journey to Uki's Land. More a soreness, really; as though Liz's cells were simply tired of being manhandled.

She blinked and saw nothing. Blinked again and saw rough-clad mountains and sunset sky, and thought briefly that those thunderbolts the Four Chiefs had zapped them with had deposited them elsewhere in Galunlati. The landscape was the same, as was the painted stick she'd been gazing at prior to departure. Except that one had been blue, hadn't it? And this was red.

Another blink and everything lined up, and she was sitting cross-legged in a ragged circle of friends, holding David's hand in a viselike grip while gaping at Sandy beside that stick.

"Devlin's," Calvin breathed. "We're back at John's!"

"Thank God for small favors," Sandy sighed, rising. Liz

twisted around as she joined her, so that she finally saw the house. They'd arrived in the backyard, with her facing the mountains, so no wonder she'd been confused. All at once she was shaking, reaching around to lock David in a hug she would've gladly continued forever. He hugged back, obviously as relieved as she. Or as scared, given what they'd learned in Galunlati: that matters were coming to a head in Tir-Nan-Og; that the Chiefs *would* help them, but in their own time; that it would require a death—

"Helluva way to travel," Kirkwood gasped, least jaded of their band.

"Helluva way to arrive, too," John Devlin drawled, stepping out the kitchen door with a wide-eyed Brock in tow. "You folks sure know how to make an entrance."

"Gotta make an exit, too," David snapped. "Shit's about to hit the fan, but it's facing Sullivan Cove, not here."

"Just as well," Devlin conceded. "I'd appreciate a briefing. 'Spect you wanta use the phone first, though."

David was already striding toward the back steps, leaving the others to fend for themselves. Liz joined him, angry at being excluded (Enotah was her county, too, and it wasn't like she was powerless herself), yet eager to learn as much as possible in her own right. Sometimes David took too much on himself, and unfortunately he was too much his father's son to admit he was in over his head. And damn those stereotypes, too!

"Got food," Devlin offered.

"Beer'd be good," Kirkwood laughed. "And we've got *plenty* of food for thought."

"Catch you in a sec," David told his host as he marched up the hall toward the living room in quest of the phone he'd last seen there. "Uh . . ." he ventured a moment later, through a frown, "where's Silverhand?"

"Gone," Devlin informed him tersely. "Lugh showed up in pre-Columbian drag, said he had a kingdom to reclaim and something about a spear, and the two of 'em hopped on a Track Lugh'd diverted here, and . . . zap."

The frown deepened. "When was this?"

"You folks hadn't been gone long. I take it you succeeded?"

"Well, we *may* have help with the big stuff," David sighed. "But I blew it on the healing water, 'cause there was bigger stuff goin' on. But if a bunch of guys with spiffy paint jobs show up, for God's sake let 'em in."

"*God's* being the operative word," Calvin chuckled, having joined them unnoticed.

"Phone," David prompted. "Sorry, but I gotta check on the folks and then the Athens crowd." Devlin passed him a portable without comment, which David accepted with a muttered thanks. "Feel free to brief John," he added to Calvin. "I got a couple of other things to do. Sorry to take over," he apologized again. "But . . . well, you know."

Devlin shrugged and sauntered back to join the group congregating in his tiny kitchen. Liz could smell coffee brewing, and someone had cranked up the microwave. Her stomach rumbled; they never had got to eat in Galunlati, and she was torn between bodily needs and supporting her lover. All things considered, Dave was doing a decent job keeping his cool over his dad; better than she'd have done if it'd been her mom or dad, if the truth were known. Or maybe it was like he'd said: once you had proof death wasn't the end, it didn't pay to fret over one individual life, even if it was your own.

"Sorry," David told her absently as he punched in seven digits, which meant it wasn't long distance, which meant the hospital. "Two days from now this'll be . . . well, let's just hope . . ."

A pause. Then: "Is JoAnne Sullivan around?" Another pause, while David fidgeted and shifted the receiver to his other ear. "Okay, I'll wait."

Liz decided not to. Dave was funny about doing personal family stuff around folks, even those he'd known a long time. She spared him a brief, wistful kiss and wandered out to the porch, wondering why she felt so safe here, when the place had been all but besieged the previous night, and discovering how great it felt to be *alone*. How long had it been, anyway, since this latest chaos had begun? Christ, her folks were probably about to have cabbages, though silence was surely the best policy for now. Or maybe telling them that

David's dad had been injured and they were giving him moral support, which was true.

All at once she was bone tired. Without thinking about it, she sank down in Devlin's porch swing. The chains creaked: a homey sound. The boards were hard, but it was a comfortable hardness. The air smelled of coffee and some of those herbs drying on the wall. The sky was shifting from purple to black, and the surrounding trees were wrapping their trunks in shadows. It was a magic time. A *between* time, yet there was nothing arcane about it. No matter what happened to Tir-Nan-Og, there'd still be magic in the world.

Lord, it was nice out here! So relaxing . . . Her eyelids drifted down. Before she knew it, she was asleep.

Not so deeply, however, that she didn't rouse abruptly when David thumped down beside her. The chains squeaked irritably. It was marginally darker, but not much, so he evidently hadn't talked very long. There were bags under his eyes, she realized, and the first trace of creases bracketing his mouth. "What's new?" she yawned.

David shook his head, then buried his face in his hands, not crying, just weary. "Pa's—He got better and then got worse, and nobody can find out what's wrong, but Ma thinks it's something Faery in the wound keeping it from healing. Something to do with blood not clotting. They keep having to transfuse him. It's a slow seepage, but steady. Coagulants don't work, and surgery would require more cutting, which would defeat the purpose. They may send him to Gainesville."

"Why don't they?"

"I'm not sure I should tell you."

"David!"

"I know, I know. It's just—dammit, it'll remind me of stuff again and . . . and make it real! But—oh, hell, Liz, it's like this: Dale and Billy have heard something wailing."

Liz felt her heart grow cold; a shiver that was not born of the cool evening wind danced across her body. "Wailing," she echoed, because she had to say something, and that was the only safe reply. Then: "Like the other time we heard wailing?"

David nodded. "I think so."

"We dealt with that, though, didn't we?"

A tired shrug, a halfhearted smile. "Reckon so."

"Nice sunset, anyway. Just in case you'd like something *good* to appreciate."

"Thanks." He slapped her thigh, as though she were one of his buddies. "You have no idea how much I'd love to just sit out here and vege, but I can't. Gotta go check on the folks in Athens."

"Don't bother," came a voice from the front door as Sandy backed through the screen. Coffee steamed in each hand, in matching stoneware mugs. She handed one to Liz and one to David. Liz inhaled gratefully, but David had fixed Sandy with a worried stare, his lips a thin, taut line. "What gives?"

"What gives is that I took it upon myself to preempt you, and the short form is *no go*. I tried your place, Dave; and Liz's; and Myra's. Nobody home, but I left messages on the off chance they decide to check down there before they come back here. The main thing is that they know which *here* to come to. We hadn't exactly decided, but best I can tell, ground zero's gonna be your home turf."

David stared at his coffee, slowly took a sip, then nodded. "Sounds like it."

"Did you expect anything else? I mean, really?"

"I guess I never stopped hopin'."

"Don't," Sandy advised, picking absently at a patch of dried ointment on her shirt. "Stop hoping, I mean. Seat-of-the-pants luck's seen us through before. Shoot, I could be dying of a snakebit tit by now."

"Luck's not infinite, though," David gave back. "Still, they've got sense enough to call here, assumin' they get back. John can reroute 'em."

"Sounds like a plan," Liz agreed, tasting her coffee and finding it finally cool enough to drink.

David twisted around to look back inside. "Gettin' dark," he observed. "I'm assumin' that nobody's expectin' anything to happen over here, what with Lugh and Silverhand gone. Somebody'd be freakin' otherwise."

"Finno says probably not," Sandy acknowledged. "Said that if Lugh rounded up Nuada, they'd likely head straight for Tir-Nan-Og. He thinks Lugh's got some secret way to contact his guard even Silverhand doesn't know about. He'll hit the ground running and issue a call.''

"Leaving us to do the shitwork," Liz grumbled.

"Leaving us to save his ass in a more permanent way if we can," David countered. "I mean, we've pretty much decided to move his country for him. Who knows if that'll work, though, or if there'll be repercussions, or if the place'll even survive."

"Silverhand knew," Liz reminded him. "He'd have stopped us if it looked too risky or thought Lugh wouldn't agree."

"Unless he's got his own agenda," Sandy cautioned. "I'm not sure I trust any of these dudes when it comes down to it. Immortality—Power—makes you cold. Makes you jaded. Even Finno's like that, and he's the best of the lot."

"Silver's not a bad egg," Devlin noted from the door. "Granted, I know him more as a poet than a warrior, and the things we've talked about have been more philosophy than fact, since I figure it doesn't do to know too much about some things. Whoever said 'Ignorance is bliss' wasn't lyin'."

"No," David agreed grimly, "he wasn't."

The phone rang. Devlin grimaced and slipped back into the house. David looked at Myra. "So Finno thinks Lugh's gonna round up his guard? What about the spear? Did he say anything about that? Like *which* spear?"

"I hope it's not *that* spear," Liz breathed, then noted Sandy's blank look. "Sorry, I forget who knows what. But the deal is that Lugh's got a spear that harnesses the power of the sun. Last time he used it, it—"

"*Moved* the sun!" David gulped. "Not ours, but the sun in Galunlati! Oh, jeeze! I'd forgot about that, since I never really saw it in use. I don't know what that means in terms of all this other crap."

"It means the Chiefs of the Quarters won't take it kindly if it happens again," Liz said flatly. "They didn't look like they'd put up with much if you got 'em riled. I—"

"David: phone," Devlin broke in from the door. He passed it out, via Sandy.

"Hello?" David began tentatively.

Liz was sitting close enough to hear someone hello back: Scott, if she wasn't mistaken. He sounded excited. David found a button that let everyone hear. "Scott? What's the deal?"

"I'd hold out for another hand, is what I'd do," Scott snorted. "Better yet, I'd fold. But I didn't call to play word games. I guess you'd better brace yourself. It's, uh—well, it's happened. Nothing yesterday, then bang-thud-swoosh: a zillion tons of stuff gets trucked in this afternoon and the place is covered up with folks. Seems they're gonna start on the onshore stuff, which they'd already designed and backed up some time ago, and work on that while I—supposedly— start surveyin' Bloody Bald. But that's not why I called—" He broke off, as though he truly didn't want to continue.

"Lay it on us, Scott. Like you said: we don't have time for games."

A deep breath. "Okay, then: they've driven the spike, Dave. Symbolic, kind of, and on shore, not on the mountain, but it *was* an iron spike. They drove it right at sunset and—I dunno, it was weird, and I think I must've been the only one who noticed it, but soon as that sucker sank in, it was like . . . like the whole goddamn Cove rang. Sounded like glass, but deep as infrasound at the same time. You've heard of the music of the spheres; this was the tolling of the earth."

"Shit!" David groaned—nor was he alone in expressing that sentiment.

"What I said," Scott agreed. "Bad thing was I had to be there to watch it and fake approval. Worse thing is that it's gettin' dark over here. Remember what they said? That as soon as iron bit the mountain, they were gonna flood?"

"One of the variations," David acknowledged.

"Whatever. You better get over here though, 'cause I think it's about to begin."

"On our way," David assured him. "We succeeded, by the way—maybe. No word from the others, though."

"Not here, either."

"Hang in there, then. Oh, wait! What about Elyyoth? He have anything to say? What's he doin', anyway? I'd kinda forgot about him."

Liz could practically hear Scott shrug. "Your folks left

him in charge when they split for Clayton. I've seen him once since then, and he was just pacin', frettin', and bitchin' about honor requirin' he be two places at once. I haven't told him the latest.''

"He'll know anyway," David assured him. "If you heard the Land ring, he did too. In fact, if I was you, I'd stick to him like glue. He might be your only hope."

"So, you guys comin' over?"

"Quick as we can."

"I'll be waitin'."

"Bye." David turned off the phone and handed it to the grim-faced Devlin. His face was even grimmer as he rose, including them all in his stare. "Better be movin', folks; it's that time." And with that, he started for the door.

Devlin caught him before he could enter and drew him aside. Liz lingered with him; no way she was letting him out of her sight now. "You need me to come?" Devlin murmured. "It's your call."

David shook his head. "Can't think why. You've helped more than you'll ever know, but this is our fight, and you've got your own turf to protect. You could still have company tonight."

Devlin gnawed his lip, then nodded. "You need me, you got more ways than one to give a holler. I can be there in a hour, and that's by normal means."

"Thanks," David replied. "And I mean that."

"No problem," Devlin said, and slipped back inside, leaving Liz alone with David on the porch. "Well," David told the twilight silence. "Here we go."

Five minutes later they were traveling, three in Kirkwood's T-bird, four in Sandy's Explorer. Clouds were darkening in the west. The first raindrops caught them as they crossed the Enotah County line. The radio was playing "When the Levee Breaks."

Liz turned it off and tried not to think about dying.

Interlude VI:
Moves

I

(Tir-Nan-Og—high summer)

A *word*, and the menhir snapped closed, looking no different than the thousand other rough-hewn megaliths that warted the Plain of Lost Stars, east of Lugh's citadel. Which is to say it was roughly thrice his height, as wide as his out-stretched arms, and patched with lichen and moss that had overgrown what might've been petroglyphs older than the Sidhe's tenure in the land. Grass waved around it, knee-high on Lugh and Nuada and the thirty other warriors who had come, by wind, steed, and water, in beast shape and their own, to join their rightful king in his drive to retake his throne. The Sons of Ailill had numbers, for now, having staged their coup when Lugh's court was abroad. But Lugh had Power and experience, and now he was free of the taint of iron, he had anger besides, which was stronger by far than youthful bravado.

He also had the spear. The Spear of Lugh, it was called, which was name enough. Goibniu had wrought it in Gorias before Lugh was born, in response to a dream he'd had. Lugh had retrieved it from hiding now, in the place he alone had known. Even in the waning light, it glittered when he flourished it aloft, flinging sparks of light about as though it gloried in once more drinking down the might of the westering sun. His cloak glittered, too: the cloak of feathers he'd

279

brought with him (perhaps wrongly, but it had seemed a gift) out of Galunlati.

Otherwise, he was clad as a man of war. Silver mail sheathed him from neck to heel, close as any fabric and pliant, almost, as the pure white silk he wore beneath, tight as a second skin. Over it was a white velvet surcoat charged with his arms: *a sun in splendor, Or.* This *particular* sun was mildly englamoured, too; for the rays whirled and twisted as he moved.

He wore no helm, however; let the Sons of Ailill know who came against them. Nor did he carry any shield. He had his warlord. He had a tenth part of his guard, but the most loyal and hardy tithe. And, again, he had his anger.

A final pause to flourish the spear, feeling already how the sun fed it Power, which Power likewise replenished Lugh's own, and he lowered it with a hiss like the air itself parting in its wake. The grass likewise hissed, whipped by a rising wind from the west that carried a hint of Power misapplied in a way Lugh didn't like but understood.

"Lord," Nuada began, likewise rearmed and rearmored from the High King's secret stores. "Lord," Nuada repeated. "There is trouble in the air, and in more Worlds than this, if I guess right."

"You do," Lugh assured him. "The Land sings beneath my feet, as it will not for Turinne. But it just cried out as well. Wounded it was, like a thorn or bee sting, yet it was pain. But," he added with a grin that bent his mustache into sickles, "it soon shall ache no longer."

And with that he mounted the white horse that had met him in the Vale of Dreaming Women; stared for a long moment at the warriors ranked around him, young, fair, and loyal, and doomed to face iron at his command; and then at his warlord and best friend, gold-clad at his side. "Now!" he cried, and set spurs to the white stallion's flanks, and turned toward the twelve-towered palace sparkling on the horizon. The wind was against them as they rode, but they were stronger than the wind.

II

(the Seas Between—high summer)

There was water beneath Arawn of Annwyn's flagship, but there was also air, for it was a ship of Powersmith make and could sail on seas or above them. Tracks it preferred but did not require, here in the Lands of the Sidhe. Oars it likewise had, but they were for show more than anything, as was the sail, which billowed regardless of wind, so that all could gaze on the sigil blazoned there—*Or, an anvil gules, within twelve human skulls in annulo, argent*—and know that Arawn had come calling.

He wondered what reception he would find here, on the shores of Tir-Nan-Og. No one had challenged him—yet—as would certainly have been the case had Lugh still sat his throne. It must therefore be true that he did not. Arawn was sorry for that. Dana knew battle was one thing lacking in Annwyn, what with the Powersmiths on half his border and Rhiannon of Ys, who didn't like to fight, on most of the rest. Otherwise—Prydain likewise had a queen, and one did not fight women unless they challenged first. Alberon of Alban was all but in hibernation, not moving from year to year from his rath in the north of his cold and gloomy Land.

What Arawn needed was to fight an equal—a friend, even—though friend and foe changed with the centuries when one was immortal. He had already—briefly—gone to war against Finvarra of Erenn, with Lugh and the Powersmiths as allies, until those damned mortal *children* had quashed it with their images of doom.

Lugh, however, or Nuada: now there would be battle indeed! How long had it been, anyway, since two High Kings hewed at each other with sword and ax and spear? Gwyddion (whatever he was: magician, man, or Faery) had once fought all day with Arawn's godson, Pryderi. Could he and Lugh dare any less?

And if Lugh did *not* sit his throne—well, it was as he had told his queen upon departure: he could aid him and so place Lugh in his debt while still getting a fair stake of combat.

Or he could feel out these Sons of Ailill and perhaps find better sport there. One—Turinne mac Angus, so said rumor— had managed to topple Lugh. And though Turinne was more wild than wily and more rash than circumspect, word also had it he was Powerful in his own right, though untrained and quick to tire. His thoughts ran differently, too, such as using mortals in his guard, and that made him interesting.

But *whatever* befell would be interesting, Arawn concluded, fingering his new-forged blade. Five breaths later, his ship crossed the border 'twixt sea and land. "Well," he announced to nobody, "Tir-Nan-Og has been invaded."

III

(Tir-Nan-Og—high summer)

Turinne grinned through the red mustache he had begun in parody of Lugh's and turned wickedly gleaming brown eyes to Brighani, his new-made druid-chief, who stood before him in the prescribed robe of woad-dyed wool, studying the map that lay between.

Only a map, yet more than a map, the landscape spread on the table had been worked in exquisite detail, showing mountains and valleys, rivers and cities, all in relief when unrolled. A slightly odd map it was, too, for it depicted the Mortal World—the Lands of Men—the Quick Folks World— however one chose to style it. What mattered was that all those places that now showed green mountains, lush fields, and sprawling cities would soon be a uniform watery blue.

The gauntlet had been cast, after all, that very day at sunset (*mortal* sunset; it was late afternoon in Tir-Nan-Og); it was his duty to meet that challenge, defeat the challenger, and claim the victor's prize.

"You are ready?" he asked Brighani, though it was not a question.

"Aye—one part is."

"One will suffice . . . for now. Rain and rain and rain. Rain without end. Rain such as mortals sing of in their oldest stories. But the waters in the earth must also rise."

"Aye, Lord, and that will be difficult."

"Not so hard as that other thing."

Brighani regarded him dubiously. "I know."

Turinne almost slapped him "*Do* you?"

"I know that however much water we pour out there, in time that Land will drink it. It will flow to the sea. Mortals may die, but mortals will return. The Land must be drowned utterly."

"And for that it must sink."

Brighani swallowed hard. "I know the rite. That is, *we* do—we think. It was used but once before, for the sinking of Lyonesse. I am not certain it will work for a Land so much larger."

"It will work," Turinne assured him. "If not for you, for someone else. But if you do not succeed, my friend, iron shall sever your soul from your body, and that drowned Land shall hold your tomb."

Brighani nodded—what else to do? And reached beside him to retrieve another map, this one thin as gossamer and depicting Tir-Nan-Og, the Tracks flat threads of gold within the warp and weft. He whipped it across the one already spread there, so that the Lands of Men showed through.

"At your leave," Turinne urged.

Brighani beckoned a servant: a sturdy bodach girl, slim for their kind and clearly scared to death. She swallowed as she approached, but her hands were steady as she held out a slender ewer of opalescent glass. A thousand like it were ranked on shelves outside, each holding water from a certain spring, and each spiced with the lifeblood of a child from the Mortal World, though Brighani and Turinne alone knew that.

"I will soon need another," the druid snapped. "See that my hands remain full."

"Lord," the girl murmured, and backed away.

Turinne didn't watch her go, nor did Brighani. But Turinne, soon to be Ard Rhi of the Daoine Sidhe in Tir-Nan-Og, watched very intently indeed as Brighani poured the water from that first ewer through the gossamer map of Tir-Nan-Og and onto the one below that depicted the Lands of Men.

And in Sullivan Cove, Georgia, and three hundred miles around, rain began to fall.

Turinne smiled and went to bathe for a coronation he'd ordered to proceed at once.

IV

(Clayton, Georgia—
Sunday, June 29—just past sunset)

Big Billy Sullivan sat bolt upright in his hospital bed and scared his wife clean out of her skin. Or at least so bad she dropped the diet Coke she'd bought out at Rabun Regional's cafeteria smack-dab in the middle of the floor in the doorway to his room.

"I wish," Big Billy growled, in the first words he'd said since he'd lapsed into unconsciousness right after she, Dale, and Little Billy had arrived that morning, "they'd stop that goddam *howlin'*."

JoAnne froze; the blood turned to ice in her veins; for a moment she actually stopped breathing.

"*What* howling, honey?" she managed, grasping the wall for support. "Ain't nothin' but the wind gettin' up. Looks like rain." Only a small part of which was true.

Big Billy glared at her, which wasn't what she needed when she'd been sure more than once that she'd seen him awake for the last time. And it was just like Dale and Billy to be out roaming around in quest of dinner she doubted any of them would more than taste when Bill returned to himself.

As to what they'd said—she wouldn't let herself believe it. That was the wind, not the family banshee, who'd appeared once before, when all this crazy shit had started, and warned of Uncle Dale's impending passing.

David had tricked it then. But David was off in who-knew-what godforsaken place likely gettin' himself killed. The one thing she knew was that that *thing* was attached to Sullivan blood. So it would be Bill. Or maybe Dale. Shoot, maybe Dale had had a heart attack; God knew he was old enough and maybe the thing couldn't tell 'em apart. Or maybe it was

Little Billy: car wreck, or something. David was gone, so it couldn't be him . . . could it?

"Get me my clothes," Big Billy demanded, yanking the IV from his arm. "I aim to die at home."

Chapter XVIII:
Cutting Edge

(Enotah County, Georgia—
Sunday, June 29—twilight)

Alec had the world's worst case of déjà vu. Only it wasn't that as much as memory, memory that said it hadn't even been three days since he'd been squinting through a rain-streaked windshield at a thoroughly soaked, storm-wracked Enotah County. The only difference this time was that he was squinting through the windshield of Myra's Dodge Caravan instead of David's Mustang, and that rather than David, Liz, Aikin, and a cat that was sometimes an enfield, his companions were Myra, LaWanda, and Piper—and Aikin, and Aife, who'd once *been* that enfield. Which was the only thing that had gone right lately as far as his specific self was concerned, if even *that* had gone right, which he doubted, given how preoccupied Aife had become.

Absorbed in the grimoire as she was, she certainly hadn't been much company on the frantic run up from Athens they'd begun two hours ago, as soon as they'd found a phone after returning from Tir-Gat. A quickie to David's folks' place had produced a very confused Elyyoth, who'd handed them off to a barely more coherent Scott, who'd given them the quick-and-dirty about a certain spike and the repercussions thereof, adding that Dave and company were back and on their way over from Devlin's. That gave Dave's crew an hour head start, which was fine, as it meant Myra's gang wouldn't have to take charge.

They had both kinds of mojo, too, though Scott had been

excruciatingly vague about what Dave had learned in Galunlati. One thing was clear, however: they had more going
for them than they'd had a day gone by.

If only it was enough.

Scowling, he shifted in the seat, downed the dregs of the
journey's third Jolt Cola (just about a day now, since he'd
slept), and tried *not* to ask the questions that were burning
his brain in two.

Like what, exactly, the spell that worked the Silver Tracks
was supposed to accomplish and, more to the point, how
were they to access it if it had sunk into Aife's mind and
couldn't be recalled? Like how Piper could sleep through all
this chaos. Like how LaWanda could stay so calm and centered and stern, almost like one of the Sidhe. Like why Aikin
hadn't figured out that maybe playing the silent type wasn't
cool when planning needed doing and his second-best friend
was about to go insane.

Like how Myra could see *anything* through all this goddamn rain.

At least it wasn't as bad as the last trip, though like that
foray, it got worse the closer to Sullivan Cove they came.

Finally he could stand it no longer. "What specifically,"
he asked Aife, "do you think we should do?"

She blinked up from the grimoire, which seemed to be
showing a bit of wear, if not actual deterioration: likely due
to its removal from the World of its making. "About what?"

It was all Alec could do to restrain himself. Instead, he
stroked the jar that contained the new ulunsuti. "About
which mojo to use: ours or Dave's or—"

"May not be our choice," Aikin called from the front.
"They get there first, they may go ahead with . . . whatever."

"Christ!" Alec spat in total exasperation. "All these
fuckin' variables! I mean, Lugh's off God-knows-where, we
have no idea what the rebels are up to besides making it rain,
and . . . and what do these folks know about us, if anything.
Never mind that Annwyn's on its way and Erenn's not far
behind."

"With a bunch of not-so-innocent workmen camped in the
middle," Myra concluded. "Though I imagine they're put-

ting them up somewhere else, except maybe those rent-a-cops Scott mentioned.''

"Like anybody'd be out on a night like this up to no good," Aikin snorted.

Myra flicked her left turn signal on, which seemed ludicrous, given the émpty highway. It took Alec a moment to realize that they'd reached the Sullivan Cove road.

No lights showed at David's house, but Kirkwood's T-bird was there. Still, when Myra made to press on to the Cove itself, by way of Uncle Dale's place, Aife's face suddenly went blank. "No," she countered, pointing up the dark frothing river that ought to be the Sullivans' drive, "turn here and keep going. We need water, and we need a Place of Power.''

"Water we got down here," Myra snorted. "But you mean—''

"Lookout Rock!" Alec finished for her. "That *is* what you mean, isn't it?''

"If that is its name. But I sense it even here. The waters under the earth, and out of the earth. Colin had a spring. We must have one as well.''

Myra was frowning like thunder. "No way the van'll make it. I'm not being anal or protective or anything; it just won't!''

Alec leaned past Aife to stare up the sodden, rain-slicked hill. "Big Billy's pickup's here, and it's got four-wheel-drive—and *I* know where he hides the key.''

"Let's do it," Myra decided. "We ain't got time to argue.''

Two minutes later, every one of them soaked to the skin, they were once again in transit, this time crammed into the F-150's extended cab, with Aikin, who had most experience with pickups, at the wheel. It wasn't that bad, actually, as Aikin steered the big Ford left and started up what had once been a logging road to commence the mile-long drive. And for a miracle, the rain had slackened now that they'd left the farmstead behind and had trees on either side. Either that or the branches screened the worst of the wind and water, save that which flowed beneath them, which was a regular torrent that had washed away most of the gravel, leaving rocks and holes and gullies you couldn't see until you were in 'em. Alec had his fingers crossed. So far so good, and whatever.

This was it, too, wasn't it? The final roll of the dice for all this Faery shit. He hoped he was ready, and to calm himself took inventory of his gear. Clothes: wet but serviceable; fatigues and a surplus flak jacket Aikin had loaned him earlier. *Gattaca* baseball cap. The pistol and ammo Aik had added in Tir-Gat. His war club. The ulunsuti. And maybe, if she remembered he was alive, Aife.

Who, Alec realized with a start, was still reading—in the dark.

And then, as often happened during long stressful journeys on rainy nights, everyone withdrew into private silence.

In spite of himself, Alec dozed. Time-compressed, rather, to use the term he'd coined to describe that fugue state when you were mostly turned off and oblivious but with one little part still aware and letting you know if anything important occurred, then turning you off again after. He'd had an astronomy class like this once, right after lunch; he'd always nodded off in there, only to awaken if the prof said something he didn't know, take a note on same, then drift off again. He'd made an A—of course.

But somehow that just didn't matter. Like graduation hadn't mattered. What *did* matter was that Aikin had just pulled completely off what passed for a road and was trying to get back on track; and, more to the point, that the headlights had caught the dark archway in the trees that marked the side trail that led to Lookout Rock.

Marked it clearly, in fact, for at that very moment, it stopped raining. *Almost* stopped, Alec amended; there was still a light mist. Aife sat up at once, as though startled or concerned, eyes darting everywhere, nostrils flaring as though she were a predator sniffing out prey.

"Power," she asserted. "Someone forestalls the rain with Power."

Alec exhaled his relief in a rush. "Like Finno, maybe?"

"So I would hope," Aife agreed. "It would still be wise to hurry."

Aikin did, sending rooster tails of muddy water a yard high

to either side as he set the heavy Ford slipping and sliding across what was usually leafy-mossy ground completely overhung by oaks and maples. Over a minute he did that, until he skidded around one final curve and nearly collided with the back of Sandy's Explorer, blocking further progress ahead.

Beyond it, however, where the forest gave way to the rocky mountainside ledge-cum-clearing that was Lookout Rock, the headlights caught moving figures. Alec was out the door before Aikin shut off the engine. Not until that moment did he realize how much he'd missed his best friend.

David had clearly missed him too and broke off lighting tiki torches to dash across the sodden moss, mud-bogged gravel, and slippery stone to enfold him in the hug he'd needed longer than he dared imagine. *This was it,* something told him. Not the end of all things, perhaps, but the end of the Faery stuff once and for all. After that, it would be back to real life. Grad school, a job, maybe a family—

He froze. *If they moved Tir-Nan-Og, what happened to Aife?* And Finno, and all those other friends?

Did that even matter when he had a tried-and-true forever buddy like David to grab him on a cold, rainy, miserable night and remind him simply by the sun-bright spark of life that burned within him that he, Alec McLean, was also alive and worth having around?

For a long moment they stood there, wet hair tangled together, stubbly cheeks brushing, breath harsh yet soft in each other's ears.

"Love you," David whispered, easing him away. Then: "I am *so* glad you're here."

Alec backed away, too, hoping David wouldn't see the tears that fogged his eyes, or else mistake them for the mist of rain that got through whatever Finno had raised to shelter them. But David's eyes were bright as well. "Guess you heard we succeeded," David said, glancing back toward the clearing. "Otherwise you wouldn't be here."

Alec nodded and eased around his forever-and-always best friend to join the others, who were likewise reuniting in varying combinations farther on. Except for Aikin, who'd stayed behind to hug David too. Which wasn't like him either.

For a moment he considered waiting, but Dave and Aik surely needed a solo reunion as much as he had, and having found himself alone, he did what he always did when he visited David's oldest, most private, and strongest Place of Power. He took in the view.

Lookout Rock was like a notch that had been hacked from the dark granite bones of Nichols Mountain and never truly healed. Flat but stony, it was an acre or so in extent and surrounded on two sides by close-grown woods beneath which lay the ruins of the lean-to he, Dave, and the rest of the MacTyrie Gang had renewed countless times. A third side fronted the mountain, and the notch cut deep there: a hundred feet of sheer stone down which a waterfall slid like the mountain's blood to form their ancient skinny-dipping site. Too many times to count, he, Dave, and Aikin—and, later, Gary and Darrell—had stripped off and dived in there. More recently, Calvin and Finno had joined their ranks. Every crisis, major and minor, that had marked puberty and adolescence had been deconstructed there. Love, sex, death, family, religion, drugs, politics, and rock-and-roll: all had paid their toll.

The fourth side gave the place its name. Open to the sky and the wind, it was a thirty-yard-long ledge that dropped straight down far enough to kill anyone who leapt off, while still offering a view Mystic Mountain would have fought an army to possess.

The lake glimmered out there and down, and more mountains, and a sprinkle of lights that were houses, though no towns could be seen. And no more than two miles away as the crow flew was the cause of all this trouble: the near-perfect quartz-crowned cone of Bloody Bald.

Hands slapped his back, startling him from his reverie, but it was only David and Aikin, drawing him over to where the rest of their crew were assembling. *All* of them, he noted, including Scott and Elyyoth. Everyone, that is, except David's clan, who were otherwise occupied, and that John Devlin guy, who had no real *business* here.

What followed was confusion, chaos, and exchange of information, then, so suddenly it startled him, decision.

It made sense, actually. David's crew had a promise from

the Chiefs of the Quarters that they'd do what they could, but no one knew when they'd show, save that it would be a time of their choosing. But since the present deluge proved that the Sons were already on the move, it made sense to try their own mojo first.

Still, it seemed ludicrous to even consider such a preposterous notion: that some screwy, incomprehensible combination of *words*, belief, water, and blood could set something as utterly alien as Tracks to work at anyone's whim. And to move a World—a big hunk of one, anyway! Why, Tir-Nan-Og must cover hundreds of thousands of square miles. How could they shift that much in one night? And where would they move it to, anyway?

And, again, what would happen to Aife, in whom the key was both inserted and seemingly stuck, if this crackbrain scheme succeeded? She was Faery, after all. If she cut herself off from that Land, she'd go mad. Granted, she could put on the substance of their World, but that was a stopgap at best. Eventually the call of like-to-like would become irresistible. What then?

Apparently Aife, Finno, and the still slightly shell-shocked Elyyoth had some notion, as they likewise did about this Silver Track thing. But the former he dared contemplate no longer, and their attempts at explaining the latter had been frustrated by terms that not only had no English equivalent but that barely formed comprehensible images in the mind when Aife tried telepathic definition.

All Alec had been able to grasp was an image of a silver river paralleling an enormous sandbar; and, farther on, an island, where the first tentative fragments of another bar of similar kind lay. The river—the Track—was to pick up sand from one and deposit it on the other until their sizes had swapped, then block itself off so that the island was surrounded by rings of both water and land. It was a screwy visual metaphor for something that was more than halfway metaphysical, but Alec thought it might succeed.

As to who would be doing the hard parts, Aife had the knowledge locked within her, all unknown, though she swore she could access it at need. She also had a fair bit of Power, now that she'd once more clothed herself in the stuff of her native World. Fionchadd too had regained most of his strength, and of his previous injuries there was no sign. Ely-yoth, while larger than either of the other Sidhe, was also the weakest in terms of Power, yet even so had more to command than the mortals.

"So let me get this straight," Scott concluded after the latest round of fine-tuning logistics. "Aife, Finno, and Ely-yoth are gonna be the movers and shakers—the ones who work the spell, or whatever."

"Right," David affirmed. "But since the Sons are bound to know what we're up to, courtesy of Finno's little umbrella here, we've gotta be primed for attack. Unfortunately, we can't fight 'em much with mojo, though Cal and Brock are already settin' wards"—he gestured to where the pair were driving colored stakes, drawing lines and circles, and chanting in Cherokee—"and LaWanda's off mumblin' too. Which means we've gotta fall back on guns and ammo, which they're gonna be ready for, seein' how we've used those against 'em already. In fact, if they're savvy, they'll send their mortal flunkies, 'cause they know it'll freak us by puttin' us in a moral bind."

"Fuckers," Aikin muttered, to nobody.

"Mind fuckers too," Liz cautioned. "Don't forget, the Sons took over those guys, no reason they couldn't get us too."

"Which means we need somebody to spy on them," Sandy concluded. "Someone to warn *us* of impending attack. Sounds simple enough: the Faeries do their thing with the Tracks; we split the remainder. Liz, I know you can scry, and Alec's got a new ulunsuti. Myra, you've got *something*, but you're not a fighter type, so why don't you help out there too? Piper, you'd best join them; you don't like to fight either, but if worse comes to worst, maybe you can pipe us out of here, or something."

Piper nodded mutely, stroking his pipes and gazing soul-fully at LaWanda, who'd just returned looking inordinately pleased with herself.

"So the rest of us play soldier?" Aikin queried.

Sandy nodded in turn. "Those that know which end of a gun the bullet comes out of should use 'em: shotguns, rifles, doesn't matter. That's you, Dave; and Aik, and me, and Scott—who can also do the sword thing if he has to, assuming Elyyoth will lend his. Wannie, you get a choice: guns or that machete I hear you're hell-on-wheels with. Or—''

"Both," LaWanda broke in tersely. "The rest—it don't work fast, and in cases like this, it only works on me. Let's just say I may not always be where you think I am."

"And *speaking* of mojo," Sandy continued, "Cal can shapeshift, and he's also got a war club with some mojo to it. Dave and Alec do, too, but seems like they'd be best used elsewhere. So, Churchy, what's your poison? Smith & Wesson or atasi?''

Kirkwood grinned. "To echo my fellow ethnic minority: both.''

"You can use mine," David offered. "Alec, what about yours? We seem to have a spare atasi and a person who shouldn't even be here." He fixed his gaze on Brock, looking long and hard at the boy as though they shared some secret. "So how 'bout, it, Badger? Wanta have a go with a war club?''

Brock, who was standing with his arms folded across his chest looking by turns scared to death and sullen, drew himself up straighter. "That'd work." He'd recovered the Ruger, too, just in case. Alec wondered if he was prepared to use it. He caught the boy's eye and gestured a silent summons. Fumbling a little, he freed his atasi from the belt loop where he'd thrust it and held it out to the boy. It gleamed in the light of the flickering torches: two feet of wood shaped vaguely like a double-bladed ax, but with the handle continuing into a knob. Good for smashing bones, capable of rending flesh if you hit hard enough. By repute, able to send off—or fend off—bolts of lightning. Cal's could, at any rate. His own? Who knew? He'd never tested it. Brock's eyes glittered as he took it solemnly. To his surprise, Alec's misted back. "Just stay alive to return it."

"Well," David announced, "best I can tell, we're as ready as we're gonna be." He glanced at Aife, then at Fionchadd, and finally at Elyyoth. "You say midnight's best to start this wingding? We've got fifteen minutes, then. I suggest we all use it makin' peace with whoever needs makin' peace with, and anything left over just off by ourselves makin' ready."

Alec found a rock near the juncture of mountain, woods, and overlook, and sat there alone, staring at the jar that held the ulunsuti. What would he see there? he wondered, when he, Myra, Piper, and Liz fed it the blood that figured so much in all this ritual and began their scrying? More to the point, what was the secret David's band were hiding and thought no one suspected, and would he live to see it revealed? They were playing for keeps now. Chivalry was Lugh's province, and chivalry was dead, as far as their enemies went. Come . . . whatever, they would receive no mercy.

Sneak attack, Aife had urged. Start the ball rolling, set Tir-Nan-Og moving, and catch the Sons before they could act.

Yeah, sure!

"Okay," David proclaimed far too quickly, "it's time."

Somehow it all fell together. Those who would work the spell—Aife, Fionchadd, and Elyyoth—stripped to their undertunics, leaving arms, legs, and feet bare, then waded into the pool, with Aife clutching Colin's grimoire. Fionchadd carried Uki's obsidian knife (*When had he got it?*), and Elyyoth simply stood there looking grim. If Alec understood things right, they'd all offer blood (not that different from what he'd done in Tir-Gat, actually), and then Aife would call the Tracks. According to Myra, they spiraled around various axes, and if you stayed in one place long enough, one would conveniently sweep by. All Alec knew was that they'd better!

And with the Sidhe all up to their knees in cold mountain water, the others took their places.

Alec, Liz, Myra, and Piper sat down in a second circle between the edge of the pool and the sheerest edge of the overlook, arranging themselves so that all but Piper had a view of Bloody Bald, with the ulunsuti jar in the center. Liz had another knife (*Lord, but this was a bloody undertaking!*), but wouldn't use it until David gave the signal.

The rest—the warriors—formed a protective crescent around the sorcerers and the scryers, with the heavy, dark mass of the mountain closing up the unguarded side. They'd alternated, too, gun-toters and blade-or-club men: Kirkwood, Scott, Aikin, Brock, David, Sandy, LaWanda, and Cal, in order from the road. They were all standing very straight, Alec noted, as though they were warriors in truth, not volunteers and halfhearted conscripts. Weapons gleamed in their hands: shotguns, rifles, and pistols wrought in the Lands of Men; swords and machetes of iron or Faery metal; wooden war clubs and Calvin's bow, made in Galunlati; and poison-tipped arrows from their foes. Most wore black. A few sported odd bits of garb from Galunlati or Tir-Nan-Og.

Wind whipped their hair, and the mist began to thicken as Fionchadd's shield, which he no longer dared sustain, began to dissolve. They had wards, of course: another circle of sticks and chanted words, but the location of the pool and the mountain had made it impossible to fix them neatly with the quarters, so that neither Cal nor Brock were certain they were viable.

Alec shifted restlessly, looking first at the overlook, then ten degrees sideways at David, who was staring at his watch; then back at his own timepiece, noting that the flashing numerals had synchronized with his heart.

"One minute," David warned. Whereupon Fionchadd flourished his knife. Liz laid hers on Alec's thigh as he reached to the center of the circle formed by their touching knees and opened the jar which held the ulunsuti. A pause for breath and he tipped the stone onto a black silk scarf Myra had provided.

"Now!" David said softly into the night. Barely a whisper that was, yet Alec heard him even above the patter of rain and the rush of sliding water. He took the knife from his thigh, slid it across his other palm without considering it might actually hurt, and closed his eyes. Around him, he sensed, more hands than his own were bleeding.

Around him, too, the torches wavered and the rain fell harder.

Interlude VII:
Road Warriors

I

(Tir-Nan-Og—high summer)

The tall thick grass of the Plain of Lost Stars had long since given way to the close-grown stubble of the Vale of Dhaionne Chainnai, as the bodachs thereabouts called the place where the famed mortal historian had dwelt after Lugh kidnapped her to write her history of Cymruw. She'd died there, too: an old woman surrounded by strange stumpy dogs, and been buried beneath a jet-black stone carved with thistles, ravens, and bears. She'd befriended the bodachs, though, and, the place having no other appellation, theirs had persisted.

Now, however, that vale, with its meandering streams and mile-off view of the twelve-towered palace, was ripe to be named again: the Vale of Remorseless Slaughter.

Lugh had expected them: these warriors in the livery of the Sons of Ailill, which was such a poor parody of his own. Turinne had to have at least one seer (though not Oisin, for whom Lugh was deeply concerned), and that seer was bound to have noted his approach. The usurper wouldn't send his best, though, if he had yet to confirm his bond to what was still not his throne; therefore these armed shapes who rose from the grass as from the earth itself would be expendable and likely halfhearted in the bargain. Most likely they were meant to delay anyone who sought to attack the palace.

As for the Bonding Rite—well, Turinne was certainly one

to take risks. He'd risked unseating a king, after all. And though the ancient Laws of Dana said one king must die (or abdicate) on the day that marked his birth for another to supplant him (and such had been Turinne's plan), the *form* of the rite was common knowledge, and it would be like Turinne to try to force his own bond with a Land already bonded and let the Land decide. It was against that choice Lugh rode.

Faster, then; bearing down on those who raised sword and spear to daunt him. Nuada was at his side. His tithe and another that had joined along the way, not all of them Daoine Sidhe, rode at his back. He thought to stop and fight, for bloodlust was strong within him, but that would waste precious time. And so he raised his spear, so that the long, strong rays of westering sunlight caught it and glittered along its length, and those who stood against him, who did not throw themselves to the ground at once, withered beneath that weapon's fire.

And the Vale of Dhaoinne Chainnai drank deep of thick, rich, heart-pumped wine.

II

(Tir-Nan-Og—high summer)

"Lord . . ." Cemon ap Cadwyr, Arawn's page and cabin boy, ventured as he padded to a stop at Arawn's back, feet wide braced on the rolling deck. "Lord," Cemon dared again. "There is—that is, the lookouts have sighted another fleet approaching."

Arawn never moved from his place at the forward railing, from which, through a curious complex of mirrors and engraved metal, he was observing what transpired in the Vale of Dhaoinne Chainnai. Yet the muscles tensed along his jaw, and the hand that held his sword grew marginally tighter. "Lugh? Or—?"

"Finvarra," Cemon panted. "Whether he pursues or shares your goal—"

"He is no fool, or else I am one," Arawn retorted. "He

will know what I know, and will have heard the news at one time and the same.''

''Will he fight with us or against us?'' Cemon persisted.

Arawn watched the empty southern reaches of Tir-Nan-Og flash by beneath him: woods and vales and a few farmsteads or private palaces; herds of beasts, and flocks of birds around the many lakes. It was too alive for him, too lush, too bright, too green. It was an implicit insult to his own dark, dry, morbid-seeming Land. And that was reason enough to contest it.

''Does it matter?'' Arawn replied languidly, not turning, though he could all but feel the boy's frightened scowl. ''Either way, we will all be bloodied. Either way, things will change. Either way there will be poems to write, songs to sing, and stories to tell.''

''Which will do no good if no one survives to hear them,'' Cemon gave back bravely.

Arawn almost struck him for insolence, then decided that such scarce-disguised disapproval was likely the bravest thing the boy had ever done. ''*Someone* will hear,'' he chuckled. ''If nothing else, we will kidnap mortals and make them give our bards a hearing. But put your heart at ease; for now I am set to contest with Lugh, and if that avails not, with Turinne. And if neither give me satisfaction, I may give Finvarra of Erenn a go. If he is as bored as I am, he would relish it. It would be interesting to rule three realms at once, whether that king be Lugh, Turinne, Finvarra, or . . . me.''

''The Powersmiths—'' Cemon dared again.

''Are very far away,'' Arawn snorted.

''Will we fight on the ground? Or indoors? Or . . . aloft?''

Arawn stroked his chin and gazed behind him. ''It is true,'' he mused, ''that I have never *waged* battle from on high.''

III

(Tir-Nan-Og—high summer)

Turinne paused with one hand on his ceremonial helm and stared through two windows at once. They were set close together in the eastern corner of the tower he'd chosen for his suite, but neither opened on the World Without; not as it was, anyway. For the openings were glazed with a mesh of clear glass and mirrors, milky-clear panes, and stained (kin to the apparatus Arawn used at that very moment, had he known). Usually they made pictures of their own devising, but now they filled another function entirely.

Now they sought out threat.

Not threat to him, however; a room's worth of windows couldn't display all those now, and he rather relished that notion. Rather, these windows showed threat to the Land itself. And while Turinne knew his own mind well enough to know that Kingship had its own enticements, this whole elaborate plot had at its heart a true and abiding love for the Land that had nothing to do with any ulterior cause.

Mortals were threatening it—Tir-Nan-Og first, but the other realms in time—and that threat, while unintentioned, was insidious. Men fought wars and men died, but the Land was always there after, sometimes injured but always recoverable. Mortal men, though, had iron in abundance, and that iron had burned through to devour the Land, and *that* Land could not be reclaimed. A finger gone, for him, was a finger that would grow back eventually. A farm or a field or a wood devoured by an iron-wrought Hole: that was gone forever.

Which had decided him. Lugh *was* the Land, but Lugh *ignored* the Land in its pain. Turinne would not ignore it, therefore he must destroy that which would be its bane: mortals in general and whichever ones were annoying the Land now.

He saw them clearly, for all it was dark in the Lands of Men. Mortals they were, and with them traitors to his own kind: Fionchadd mac Ailill, Aife of Tir Arvann, and Elyyoth whose lineage he did not know; all engaged in some complex *working* whose nature he couldn't tell, for the window showed only threat, not reason, distance, or kind.

But the place he *did* know: a place he'd heard of in the Lands of Men that had almost as much Power as some parts of Tir-Nan-Og.

But he had time yet. It was far too dangerous to stake his claim before sunset, and so minor a skirmish as he had in mind didn't require his presence. Besides, his warriors were restless. They'd vowed revenge on this very same band of mortals, and who was he to say them nay?

"Fetch"—he counted through the window, speaking to the guard who lingered by—"fetch a tithe; half of it mortal, half of it Sidhe. Go to that place, slay all you find there, and return with their heads to me."

IV

(west of Clayton, Georgia— Sunday, June 29—near midnight)

"This is a crock," JoAnne Sullivan grumbled from where she was driving Dale's big Lincoln far too fast for slippery mountain roads; antilock brakes and traction control notwithstanding. The wipers beat at the downpour: fierce as her anxiety, steady as her pain.

Safely ensconced in the back seat, Little Billy blinked stoically and tuned out her latest tirade on why his dad should've stayed at Rabun Regional, how he shouldn't have gone off to fight in the first place, why that wailing he and Dale still heard now and then really could *not* be the family banshee. And finally, and most forcefully, how a stick in the back was just flat out not an acceptable reason to die. Dale, in the front shotgun, had tuned her out, too, by the expedient of playing 'possum. Which was just as well; it left Little Billy alone with his pa—his *dad*, rather; he'd never liked that old-fashioned term Davy, against all sense, continued using.

Might not be a problem much longer, though, 'cause Big Billy looked pale as a ghost, and if truth were told, wasn't hardly breathing. Frankly, it was a miracle they'd released him, and if Bill hadn't threatened to sue, and had Dale to back him up (and himself, too, if an eleven-year-old counted), they'd still be back there waiting.

"A man's got some rights," his dad had said, staring his mom in the eye. That was what he'd been saying when he and Uncle Dale returned from a lightning raid on Hardees. "And one right a man's got most of all is the right to say when and where he'll die if he knows he's dyin'. I don't *know* I am, but I *think* I am, and something else has a pretty good idea that could happen too. Now help me or go away, 'cause I've said what I'm gonna do."

They were doing it now, though later than his dad had wanted by about two hours, 'cause it *had* been after hours, and there were some things hospitals had to bend the law to do. But home wasn't far now, maybe ten miles, and they'd have been there long since if not for the incessant rain.

Little Billy wondered what he'd find there. That Elyyoth guy, who'd been from Faerie and told him tales of wonder when fretting over Davy threatened to drive him crazy? Maybe. Water? That was for sure; but what else? War, somehow, some way, and likely fought with magic. Shoot, if he was a little older, he'd be in there, too, Mom or no. Christ, Brock wasn't but a couple years older'n him, and he'd been in the thick of things. On the other hand, fighting meant you might die, and he didn't think his mom could stand it if him, or Davy, or even Dale, died too.

Which sounded like he'd given up on his dad, which he hadn't. Without thinking about it, he did something he'd never done in his life. He reached over and grasped his father's hand.

Chapter XIX:
Life's Blood

(Lookout Rock, Georgia—
Sunday, June 29—midnight)

David wished he had a better view of what was going on behind him, where Aife, Finno, and Elyyoth stood knee-deep in what had always been, to him, sacred water, beginning to work their spell. He dared not turn full around, however; not while he was on guard. Against *what*, he didn't know; though it was absurd to assume they could actually pull this off without a glitch. Well, perhaps in a perfect world, but they'd surely blown their luck quota by now, and they'd *need* luck in spades to avoid detection.

Or simply to stay alive. All he knew about Turinne was that he was ambitious, didn't think along traditional Faery lines, and was far more ruthless than Lugh; witness his execution of poor Oisin. Opposing him wasn't good odds.

Their best chance lay in the rebels' getting close enough to have at them with something besides magic. Bullets, they'd already proven, could put serious hurt on Faery bodies: smashing joints, breaking bones, and disrupting senses, if not slaying outright; plus those injuries took Power to heal, which was Power the injured couldn't access in a fight. Steel shot was even better, because not only did it hurt but the Sidhe actually feared it. David's concern was that Turinne might be canny enough to pit them against ordinary people.

Best not think about that, he decided, as he turned just in time to catch the flash of obsidian as Fionchadd slashed one palm, then shifted the blade to the other and sliced the free one in turn. Blood dripped into the pool: an offering of Power to the water, as he offered the knife to Aife, who followed suit. Elyyoth would as well, but Elyyoth was out of view.

For himself, Brock was to his right, Sandy to his left, Alec and Liz behind and to the left: them and the wind and the rain and the night and what was still, and forever, a magnificent view. And so he stood and waited; poised, but not tense; no longer tired, or beyond it; shotgun in hand, Beretta at belt, odd lots here and there; black fatigues, black sweatshirt, brown sleeveless jacket bristling with pockets; an ugly green boonie hat that fended the rain from his eyes.

And, he suddenly realized, an iron medallion around his neck whose origin he still didn't know. He fingered the chain and looked down at Brock, whose gift it was, the boy dressed more or less as he, but bareheaded, and with his flag of hair twitching in the wind and Alec's atasi held two-handed before him like a battle-ax. "I haven't forgotten," he murmured, nudging Brock with his elbow. "The medallion, I mean."

"Woman gave it to me," Brock mumbled. "Like I said. Supposed to be protection against the Sidhe."

"Thought you bought it."

Brock shook his head, took a deep breath. "Gave it to me for a tumble—my first, actually. I don't think she was human. Said she needed a mortal's first seed for her own conceiving."

Christ! David thought, *dead Sidhe sometimes had to link their souls to a new conception.* "Did this woman have a name?"

"Neman," Brock replied, barely audible. "She said I was to give that to you to settle a debt. She said it was interest on a death."

David's breath caught. *So that was it!* Neman, the part of the tripart goddess who gloried in what had come to be called friendly fire, had contrived his namesake uncle's death in Lebanon. He, in turn, had inadvertently precipitated her sister's doom: Morrigu, Mistress of Battles, who by rights should've overseen all that transpired here. Clearly that had shaken Neman, and equally clearly, Morrigu sought rebirth.

And because Morrigu ruled honor and fairness in battle, her sister had felt obliged to honor him in turn and had empowered this talisman made of what to her would've been the deadliest metal to shield him from her own kind.

That made as much sense as anything, anyway.

"Thanks," David murmured, and fell silent, gazing out at the ominous woods. Wondering, as his eyes probed every shifting shadow, how many others had stood like this: forlorn and frightened in the dark, waiting for their deepest fears to manifest. Devlin had, and lost a hand trying to save a friend. David-the-Elder had, and lost more than that in the long run. Dale had, and his father. He was no less than they, no more important in the grand cold scheme of life. And here he was. Waiting. A soldier—almost—in the night.

The *words* weren't there, and then, quite simply, they were.

Aife didn't know whether her eyes were open or not, though they had been when she'd drawn the knife across her palm and let her blood fall into the pool. Carefully, she'd done that, for she'd known without consciously learning as much that if the pool touched a wound, it could suck you dry. That had been Colin's doom; that was what had almost destroyed Tir-Gat. He'd been Powerful, too; more Powerful than herself, Fionchadd, and Elyyoth together. But his had been the need for stealth, to steal a little at a time from Alberon: a hill, a tree, every third stone in a mountain. Such subtlety was useless now; what she needed was control and direction. But first she had to find a Silver Track.

And so they'd fed blood to sacred water and sent it questing. Blood to awaken water, to wake more water, to touch all water and be aware. Even the water in the air, perhaps, for she could feel the touch of Power in it as it fell.

And so she watched with her inner eye, feeling the water around her feet, and through it, all water everywhere; all the while recalling the touch of the Silver Tracks Colin had so carefully described in *words* no mortal could ever translate.

Nothing . . . Nothing . . . Farther and farther, down near Athens now; and then she *touched* one, and more of Colin's *words* awoke, and she began to summon it *here*.

*   *   *

Alec stared at the ulunsuti and tried not to think of the crimson septum that divided the oracular stone as a metaphor for the barrier he sensed rising between him and Aife.

Barriers . . . human and Faery. Mortal and Sidhe. Blood from the Lands of Men and an organic jewel from a monster from Galunlati.

Blood.

His hand glistened where he'd sliced it to prime the stone before passing his knife on to Liz, who'd passed it to Piper, thence to Myra, and so back to him. They were watching him, too, which he hated. "Okay," he whispered, so as not to disturb Aife's spell, "let your blood drip on the stone, no more than a drop or two until we get a sense of it. Yeah, that's right. C'mon, Piper, you too."

Piper's face was white as snow; the poor guy was actually trembling. Alec was beyond sorry for him. He hated this stuff because it disrupted his life and what he'd grown up assuming were the universe's givens. Piper hated it because it scared him to death. At least Myra was here: Piper's most tenured friend, that bond as old as the one 'twixt himself and Liz, if the two of them even *were* friends.

Scratch that; they were. She was getting anxious, though; he could tell. And so he took a deep breath and reached out to clasp the hands of those nearest. Liz's were soft and silky, Myra's competent and hard. "Okay, like I've told you, it works best if you just worry at it. Think about threats, but not specific threats. Keep your eyes open as long as you can and stare at the septum. Pretty soon it'll take over."

"Been there, done that," Myra affirmed. "Don't worry."

Alec didn't reply. Years of much-begrudged experience had made him more facile at scrying than he imagined, and before he knew it, the septum had become the whole world, and he was flying.

There was no *other* way to describe the sensation, though he had no sense of giddiness, only of cool observation. Nor could he tell precisely what he saw, save that it seemed to be their own World. Which made sense, given that Liz or Myra could be directing as easily as he. Christ, both of 'em were stronger-willed than he was!

At any rate, chaos had clarified into Sullivan Cove and that yucky bunch of make-do structures out at B.A. Beach. A shift, and he glimpsed Dale's Lincoln approaching, though what that portended, he didn't know. Someone was worrying about the elder Sullivans, though, or concerned about what would happen should David lose his dad.

A jerk, a mental twitch, and they looked on Tir-Nan-Og and Lugh's palace, now bathed in fading light, which meant time between the Worlds was out of synch again. The place was alive, too, with hundreds of half-seen figures on horseback, afoot, or aloft, all converging on Lugh's citadel. He hoped Lugh was there as well; that these were warriors come to aid him, not riffraff come to storm the palace or witness the crowning of a mortal-hostile king. And then he saw the ships: two whole armadas aloft, one Arawn's, one Finvarra's, likewise intent on the palace. He breathed a sigh at that: whatever they faced here, far more was occurring in Tir-Nan-Og. Maybe with enough distractions there, no one would heed a band of half-mad mortals a World away.

Another shift, and a dark-clad troop appeared from nowhere amid a ruined circle of standing stones and charged straight toward them—in Faerie, of course, but right in their direction. And then golden light flared before them as a Track awakened, and Alec lost them—unfortunately, because at least half those figures, though they wore Turinne's livery, were men from his own World.

The stone had shown them specifically, too, which meant they were a threat. And then he recalled something that made his bones go chill. Those men had stepped on a Track. Tracks laced through the Worlds like laser light in a room full of mirrors. Two ran close to David's place: disturbing, but still a fair way from here, plus anyone approaching from them would surely make *some* noise. But there was a third, which no one thought about because it didn't link to their World directly. He'd been on it exactly once, when they'd sought Ailill's sister, Fionna; and that Track entered this World from the blank stone behind the waterfall!

Thinking it *showed* it; showed his fears were true. Liz clearly realized it as well: that they'd left one whole flank unguarded. Alec had no idea whose voice it was, Liz's or his own, that yelled warning.

David felt the burning in his eyes the instant he heard Liz scream. Burning meant Power in use, and his eyes had been burning already, from Aife's spell. But he'd learned to tune that out so that it was no worse than bad eyestrain. Now Power was awake again: close by and with no warning, as though someone had opened a door onto chaos.

Another scream: warning or fear . . . an oath in the language of Faerie. And then sharp, harsh cracks, like distilled thunder.

Gunshots!

Fucking *gunshots*!

More shouts followed, and there was splashing and yelling, someone roundly cursing the weather, and far too human laughter.

David spun instantly, wondering how anyone could possibly have come at them from the back, and then *remembering* how: the Track they'd all forgotten, that opened through solid stone on the unguarded side of the pool.

"Down," he growled at Brock, diving for cover behind a knee-high boulder, but Brock was already down—and groaning, though his face looked fierce and grim. Around him other wet, dark shapes were ducking for cover as well; at least there were rocks and logs aplenty. His concern was for the unarmed, the folk in the pool, who'd been right in the line of fire; but also Liz, Alec, and the rest, who were off to his right and not in direct view of anyone emerging from the waterfall. Which might buy them time to fumble out the weapons he'd insisted they carry.

But where were their assailants? The Track terminated behind the falls, but it was narrow; one person at a time was all that could navigate it. Which meant—

Shotgun up! Firing—straight at the shape moving behind the water; at the same time noting that their three Faery allies were nowhere to be seen, which meant, he hoped, that they were underwater. *Wait!* Aife was still standing, though she'd staggered back. And was that blood on her shoulder where there should be no blood, according to the rite? What was she doing, anyway, out there in the middle?

"Oh, Jesus! I'm hit!" And that *was* Alec! David's heart stopped cold in his chest, though his finger went right on twitching: shooting a dead man who pitched straight out of the waterfall to land in the sacred pool. Two others followed, springing through and fanning out to either side. And the shotgun wasn't loaded! Fingers fumbled for shells while his frantic gaze found Alec, two yards away, lying on his side, staring at a long red gash along his forearm, while Liz leaned over him, pistol in hand. He glimpsed Piper's frozen face, and then the shotgun loaded itself, and he was questing for targets. His side were getting their bearings, too, and bullets were flying from every quarter, notably LaWanda, who was pumping 'em out like Dixie—and had just taken out the second foe, who was certainly mortal.

More replaced him at once; and a bullet zinged close to David's head. Lightning cracked from the left to smite the falls, and he glimpsed, cut out in stark black-and white, Kirkwood wielding the atasi, apparently from blind reflex. Anything it hit could conjure a bolt if the wielder was angry. And anything that hit it as well, evidently, since the guy was using it to *parry* bullets. The boy liked to live dangerously. Then again, he was kin to Calvin.

"Damn! Fuck! Hell!" Brock groaned beside him, not fighting at all as he clutched a bloody calf, but David dared not check on him when he had Bessie reloaded and hungry for fodder. There was plenty of it, too: warriors—mortal and Faery alike—crowding from behind the waterfall. At least none had Uzis or anything like that, or they'd all have been mincemeat. In fact, many of the humans looked like good-old-boy hunter types; and come to think of it, a number had gone missing the last few years, all through the South.

But where was a target? If only Alec weren't so close . . .

Fuck it! He fired at a pair of wide white eyes that suddenly squinted down a barrel before him. The shotgun roared. The man staggered backward into his fellows. Something ripped along David's head between his skull and right ear. Sudden aching warmth. *He'd been blooded!*

The world vanished. Returned. Vanished again, then returned to stay, but with a killer headache that hinted of concussion.

He ducked instinctively, peered up again, seeking another target—and caught a faceful of spray as Fionchadd exploded from the pool right in front of him to seize the foremost man by the belt and drag him down to an assignation with the obsidian dagger flashing in his hand.

More lightning, to his right, this time from Calvin, who was jumping up and down and screaming as though every ancestor he possessed had crowded into his head and was cheering him on together. Bullets spat at him, but miraculously none hit.

And then silence, as everyone seemed to run out of steam at once, giving David time to take stock. The attackers—mortals in the vanguard—had got no farther than the middle of the pool but couldn't retreat for the pressure of forces behind. At least four were floating facedown, and three were making tracks for the relatively unguarded shore farthest from the overlook: toward Kirkwood by way of Aife, who was simply sitting waist-deep in the water looking shocked—*wounded by iron!*—and bleeding into blood-starved water.

Alec and Liz seemed to be okay. They'd found shelter behind the largest log around, and Piper was lying flat on his face beyond, with his pipes beneath him: probably the smartest thing he could do. Myra, who'd apparently lost the gun she hadn't wanted to start with, was cursing and throwing rocks at anything that moved.

He couldn't tell much about the rest without looking too far afield, but Aikin, LaWanda, and Sandy were choosing *their* shots with care and making them count. The atasi crew were holding their own, which left Scott, who'd expected to fight with Elyyoth's sword but had wound up scrunched behind very sparse cover indeed, fumbling frantically for his shotgun.

And Brock, who lay closest: first of the fallen.

"Hang in there, kid," David grinned. "Just hurts; you ain't dyin'."

"I'm tough," Brock breathed, feeling with wet red fingers for the atasi which had wound up under him. "Just gimme a minute."

A *word*, then: Faery Gaelic, shouted at the sky.
And more lightning, this time aimed at them.

"Fucker!" LaWanda spat, burying her face in her arms as
a shrapnel of rocks rained down, shrapnel that merged with
the rain itself, which was getting harder as the Faery boy's
shield wore away. "Fucker!" again, as another bolt struck
and turned the World stark white, catching her with eyes
open, too late to blink.

Which gave her a chance to see the third bolt actually
switch directions and veer toward Calvin's atasi, where it
was reflected back at the serious-looking Faery who'd called
those bolts down from the sky.

Wouldn't call no more, though, 'cause Aik had shot him.
Shotgun, too, which meant iron pellets, which meant that
sucker wasn't risin'.

But which gave her a chance to. She snapped off a pair
of rounds at the nearest mortal: a woman of the sensible-
shoes, angry-at-men, short-haired type, with a dash of good-
old-girl thrown in. Which looked damned funny in Faery
livery. Bitch wasn't laughing now, though, with bullet holes
in her too-large titties.

LaWanda saw the woman's mouth round into an anguished, shocked *O*, and realized with sick fascination that
she'd just killed her first, and she prayed only, white woman.
Her only mortal, period, she hoped; her other shots had been
calculated to wound. And wasn't it just like men, too; sending the "not-like-mes" in first? Blacks before whites. Aussies before English at Gallipoli. Irish foot before English
archers in fourteenth-century Scotland, if you believed
Braveheart. Mortals before Sidhe.

But they were all enemies, all trying to kill her friends
(and remind her to take Myra aside after this was over and
teach that gal to *shoot*). And all of a sudden there weren't
many mortals anymore, and the whole pool was swarming
with pissed-off, rain-soaked Sidhe. One of whom had pre-
tended to be a floater until he made it almost to shore—two
yards from her—whereupon he leapt straight at Myra, who
lay between.

LaWanda shot him. Shot *at* him, rather; the automatic was

empty. Okay then: blade on blade, and she jumped up, rolled, and met the man's sword with her machete before he knew what had happened. Blade didn't like hitting iron, either, and clanged tinnily as the man jumped back—on one leg, her follow-through having hamstrung the other. Myra promptly fell atop him with Alec's dagger. Faery blood spurted from severed carotids.

Guy had friends, though; at least two, both of whom rushed her with swords upraised in opposing hands, which wouldn't be good if she got scissored, protective juju or no. Myra stabbed one in the foot; Alec, who'd got himself winged early on, tripped the other by rolling into him—which brought him down smack on top of Liz, who was trying to reload, effectively immobilizing her. The guy's lips—he looked like the prettiest Guess model imaginable—had already curved in a wicked grin when LaWanda slammed her machete into his skull.

She didn't stop to survey the damage, but Liz didn't look real happy under there and was bleeding from a scalp wound that could've had a dozen sources. "You okay?" LaWanda demanded. "If not, play dead."

"Won't take much playing," Liz chuckled, head falling into a pool of someone else's blood.

LaWanda hated to abandon her, but she was probably in the safest place she could be. Myra, Alec, and Piper (who'd anticipated Liz's action) were her main concerns. In fact, she was surprised she wasn't standing over Piper defending him above all else. Wouldn't hurt if she was closer, though! Stepping over the body of the Faery whose head she'd sundered, she leapt toward her lover.

And spun half around as something smashed into her thigh right above one of the wounds Yd had given her, knocking her to the rocky ground. *Gunshot,* she knew right off; she'd thought they'd taken out all those motherfuckers. Hurt like a son of a bitch, too, though the force surprised her more than the pain, which, being on top of something that hurt already, wasn't as bad as it could be, though it might've messed up a tattoo she'd lately had done there. In any event, it probably wouldn't be fatal, thanks to certain protections.

Best stay off it, though, and so she crawled up between

Piper and Myra, behind their log, and decided it was time to reload the automatic.

Calvin, who was crouching behind her in the shadows of the biggest boulder on that side of the clearing, saw her and muttered a terse, "You reload, I'll cover."

It took but seconds, which, however, she hadn't had earlier. It also gave her time, first of all, to fight down shock, which was threatening to blindside her, but also to assess the battle. First wave, mortals with guns, were down. Second wave, Faeries with mojo and swords, were doing better because they were rasher and probably used to dying. Shoot, the Death of Iron was likely no more real to them than death of any kind had been to most of her party until tonight.

Her party—they seemed okay, but she couldn't see the kid, who'd been on David's other side. "Dave?" she yelled, because it wasn't a bad idea to check now and then on your commander. But he was busy: shooting the chest out of a blond Faery who'd also tried to play the floater game. The Faery fell, but his sword came down anyway—right at David.

David rolled. Brock either couldn't or didn't, and the atasi the boy flung out to block the blow imperiling his friend didn't quite get there in time. Blood blossomed along David's sleeve—blessedly his left one—even as the war club caught the sword on the follow-through and reduced it to slivers of light. *Some* of it. The blade shattered and bent but continued down, wielded by dead hands.

And caught Brock with weakened but still potent force at the juncture of arm and shoulder. The kid screamed. David's face went white as paper, eyes blank as the blind, which a blast at that range might well have effected.

And then the third wave arrived and she had no more time for observation.

Brock was pissed as hell, and not because he hurt so bad he'd have done anything he could imagine to stop it—*either* it: the one in his calf, which had hurt more than anything he'd ever felt; or the new one in his shoulder he couldn't see, but which he knew was awful, because that arm just wasn't moving.

No, he was pissed because this was his second battle, and he'd spent the first cowering, and had determined, at any cost, to be as good a man as all these excellent friends, which meant holding his own no matter.

He'd spent his fifteen-minute psyching time thinking about it: how a man had to control his own mind, and if fear came calling, it was to be told to go away, because fear got you killed, and you could offer it tea later, when you sat around BSing. This was to have been reflex: cold and calculated as a video game.

There was to have been no sneak attack. No pain—you didn't see that in the movies, just guys grimacing—no stench of blood, no taste of bile and adrenaline and dirt and bloody water in your mouth, and no fucking rain to complicate everything, including choosing your target.

At least he'd told David the truth about the medallion. And at least part of him would survive in the child that woman was carrying: half-human, but all Faery.

As for the battle—gosh, there *was* a battle, wasn't there? Was still shouting and yelling and bullets going off and lights flashing and faces he knew blinking in and out like strobe-lit masks in an arcade.

In a quirky, drifty, unreal kind of slow motion.

But he had to help too! Sure he hurt, but Dave had it right: pain wasn't dying, and he had a good leg and a good arm, and a brain that was no slouch either.

But where was his atasi? He fumbled in the mud for it, but couldn't find it. "Club," he choked, to the quick-moving, wild-eyed shadow to his right.

"Huh?" David gasped, even while shooting—handgun now.

"Club," Brock repeated, though it cost him.

"There!" The weapon appeared at his side as by magic. He grabbed for it, missed; ducked something that whizzed past his face. And found it again with fingers that were slick and not nearly as strong as they ought to be.

There was a dead man right in front of him, too: blond and young-looking, with half his pretty face burned off, and one whole arm charred to the bone. Made a good shield, anyway, though Brock was damned if he knew what he could

do besides parry bullets. God knew he couldn't run screaming into that mess that had just exploded at the water's edge,
where at least five people went at it with fist and tooth and—
claw, if he wasn't mistaken. One was Dave, which wasn't
good, since his buddy had taken one in the arm trying to
shield him. One might be Finno. The other good guy was
Elyyoth, who'd reclaimed his sword and was having at someone his own size with the hilt. Guy knew his way around a
blade, too, which made sense, given he was one of Lugh's
guard. *One, two, snicker-snack*, and an arm flew off—a rifle
still clutched in its hand.

Whereupon Elyyoth's eyes went very wide indeed, and he
toppled forward, a hole the size of his fist in his back, where
a mortal had let him have both barrels of a shotgun at point-
blank range.

Blood splattered Brock's face—his *mouth*, for Chris-
sakes—and he choked and retched and tried to stand and fell
because he'd forgotten his leg didn't work. For that matter,
he'd mostly forgot that it hurt, which ought to bother him
but for some reason didn't.

He *was* getting light-headed, though, and things were going weird and distant, but he thought most of his folks were
still up and running. The Indian crowd—*his* crowd—were
doing fine. Aik, LaWanda, and Sandy were like clockwork.
A few were befuddled. Elyyoth was . . . dead.

And David, Alec, and Liz, who'd all been so nice to
him . . .

The last two he couldn't see, but Dave was right in front
of him, embroiled in the pitched hand-to-hand in the shallows. He couldn't help anyone else—

Hey, but maybe those folks wouldn't be looking for someone his size, if he stayed in the shadows . . .

"Motherfucker hell!" LaWanda yelled, five yards to the
right, clutching a hip that was already bleeding twice, though
she tried to rise.

"Shit!" Scott spat, right after, on Brock's other side. He
heard Scott's pistol fall, but couldn't spare time to assess his
damage, because Dave was down flat on his back, and his
gun was empty and there was a man twice as big as him and
Brock together jumping on top of him—weaponless, but

with hands the size of baseball gloves. Hands that clamped around Dave's throat.

Dave grabbed at wrists as thick as his legs, and was wriggling and thrashing for all he was worth—a lot, actually; he was a pretty decent wrestler—but his eyes were already bugging out.

Brock started, realizing he'd gone into that dreamy fugue again. This time, however, he knew what was causing it. But he also knew a friend was in trouble, and that that friend had no hope but him, and that he once more had a weapon.

His leg wouldn't hold him, but he rose on it anyway—stiffly—and used it to prop himself up long enough to lunge one-handed at that man and bring his war club, with all hundred-odd pounds he possessed behind it, down on that man's skull.

It exploded into light. The air smelled of ozone, blood, and burned hair. The man slumped atop David, who was trying to catch his breath and crawl from under a corpse.

Brock stared at him. David stared back, blankly at first, then recognizing him. He grinned a grin that would have lit the whole clearing. "Thanks!" he panted, and collapsed. It was the last thing Brock ever heard, too; because Brock-the-Badger No-Name, who had been born Stanley Arthur Bridges, was dead.

Aikin felt the tide turn against them as though it were a literal change in the wind, which perhaps it was, since the Sidhe could control such things, and the latest wave—the fourth wave—of attackers were Faery. Made sense, he supposed, alternating like that—as he slapped another magazine into the Glock, since the shotgun took too long to load and he'd dropped a whole box of shells into the effing pool.

Nope, it didn't look good for the home team; with Elyyoth dead, Aife bleeding like a stuck pig from the shoulder, and Finno who-knew-where. Oh, the Redskins were doing fine, probably had medicine bags or something; either that, or charmed lives, though he'd lost all respect for Cherokee mojo when the wards hadn't kept these fuckers out. Of course, they hadn't warded the mountainside, either, because nobody had remembered there was a Track in there. But they weren't everybody.

The rest—well, the noncombatants had performed as expected: all down or muddling, though Liz, Alec, and Myra were doing their best. Shoot, McLean had finally got his ass up and running and was skimming around the edges, cutting the throats of every downed foe—every *Faery* foe—who dared move. The kid? Who knew? Didn't look good, though. The others, the ones he'd termed the big guns, which was basically him, Dave, Scott, Sandy, and LaWanda—well, he was the last man standing, and all of a sudden he realized it was really down to him and Cal and Kirkwood, only Cal was all the hell away on the other side with a bunch of fresh new bloodthirsty Sidhe pouring out of the waterfall, swords in hand.

At least they weren't using mojo; couldn't, if what Finno said was true: that you had to concentrate to do it right, and most Sidhe weren't much better at it than most mortals were at foreign languages. Capacity was one thing, skill and strength another.

Bloodlust was a third, and he'd had plenty of *that* tonight; and stayed cool, calm, and collected, and chosen targets just so, and hit most of 'em, and avoided taking out his friends, and all that. Except that all of a sudden he'd realized he was standing all but alone amid the dead and dying, a good chunk of whom were his buddies, and that he was grade-A, number-one prime target. And that four sets of Faery eyes were looking straight at him.

He stepped back, wishing he had that fucking ammo that was scuba diving down by Aife's foot; took another, and debated turning to run.

"Aikin!" someone yelled; Alec, it sounded like, though it was hard to tell above the moaning (not much shouting anymore) and the steady hiss/roar of the increasing rain. "What?" he yelled back through a faceful of streaming water.

Alec yelled again, voice wild and desperate and full of pain. Another word this time: not his name.

". . . horn."

Horn? He blinked, then cursed himself for having forgotten what he'd come to consider a nuisance, there at his hip.

The horn Deffon the gryphon had given him!

He'd said he'd come. Would he still?

And would he be in time?

The nearest Faery was favoring him with a far too evil grin and stepping forward. Without a second thought, Aikin yanked the horn from his hip, raised it to his lips, and blew.

Interlude VIII:
Within Walls and Without

I

(Tir-Nan-Og—high summer)

The wall was polished white marble quarried in Annwyn, and vanished into a haze of glamour to either side. It was higher than the conifers from the Mortal World that made a grove beside it on that least precipitous face of Lugh's Peak, and as thick as the greatest of those trees was through. It was beautiful, too; for intricate, yard-wide friezes made bands of knotwork, zoomorphery, and calligraphy at intervals along it, and double doors ten times a man's height tall were set an armspan deep in the center, there where Lugh's surviving guard and the bulk of his old court sat their mounts before them, contemplating entry.

Those doors were the tenth most complex constructions in Faerie, and not only for the designs worked upon them. For they were made of every known substance in that Land save those which quickly decayed, and included many of them, like ice that never melted and Fire frozen in Time (a Powersmith specialty). Never mind bones of the Daoine Sidhe, bodachs, and selkies; gryphons, enfields, and wyverns—and jewels, woods, shells, fabrics, paper, glass, metals—even insulated iron. All these made up Lugh's doors. He confronted them now: the one barrier between himself and his palace— them and a building's worth of battle, for word had it from a turncoat survivor of Dhaoinne's Vale that Turinne had summoned all the Sons of Ailill to witness his coronation.

All, save a tithe who'd ridden out like the Fomori themselves were on their tails shortly before Lugh's arrival. Where they were, he had no idea, nor cared. Perhaps seeking some artifact needed to seal the ceremony.

The rest—he would fight them, though the Spear was not so Powerful now that the sun was setting. Mortals, he would blast ere they came near enough to wield their iron weapons. Sidhe he would disperse more slowly, so that he might savor their deaths as they would have savored his. No amnesty *this* time. Nor had Nuada, who championed such things, urged it.

"Well, Lord," Nuada murmured at Lugh's right, in that place he treasured most. "It seems that the vintage of the day is blood, and not only in this World, or I miss my guess. Soon enough you will stain your white halls with gore and the lives of those who follow you and defy you alike. But hear this: take your Land now or lose it forever! I know this, for the Power of my house is upon me, and I know that the Land will resist this choice!"

Lugh grinned at him, impish as a boy, then brandished the Spear aloft. And then he looked at those massive, enormous, wonderfully wrought doors and whispered a *word*, so softly not even Nuada could hear.

The panels promptly split from top to bottom, but instead of opening, they dissolved, like the leading melting free of a burning stained-glass window.

"Lord—" Nuada gaped, aghast.

"I will not be sealed in against my will, nor have my forces sundered from me or myself from them." He twisted around in the saddle and regarded the host at his back. "Ride or dismount, I care not, only follow. Little time remains and we must use it to advantage. When in doubt, kill, and let wergild be on Turinne's head!" And with that, he leveled the Spear straight before him and rode into his palace.

The first man he met fled in terror. The second groveled and was ridden down. The third, fourth, and fifth stayed to fight, but Carmagh, Lugh's squire, slew them with blowgun darts before they could find their ground.

Then came the first cross corridor—and attack. Swords flashed, shields glittered, voices chimed like bells of brass, and marble echoed with the songs of metal against metal, hand against hand, and life against life.

The pavement in their wake was far more crimson than white.

II

Lugh's famous twelve-towered palace blazed before the sun like a mountain aflame. The fires of sunset washed its walls with glowing red, vivid orange, and twilight purple. But the building itself blazed as well, for every window held a light, and every single one of the countless stone embrasures that crowned towers, walls, and turrets alike bore a torch. Banners flew there: Turinne's and the Sons of Ailill's.

But not Lugh's—yet—though Arawn doubted the returning King would suffer usurpation uncontested, if contest it he could. What amazed Arawn was the haste with which Lugh had raised such a formidable force. Most were older than most of the Sons, so said rumor, which made them slow and predictable, for Sidhe. But they were also wily and more experienced, and some had faced up to iron.

Iron—Arawn stroked the never-sheathed blade that hung at his side. It was *not* made of that metal, though he would've liked to own a mortal blade as a curiosity. In any event, he was still debating who should taste it. If Lugh and Turinne met, one would die—likely forever—and he would have only one foe. If he caught them before, however, it was possible he could meet them both with blade and battle. Or—

He froze, for the instrument he'd been consulting on his forward rail showed a strange new image: a mountainside outcrop in the Lands of Men, around which close to a dozen mortals engaged a troop of Turinne's in what looked more ambush than battle. The mortals were holding their own, too, though several were down, and, now he looked, they did number a few of Faery kind among them, notably Fionchadd mac Ailill, who had become quite a problem indeed.

It was an odd mix, actually: steel weapons, both bladed and *guns* (or whatever they were called); and what looked like simple wooden clubs but clearly weren't; ranged against more guns, swords, and what minor-level sorcery the rank-and-file Danaans could conjure while engaged. It was raining, too, which always made combat interesting, as did the fact that half those in Turinne's livery were mortals.

"This I must see with my own eyes," he told the gaping Cemon. "Tell the captain to steer the course I give him."

III

Arden mac Alben sometimes wondered why he'd joined the Sons of Ailill. Boredom, perhaps; or the need for change. What he hadn't bargained for was standing guard in the vast white emptiness of Lugh's high-arched audience hall watching mortals disperse the iron cage they'd erected around Lugh's throne.

He could feel its heat even here, a dozen paces away: iron bars, iron bands, and iron bolts and other fasteners; all transported separately by unsuspecting mortals and assembled in haste around Lugh's judgment seat, which was not only the symbol of his sovereignty but also his actual linkage to the Land. The Land hated that prison, too, he could tell, in spite of the precautions Turinne's mortal overseer had contrived to soothe it, notably the lavish use of wyvern skin insulation at the four points where the stuff of the Mortal World rested on more refined Faery matter. Even so, the floor smoked a little, and new depressions showed in the stone beneath those metal feet.

At least it was two thirds gone now, and the remainder wouldn't take long to disassemble, now that key bolts and junctures had been removed. Then came the cleansing, the scouring of blood, and the coronation. Not the ceremony it would've been, but effective nonetheless. And once the Land accepted Turinne, *then* there'd be time to—

The ground shivered, gave a little jolt, as though something vastly heavy had slowly begun moving underfoot. He knew that sensation, too, for he'd felt it often in his youth in the quarries of Annwyn, from whence half the stone in this palace had come. It had been play then: boys standing on fresh-cut stones which rested on smooth, round rollers—

then pushed into movement and set racing down those perilous, steep roads. This felt exactly like that: the merest of
movements, but implicit within it the certainty of continued,
ever more rapid, progress.

Again! Or the same—but stronger.

The palace shifted ever so slightly; marble dust drifted
down. A mortal braced for balance against the cage and came
away unscathed. A Faery did likewise and jerked back a
smoking hand.

A third time, and the movement became ongoing, so slow
and insidious one wouldn't notice it if one weren't attend-
ing—like breathing or the pulse of one's heart.

What could be causing it, though? There were no earth-
quakes in Faerie, though the Tracks and Pillars could do
strange things sometimes. Or perhaps this was the Land's
preemptory response to what Turinne soon would dare; as
though it would wrench away from that confrontation.

Or embrace it.

One thing was certain, however: Tir-Nan-Og *was* moving.

"Go tell Turinne," he told his page, a wide-eyed bodach
girl. "Tell him the Land is resisting."

IV

(Sullivan Cove, Georgia—
Monday, June 30—just past midnight)

Big Billy Sullivan almost didn't recognize his house,
though everything was the same as when he'd left it, save
that his pickup was gone, for which he imagined there was
a reason. Other than that, it was the same yard: half grass,
half mud, mostly all water now; the same porch in need of
paint; and the same clapboard siding he'd intended to up-
grade as long as he and JoAnne had been married. Same
outbuildings, too; same worn boards on the porch; same li-
noleum in the kitchen; same tacky-looking brown shag in the
den he demanded JoAnne help him into.

But it was not the *same*. Maybe it was the clammy, un-
seasonable chill, or the light (something *weird* about the

light); or the odd little things that had moved. A gun here (with a note from Aikin, saying he'd borrowed it); a pair of boots there that belonged to none of his clan. A cloak somewhere else that had nothing in common with any fabric he'd ever encountered. The scent of whatever Elyyoth smoked in that weird pipe he'd brought with him out of Faerie.

Or maybe he was simply seeing it with observant eyes. Eyes that would drink it down and remember.

"Beer'd be good," he told JoAnne as she and Dale and Billy (who was stronger than JoAnne now) eased him down into the leather lounger they'd bought with some of the gold that turned up on the porch now and then. He didn't add that whatever piece of his innards had been nicked when that stick went in had just split most of a seam and was now bleeding much more freely. It wasn't a *bad* feeling, exactly; kinda like being filled up with warm water. But no way it portended anything good.

Who'd've thought it, though? To have survived the 'Nam and all the shit that went with it, and then die from a poke in the back! And the thing was, no one would know what Dale had confided (that David had told the old man alone): that just as iron could eat away at the substance of Faerie, there were metals there that could do the same to the stuff this World was made of. The stake that had got him had been bound with some kind of greenish metal. It had broken; the metal had dissolved because of the iron in his blood. But suppose a sliver of that metal *hadn't* dissolved, or dissolved more slowly, or reacted with mortal iron? And if it was a small enough piece, it might not show on X ray.

Which didn't really matter any more than it mattered that a .44 got you 'stead of a 30.06.

What *was* important was the road he'd took to get here, and nobody but nobody, and certainly not his wonderful, strange, frustrating older boy, would ever be able to say he hadn't done his best. *Whatever* happened tonight, Big Billy Sullivan had gone down fighting.

It didn't even hurt much, though he was really tired and kind of thirsty and wished JoAnne would get back with that beer. In the meantime, he wondered if that ongoing wailing didn't sound like "Amazing Grace."

Chapter XX:
The Darkest Hour

(Lookout Rock, Georgia—
Monday, June 30—past midnight)

Sound called David back to consciousness.

He'd heard the Horn of Annwyn once: that which summoned white hounds with red ears to appear from some place that was not of Faerie to devour both the body *and* the soul of whatever they were set upon. It had been on this very ledge, when he, Liz, Alec, Nuada, and a bunch of Faeries he hadn't heard from since had blundered from that same hidden Track that lay behind the waterfall straight into the clutches of Ailill and his half-mad sister. That horn had saved his life then, but he wouldn't have said the sound was sweet.

The horn Aikin had just winded, however—perhaps it was merely the fact that it was the first thing that registered clearly after he'd roused from some kind of blackout, but he doubted he'd ever hear anything so beautiful again: high and pure and clear, as though all music were distilled into that one note.

The air trembled. The hiss of rain and the mumble of the waterfall vanished, as though they likewise hearkened to that sound. The Faery warriors wading thigh-deep through a pool full of blood and floating bodies stopped where they were as well.

Which proved their undoing.

For the barest instant, the pool glowed silver as though lit from beneath, then erupted around those gaping warriors: water first, followed by solid shapes—two, three, *five*—each with a lion's body and the head and front talons of an eagle. Three had wings, two did not, though light pulsed from junctures in furred body armor.

"*Gryphons!*" David gasped as he shrank back in dread and awe. Horn or no, the way things had gone tonight it was no given that anything from *there* that showed up unexpectedly could be presumed an ally. And maybe these beasts weren't. But the first to emerge—one of the big males—dragged a talon along the chest of a Faery who *might've* moved to block his way, ripping him open for his trouble. The warrior died screaming through a torn-out throat, courtesy of a second swipe. Might as well have died, anyway: the pain forced his soul from his body, which was as close as the Sidhe came to death when iron wasn't involved. Unfortunately, he tumbled into David, sprawling him across the bulky mortal he'd seconds before crawled from underneath.

From fighting for his life, David was jolted into playing spectator at what strongly resembled a Roman gladiatorial combat, save that none of the humans were Christian (and the mortals among them were apparently all dead), and most of the lions had wings. And of course there was the small fact that the carnage was taking place in a pool of mountain water.

"*Fuck!*" Aikin gasped, staring at the horn as though it had bit him. "Did I do that?"

David didn't answer, concerned as he was with keeping one eye on the combat (which was obscured by vast plumes of red-tinged water amid which gryphons bit and tore, while Faery warriors had at them with swords, then hands, and finally, in one case, bloody stumps) and, more to the point, with getting his ass out of there.

His and Brock's, ideally, since he doubted the kid had prospered from saving his life just now, which was the last thing he remembered before he'd gone out. Shielding himself from a particularly strong swath of spray, he freed himself from the bodies sprawled atop him, crawled over another, and finally reached the boy, who was lying face down in a shallow depression. He reached out and nudged him in the ribs with his free hand, oblivious to the blood dripping there.

And almost threw up on the spot.

"No *way!*" he mouthed, flinching away. "No fucking way!"

The kid was *dead!* No way he'd be so limp otherwise. But . . . he'd just been *alive!* Alive enough to cleave a man's head with an atasi!

All at once the battle didn't matter.

Nor did he care when he rose shakily and began firing aimlessly into the corpse of the man who'd tried to skewer him, who, as best he could tell, had cost Brock his life. It was stupid, crazy, and dumb, and utterly irresponsible, here on the fringe of what logic suggested was no longer their battle. But he had to vent *some* anger *right now*, and the only live things he could access were on his side.

The Beretta clicked on an empty chamber.

David sat down with a thud, staring at nothing save Brock's smooth, blood-spattered face. At least the kid's eyes were closed and he looked fairly peaceful. He didn't dare look at the awful gash in his shoulder, though, nor did he heed the steady trickle of his own blood down his arm. Or the ever-increasing pain.

He didn't notice when the sound of splashing diminished into the familiar rain-hiss and waterfall-rumble, and scarcely heeded more when all five gryphons, none the worse for wear, calmly knelt before a very confused-looking Aikin.

He heard something about a debt fulfilled (there was a lot of that going around), and springs being to Silver Tracks as Pillars of Fire were to Gold, only not exactly because the water and Silver only touched, as opposed to there being an actual identity in the other case.

And he flat didn't give a damn, any more than he gave much of one about the fact that they'd apparently just won. As for the grandiose plan that had brought them here—well, Elyyoth and Aife were out of it, and Finno was AWOL entirely, though he'd been awfully close to the bad guys when the cavalry had arrived. No way they'd finish the Track stuff now. No way in *hell* Tir-Nan-Og would ever be moved—that way.

Nor did he care when Aikin whispered something to the biggest gryphon, which promptly led the whole pack of them in a series of graceful dives back into the pool, whence they vanished as though sucked down a drain.

And he cared little more when Liz uttered a strangled gasp and laid her hands on his shoulders. Her grip tightened, and he knew she'd also seen. "I got him killed," David spat. "I fucking got him *killed*. He was just a kid and he—"

"Don't go there," Liz warned shakily. "He knew what he was doing. If not for him, I wouldn't be standing here saying"—she paused, swallowed—"saying we won."

David shook his head, which ached like a son of a bitch, never mind his arm. "Wasn't for *me*, somebody wouldn't be havin' to call his sister and his mom sayin' he wasn't comin' home again ever."

Silence. David was dully aware of the others collecting themselves, assessing the situation, tending wounds, inquiring after others. He supposed he ought to make an announcement: apprise them of their loss, which only Sandy among them had noticed. She'd withdrawn at once and now sat alone, grieving silently, but otherwise intact.

His worst wound was inside. Oh, he had a nice graze along the side of his skull that'd make a handsome scar, and there were a pair of ugly red gouges on his left arm, one of which bled persistently. His throat felt tight, too, as though fingers still dug in there. But the worst pain was not of the flesh.

Calvin staggered over to join them, took one look at Brock's body and sat down abruptly. "Is he . . . ?"

"Oh, yes!"

"I loved that kid!" Calvin choked, gaze fixed stonily ahead.

"Me too," David managed, slapping a red-stained hand on Calvin's thigh before burying his face in his hands. "Sure as hell didn't deserve it!"

"Nobody does. Neither did Elyyoth."

More silence, but for the hiss of rain, the lapping of troubled water, and the sound of someone rising from the pool to slosh clumsily toward them.

"Just like the song," David mumbled, because he had to keep talking or go crazy. "He'll never get to fall in love, never get to be cool."

Calvin shook his head. "Think he made the second one."

"Two ends of time," Liz quoted another song. "Neatly tied."

"I can't stand this!" David gritted—and stood.

Fionchadd appeared from the shallows. He was dripping wet but none the worse for wear. "It is working—I think!" he breathed. "I must help Aife."

David blinked at him and saw that the sloshing had been the Faery woman's approach. She stood before them now, looking gaunt, grim, and haunted—and tired unto death; yet still beautiful for all of it. Blood oozed from the shoulder that had taken the bullet, spreading into the wet fabric of her tunic. Alec was beside her, nearly invisible behind Fionchadd, but supporting her all the same. The wound in his forearm glistened darkly, but was minor or he'd be tending to it. "Sacred water has drunk deep tonight," Aife whispered, as though that effort cost her deep as well. "Yet as best I can tell, all this blood, from friend and foe alike, has called a Track, bound it to us, and set it to working that which was in my mind when we were attacked. Our enemies have aided us unaware."

Myra scowled at her from where she was helping Piper tend a protesting LaWanda. "So let me get this straight, we only needed a little blood, and got—"

"A river. Maybe too much. Maybe more than I can control. But for better or worse, Tir-Nan-Og *is* moving."

"Yeah, but where?" Liz wondered.

Aife's face went grimmer still, if that were possible. Certainly she showed no sign of her recent victory. "Where I wanted, maybe. Or perhaps it will go where the Track takes it. Perhaps Tir-Nan-Og will be torn apart and destroyed."

"By a bunch of fucked-up mortals tryin' to save it," Scott growled.

"Tryin' to save our World," David corrected bitterly—even good news left him numb right now. "At a price nobody's ever gonna know."

"Goddamn it!" Alec shouted. "Can't you people fucking *hear*? She says she's not done. She's gotta try to control it—and she's worn out!"

"We all are," Myra sighed, patting LaWanda's leg and rising. "Tell me what to do, and I'll try."

"Better make it snappy," Kirkwood broke in, gazing toward the overlook behind them. "We got more company."

"Good!" David snarled. Steeling himself, he reached over and eased the atasi from Brock's lifeless fingers, then rose to his full height and stared at what was approaching. "I *feel* like killing right now."

For Alec, it was another case of déjà vu. Once before—the same night they'd blundered out of the Tracks in the cliff and heard the Horn of Annwyn summon Ailill's doom—he'd stood up here with his friends watching ships burn their way out of thin air to hover just beyond the precipice, supported by nothing. Those had been *Lugh's* ships; their errand, mercy and conciliation. This armada of baleful, dark-hulled vessels bore the arms of Arawn of Annwyn upon their billowing sails. And Arawn had no love for them at all.

Aife inhaled sharply, though from pure frustrated alarm, or the pain in her shoulder, he couldn't tell. "Help me," she mumbled. "Others will deal with Arawn, but the Tracks must be mastered *now*."

Alec glared at her. "I already said I'm with you."

"Give your strength of will, then, for mine may not suffice." She gazed down at the water that swirled about their feet. "Of blood, beyond hope, we have enough."

"But the ships!"

"Others will deal with them. Now aid me or ignore me, but come. We have no grace any longer. Fionchadd, I need you—and anyone else. Now!"

Alec spared one final glance at the fleet massing beyond the precipice, noting that a tall red-haired man with somewhat the look of Lugh, though sterner and angrier, stood in the prow of the nearest vessel. Arawn, Lord of Annwyn, without a doubt.

And then Aife took his hand and led him into deeper water, oblivious to both their wounds.

Kirkwood hesitated barely a second, then strode up to stand beside Calvin, Scott, Aikin, and a very wild-eyed David where they faced the armies of Annwyn across a gap of air he could've leapt when he was younger. Cal and Dave had atasi, as did he. Aikin had his shotgun; Scott, Elyyoth's sword. A ragtag bunch they were, too: bloody and dirty and wet. Yet here they stood, staring down the king of a country that two days ago, in spite of what Cal had told him, he'd never believed existed.

Arawn gazed at them hungrily, likely weighing their strengths, as Kirkwood had seen opposing sides of *anetsa* games do as part of their pregame psyching. He glared right back, refusing to be baited. No one spoke, as though each side conceded first move to the other. A pair of tall warriors eased up to flank Arawn. Both wore helms and cloaks and carried swords, which they unsheathed together and laid casually on their shoulders, at rest but still a warning. Arawn likewise raised his, still not speaking.

"What do you want?" David demanded at last, a hard, impatient edge in his voice. Kid sounded fey, if truth were known; not that Kirkwood blamed him. "Fight us. Help us. Or leave. I really don't care right now. Just do it and get it over."

Arawn's lips curled; his eyes narrowed angrily. "I see we missed the battle we came to witness, so perhaps you should provide us with another."

"Whatever!" David retorted recklessly.

Faery eyes flashed in more than one face. "You fought the ashes," Arawn purred. "Would you now face the fire?"

"Whatever," David repeated. (*Stalling,* Kirkwood realized. Buying time for Aife. He hoped that was his only agenda.)

"I could *burn* you to ash where you stand, little mortal!" Arawn hissed. "Lugh has spoiled you, but not all the Sidhe are like him. Even now he fights for his throne. If he wins and we slay you, we rid him of the last impediment to his plan. If Turinne wins, we remove a nuisance from his borders."

"We've got steel!" David warned. "We've got stuff you never even heard of!"

A brow quirked upward. "And we do not?"

David squared his shoulders and took another step forward, which brought him perilously near the edge. He was scared of heights, too, Cal said. So, good for him. "I'll fight you, then," David challenged. "Man to man. But only if I can name the weapons."

"That choice by rights is mine," Arawn drawled. "Yet I am curious." He leaned forward expectantly, hands draped across the quillions of his sword.

David swallowed. "No steel from my World. No Power from yours. Weapons neither of us truly know, but with both force and Power in 'em."

"What would these weapons be?"

David flourished his atasi, bright with more than one kind of blood. "War clubs from another World, that take a man's skill and strength to wield, yet which contain their own Power."

Kirkwood's mouth popped open. *What the hell was Sullivan trying to do?* The kid no more knew how to "wield" an atasi than the man in the moon. Shoot, he barely knew how to use one himself, and most of the flash stuff tonight had been desperation more than skill.

Arawn, however, seemed to be considering the possibility. Good. Maybe Dave *had* bought Aife some time—if only he didn't wind up paying for it later.

And still Arawn considered.

Aife's hand was cold where Liz held it fast, adding what strength she could to the woman's own. It was failing strength, too, but in that she was no different from the rest and better off than some—like poor little Brock. Or Elyyoth, whom she'd barely known, or LaWanda, who was shot so full of holes she might never walk again without limping. It was a miracle no one had been permanently maimed, and only two had died.

It was more of a miracle she was standing here up to her butt in cold mountain water when the love of her life was over on that ledge bullshitting the King of the Annwyn Faeries, who was also in some screwy way a Lord of the Dead. She wondered what a bullet from this nice little revolver in her belt would do to all that arrogance.

Blow things all to hell, probably. Besides, it wasn't her fight. She'd thrown her lot where strength was needed most: in helping Aife control her spell.

It was an odd sensation, actually; rather like bleeding to death. It hurt, but required no effort to maintain, leaving her free to observe, though her head felt strange, almost like being high. Mostly, she watched David. But sometimes, too, she gazed at Piper and LaWanda, who were off by themselves consoling each other over the death of Brock. Or at Alec, across from her, who'd aged a decade in the last hour and looked as rough as she'd ever seen him. Finno was simply *there*; slack-faced but unwounded. Sandy and Myra were present as well, and Aik had veered their way before choosing to stand with David.

A yawn ambushed her. She closed her eyes against the slow, steady rain she'd all but tuned out, it had become so pervasive. And immediately lost herself in Aife's effort. Indeed, it was as though the border between them had dissolved, so that she felt with Aife's fingers and saw with the Faery woman's inward eye.

And what she saw! Silver Tracks: a dozen at least; all twisting, merging, surging like a spiral river *toward* Tir-Nan-Og, then *through* it and beyond to another place whose position in space and time she couldn't comprehend.

Do not try! Aife demanded. *I alone must aim the spell. A little longer, and Tir-Nan-Og will be anchored. Only then dare we rest.*

Liz scowled, having caught something darker, there in the back of Aife's mind. A second agenda, perhaps? Or merely a misgiving?

Only a little longer, Aife repeated. *Pray the others can forestall the Dark King.*

Dark King. Liz pondered the phrase absently, realizing how little she knew about any of this beyond its impact on her own life. *Dark King.* Was Lugh therefore the Light?

Abruptly, there *was* light—and thunder, too, as lightning struck close by.

Reflex opened her eyes. She saw Alec only in passing, as her gaze darted first to the standoff at the precipice, then to what had drawn every other set of eyes.

She didn't see the man initially, lost in rain and shadow as he was. But then the rain was swept away, and the shadows by the woods clarified, and what she'd taken for a shrub by the entrance to the trail stepped into the sputtering torch-light.

A tall, muscular man clad in black buckskin studded with patterns of polished hematite, with an atasi at least a yard long in hands far blacker than this or any night.

"Asgaya Gunnagei!" she breathed. The Black Man of the West. Chief of Usunhiyi, the Darkening Land, in which lay Tsusginai, the Ghostcountry.

Who was *also* a Lord of the Dead.

They had come! The Chiefs of the Quarters! One was here now, and the rest were surely close behind. It really *was* going to happen! They really *were* going to move a World, even if Aife failed—which might well happen, the way she was fading.

Sparing the barest glance toward the group in the pool, Asgaya Gunnagei strode toward the confrontation at the cliff. David and Aikin eased aside, relinquishing their place on the precipice. He accepted it without acknowledgment and stood there, staring at Arawn.

"The dead of this place," he said coldly. "Are mine!"

David didn't know whether to be relieved or terrified. Beyond hope, someone had stepped in at the last instant to save their asses. Or maybe not the last instant, given that the Chiefs of Galunlati had oracular stones, a tendency to spy, and a vested interest in events in the Lands of Men.

And a promise made to aid them.

It was all going to be all right!

Or were two Lords of the Dead about to come to blows?

"This is not your Land!" Arawn snapped.

"Nor yours," the Black Man replied amiably. "The dead are another matter."

"The dead themselves choose most often, so I have heard. My kind do not die that way, and in spite of what mortals say, I have little traffic with their dead."

"It appears that you would make some," the Black Man noted.

"It appears," Arawn hissed back, "that they have made a fair number themselves!"

"Only one of which concerns me . . . now."

"You would make an interesting foe, Asgaya Gunnagei," Arawn drawled, leaning back casually. David wondered if he was scared or merely assessing.

"As would you, Arawn of Annwyn," the Black Man echoed. "Perhaps we shall test each other someday. Or perhaps our armies will. War one day, games the next. Anetsa and hurley: they are not so different. Or maybe toli."

"Perhaps," Arawn agreed.

The Black Man cleared his throat and tapped his atasi meaningfully. "It would seem to me, oh Outland King, that your attention might better be placed elsewhere. What happens here is beyond your stopping or mine. What happens there could go either way. Perhaps you should . . . observe."

"Perhaps," Arawn conceded with a mocking bow, "I will."

"Now might be advisable."

David didn't hear the *word* Arawn gave his fleet, though the anger that drove it throbbed in his skull like a decade of colds borne all at once. It was clearly an order to withdraw, however, for every ship in that fleet—and in the second that had stealthily massed behind it—slowly pivoted around its center. Those behind Arawn's flagship parted for their King to sail through and closed behind them. The air shimmered, though it was hard to see, for the rain had returned beyond the ledge. And then, like salt dissolving, they were gone.

Leaving David standing behind Asgaya Gunnagei. " 'Bout time," he muttered recklessly, too tired to say other than what he thought.

The Black Man rounded on him, knocking his atasi from his hands with one casual blow from his own. It crackled feebly, a spark where before it had commanded lightning. "I am not Uki!" the Black Man spat. "I come of my own time and choosing!"

"So you said," David snapped back, anger making him rash, as reason fought to overcome it. "Adawehiyu," he added wearily. "It has been a trying night."

"Not for you alone," the Black Man growled. "Many seek my realm, or its reflections on other sides."

David didn't look at him. He really did *not* have patience left for verbal sparring. He wanted this resolved so he could get on with the rest of his life. They were at the critical juncture now, with one spell in place and apparently working. He had to keep things moving.

"I come alone," the Black Man informed him.

David gaped at him. "No way!" he blurted, aware even as he spoke that he sounded like a pouty kid. "You promised you'd help move Tir-Nan-Og!"

Asgaya Gunnagei lifted a brow the color of a coal mine. "And is Tir-Nan-Og not moving?"

It took a moment for the words to sink in. "It . . . *is*?"

The Black Man nodded. "What we would have done, your other allies have discovered on their own and effected already. We could do no more than they. You do not need us."

"Then why're you here?" Aikin protested, sounding as angry as David felt.

"Because someone here has *died*. Someone who dared my Land before and so won great honor."

"Brock!" Calvin whispered. "You've come for Brock!"

"He is not of my Land by lineage, but still it is his right."

David gnawed his lip as logic reasserted. "The . . . death!" he dared. "Was it Brock's? Or those guys we fought, who died in the pool? Or . . . what?"

The Black Man glared at him. "What you are about requires the power of Life. It has cost one death freely given and a score sold unaware. It may yet cost another."

"What—?" David began, not wanting to believe what he'd just heard.

The Black Man wasn't listening. Wordlessly he made his way back to where the remainder of their companions stood locked in some kind of half-assed trance in the middle of the pool. David followed him. Fuck danger or decorum, Brock was still his friend! And Cal's even more, as he slowed so his companion could take the fore.

"Poor little guy," Calvin murmured when the Black Man knelt beside the slight young figure who still sprawled where he'd fallen: pale face half buried in gravely mud, black hair slicked to his skull where it wasn't floating in water.

"Whatever happens," David whispered back, "it'll be better than what we've gone through."

"Yes," the Black Man agreed, not turning. And with that he gathered Brock into his arms and waded into the pool. Ignoring the circle still at work there, he marched straight for the waterfall. Nor did he stoop as he passed through, though the water steamed where it touched his skin.

David watched unblinking, eyes afire with unshed tears. Cal did too. All at once they were sobbing. Calvin's arms enfolded him; he hugged back. And for a while two grown men bled sorrow into the night.

Music found them there: Piper, still alive and functional, still with his Uillcann pipes. He was playing "Green Fields of France."

Interlude IX:
Edge of Battle

I

(Tir-Nan-Og—high summer)

Lugh was beginning to think that perhaps he should not have built such an enormous palace. He hadn't *intended* to, of course, but even one room added per year for a thousand years amounted to quite a number, and the place was ten times older.

They were in the old parts now and still on horseback, though that was becoming more difficult as corridors became narrower, ceilings lower, and floors more slippery, never mind the stairs. The straight ones they could manage, but not the tightly curved ones, which affected the route they chose.

He could've abandoned his steed of course: faithful golden Sunstorm, ninetieth of his line. But though he still held the advantage as he and his burgeoning band bored ever deeper into his citadel, height, mass, and a longer view were virtues that couldn't be ignored. And now, though he was as sure of victory as he was certain he'd confront Turinne, still he was loath to relinquish whatever advantage he commanded. A man on foot *might* have presence; one on horseback always had more.

They were approaching an intersection now, the narrow corridor they trod giving onto a wide one more than halfway to his throne hall, where lay the heart of his realm. Closer, and he knew with senses subtle and obscure that ambush waited there. A brow cocked at Nuada bestowed him the favor of the charge. Heels touched silvery sides, and Nuada surged forward, bent low, sword in hand. Carmagh thundered by on his left, likewise poised for attack. Forty strides... thirty... twenty...

Men poured from either side in the livery of the Sons of Ailill, all afoot. Nuada took the head of the foremost. A second knelt to fire one of those coward's toys from the Mortal World. Lead rang off granite and chipped the horn from a carved unicorn, but Lugh was ready. Such they might use, but such could not prevail against something as simple as air—when Lugh summoned winds to aid him. Shot flew indeed, but shot turned aside in the tiny tornado that rose between the foe and Nuada. Let them have their fun, take their risk; he would do the rest.

"Throw down your weapons!" Nuada roared, as his sword clanged loud against mortal metal. "Throw down your weapons and save your lives, mortal men and Faery!"

"Throw down yours and *die*!" someone yelled from the side, releasing a barrage of shot. Nuada caught it on his shield, faster than any mortal could have imagined. Pellets made patterns in the intricate boss, and the metal smoked but held firm.

Nuada's eyes all but smoked, too, as he wheeled in that impossibly narrow space and charged. The mortal who'd fired upon him stood still for maybe two seconds, pondered his weapon for a second longer, then turned and fled. Nuada rode him down, and the three behind him, trapping the rest between himself, Carmagh, and Lugh's still-whirling wind. One dared the latter and got the meat stripped from his bones. Another ran, to be felled by a dart from Carmagh's blowpipe; a third stabbed himself in the heart. The remaining two sent their weapons skittering down the hall and bowed their surrender.

"Accepted," Lugh said calmly when he arrived. "Now take their heads. It will give Turinne more at which to gape." A moment later, their souls fled, but their eyes still wide and staring, and the stumps of their necks still leaking gore, Margol mac Edril and Finocris ab Istyn jeweled either side of their rightful King's saddle.

"Well, my lord," Nuada chuckled as they continued on. "What odds do you lay against further interruptions?"

II

Coward, thought Finvarra of Erenn as he watched Arawn's fleet depart that place in the Mortal World they'd turned aside to investigate. *Coward and fool!* For a moment he considered blocking his fellow King and giving him the battle he so clearly desired right there within Lugh's precious World Walls. But though Arawn himself was mighty, his grim dark Land held little to be coveted, and to slay—or defeat—Arawn was to make oneself heir to his realm, which was in truth no prize.

Tir-Nan-Og, however, was another dish entirely. Who would not desire a realm such as that?—which Finvarra had never seen from on high ere this voyage, and was looking forward to seeing again, now that that foolishness in the Mortal World was concluded.

But shouldn't they be there by now? Surely they'd been long enough *within*. Yet *within* continued unabated, nearly as full of nothingness as a Hole. Perhaps it *was* a Hole; perhaps the Lands of Men had burned through the World Walls right here, by pure blind luck.

"Lord," his captain ventured beside him. "Where . . . ?"

"There," Finvarra sighed, then choked on his next word.

They *had* reached Tir-Nan-Og. The western realm of Faerie lay beneath them, green and rich and mellow. But something had *changed*. Or was changing. This high up he could see it easily; the air itself shimmered around them with some strange new silvery Power.

Silver and Power. Alberon and a usurper druid. A tower in a World near here in which he'd imprisoned Fionchadd. Another he'd never accessed. A threat overlooked until too late.

Not that it mattered when such a spectacle lay below. For it was as though the Land itself was alive, the hills, ridges, lakes, and streams like fur on some great monster's back, remaining fixed in place, yet moving as muscles flexed beneath the skin. There was method to that movement, too: a slow spiraling along the grain of the World Walls, like liquid forced outward on a potter's wheel, then sucked upward at the edge by a sponge.

"Dana help us all," Finvarra gasped. "Tir-Nan-Og is moving!"

III

Turinne snugged a heavy gold belt around a waist still trim beneath four layers of silk, wool, velvet, and leather, and one of silver mail, and regarded himself in the wall, which was also, for this time, a mirror. He looked a King well enough: tall as Lugh and more muscular, though not so well proportioned, and younger, though that didn't truly show. He'd shaved off the mustache, however, and wore his red hair longer in an elegant tail.

He was not so much a fop as Lugh, though, and had chosen warrior garb as much as that of scholar, craftsman, or bard—which meant mail showed at wrists and throat and underlay his robes to afford his body protection against conventional weapons. Iron—that was another matter, but it was not important, for Power was Power whatever transpired, and had no regard at all for *any* metal.

Still, he was a fine figure: crimson hose and underrobe, emerald tunics layered over them, each embroidered with gems along collar, cuffs, and hem, each a hand's width shorter than that beneath.

And over all a cloak bearing the arms he'd chosen for himself as High King: *per chevron inverted argent and gules; in chief a sun-in-splendor, Or; pierced of a dagger, proper; goutee de sang*, as mortal heralds would blazon it.

There was also a sword, though not the sword of state, for he couldn't yet access the place where it was kept, no more than he could access Lugh's most official crown. For that, for this time, his own helm would suffice, which was more than fine enough. Mortal work, too: stolen from an unmarked Irish rath.

For when one got down to it, what made a King of Tir-

Nan-Og was the bond with the Land, and that merely required a particular dagger, and that he certainly *had* found.

"Lord," said his page, from the doorway, "time draws nigh if you would do this thing tonight. And surely . . . surely you know that the palace has been breached and Lugh Samildinach advances with an army at his back."

"I know," Turinne replied calmly. "I go to meet him. For good or ill, this thing will be resolved now."

IV

(Sullivan Cove, Georgia—
Monday, June 30—the wee hours)

Big Billy Sullivan was dreaming. He hadn't moved from his lounger since returning home, but had been drinking steadily. Not to get drunk, however (indeed, he was stone cold sober), but because he had thirst unending and a strong suspicion why. He was also tired, which was why he'd drifted off, which was how it was he was dreaming.

In his dream there were four boys. Three were blond and good-looking; the fourth was a stocky redhead. Two were brothers and all but identical; the others were also brothers, but not quite so alike. One of each set was named David, and one of each set was named Bill—the smallest (though they were all the same age, somehow—say fourteen) and the largest, who was himself: the one with the auburn hair. And in that dream they were *all four* brothers, yet also all best friends. And they were playing soldier; only it wasn't playing, all at once; it was real, and they were shooting real bullets and people were shooting back, and the stone fort they'd rallied in (which had started out as a cardboard box, then progressed to an abandoned outbuilding at Uncle Dale's) had disappeared, so that they were vulnerable from every side. And then they all got shot and he could actually feel the bullet boring toward his heart. But instead of dying, they collapsed together, clasped hands, and held each other as though their hard strong fingers held life itself, and swore not to let each other die.

And then they were all well again, and no longer boys, but four kings of four lands, and they warred with each other yet still loved each other, but now they loved the land more and it was over land that they fought.

And then it was no longer a dream, nor yet was he totally in his body. Instead, he looked through other eyes—*David's* eyes (his son, not his long-dead younger brother)—and felt grief fill his heart from some great sorrow, and saw war there as well: the horror he'd known himself in a far-off jungle country.

And then someone was shaking him and calling his name (*Was* that his name? What *was* his name, anyway? David or Billy or Dave or Bill?), and he awoke to see his wife staring down.

"A boy ought never to have to kill a man," he whispered. "And a man's no man that ever, ever, ever kills a boy."

JoAnne regarded him curiously, tears bright in her eyes. He smiled and took her hand. "And you know what, sweetheart?" he confided. "Inside us, we're *all* boys."

And for the first time in years, Big Billy Sullivan cried.

Chapter XXI:
Earthshaking Events

*(Lookout Rock, Georgia—
Monday, June 30—very early)*

It was funny, David decided numbly as he and Calvin eased free of each other's arms, how big things and little things were weighted in one's heart. Like tonight, for instance. He'd just seen two demigods nearly come to blows, and it had scarcely fazed him. But a mere mortal boy, whom maybe twenty people alive really knew—losing him had all but taken him apart. What Aife was about right now could well save several Worlds, but all *he* cared about was the fact that no one had saved one runty teenage kid.

What was it? Maybe two minutes from Brock's first wound to his death? And how long had the Black Man and Arawn engaged in their pissing contest? Not even half that long. Everything was out of balance, and absolutely *nothing* was fair.

Calvin started toward the pool but paused to look back at him. "Gotta keep on," he urged. "Time for this later, some things you *gotta* deal with now."

David didn't move. "It's just that I wasn't *done* with him. He got ripped out of my life and he's just . . . *gone*." A pause to swallow, as tears hovered close again. "It's not like my dad. Whatever happens to him, we've made some kind of peace. Me and Brock didn't. He was just here and then he wasn't, like a great piece of art forever left unfinished."

"Yeah," Calvin acknowledged, "I know. But we gotta go

on. I mean, look, guy: Aife's got something goin' on, too, and that's also unfinished!''

David swallowed hard and let Calvin lead him into the pool. The water was cold—which shocked him—which was probably good. And his friends were out there, holding hands in a circle centered on Aife, a handful of bloody, dirty people trying to do the most improbable thing he could imagine: trying to move a World.

Without him, when it was at heart his quest. Squaring his shoulders and sidestepping far too many floating bodies he didn't want to think about right now, he waded into the deeper water near the center. And found himself chuckling giddily, having realized how much it reminded him of a country baptizing.

Except they weren't generally held at night, and he doubted anyone present was a card-carrying Christian, save maybe Piper. They were all present, too, but LaWanda, who had leg wounds and didn't dare enter water that might suck her dry, and Piper, who likewise remained on shore, playing softly on the pipes.

David tried to focus on the music as he freed Alec's hand from Liz's and inserted himself between, while Calvin eased in on the other side. It was actually kind of nice. Cold water around his legs; rain (back, now that the Black Man had left, but fairly gentle) upon his head and shoulders, slicking his hair into his eyes. His best friends' hands. The melancholy droning of the pipes that was oddly comforting. A deep breath, and he closed his eyes and felt Aife's Power touch him and start to draw.

The warmth of that connection pulsed through his hands and up his arms like Christmas lights on a string, but *including* his thoughts, so that he knew certain notions were his alone (like the filaments of those lights), but that the light *he* made merged with all the light around him. He was blind, too, yet he was seeing with . . . *cosmic* eyes, though exactly what he witnessed, he wasn't sure. It was like a real landscape but with every source of energy that pervaded it also visible, so that he could see winds push and froth past each other, and watch tectonic forces underground slide and shimmer like black oil upon still water, and even perceive what must be gravity as tiny sparks leaping between every single thing, like iron filings around a magnet.

But under it all—and over it all and *within* it all, to-gether—was a lattice of gold that existed in the three di-mensions he could sense right now and surely continued into more. Those had to be Tracks—*golden* Tracks. But there were silver ones as well, sliding neatly through the spaces between. And while every one of the gold Tracks was straight, the silver ones were curved. Even as he watched, those silver Tracks wove ever more pervasively through the physical Land.

They touched a tree, a leaf, a mite upon that leaf, and it dissolved and went sparking and tumbling down that shim-mering length. But if one followed it, why, somewhere far-ther on, it surfaced again, intact. And that was happening over and over *everywhere*: in forests, plains, and Tir-Nan-Og's few villages (it had no true cities), and every place between. It touched beasts, too, and bodachs and the Sidhe, apparently without their knowing; and it was as if they were reflected in some more distant place, and for a moment both were equally real, and then the reflection alone was. One could be moved that way and not know it any more than one felt it when someone moved a mirror in which one's image showed.

It's working! He told himself, completely caught in won-der. *It really and truly is working!*

But not perfectly, for when he'd joined that curious circle, the movements had been as smooth as a laser-cut edge, as precise as the gears in a virtual machine. Even his added presence had caused no obvious disruption. But now, it was as though a machine was wearing down, as though the small-est gears in that vast complex mechanism now and then skipped a cog, or a spring lost a fraction of its tension.

And *he* knew where that weakness lay.

Aife!

A thought that was not thought acknowledged it; a cluster of images explained. The Power alive in the pool had to come from somewhere, and in practice it came from life, since Power was the active aspect of spirit as energy was to matter. But once the pool began to draw it evidently couldn't be stopped. And Aife had been wounded, then fallen into the hungry water. It had sucked at her wound at once, never stopping, even when she stood, but continuing to reach up from its surface through her clothes to the skin of water that sheathed her wound. In effect, she was bleeding to death. Her only hope was that they would finish their task before she succumbed.

David felt her terror, as he felt the strength of her resolve. The movement was well along now; indeed, the Land itself was all but relocated, there only remained the sealing-off to conclude. Already she'd begun: finding the heart of Tir-Nan-Og and withdrawing the Tracks from that center, feeding those farther out, making them larger, thicker, *deeper*; pouring them into a moat of time/space/matter that could never be forded by anyone approaching from the Lands of Men, even to drowning the Tracks that led there from that World.

It would still be accessible from the rest of Faerie, he/she/they knew, as a bridge could span a river. But the river itself would never reach up to the bridge.

Which was interesting but hardly helpful, and the worst thing was there was absolutely nothing he could do. Oh, he had blood, but the pool was already sucking at that the way it sucked at her: through wet clothes and skin to his various open wounds.

Which *might* soon be a problem, but not yet.

But what else could he give? Desire? Passion? Strength of will?

"Things have Power because you give them Power," Oisin—bless his name—had said. And he suspected that a decade's worth of love, enjoyment, and passion had empowered what had until then been an ordinary pool. Or added to it, since David-the-Elder had felt the same about it, and probably two centuries of kin before that.

But if he'd had Power to manage that, perhaps some remained to contribute now.

But how?

Like Alec said: by simply worrying at it? Or—

Think, that which was Calvin broke in, *that you're doing it for Brock*.

David hesitated, fearing to go there again. But then he

recalled the things he'd liked about the boy, and then not those *things*, but simply the liking itself. And suddenly Power was rushing out of himself in a rising flood as he freed emotions he'd never dared expose.

Liz felt it, too, and in that odd dispassionate analytical way she had, likewise found the method to his act and followed. An instant later, so did Alec.

All at once *they* were the driving force, freeing Aife to focus purely on shaping her working to its final form. She was still weakening, though; David felt her slipping as his Power surged into places hers instants before had been, even as she withdrew further.

But they were almost done. The "moat" was complete. There only remained their own retreat and tying off the "loose end" with one final cauterization of Power.

. . . decided . . .

. . . doing . . .

. . . *done!*

It was over. They'd done it! Tir-Nan-Og had indeed been moved. He could feel their Power receding; see it, even; for as it slid from around the Tracks and Pillars, each one sparked as that Power touched it and whirled on by, leaving Tir-Nan-Og alone, an island in an ocean of formless dark.

But the drawing had not abated, so that he felt himself starting to gasp, in that flimsy shell that was his body. Seriously alarmed, he tried to retreat but *couldn't!* He was no longer feeding Aife; rather, she was draining *him*—and everyone else besides.

Not my fault! she cried. *My self seeks to survive.*

What? From Alec.

David's heart fluttered. He felt sick, what part of him could feel at all.

My life! Aife repeated. *To end this all, the spell must have a life.*

David felt her desire even as he felt Alec deny it. *No!* Alec screamed, there in that not-place. *No! No! No!*

I would never make you happy, my Alec. If you would make me happy, slay me now!

NO!

YES!

NO!

I will, came another presence. *And may Alec's wrath fall on my soul!*

No! David had no idea who that had been.

But he knew when it was finished. He gasped as Aife's final pain flashed out to fill the world. His heart stopped, then restarted, faster. His lungs went numb. His brain froze back to a soup of chemicals.

It was like a rubber band stretched to breaking, then released. One moment he was part of everyone, Aife in particular. The next, he was himself: rain-soaked and shivering in a pool of cold mountain water.

Gazing at Aife standing there with closed eyes and Fionchadd's dagger in her heart. She balanced briefly, in a tunic of black silk that had become her pall, then slowly slumped backwards into the water, where she floated amid a cloud of drapery and hair: Millais's *Ophelia*'s dark twin. Her face looked very peaceful.

David closed his eyes to blot out the image. And because he still clutched Alec's hand, and Alec still held Aife's, he caught her final thought. *Farewell, my Alec: I truly did love you—and truly, truly I am sorry!*

And then, like one of those Christmas lights winking out, all that made her real was gone.

Alec's hand tightened so hard David felt bones start to grind. He had no choice but to free his other from Liz's to lay it on his best friend's shoulder. "Gotta let go, man. Me *and* her. She's gone."

"Gone," Alec echoed numbly. "Gone."

"I am sorry," Fionchadd offered. "Hate me if you will, but her life was her own to give or keep."

"I know," Alec acknowledged shakily, releasing David's hand. "But eventually she'll return. I just won't be there to see it." He paused for a deep breath. "Not that I won't be *around* to see it; I just won't make the effort."

"*Can't* make the effort," Aikin corrected roughly.

Alec stared woodenly. "That hasn't stopped us—*any* of us—before. No," he added, "I *mean* won't."

"If you can make yourself believe that," Myra murmured, reaching over to hug him, "you've already started healing."

"I never really had her," Alec choked. "She was like a painting. Never real. It's easy to let go of that. Once you know it only *was* a painting."

David swallowed hard, reminded too forcefully of Brock. "Am I right, or did we really and truly get this thing done?"

Fionchadd closed his eyes, looking sick, tired, and very, very pale. When he opened them again, those eyes looked centuries older. "Tir-Nan-Og no longer touches this World. It is as if . . . as if it had once been the second level of a building of which this World is first, and is now a thousand levels higher. The Tracks still reach there, but are tenuous. As for the rest of Faerie—since Tir-Nan-Og is the strongest of the realms, I think the rest will feel its call and . . . follow."

"Which means," David said bleakly, "we just drove magic out of the World."

"Nothing is without cost," Fionchadd countered. And without further word, he slogged toward the shallows.

"I wonder," Aikin mused as he joined David, Alec, and Liz on a boulder, "what's goin' on with Lugh?"

"It's not raining," Alec chuckled edgily. "That should tell you something."

"Aye," Fionchadd agreed. "It says the drowning spell weakens with distance."

"So what now?" Liz asked, to nobody.

"Deal with these bodies, for one thing," Scott said, looking hard at Fionchadd. "Any ideas?"

Fionchadd shook his head absently. "At the moment I am pondering what I am going to do with . . . me."

Interlude X:
Claims

I

(Tir-Nan-Og—high summer)

... more doors, but these were the final set before the ones
Lugh sought. He was angry now and impatient at all this
blood, all this carnage, all these not-so-loyal subjects slain
in vain. The palace was littered with them, in all shapes,
races, and sizes, not all of them even vaguely human. One
could trace his progress through the halls by wet, red
horseshoe prints; sprawled, often headless, bodies; and sundered body parts.

And weapons. Faery weapons he kept; mortal ones—
swords, guns, or whatever—he ordered thrust into a bag of
wyvern hide for disposal later—into a Hole.

But all that was behind him, as a *word* sent another barrier
crashing down, this one a massive slab of heavy hammered
bronze. Six armspans high, those doors had been, and they
crushed a dozen defenders beneath them as they fell. The
rest cowered back or were swept there by the force of Lugh's
spell.

And then he confronted the final portals. These were solid
gold and *twenty* armspans high, and had been made by an
Italian craftsman whose death in the Lands of Men had been
a fabrication. Lugh considered dismounting but changed his
mind and eased Sunstorm up beside the juncture. No *word*
opened these doors, and no spell; only the merest touch of

a finger. *His* finger. An army of muscular mortals could not have budged them otherwise.

Silently they swung back, and very slowly. Lugh used that time to position himself for maximum effect, as the panels parted enough for him to steer Sunstorm through. And though he'd entered what lay beyond countless times before, beholding his throne hall from the entrance always took his breath away.

He had no idea how long it was or how wide. And no notion whatever of how high, though the doors he'd just passed had always seemed too small to be in scale. He had merely drawn it like he wanted, shown that sketch to his builders, and they had raised his dream: a fantasy of pure white pillars soaring to a distant, marble filigree sky. Paving stretched ahead: mosaics in subtle pale colors but impossibly intricate designs; and beyond the pillars gleamed windows that could also be murals or mirrors, but which let in whatever light he desired, for those panes could store such things. Turinne had anticipated him, too, and commanded them to twilight.

Which suited Lugh fine. This *was* twilight, of a kind; though more as the Sidhe reckoned that hour: the beginning of the day, not the languid end mortals ordained.

Something would end today, that was for certain. Or someone.

In spite of the eagerness that surged within him, Lugh held back, deliberately letting his shape be cut out against the brighter light behind him. It gave his eyes a chance to adjust, too; the room was that big and that much englamoured. Indeed, it took a moment to locate his adversary, though he'd never doubted he would find him here.

Turinne entered on foot from between two pillars to the right of the distant throne, which was the route that led to Lugh's quarters, which surely meant he'd found an important something Lugh kept hidden there. A chill raced over the High King, born alike of dread and anticipation, for he'd counted on the absence of that something to validate his cause.

Turinne had it in his hand: the plain, white-bladed knife through which King and Land were joined. He made sure

Lugh saw it, too: that shard of white fire against all that fine green fabric he wore beneath an amazing heraldic cloak.

But Lugh had a fine cloak as well: feathers from the birds of Galunlati. A wind he summoned made that plumage flutter, even as it sang through the mouths of the heads bouncing before his knees to either side. And then he set heels to his horse and paced slowly and steadily down the center of the hall toward the throne.

Lugh was playing for effect, but Turinne knew its value as well, though who either of them was trying to impress, Lugh had no idea. He had his scraggly army at his back; Turinne had brought his partisans, who spread out behind the throne in a solid wall of dazed-looking mortals spaced every third one with grimly competent Sidhe. The vast echoing space between the two was empty, save for an unclaimed throne.

Three things could happen now. Turinne could bond with the throne and let the Land choose its own master. He could command his mortal guardsmen to open fire on Lugh and his ragtag army, but that was the coward's way, the dishonorable way, and a way of which the Land would not approve. Or he could face Lugh in combat, which was likely the choice he favored; for now Lugh was close enough to see what he suspected he was intended to see: the glitter of mail beneath all that finery. Lugh had to admire him for that; standing aground to meet an armored king on horseback spoke of courage, competence, or simply chivalry that carried its own impact.

And then they were close cough to speak.

"Yield to me, Turinne mac Angus mac Offai!" Lugh thundered. "Throw down that which you hold, which you surely know is no mere weapon, and surrender to me. I will let you live."

Turinne eased around to block access to the throne. "Aye!" he shouted back. "But there is living and there is being alive. Are you certain you mean not the latter? The fate I gave *you*, perhaps? Ten thousand years in the Iron Dungeon, with iron dust blown in? Ten thousand years devoted purely to pain."

Lugh grinned wickedly. "That *had* occurred to me, and

anticipating such subterfuge proves you do think somewhat like a King."

"A King cares for the Land," Turinne challenged. "So do I."

Lugh's breath caught, for Turinne had just stated his strongest case. He *had* been lax, too caught up in the complexities of human history (at the time) to pay proper heed to his realm. "We can settle this easily enough," he replied, as his army crowded 'round. Turinne's troops fairly twitched in alarm.

"And what might that way be?"

"We could do as I know you have considered, and let the Land itself choose."

Turinne's eyes shifted to the knife in his hand, a gesture which Lugh of course noted.

"I would rather fight," he countered. "That way lies more honor."

"The Land honors life more than death," Lugh retorted. "Did you know her as well as I, you would know that as well."

Turinne folded his arms. "Explain yourself; I will listen."

Lugh paced his horse two steps closer. "I will dismount. We will each march up and kneel before the throne. And then we will proceed with the dagger."

Turinne's brown eyes narrowed. "No tricks?"

"You ask it? I have said it."

"Very well," Turinne conceded. "So be it."

Slowly, deliberately, Lugh dismounted, tossing his reins to a troubled-looking Nuada. He caught his friend's eye and grinned the most subtle and sly of grins. And then his feet were on cold, slick marble and he was striding toward the throne. Turinne met him there, looking young and fit and confident—and pleasantly troubled as well.

"What is it you will?" the younger man demanded.

Lugh took a breath. "You know the rite: this throne is part of the Land beneath it, by unbroken linkage: stone-to-stone. To be King is to join with the Land. To join with the Land, one rests one's hand on the Throne's right arm and stabs that dagger through it. The rest is decoration."

"And how are we to chose which of us makes first claim?"

"We go together," Lugh informed him. "You place your palm on the arm, I place mine atop it—or beneath, if you so say; it matters not to me. We then place our other hands on the dagger and stab through flesh into stone."

"And that is all?"

"That is how it was done for me."

"Well, then," Turinne agreed, "let us do it."

II

For the second time since arriving in Tir-Nan-Og, Arawn of Annwyn was late. That business in the Mortal World was troubling, too; and he'd spent most of the voyage hence cursing himself for not investigating those events more thoroughly. But he could already smell the sweet scent of the kingdom on which he planned to feast, and that, as much as that . . . *being's* taunts, had urged him here in haste.

Nearly too late at that, because somewhere between their arrival at what was surely the mortal boy's private Place of Power and their reemergence in Tir-Nan-Og, some fundamental change had wracked the Land. It spoke of Power applied subtly but in profligate amounts, and of a heretofore unknown brand of sorcery. Terms didn't matter, though, when the end was the same. Tir-Nan-Og *had* moved.

So it was that he'd almost watched too long, then had to use Dana's own skill to enter into the palace unopposed and unaccompanied save for Finvarra (and damn his hide for that: to wait until they were beneath Lugh's roof—and therefore his protection—to acknowledge his presence here). But that was for later—a diversion perhaps, now, given that Lugh looked to be gaining ground fast. And if Lugh commanded the Powers Arawn suspected he did, this might *not* be a good time for confrontation after all.

They reached the hall from the door opposite that through which Turinne had entered, and were just in time to see both men kneel before that empty chair of earth-dark stone. A pause for breath, and Turinne placed his hand flat on the throne's right arm. Lugh laid his atop it.

Another breath, and Turinne raised the dagger, high enough to reveal it to all who gathered there. Two of his guard, two loyal Sons of Ailill, applauded spontaneously, but Turinne silenced them with a glare. "At your will," Arawn heard him whisper, the words still audible, courtesy of the room's perfect air.

"Aye," Lugh murmured back, and wrapped his hand around Turinne's.

"At sunset precisely, a gong will sound," Lugh advised his adversary. "When that stroke sounds, we stab."

For five heartbeats they waited: the claimants to the crown; their friends, warriors, and seconds; and two rival kings who had come to claim the bones.

Another pair of heartbeats. Then, so deep it was as though the palace itself resounded: a muffled, earth-deep *bong*.

Lugh's hand tightened; Arawn saw the tendons stand out there. Clutched in two fists, the dagger swung down . . . closer . . . closer . . . almost touching the flesh of the topmost hand . . .

Lugh shifted his weight, which upset the forces on the blade. And in that instant of wavering indecision, his grip tightened again like a spring-trap, and he acted.

It was over before Arawn saw. The dagger had indeed tasted flesh, but that moment's uncertainty had cost Turinne his life. Lugh's ploy had been simple: confuse his opponent at the most critical moment, then make him relax, then strike—not down through the hands but inward, suddenly, with Lugh's greater strength, into Turinne's heart.

Arawn heard the sharp gasp, the hiss of incredulous anger, that filled the Sons of Ailill. But the word he heard most clearly, and from Turinne, was "Forsworn!"

"No," Lugh snapped, as he casually removed his blade from Turinne's body and let it slump aside. "You yourself named your doom."

"I . . . do not understand."

Lugh grinned a malicious grin. "My precise words upon proposing this were 'we will proceed with the dagger.' I did not say with what we would proceed. My words upon agreeing were 'I have said it'; yours were 'so be it' and 'let us do it.' I never said what 'it' meant, nor did you, leaving me free to choose what sense I would."

"It was implicit," Turinne gasped.

"Ah, but only the *explicit* can be true."

"It is trickery! I would have thought better of you."

Lugh regarded him coldly. "You tricked me as well: with poison from the Mortal World, when the Laws of Dana gave you the right to call me out. And do not forget, you are a traitor: be glad I do not scour your soul with iron!"

He rose then and turned toward his followers, leaving Turinne to die where he fell. He would return, of course; his *soul* would. But it might take ages for him to build another body, and Lugh, Arawn knew, would be watching.

"Long live the King!" Nuada shouted. "Long live the Ard Rhi of Tir-Nan-Og! Long live High King Lugh!"

Arawn stared Finvarra straight in the eye, grimacing sourly. "Long live," the two cried together. "Long live High King Lugh!"

Lugh turned to face them, smiling far too smugly. "Greetings, brothers!" he cried graciously. "And welcome to my court! One boon alone I claim of you, which is that you re-acclaim me, and the words be, 'Long may Lugh Samildinach reign as High King of *all* the realm of Tir-Nan-Og.' Or, you may face iron too."

As one, they blanched. As one, they also responded.

"Now," Lugh sighed, turning once again to sit on his throne, "would someone please tell me why my Land has moved?"

III

(Sullivan Cove, Georgia—
Monday, June 30—very late)

Little Billy stared at his father's face. At his nose, more specifically, wondering if the bristly hairs in his nostrils still stirred. They did, which was a relief. Big Billy really was breathing; he could hear the soft, whispery, hiss—hear it when his mom hushed, anyway, which wasn't often. She was in the kitchen now, making up another pot of coffee to divide among herself, Uncle Dale, and him. His dad was beyond drinking, and had been ever since he'd woke up with a wild-eyed start, made that comment about killing boys, and started crying, then gone back to . . . sleep. That had really put the wind up Little Billy, too, because it was full of—what was that word David used? Oh, yeah: *symbolism*. For sure there was more to it than just a dream.

And the howling—wailing, or whatever—that was still going on too, though it had kinda subsided into a distant sob like a big diesel engine very far away. Once, he was certain it had ended, and his heart had all but stopped because he had a strong suspicion that its ending meant his dad was dead. He hadn't been. Thank God. But the whole thing still freaked him because he knew something magic was going on close by; he'd learned to sense such things, or else it was in his genes the same way it'd been in David's *and* David-the-Elder's. In any event, it was like Life and Death fought some enormous battle that sent ripples even here, and that the wailing ebbed and flowed with the tides of that weird-ass battle.

One thing was certain: nothing would be the same after tonight. In the meantime, maybe he should—

He froze in the act of rising and stared transfixed at his father. The wailing had returned, louder than it had ever been. Louder again, and the nose hairs slowly stopped moving, and an unmarked tension along Big Billy's jaw relaxed as his mouth fell open with a rattly hiss. And then the hairs stirred again.

"No!" Little Billy gritted. "This *isn't*. You *aren't*—not yet!"

And with that he rose and stalked through the kitchen door. His mom, who was at the counter making sandwiches, raised a brow as he passed. Uncle Dale was snoozing in a chair. "Goin' to check the rain," Little Billy announced, easing out the screen door.

He *was* gonna check the rain, too: up on Lookout Rock, the place where something told him the only remaining chance of helping his father lay. Funny, though; it wasn't raining now, and the sky had gone utterly clear, as though the thunderous cumuli had never existed. There was also something screwy about the western horizon, too, but he couldn't figure out what. Nor did he care. Not remotely.

Chapter XXII:
Going Home

(Lookout Rock, Georgia—
Monday, June 30—the wee hours)

"Oh, my God!" David groaned, staring at Fionchadd through sodden, bloody hair. "You're cut off here, aren't you?"

"What?" Kirkwood grunted, drifting over to join them, atasi in hand. One of the few who'd survived the night unbloodied, he was more alert than most of their cadre, a couple of whom, notably LaWanda, seemed dangerously close to shock. David doubted he was entirely in his right mind himself, and knew he wasn't when he thought about Brock. He scowled at his Faery friend, who looked like something the cat had dragged in after gnawing on it a while.

"Madness," Fionchadd mumbled as though to himself, beginning to pace. "As best I can tell, I am indeed cut off from Faerie, yet my body is substance of that Land, and that link is never severed. Faerie will begin to draw on me. It will be subtle at first, a minor irritation, but will grow stronger day by day. Eventually . . . one goes mad. No one knows what happens then."

David shrugged helplessly and picked up his atasi. "Christ, Finno, I don't know what to say. I mean, you knew the risk. You should've covered your ass."

The Faery regarded him levelly. "Would you have?"

Another shrug, a wary smile; the first in what seemed like hours. "Probably not. But hey, we'll figure out something.

In the meantime, you can stay with me and Alec down in Athens.''

"Or me,'' Kirkwood chimed in. "Wouldn't mind pickin' this boy's brain a while.''

"I was fixing to suggest the same thing,'' Sandy inserted, ambling up with Myra, with whom she seemed to have bonded. "Sit on the porch, drink beer, and discuss Faery physics. Like what's this stuff about changing 'substance' mean, anyway? Best I can figure it involves one of those quirky subatomic things like charm or spin, or something. Like positive to negative, only you don't get antimatter or anything.''

Fionchadd regarded her woodenly. "I would be glad to discuss these things. But still—''

"Guy wants to go home,'' Calvin said from where he was inspecting the nearest body.

"We already knew that,'' David grumbled.

"No big deal,'' Calvin replied easily, flopping down beside Sandy. "He's still got his boat, right? It's in splinters, but maybe it could be fixed. Plus''—he squinted at Fionchadd in the uncertain light—"correct me if I'm wrong, but aren't you part Powersmith? But that's not the same as Faery, right? So can't you still get to their place from Galunlati? And from there to Faerie?''

"Right!'' David took up eagerly. "And we *know* how to get to Galunlati!''

"Unless,'' Liz cautioned, "we moved those places along with Tir-Nan-Og.''

Fionchadd shook his head. "We did not. I learned the spell as Aife did. It was quite specific.''

"Well then,'' Kirkwood concluded brightly. "You're okay! You hang around here a while, put some meat on your bones, and when you start gettin' antsy, Cal here ships you off to Galunlati, and you make your way back home from there.''

"Yes,'' Fionchadd considered. "That actually does sound possible.''

Liz nudged David with a knee. "What about Alec?''

David looked up from scouring the atasi with a rag he'd picked up somewhere. And saw his friend—his *best* friend—

squatting by the edge of the pool farthest from the mass of floating bodies, staring into that cold, wet, mirror-darkness, sometimes stirring it with a stick. Aife was where they'd left her, floating on her back as though she had no weight at all. No one had touched her, though Fionchadd had flung the remains of his cloak over her face, through which, by what couldn't be entirely luck, some of her beauty still showed.

Again, David sighed. "He'll be okay. I think he really has given her up now. In fact, I think he had a pretty good idea beforehand it'd never work. He needs to be his own man for a while, and never would've been with Aife. No way they could've ever been equal partners."

Liz nodded. "Better keep an eye on him, though."

David nodded back. "Never fear."

"I, uh, hate to mention this," Scott drawled, "but we really do have to figure out what to do about these bodies."

"Anyone make a count?" Sandy wondered.

David craned his neck. "Aik's doin' one now. Prob'ly pilferin' everything in sight for weapons, too; not that I blame him. Somebody oughta get something out of this."

Liz snorted.

David rose, aware as he pressed down how sore his arm was, like his headache, which reminded him of his possible concussion every time he moved. His arm really was a mess, too, with a deep oozing furrow four inches long in his left biceps, where a bullet had winged him pretty damned solid, with a sword-scrape right on top of it. Probably should've bound it up a long time ago. Except, Christ, he'd only had it maybe ten minutes! Which seemed impossible. He ripped at the sleeve—and winced. As soon as they got things squared away here, he'd . . .

What? By all reasonable standards, this whole cruddy mess was over. They'd achieved their goal: had moved Tir-Nan-Og, so that it was no longer threatened by the new resort down at Sullivan Cove. But *that* problem still remained: the rape of his ancestral land, and he doubted Mystic Mountain Properties would be sympathetic.

And there was still the matter of his pa. A nap would be nice too. Food. A bath in very hot water. At least it wasn't raining, though it might as well have been, for a thick summer fog had risen, completely veiling the world beyond the ledge. Which was just as well; he didn't want to contemplate the last thing he'd seen out there. Shoot, for all he knew, Arawn's crowd could've escaped . . . whatever, and be on their way back now. Maybe they should post another guard.

In the meantime, they really did have to do something about the bodies. And since calling the authorities was not an option (no way they'd be able to deal with those sorts of questions), he supposed they'd have to consider arcane alternatives. In any event, they had to get 'em out of the water and try to identify 'em, especially the mortals—not that he expected to find IDs.

"So how many we got?" he asked Aikin as he picked his way along what would never again be a peaceful shore.

"Thirty-two—I think; critters weren't picky about tearin' 'em up. Plus Elyyoth and . . . Aife."

"Separate deal," David told him. "We'll ask Finno how they handle this kind of thing in Faerie."

"The rest?" Scott wondered.

David looked to Aikin for advice. "Burn 'em, maybe? The Faeries anyway. Or just leave 'em and let nature take its course. I mean, their bodies don't seem to hang around long over here."

"What about the mortals, though? Can't bury 'em. Can't leave 'em. Can't report 'em, either."

"And I'd just as soon Ma didn't know," David finished.

"Won't get any easier," Aikin prompted from beside the nearest body: a slender, rather hard-faced Faery woman. "First thing I guess is to lay 'em all out in a row. You guys wanta give me a hand?"

"No," David muttered, but joined him. "Head or feet?"

"Alternate," Aikin gave back. "I'll take head this time."

David frowned as he hunkered down at the fallen warrior's boots. No obvious wounds showed on her body, so he wondered how she'd died. But then Aikin twitched the hair away from her throat and he saw. She was one of the ones Alec had dispatched.

He wondered if he was up for this; not only from the pain in his arm but from—he faced it squarely—the way it would remind him of Brock. Still, it had to be done, and he was no better than the others, and indeed no more affected. Steeling himself, he reached for the warrior's ankles.

And flinched back in horror, for his fingers had gone in too far!

He touched her again—higher.

Same effect.

"Oh, shit!" spat a startled Aikin. "Oh, fuckin' bloody friggin' damn!"

"What?" Liz wondered, looking up.

"Finno!" David called. "You got any—?"

Fionchadd padded up beside them and regarded the woman with cold, dispassionate eyes. "Two things," he observed. "First, without spirit to maintain it, and with all Power fled, and being made of the stuff of another World, there is little to bind these bodies together. Too, the pool drank deep indeed. It drank blood, aye, for blood contains much Power. But it also drank of more subtle . . . energies, you would say. And since we were wet all over, it could draw Power from virtually everything."

"Hmm," Sandy inserted, from behind Calvin. "Makes sense. I mean, think, folks: how much energy would be required to move a mass the size of Tir-Nan-Og?—and it *was* a physical mass, no mistake! And then remember how much potential there is in a person's atomic structure if you could tap it. Play with Einstein a while, and you get some amazing numbers."

"An A-bomb channeled through Aife?" David snorted. "I don't think so. No, scratch that," he corrected. "Don't *want* to think so."

"Me neither," Calvin agreed, looking pointedly at Fionchadd. "But what *you're* saying is that if we leave 'em here, they'll eventually just dry up and blow away?"

"Yes," the Faery agreed. "Flesh first, then clothing, then stone and metal. Those last, however, you may have to salvage."

"And the mortals?"

"Same thing, but slower. I *think*," he added, "that the spell still lingers here in this spring and would gladly suck the rest of these bodies down. I think that would provide the final . . . sealing."

"Whatever," David grunted. "Let's just get movin'."

It took less than ten minutes, with all the men save Alec and Piper pitching in. The women, by choice, stayed away, but Piper played a suitable lament. He settled on "Flowers in the Forest."

Nor was it as bad as David expected. Over half of the bodies in the water proved to be essentially floating shells and were all but dissolved already. Submerging them helped, so all that remained was to wade them into deep water and hold them down for a while, after first stripping all Faeries of weaponry and jewels. *Wergild*, Fionchadd proclaimed, for Brock, Aife, and Elyyoth. And while the metal would eventually wear away, gems, silver, and gold dispersed very slowly indeed.

The humans were a larger problem, mostly because their clothing, being Faerie in origin, didn't seem to be lasting as long as their bodies. Finally David remembered the ropes that had bound their latest lean-to together, and with them and the numerous stones that littered the lookout, they weighted the corpses. A day—two at the max, Fionchadd said—and they'd dissolve as well. Their weapons, they'd cache nearby for the nonce, then retrieve someday for burial in the Sullivan family cemetery.

Of Elyyoth, there was no sign. Then again, he'd been among the first Faeries to fall and had died in what was then very hungry water.

Aife's fate was Alec's decision. "I don't want her with the rest of them," he said. "Otherwise, I . . . I don't care."

Fionchadd gnawed his lip. "I could blast her with Power— I have enough for that. But I would rather spend it healing your injuries."

Alec smiled wanly. "Actually, I was thinking there's probably enough dry wood left in the lean-to for a pyre."

By unspoken consent, David and Aikin went to accomplish that, leaving Fionchadd, Scott, and Kirkwood to handle the removal of Aife's body. Being the last casualty, and having died as affairs were resolving, she was almost intact, though Calvin commented on a disquieting lightness when he and Kirkwood lifted her onto the makeshift bier. Fionchadd shrouded her with his cloak. David laid an arm on

Alec's shoulders. "Hang in there, big guy. We're almost done. You want us here, we'll stay; you want us gone . . . we're outa here."

"Stay until sunrise," Alec said. "That'd be a good time, I think."

Sunrise was an hour away by David's estimation, and while he was desperate to get to a phone and check on his pa, he was too fried to even think of leaving yet. With his fellows, he found towels and dry clothes in one or the other vehicles and changed. A few napped. Wounds were tended, notably David's, Alec's, and LaWanda's. Scott and Kirkwood stood guard, though everyone retained a weapon.

It was David who remembered the ulunsuti. It lay where it had rolled during the first attack: lodged beneath a piece of driftwood with the pot that held it not far away. He touched it cautiously—and jumped back in alarm when the crystal pulsed with light. "Folks . . . !" he yelled.

Calvin was there in a trice, with Kirkwood and Liz close behind. David hadn't moved the stone since it awakened, but had never let it out of his sight. It was still glowing, too; more brightly by the moment, in fact, and as David stared at it, images took form, in the crimson septum first, then reaching out in a glare of light to fill a circle maybe two yards across. A face appeared within that circle: black hair, dark eyes, pale face, long mustache. Crown. It wavered briefly, then stabilized into the image of Lugh Samildinach— on his throne—with a dagger thrust into its arm by way of his hand. He too looked freshly bathed and dressed.

"Greetings, Lord," David coughed, because no one else seemed inclined to speak. "You've, uh . . . found us."

"Not without difficulty!" Lugh laughed. "It seems the maps hereabout have . . . altered."

"We had no choice," David protested. "If it's caused you trouble, I'm sorry. But a man's gotta defend his own place."

"A fact that is not unknown to me," Lugh replied neutrally. "And a situation I can certainly understand."

David nodded. Waiting. Clearly Lugh had his own agenda. "I doubt we will meet face-to-face after this," the Faery said eventually with an air of genuine regret. "We have gone far together, you and I and these others. We have fought and lost and fought again and won. We have learned from each other as well, though I doubt I need to tell you that! But what you have done here—it was . . . *is* . . . unthinkable! Yet you have done it. Had I considered such a thing, I would have investigated it. That you *did* consider it brands you a wiser man than I."

David puffed his cheeks and asked the question he knew he had to ask or regret it the rest of his life. "So, are you pissed at us, or what?"

Lugh's brows twitched. "A man does not like his property put at risk; I have therefore some right to be angry. A man *does*, however, like his property protected, and you have done that as well. So let us call the payment even."

A deep breath and one final question. "What about your plan? You still gonna flood the Cove if they start buildin' that resort there?"

Lugh countered with a cryptic smile. "That place is no longer a threat."

"Not to *you*!" David muttered, and would've said more had Liz not elbowed him in the ribs.

To David's surprise, Lugh rose from his throne and bowed, though his hand never left the arm. "I thought it right we exchange farewells," Lugh told him. "So in my name and Nuada's and everyone else you know here: farewell!"

David bowed in turn. His eyes were misting. "Farewell," he whispered, and turned away, hearing the others likewise call "Farewell."

Eventually they all made that final formal parting, even Alec, though it cost him dear. Fionchadd alone spoke more than a few words, but David never heard them, for they were in Faery speech. Still, his Faery friend looked the better for that encounter.

Sunrise was threatening the sky when a tight-faced Liz returned the quiescent ulunsuti to Alec. The fog beyond the ledge shimmered with pink and gold and orange. David had just decided he might possibly be able to snare a moment's shut-eye when he heard someone running—staggering, rather—up the trail, virtually out of breath. "Cal," he warned, hand on the Beretta. "There!"

"Got 'im!" Kirkwood laughed from the entrance to the trail, flourishing a kicking and twisting Little Billy, whom he'd corralled by the collar. "This belong to you?" he asked David with an evil smirk that turned to an agonized grimace when the kid's heel caught him smartly in the crotch. Kirkwood slumped backward. Little Billy sprawled on all fours, but picked himself up at once, full of outraged dignity. Which washed from his face as soon as he saw David, to be replaced with anguish mixed with tears.

"Fuckin' fog!" the boy sobbed as he flung himself onto his brother. "Slowed me down like hell—sorry, like *heck*. Oh, dammit, Dave, who gives a fuck about . . . about words, when—" He broke off, tried to compose himself, swallowed hard, then tried again. "I . . . don't know what you guys are doin' up here, but you . . . you gotta come home right *now*, Davy! It's Pa!"

David's heart nearly leapt from his body as he stared his brother (not much shorter than him now) straight in the eye. "What about him?"

Little Billy gaped, wide-eyed. "He's—Davy, I think . . . I think he's gonna *die*!"

"Aik!" David yelled. "Liz. Somebody! Car keys! *Now!*"

"No need for haste," a voice purred from the forest.

David nearly jumped out of his skin. Calvin and Liz (but not the groaning Kirkwood) went instantly on guard.

David searched the forest frantically, but even so, it took a moment to make out the shape slipping silently from among the trees. Female (but he'd known that by the voice), smallish, oddly dressed, and eerily familiar.

Calvin recognized her first. "Okacha!"

David's tension dispersed so quickly he almost collapsed. "'Kacha—what? I mean, I don't want to be rude, but my pa—"

"Will be fine if you do not spill this," Okacha replied, extending a narrow-necked pottery phial sealed with wax. She held another in reserve.

Little Billy looked seriously suspicious. "Huh?"

Okacha's eyes danced with an amusement David didn't appreciate, a fact she soon keyed in on. "Sorry," she murmured. "Sometimes I forget how fear can screw you up, and that not everybody's gonna chill just 'cause I know it's okay for them to. Anyway, the message I have is this: Uki and the others saw everything and applaud your actions and your courage and your wits. And they know, as you didn't until your brother got here, that your father lies in peril of his life from a shard of Faery metal that won't let his wound heal. They'd prefer this didn't happen, however, so they send you that phial, with another for yourselves, if you need it.''

David regarded it dubiously. "What—?"

"Water from the Lake Atagahi," Okacha replied. "*Healing* water. If it can't save your father, nothing can. In any event, it'll certainly be useful."

"Thanks," David breathed, at once relieved, excited, and frightened. "And if you don't mind, we'd better get to it. Feel free to come along, as soon as somebody gets me some keys."

"You hang on to that," Aikin told him roughly. "I'll drive."

Epilogue:
Spoiling the View

*(Sullivan Cove, Georgia—
Monday, June 30—dawn)*

David held his breath. So did Little Billy. So did their mother and most of the other people crammed into the Sullivans' den. *Was it enough?* That tiny trickle of healing Atagahi water Sandy and Kirkwood, who between them *almost* constituted an EMT, had finally managed to get down Big Billy's throat.

How much *was* enough, anyway? And how long did it take to have any effect? He didn't know—couldn't remember—was too wired to focus. The bottom line was they'd done the last thing they could to save his father. Might work; might not.

No one spoke. David held tight to Liz's hand and squeezed his mother's reassuringly with the other. She looked tired. Worried. Dubious. Angry. And put out.

In serious need, David thought, of some coffee-an'-'shine—without the coffee.

Big Billy's lips worked. Every head in the room craned forward, but nothing followed. No response. A nod from Kirkwood, and Sandy pressed the phial once more to his mouth. It was still half full, David noted: good stuff to have around in light of their other injured, the most serious of whom was LaWanda, who was probably good for a whole phial herself.

A noisy slurp, and Big Billy swallowed. But that was all. Or had his breathing eased?

Silence.

Footsteps on the porch. Dale promptly sauntered off to see who it was, to return a moment later with a bleary-eyed Alec in tow. Alec eased up behind David and leaned forward to knead his shoulders and whisper in his ear. "Aife can wait. This can't."

"Thanks," David murmured, patting his hand.

The clock ticked. People began to stir. David wanted away from there so bad he could taste it, not because he didn't care about his father but because he cared too much and had been through more than anyone should have to lately and just couldn't stand not knowing. "Gotta—" he began. And froze.

Big Billy's lips had moved again. His breathing was stronger, and his eyelids were stirring. "Pa!" David called, easing closer. "C'mon, Pa, you can do it! I'm not finished with you yet!"

"... boy ..." Big Billy mumbled. "Boy."

"Right," David acknowleged, nodding vigorously. "It's your boy."

"Two boys ..." Big Billy slurred, "... got two boys."

"Right," David repeated. "Other one's right here. You wanta talk to him?"

"I want," Big Billy announced clearly, opening his eyes, "some coffee-an'-'shine."

"You do not!" JoAnne squawked in outrage. "why, Bill, you—why, Bill—!" She didn't finish because she was on her knees sobbing, burying her face in her husband's rough red hands.

David grinned at his pa over his mother's head. Bill grinned back, lopsided. "Feel real funny inside," he rumbled. "Feel like some kinda clot's dissolvin', or something— an' like something's—I dunno, kinda pullin' together. Weird."

"'Course it's weird," David retorted. "One of my friends did it."

"'Preciate it," Big Billy yawned. "Now, if you folks don't mind, I reckon bed'd look pretty good." And with that, he levered himself to his feet and lurched toward the door. David's friends—everyone who'd been on the mountain, plus Darrell and Gary, whom Myra had summoned and de-briefed—parted before him as though he were a king. David started to follow him, but JoAnne shook her head. "See to these folks, you and Dale. Get 'em fed and bathed and whatever they want. I gotta spend some time with my man."

David started to protest, then thought better of it, then changed his mind again. He was still waffling when he heard the throaty macho rumble of a big-bore motorcycle crunching up the drive. By the time he'd made it to the back door, the rider was striding through the yard.

"John!" he yelled joyfully. "John Devlin! Get in here!"

The Ranger looked a little crispy around the eyes, David noted, wondering what kind of night he'd had, and cursing himself for not checking in. "Well," he offered through an uncertain grin, "welcome to chaos."

Devlin's brows quirked upward. "Looks like a lot of company, but *not* chaos."

"Yeah, well," David sighed, "it's a long story."

"Which reminds me," Scott sighed in turn, "I gotta scoot. Don't mean to be rude or anything, but I need to check on some dudes. Don't want to, but—you know."

David slapped himself on the head. "Oh, bloody hell! I forgot about the blessed developers! Shit, here I thought this was all over, and we've still gotta deal with that!"

"That," Liz reminded him pertly, "is why we got into this."

"Developers?" Devlin echoed casually. "What's the deal?"

David scowled at him. "Didn't we tell you? Hell, John, I don't know who knows what anymore, but if we didn't—"

"Quick and dirty," John broke in. *"What's the deal?"*

"The deal," David growled, "is that an outfit called Mystic Mountain Properties took one look at Bloody Bald and decided to build a resort on top of it, with a marina in the Cove."

"Bloody Bald . . ." Devlin repeated carefully.

"Right."

"That would be a . . . mountain?"

David rolled his eyes. "You could say that. Mountain

here, mountain in Faerie too. Heart of the trouble, 'cause the Sidhe decided it was sacred, or whatever.''

"Mountain," Devlin repeated, eyes twinkling.

David's eyes narrowed. "There something you're not tellin' me?"

"Maybe," Devlin grinned, "you oughta pay more attention to what's goin' on around you. Man oughtn't to take his local landscape for granted."

"What—?" David began, then broke off and pushed past the smirking Ranger onto the porch, thence down the steps and into the yard. It was the first time he'd been outside since daylight arrived and with it the lifting of what had seemed to be a quite normal fog. Thus, he'd had no reason to peruse the local landscape. He did now—and gasped.

There had never been a really good view of Bloody Bald this far out the Cove, and most of it had always been masked by trees so that only its white quartzite peak showed.

Now, however, that peak showed no longer.

"Oh, my God!" David breathed. "The whole damned *mountain's* gone!"

"Gonna be some pissed-off boys over at Mystic Mountain," Scott chuckled, stepping up behind them, vanguard of a horde that had likewise come to gawk. "Gonna be some pissed-off money men down in Atlanta, too, 'cause that mountain was the whole damned draw."

"No marina?" David mused. "I mean, won't they want to cut their losses?"

"Maybe," Scott replied. "But I wouldn't worry about it."

"Nor would I," Liz giggled right behind him. "Besides, after last night, you can always buy 'em off with Faery gold."

"Right now," David laughed, his tummy rumbling, "I'd rather just buy breakfast!"

Scott Gresham's Journal

(Monday, June 30)

Well, it's over. I *think* it is, anyway, though we shall see.
Still, I feel pretty good about it. Mostly, frankly, I'm just
tired and sleepy. I don't remember the last time I got any
shut-eye. Not last night, that's for sure, with that nice little
mountainside pool all of a sudden turned into a war zone,
and me having to play soldier, which actually made me feel
pretty decent, because it let me actually do something active,
something I could see and that everybody else could also
see. (Yeah, I know that sounds like ego, but as messy as this
all is headspace-wise, I need for folks to know I did something too.) And shooting let me vent a helluva lot of anger.

I also killed some folks—or shot at 'em, anyway—and
I'm not sure how I feel about that *at all*. (And of course I
won't be able to see a shrink about it either, but what else
is new?) I've rationalized it by saying I mostly shot at Faeries, and shot to wound, and that those folks probably
weren't real sterling examples of humanity anyway. But still,
I wonder. Something tells me we're all gonna spend a lot of
time deconstructing this. Oh, well!

Anyway, I *think* I've done the right thing. I stayed on the
side of the good guys, which was harder than folks might
think, especially when what's good in terms of your own
best interests may not be good in terms of the big picture.

As for Mystic Mountain: who knows? Their big stake in
all this was Bloody Bald, and there *is* no Bloody Bald anymore (and I don't have to explain why either, because *I* obviously didn't do it, nor see it done; but if they bug me about
it, I'll just quit). The marina was supposed to be mostly to

support the ferry out to the lodge in the mountain, so I don't know if they'll build it or not. They might, to cut their losses; and the Sullivans may have to live with that. But nobody's gonna flood the Cove now, and that's what we were really fighting for.

As for me. I can probably get my old job back at the newsstand. Plus Finno's said he'd help me find some gold and jewels and stuff on my own, which is what I really want to do, because I'd rather be my own man and not be beholding to anyone.

Bottom line, when all is said and done: I've passed through the fire and come out on the other side, tempered, or harder, but better made (wonder where *that* came from?). I think I've done the right thing. I think things are gonna work out for most of my friends. I think I'm gonna be happy.

I think things are gonna be okay.